Fire in the Marshes

*A Tale of Justice and Vengeance in
Medieval Holland*

Noah Verhoeff, 2025

Contents

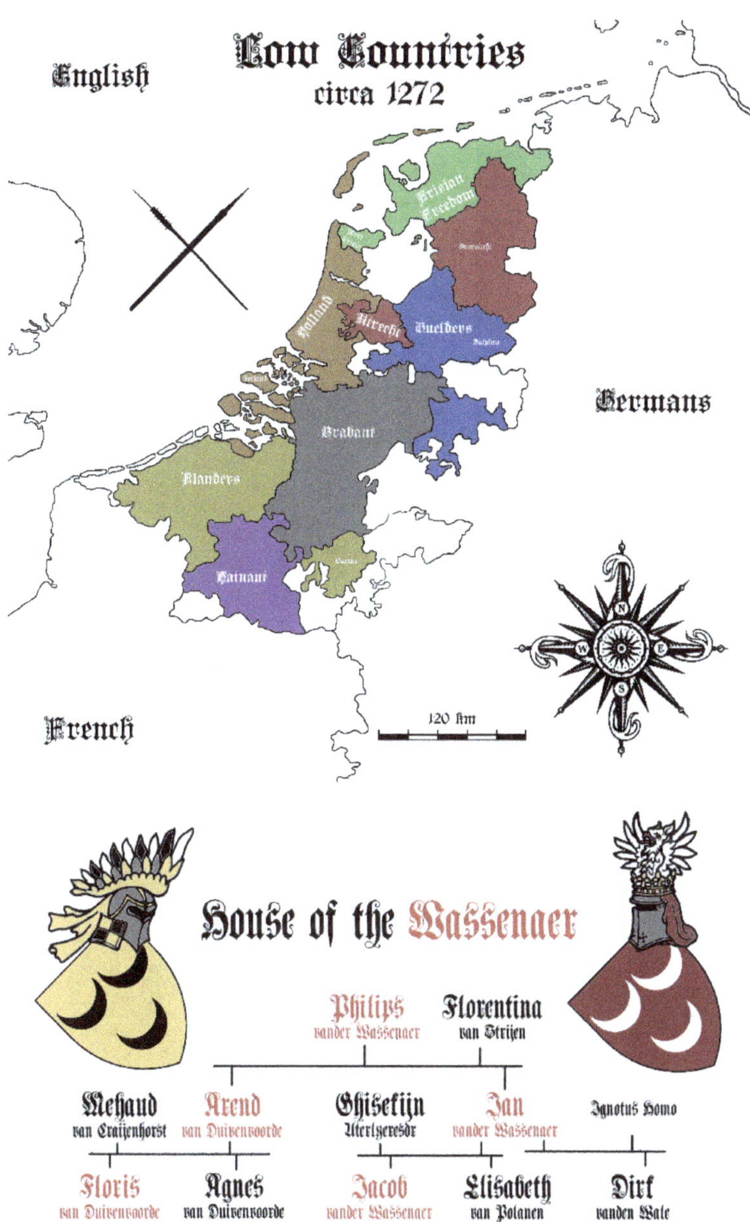
English
Low Countries
circa 1272
Frisian Freedom
Holland
Utrecht
Guelders
Zutphen
Germans
Zeeland
Brabant
Vlanders
Hainaut
French
120 km
House of the Wassenaer
Philips
vander Wassenaer
Florentina
van Strijen
Mehaud
van Craijenhorst
Arend
van Duivenvoorde
Ghisekijn
Uterlyeresdr
Jan
vander Wassenaer
Ignotus Homo
Floris
van Duivenvoorde
Agnes
van Duivenvoorde
Jacob
vander Wassenaer
Elisabeth
van Polanen
Dirk
vanden Wale

Florens (Floris) V
Gerulfing

Count of
Holland

Brederode
De Vriese
Lords of Leyden
City of Leiden
Reimerswaal

Duivenvoorde
Knights Templar
Wassenaer
Raephorst
Borselen

Pendrecht
Egmont
Kerekhove
Oudshoorn

Jan I of Nassau
Prince-Bishop of Utrecht
Lodewijk of Heyen
Renier of Heyen
Wollefram of Heyen
Renesse
Oudart
Ghijsbrecht of Amstel
Arnoud of Amstel
Woerden
Abcoude
Velsen
Wateringen
Scalmen
Drongelen

Chapter 1. The Barter: Piet

"I'm sorry, Mrs. Lijsbet, but I simply don't play dice. That's far too many guilders for a mortgage — even if it's bet on all the barley you can muster," Lord Hillebrant said with the apathy of a man who'd never felt hunger a day in his life. Rain pounded on the clay roof tiles. I peered out the window to see a stray cat shielding itself from the rain on the windowsill. It looked back at me, just as fatigued, and just as hopeless.

"Please, my Lord," Mother said. "It's almost harvesting season. We can pay you back in full, and more by Michaelmas." I watched while the expression on Lord Hillebrant's face didn't change one bit. He just sat there, fingers crossed, gold rings on each finger, and a great gold livery collar on his shoulders. He was shriveled and dry — like a dried apple, wrinkled and weathered with age. He was spared from the rain. We, on the other hand, were soaked through. Wet. Wet all over — our hosen squelched as we walked through the streets of Leyden. It was not uncommon to see rain. This time of year, it rained more days than not. On the ones that we were spared a downpour, we smelled its sweet, damp, mossy remnants. Days when the sun was bright, were scant, and taken as a gift from Heaven; a sparse reminder that there was something to look up to. But today was a day befitting of rain. It would appear that the little hope Mother had shown on the long trip over here was still too high of an expectation.

Seemingly reading my mind, the lord spoke. "Damn roof tiles," he said, changing the topic dryly. He looked up as if he could see them between the wooden floor beams above his head. "The Count orders us to install them. Fireproof he says — safer for the city. I can't hear a bloody thing with that racket."

"My Lord," Mother began once more, "I'm begging you."

"Tell me, who is your liege lord, Mrs. Lijsbet?" Lord Hillebrant stroked his great blond beard.

"Heer Arend van Duivenvoorde, son of Philips vander Wassenaer, Baron of Duivenvoorde Castle, my Lord," Mother replied with haste. She wished to add more, but the old lord cut her off.

"Jaja, I know him well. He's a daring man, isn't he?" he asked rhetorically. He wouldn't expect someone of our status to pass judgment on the personality of a noble. "A descendent of the vander Wassenaer lineage, I believe," he added, flaunting his knowledge. What he just uttered meant little to us – we were serfs, not heralds. Seeing that Mother wasn't interested, he cut to the point. "And why has he not accepted your offer? It would seem that it is his responsibility, not mine."

"Heer Arend is on pilgrimage to the Holy Land, and his wife won't listen to us," Mother replied.

"Have you tried the Jews?" Lord Hillebrant's face flashed a smirk. "Those lot are often eager to accept an offer like yours. In fact, they're only a few blocks downriver. They trickle in from all over the place. You know they've had a rotten lot – all the killings and lootings. At least the Count likes them."

"I have," Mother said. "They offered to take it up with the same amount in interest," she explained, "a better barter than your hand." Then she snapped, "Your purse is closed tighter than that of a Lombard merchant." I saw a change in the old lord's expression now – seemingly a snap to attention. Perhaps Mother had been too curt with him – the nobility tended to be quite soft. But Mother was a fighter — she made sure to speak plainly to whomever she came across, including Lord Arend, and even Lord Hillebrant here before us.

"Mrs. Lijsbet, there is simply nothing I can do for you — you are only entitled to mortgage your crop yield to your own liege lord, and if he is unwilling or unable to agree to your proposition, there is little more that you can do." The lord yawned. "Now I imagine that it will be quite a walk for you, and the sun will fall in only an hour or so. You do know that it is illegal to roam the city of Leyden at night?" he asked condescendingly. I would have expected no less from a burgher, to look upon us like that. Not to mention a noble burgher, likely seeing us as no more than cattle or rats. We are people of the land, that is all we are. We *are* the land, for all they care.

"We are serfs, not idiots," Mother replied, collecting the folds of her kirtle gown and apron in one hand and lifting herself from her seat with the other. In truth, I didn't know much about the situation — I was too young. What I did know, was that, since Father had drunk himself into the river, Mother had been visiting Leyden often. Every time she brought me along. She called me her little helper and said that I'd ward off the bandits and evil spirits. In reality, I think she just wanted me to carry her groceries from the market.

But the truth was that I was hungry — we all were. We had waited for the barley harvest, but Mother said that our grain ark had been getting a little too light. That meant that instead of a bowl of pottage for me and my brothers and sisters, we got only half. No cheese nor eggs neither — mother and I only took them to the market to sell for coin.

Mother made her way to the door, and gestured for me to come. She coughed into a handful of her wimple and then looked to the crucifix hanging above the door to whisper a quick prayer to herself. I hated seeing Mother like that. Whatever this man's complex words meant, all I knew was that he had put a disdainful frown on Mother's face. She looked quite sad, and she only coughed when she was unhappy. Well, she coughed when she laughed too — although she laughed little these days. She had told me to be polite because Lord Hillebrant was a noble, but I couldn't leave without speaking. She stood up to him, if only for a moment. I decided to, as well. I turned to him.

"We're hungry!" I shouted at him. "Mother says the grain will run out! We have no coin to buy pies or salt herring at the market! Can't you see she's sick?" I started breathing heavily. In all honesty, I wanted to cry, but Father always told me that I had to be tough, like an ox, and reserved, like a wolf. Especially for Mother. Lord Hillebrant changed his expression, finally. His eyes drifted to the cross above the door, and he let out a deep sigh.

"Come back," he said. "Have a seat." I looked at Mother, and she reassured me that it was okay. I saw a sparkle in her eyes. Whether it was hope or pride, I was uncertain. The lord, on the other hand, changed his tone greatly. He spoke to me in a way far warmer than that in which he had spoken to Mother; like a blanket of fine linen and ermine fur. "I apologize, young man. I am deeply sorry to hear about the passing of your father. Tell me, what is your name?"

"Pieter," I replied. "Well, everyone calls me Piet."

"And how old are you, Piet?"

I frankly didn't know. I looked at my Mother, who said, "Seven years old, my Lord." He looked inquisitively at me. He scanned me up and down before turning to Mother.

"You know, that is the age that most apprentices in the city begin their work."

"I know, my Lord. I would buy him one if I had the means — but we're struggling to get by as it is. Our Liege Lady said we will need to pay the hariot tax on the land if we wish to keep it, and the merchet if I wish for my husband to be buried by the church. Of course I do! We can't even pay these dues as it is. Besides, we're serfs. We can't simply get up and leave — we need permission from the Lady of Duvernvoorde. She'll demand a chevage payment — more money we don't have. Or worse, she'll ride us down with her knights."

"May I offer you some advice?" Lord Hillebrant said.

"Go on," Mother replied. Lord Hillebrant gave a brief snort. He seemed to find Mother's candid nature amusing.

"Mrs. Lijsbet, I know that you are doing all that you can for your children. You wouldn't have come here if you weren't. I certainly respect you for it — there is little more we can do in this world than try our absolute best, for our children most of all. Now, as I am sure you have come to realize, I am a pragmatic man. Like I said, I don't play dice. I wouldn't be here if I did. So, tell me, how many children do you have?"

"Three girls and five boys, my Lord," Mother replied. "I love them all deeply."

"I wouldn't doubt it. In truth, your prospects appear grim, Mrs. Lijsbet. My best advice, be it however taxing on your heart, I would say that you should marry off your girls as soon as you can, to boys their ages, of course, and to try your best to apprentice off the younger boys. The older boys can aid you with the harvest, well, to harvest what selions of farmland you have not gifted as dowry or sold for your apprenticeships. Perhaps your liege Lord… well… liege *Lady* may send some hands to aid with the threshing and cultivation since I'm sure she wouldn't want any of her barley going to waste."

"My Lord, I can't simply buy them apprenticeships. As I said, we are serfs…"

"Ah, well the burghermeister of Leyden and his aldermen have recently decided to allow serfs to escape to the confines of the city. If your sons manage to live here for a year and one day, perhaps they can work in a pub or a snackshop, they will be granted asylum. As the old saying goes, city air makes one free," he said, hoping to bring a bit of light-heartedness into the conversation. Mother did not indulge him. He continued. "If your liege hasn't found them and brought them back by then, it signals to the Count that they are unable to keep their own peasants, and thus you are free to live here as free peasants. In truth, the aldermen and the rest of the burghers here simply want to keep the city growing. The more citizens they have, the more power they wield, and the better they are able to keep the hands of the feudal nobility out. I can understand them — I'd hate to plough a crop all day just for my yield to be given to some lord. Granted, I'm here upholding the Count's law. I suppose it's a little better than riding about on a warhorse in some castle somewhere." The Lord paused. "Anyways, I get ahead of myself. As for your son here, he seems like a charming and polite young man. With a healthy dash of courage, of course. Strong, red hair, good teeth, and a true farmer's build. He's hungry, I can see that, but he also clearly knows how to guide a plough. It so happens that I could use a page boy, well, I suppose I could accommodate one."

"My sweet boy Piet? Fine jest. I'll be on my way."

"Settle down Mrs. Lijsbet, I mean no offense by it."

"Oh no? You think I would part with my son just like that?"

"On the promise of a noble's life? Compared to starvation? Yes," he said. Mother took a moment to consider, tempering herself now.

"Lord Hillebrant, I will not simply hand my son to you."

"Mrs. Lijsbet, do you know what becomes of a page in a noble's court?" Lord Hillebrant asked. Mother did not reply. I think she didn't know but didn't want to appear simple — that's what I do when I don't know something.

"I will tell you. I can offer your son a far better life than he might have on any farm. In truth, I will essentially make him nobility. After pagehood, your son will become a squire — perhaps to my older brother, or perhaps to another close friend of mine."

"Not yourself? Have you your own squire?" Mother

asked.

"I am by no means a fighter," Lord Hillebrant said. "I am merely a lawman here in the name of the Count. That sword you see hanging on my chair behind me is mostly ceremonial, I'm afraid." He looked down at his belly. "And I wouldn't be much use swinging a sword now anyways," he joked. "Anyways, eventually, Pieter will be knighted, and become a noble. Granted, you must understand that it is extremely uncommon for a boy of your son's status to become a page. He is a child of the land. Most of his stock would live and die on the same plot in the same fief. But, if all these years in Leyden with these merchants and burghers and artisans has taught me anything, it is that men are made of the same blood. God gives us our birth, but our lives are what we make of it. Fifty years ago, one would not have seen a single low-born man carry a heraldic coat of arms. Now, you see one flying on every manor house in Hollant, for every merchant, burgher, alderman, and guildmaster. Times change, Mrs. Lijsbet, and, by the Grace of God, I wish for them to favour your family in the little way I can will them to. Please know that it is out of charity that I do this." He paused and appeared to think for a moment, looking down to his interlocking fingers which now sat like a prominent paperweight upon the loose papers that riddled his desk. "Charity, and I so happen to empathize with you, Mrs. Lijsbet. I too have lost someone dear to me." A grim expression pressed on his face. "Two people, actually." His bright, green eyes darted about the murals on the plastered walls. It took him a moment to muster the courage to speak. "Not two years ago I lost my own son. He was not much younger than your boy, Piet." Mother gasped. For the first time now she appeared surprised and ashamed. Her pale cheeks grew the slightest pink. "His mother died during childbirth. I was left alone."

"I am so sorry, my Lord. I had no idea…"

"Don't fret about it. I'm no gambling man, but I'd still wager my last guilder that nine in every ten houses in Leyden's lost a child. Little Buyc, that's what we called him for his little belly at birth, was a sickly little elf of a lad — never grew past my belt. He passed in his sleep. We had a doctor come to heal him when he grew particularly feeble, but he came from Ghent two days late. We fear he had the sugar disease."

"The sugar disease?"

"Yes. The poor boy loved his sweets — as any young boy would. He ate no more honey nor candied fruit pies or sweet loafs than any other boy his age. Well, any other boy of standing. But, one of our servants in the manor, when clearing his chamber pot, noticed that his urine smelled of sweets." Mother made the sign of the cross upon her chest.

"Ah, the honey curse. Our Priest says it is a punishment from the Heavenly Father for those who grow fat."

"That is certainly it. But, young Buyc was a bony young lad."

"I am sorry to hear this, my Lord. My thoughts are with you and your young son's soul. I've had two of my own pass— one was birthed cold and the other caught a fever…"

"Please, Mrs. Lijsbet, you have enough to think about."

"But to lose your wife as well? I can't imagine what

torment that must be. I truly am so sorry for your loss."

"If I might ask. What gave you comfort, when your own children passed?"

"Well, in the country, young children who don't make it are changelings. They say that the wood elves have taken your child at birth and replaced him with a changeling. Although, I'm sure it is far more difficult for the elves to steal a baby from a gated noble manor such as this than from a village house, I believe they only swapped your little Buyc with the changeling, and your real boy is growing tall and mighty with the elves, happily and peacefully," Mother said. It was true — some of our neighbours had changelings for children. Luckily, none of my brothers or sisters were stolen by elves. Lord Hillebrant seemed to be feeling how I had just felt when I was also fighting back tears. His cheeks were red, and his eyes glistened like the sea.

"Your words do certainly comfort me, Mrs. Lijsbet," he said, fighting back tears.

"It can't be easy bearing that weight. I truly pray for you, my Lord," Mother said. "And I hope my son lives up to be the mighty warrior you see in him," she added, now feeling her own esophageal contraction. I looked at her, and she returned my expression with a face of reassurance, behind which was most certainly a deep sadness. I will never forget the warm smile she gave me — that everything would be okay. It would not be okay. It would be a month of okay until the okay went away.

"I'm sure he will," Lord Hillebrant said, looking at me. "He's destined to be a gentleman — just look at him." He smiled and turned to Mother. "I will send out a party to fetch him once the harvest is done. You can rest assured that he will be fed, clothed, housed, and given a bright future. I sincerely hope the best for yourself and the rest of your children as well. I will put in a good word with my friends in the baker's guild — perhaps they can make pies for a few years before they earn themselves an apprenticeship in a bakery." Lord Hillebrant returned to me. He seemed to struggle to find words. After a quick moment, he asked me, "Young man, what do you know about chivalry?"

"Very little. I'm just a boy… and a farmer."

Lord Hillebrant smiled. "But surely you have seen the knights of Heer Arend before? Had your father ever taken you to watch the tournaments here in Leyden?"

"The knights come to collect our dues to our lord. They take our harvest," I replied.

Perhaps it was the way I had said it; the slight quiver in my voice, or perhaps it was an expression on Mother's face — in truth, I had not been paying attention to her at that moment — but Lord Hillebrant gave me a solemn look of deep understanding.

"Ah yes, for they too must feed, Piet," he said. If he had told me that he believed in what he said, I would have called him a liar. They were words spewed out simply to avoid a conversation; one which I would have been eager to have. One that I still am. "But they are not the emblems of chivalry I would hope you might aspire to." He took a moment to consider how he might continue. "Have you heard the Song of Rolant?"

"Jaja," I replied. "Sometimes minstrels will sing it when

they come through our village. My friends and I always listen. It's one of my favourites."

"Very good. And can you tell me what exactly these minstrels are singing about?"

"Yes!" I replied excitedly. I had no idea of why Lord Hillebrant wished to quiz me on the tale of Rolant, but I would never shy away from reciting my knowledge of old heroes.

Grandfather would always tell me tales of the Knights of the Round Table, Saint George and the Dragon, King David and his battles with Saracens, and the Paladins of King Karel the Great. "There once was a king named Karel, who ruled all of Christendom. He was King of Rome, and France, and Germany, and even the Low Countries. He had a retinue of twelve hand-picked knights, each the most valiant and chivalrous in all the realm. Of these knights, the best was Sir Rolant. He battled the Saracens in Spain, and…"

"Prima, Piet, you are a gentleman and a scholar. Quite the expert on Carolus Magnus. But, more importantly, can you tell me now what the tale tells about chivalry?"

"Yes, the minstrels always tell us that a chivalrous knight fears God and is faithful to the Church, serves his liege lord with valour and loyalty, and protects those who cannot defend themselves."

"Good," Lord Hillebrant said. "I know that you are not under my tutorage yet; however, it is time for your first lesson. Those chainmail-clad ruffians who call themselves knights under the command of Heer Arend — which of these laws have they broken when they take more than their fair share of your harvest?"

I looked to mother — I didn't think that I should answer this question truthfully. She only looked intrigued, and somewhat confused. "Have they been unfaithful to God?" I asked. "Father Wil said that we should love our neighbour, but I don't think they love us very much." Surprised, Lord Hillebrant looked to Mother, who returned his expression with her own look of pride.

"Impressive. It would not seem so. But, unfortunately, God Almighty has divided us into those born of noble or peasant status, and, as such, those knights have only done their duty to the Lord. Where they fail, however, is in defending the defenseless. You and your family, well, you appear to be a strong little lad, but your family is not made up of warriors. You have no ability to fight back by strength alone." Lord Hillebrant passed me a signet ring from his left index finger. I studied it closely for a moment, examining the sigil. It was a green shield with two stretched white letter *z's* standing side-by-side. "That, young Piet, is the weapon shield of House ver Heyen — the house to which I belong. Those symbols there are wolf hooks."

"Wolf hooks?" I asked. I didn't know what those were.

"Yes, wolf hooks. You may not need them on your farm, but, since the pagan days, trappers throughout the Low Countries have placed these hooks, attached to strong chains, buried deep in great chunks of meat and animal carcasses."

"What for?" I asked curiously.

"To catch wolves," Lord Hillebrant replied. For the exciting topic of wolf-hunting, he appeared to have little excitement in his voice. He was as serious as Father Wil of the village church. "Wolves represent all the predators that would seek to attack and overpower you. They stalk you in the wild, when you are most vulnerable. They overpower you with the talents they were born with, and when they cannot, they attack you with many at once. There are few animals more dishonourable. It is through cunning and ingenuity that you will outsmart these opponents and defeat them. That is what we do, lords and ladies of House ver Heyen, we turn predators into prey. We set traps, and hunt wolves. My hook is the law. No sword can cut through the steel bars of a dungeon cell. But, Pieter, when you join this house, you must come to learn this — that we defend the defenceless. I don't know what your wolf hook will be. Perhaps you will be a skilled fighter, or perhaps a skilled politician. Whatever it may be, you must swear to always use your power to do what is right, and rid this world of the wolves that would seek to harm those who cannot defend themselves."

"I swear," I replied. It sounded convincing enough — he seemed quite enthusiastic about it. If this was to be my new life, I figured there would be little point in challenging Lord Hillebrant's words. I suppose he was to be my liege, and, like Rolant, I would have to become loyal to him. I decided to start right then.

The endless, golden fields were all I'd ever known. Duivenvoorde, like every other fief in the low countries, was flat as a plank of wood. And wet. When the ground wasn't soft and supple like the clay near the riverbed, it was sandy and granular like a fistful of grain. It melded around our clogs like the dough beneath a kneading fist. Instead, the earth in the city felt far different. The water in the soil on our farm was wetted by the polders, which even soaked the dirt roads along the dikes. In the city, on the other hand, our clogs clopped like horseshoes on the cobblestone roads. They marked us out as peasants, no, worse than that alone, they marked us out as serfs. At the end of the day, we were just common people, not unlike most others we saw on the streets, but those clogs meant that the burghers saw us as three things in particular. Uneducated, poor, and unfree. And, by most metrics, it was true. I, a boy only seven years old, couldn't spell more than my own name or count further than one hundred. My mother wasn't much different, although she also knew how to actually read the signs we passed as we trod through the streets. She'd quiz me as we passed by them.

"Piet, what does that say?" she'd ask, pointing to a sign.

Most of the time, I'd either recognize it, proudly saying, "Barbershop" or "Hot Pies," but other times I'd simply shrug and let Mother teach me.

The streets themselves were busy — far more crowded than the village dirt roads of Duivenvoorde. Often, we'd walk alongside a canal to make our way through the city. They smelled foul. While they offered some duly desired open space, I think a few of the burghers sneakily dumped their chamber pots into the canals when they lived far away from the collection sites. And those sites were the worst of all. Some of the streets we passed were called Strontstrat or Kutstrat (shit street), or Pis Steegje (piss alley). They smelled even fouler. The pis steegjes were often behind alehouses where workers might be seen emptying their guts onto the side of the wall. Mother and I could see large cultures of plants growing on those very walls, seemingly from between the brick cobbles. The strontstrats were the worst. Those were the thin alleys where all the cesspits were. We occasionally saw gong workers, perhaps one of the few professions seen upon as more lowly than serfdom, shoveling all the waste to sell to gong farmers. We'd often see gong farmers visit Duivenvoorde. They sold us our manure.

"The sun's going to sleep soon," Mother said as we walked. I looked up, above the line of thatched roofs that shielded the street below, to the grey clouds where, indeed, I saw a beautiful orange painted across a sky striped by rising streaks of chimney smoke. "We'll have to sleep in an inn tonight and head back tomorrow," she said. I obliged obediently and followed her as we walked. As we made our way through the streets, the number of people began to dwindle, and windows began to glow orange with the light of fireplaces, rushlights, and candles. Inside homes we saw and heard people eating their light suppers, playing games, singing, dancing, reading, and what have you. We were out in the rain, soaked through, although, in all fairness, the downpour had begun to thin.

Different buildings each had signs protruding from above their doors, many of which were heraldic coats of arms of various wealthy merchant or noble families. Others were simple signs that signified what one might find inside, such as a pair of scissors for a textile cutter, or a pig for a butcher. Alehouses tended instead to pick signs with more unique designs, you could hear them before you saw them, so a tankard above the door would do you little good. Inns too. The one that we eventually decided to stop at was called the Saint Christophel Inn — Mother said he was the patron saint of travelers. Their sign showed an old Saint Christophel trudging his way across a river, carrying a baby Christ on his back. Mother said she liked the sign, so we'd stay here.

When we stepped inside, we were hit by the warm air emanating from the hearth.

Several tables had been arrayed where travellers sipped on their ales and ate hearty meals of various meats in honey or vinegar, eggs, cheese, salt herring, and various pies, all served on deliciously smelling trenchers. The scent of the spiced sauces smelled delicious. Before forgetting, I quickly looked to my feet. Father always taught me that you could tell how clean an inn was from how clean the rushes were on their floor. Sure enough, despite the late hour, they were almost pristine. It meant that they had been changed very recently — a sign of a dutiful host. Only seconds after we entered, a cheery, older woman addressed us.

"Oh, welcome, welcome! In you come," she said with a warm smile. "Best get yourselves out of the rain." The lady had a tray of used wooden plates in her right hand. With her left, after quickly cleaning it off on her apron, she gestured to a corner of the room near the window. "There's a table for you right over there," she said, ushering us in. The room was crowded and full of travellers eating and drinking and conversing with one another. One of the tables, particularly rowdy, appeared to be sharing stories from their travels while on pilgrimage. When passing by, Mother covered my ears. I think one of the men spoke about a maiden he fancied.

"Berta, fetch these lovely people some ale," the woman

instructed to a younger serving girl, who scampered back into the kitchen. "And make sure you only serve small beer to the little lad," she chuckled, "wouldn't want to have him sloshed."

Mother sat down before me, and then gestured for me to sit down as well. I sat down right next to her — both of us had a full view of the inn. I had never been in an inn before — it was quite exciting. I had always heard tales from travelling merchants and bards about funny escapades which happened here, but I hadn't expected to wind up in one tonight. I think that our meeting with Lord Hillebrant had taken longer than expected. That, and Mother and I struggled with finding his manor to begin with — Leyden could be a confusing place at times. The room was warm, far warmer than it was outside. And dry, so dry. The building had sturdy brick walls which nicely kept in the heat — something which I noticed was much more common on the bigger buildings in the city. The smaller ones, like homes and small stores, were all made of wooden planks, and the occasional home was made of wattle and daub — much like the houses in our village. Finally, after hastily washing her hands with some black soap in a big tub near the kitchen, the lady, little and stout, made her way over to us. Mother looked far less enthralled than I was; I wasn't sure what she was nervous about. The last approaching seemed to make her most anxious of all.

"Hello lovelies. My name is Aleydis, and I'm the landlady here," she said with a smile. "The Saint Christophel is the finest Inn in Leyden, I can assure you."

"Pleasure to meet you, Aleydis," Mother said. "My

name is Lijsbet, and this is my boy, Pieter."

"Handsome young lad." Aleydis ruffled my hair. "What can I do for you this evening, Mrs. Lijsbet?"

"It looks like we won't be making it back out into the country today. How much for a place to stay?" Mother had a weary look on her kind, gaunt face, as if she already suspected the answer would not be what she wanted.

"One guilder for you, and a half guilder for the boy," the landlady said. "You'll have your own room," she added. Upon hearing this, Mother couldn't help but begin coughing again. I tried to calm her, and Berta came with the ale which helped.

"I'm so sorry," Mother said.

"God bless you, dear," Aleydis replied.

"One guilder and one half?" Mother asked to confirm, reaching into the coin purse strung onto her belt.

"You know what? The boy stays for free," Aleydis said with a smile. Mother was incredibly grateful, and couldn't thank the kind woman enough. She also ordered one bowl of pottage and bread for each of us — the first time I'd had pork in a while. They only cost Mother a few more groten — far smaller coins. Hungrily, the moment it arrived, I dunked my bread into the stew and began to eat. Every bite tasted better than the last — it had been so long since I'd had food with flavour. Even the bread was buttered! I ate and chewed a full-sized portion until I couldn't anymore; not because I couldn't fit more in my stomach, but because every single crumb and drop of broth had been eaten. I felt full. I felt amazing. I felt like I had energy again. I felt like I could finally think for a moment. What in the world had happened today? Noble to noble, merchant to merchant, and not a single one of them accepted Mother's offer. And the last man, Lord Hillebrant, wanted to take me on as his page? No, more than that, Mother had accepted!

"Mother, I don't want to be a page," I said emphatically. She stopped eating for a moment.

"What do you mean?" she asked warmly.

"I mean, I don't want to leave the farm. I want to stay with you and my brothers and sisters. I want to tend to the pigs. Will there be pigs with Lord Hillebrant?" I asked. I honestly didn't know. But, I was quite content with my life as a peasant boy; I worked, and played, and ate, and slept. There was none of the intricacy that I saw in the city, of how to act or dress. You just… were. And the older boys and the men seemed content too. They worked in the day, and then they headed to the alehouse to drink and play games and sing and dance together. That seemed like a merry life. The city, on the other hand… Beggars riddled the streets — what if I ended up like them? And the nobles, they were all so cold and formal. I didn't want to become like that.

"Oh, love, don't you worry. Lord Hillebrant will take good care of you. He has a lot of guilders, you know? He might buy you a pet pig if you're good, I'm sure."

"But I don't care about guilders. I just want to be with all of you."

"Pieter, your brothers and sisters may not be staying in the village for long either. You heard Lord Hillebrant — they'd ought to venture out and make names for themselves.”

“But why can’t we just stay?” I was growing teary-eyed. I felt my cheeks redden.

“Can’t Uncle Max help with the harvest? I’ll take care of the pigs all by myself. The chickens too.”

“Piet, we simply don’t have enough hands. Your little brother, Filips, will have to go off to the monastery, I think. And your big brothers, Maurits, Sam, and Thiel will have to work for the bakers, like Lord Hillebrant said. And Uncle Max has better things to do than to help us farm. He’s a blacksmith, not a serf, like us.”

“What about Merin and Florie? Or sister Yda?” I grasped at everyone left.

“Your sisters? Oh, well, I suppose your sister Yda is of age. She seems to fancy that boy Maarten — he is a handsome young man, I’ll give her that. And Merin and Florie might also find work at a nunnery, or, perhaps your uncle Max might be kind enough to take them in.”

“But they’ll all be gone! And we won’t see each other anymore,” I protested. “Oh, Piet, I know. It’s hard. I’ll come visit all of you if I can.”

“But what about you? What will you do? You can’t stay all by yourself?”

“Oh, I’ll find something somewhere,” Mother said. “Don’t you worry about me.” At that moment her smile cut like daggers. In no world was that the truth — I could tell it hurt her just to say it.

“Nay, I will stay with you. I will run away from

Hillebrant and I will come and live with you in the village!" I stomped my clog down on the wooden floor boards. The whole inn turned to see me, thinking that something had happened. Embarrassed, Mother lowered her voice into a bitter whisper.

"Have you lost your wits, Pieter? You may not see it now, but what Lord Hillebrant wants to do for you is possibly the greatest thing that will have happened to you. Praise God for it, foolish boy."

I would have continued, but a tongue-lashing was far from how I wanted to spend the evening. I instead sipped from my tankard.

When the sun finally ducked its head below the farthest row of thatches and roof tiles, a sharp bell rang out which bellowed across the city. The curfew bell. I looked out of our suite's window, watching as every cooking fire and hearth in sight across the street was covered up — left to smoulder throughout the night and reignite in the morning. Mother smothered our fire as well, leaving nothing but smouldering ashes to keep us warm. A few rushlights kept themselves going as I saw artisans and workers of various kinds continuing their trades well into the night. While the streets were devoid of all pedestrians and riders aside from the urban militiamen, who brandished bright torches as well as long, two-handed, clubs with spearpoints. Or, spears with club heads. Goedendags, the men of our village called them. Father had wielded one when he went on crusade. He said they were only wielded by the men of the Low Countries, and among the men of the Low Countries, it was what most of them wielded. Was this going to be my life? The men who came to the village to collect taxes were certainly not nice men — I never wanted to become like them. I was just a boy, a peasant boy. I knew grains, and harvests, and how to collect fish net traps from the river. I knew how to feed the pigs, and milk the cows, and collect eggs from the hen coup. I didn't know how to serve a lord. What did a page do, anyway? I didn't think they'd have them swinging swords — I couldn't lift one if I tried, I was sure. So what was I to be? A servant? A bookkeeper? A cook? A groom? I'd find out soon enough — the harvest was to come soon, and Hillebrant said he'd collect me when the harvest came. I didn't know what to do. What would I tell Yda and Maurits and Sam? What would Thiel say about it? And little Filips — he was barely old enough to stand. Would he even remember me in a year or so? Would I recognize him if I ran into him again someday? At the monastery, perhaps? I changed out of my day clothes and, in my braies, hopped into bed, where Mother waited to embrace me in her arms. The linen smock gently hugged me tight, while the thick sheep's wool blanket lay over us. We kept warm together throughout the night — the straw bed was nearly as comfortable as the one at home. After a long day of walking and thinking and life-changing events, I took a few deep breaths, closed my eyes, and with a yawn, I slowly, softly fell asleep.

Chapter 2. The Humiliation: Piet

The rooster woke us up bright and early. The orange light of the morning sun gently peeked into the window. My brothers and sisters and I all hopped out of our straw beds, ready to start the day after a quick yawn or two. There was no time to spare, never during the harvest. Only in our braies, my brothers and I all raced to slip on our hosen, one by one, then our tunics, our belts, and our hoods. Last but not least, we all put on our turnshoes. I helped Filips tie his leather laces — his chubby little fingers were too young to tie them on his own. My day proceeded as usual. As I stepped out of the house through the narrow doorway, a brisk sea breeze slapped me across the cheek. We were not far from the sea, and sea breezes blew strong and tasted salty, although we became quite used to them. Windmills thrived here — Lord Arend even had one built in Duivenvoorde a few years ago. Also, because of the sea, seagulls were never far from sight. They sang their rasp calls as they soared above us.

Sometimes I imagined what it would be like to fly like them, or like a dragon in the old tales, battling knights, hoarding gold, and munching on cattle. Enough daydreaming. First things first, I tended to the pigs and chickens in the market garden out back. Six eggs today. The little piggies were fattening nicely. The rooster, grouchy as always, had a go at playing his tricks on me, hiding in the back of the henhouse and poking his beak out at me when I came to reach under him. The pigs, on the other hand, were quite docile — minding their own business for the most part, and happily accepting the old vegetables we had in store for them. Then, I watered the vegetables in the market garden with the sprinkling pot, taking care not to waste a drop of water. We were nearly through with the water the last I'd checked the trough — I'd have to fetch some more water from the well. Or I could just ask Merin and Florie to do it — they'd be happy to run any errand as long as they did it together. I nearly dropped the sprinkling pot when Mother called that it was time for breakfast. Scrambling, we all rushed to take our place at the table. Breakfast, as usual, was bread and ale — the morning meal of all good Christians, as Father Wil said at Sunday mass. We could always rely on a piping hot loaf between the nine of us at the breakfast table. The scent of savoury barley or rye always marked our mornings. At breakfast, Mother gave us each our instructions for the day. In order from oldest to youngest, she'd read out what had to be done and who was to do it. My task was to take one of our sickles down to the blacksmith, Uncle Max, to be repaired, and while I waited, I was to check on our fish traps down by the mill — it was a simple enough job for the morning. Most of breakfast was spent joking around with my brothers and sisters, while Mother made sure that little Filips got all his rye pottage in his mouth instead of on the floor rushes. Our house cat, Vlam, spent breakfast time dodging Filips's rye porridge as if it was a game. We called her Vlam (flame) because she was a bright orange. She didn't need any food to break her fast — she'd spent the night hunting mice. We could hear them fiercely battling throughout the night, waking us up from time to time.

When we'd all finally finished our chunks of bread, we got to work. I walked with Maurits, Sam, Thiel, and Yda to the barley field. Maurits and Sam were to cultivate today.

They had quite a few selions to clear out, so it would be a long day's work for them. Yda, on the other hand, would collect the barley that they'd cut before her with their sickles. It was an efficient process — everything we did was out of pragmatism and efficiency. We needed to cultivate as much as possible, produce as much as possible, and not waste an ounce of sweat. We had none to waste. Thiel, on the other hand, would be threshing the barley collected yesterday with his great flail, and collecting the barley grain in a great barrel. As we walked through the village, we said hi to all of our neighbours. Everybody knew everybody here; that's simply how it was. These families had been here since King Karel, and even before that. Nobody truly knew, but they had certainly been here longer than the King of the Germans ruled over us, and even longer than the Counts of Hollant managed these lands. The farm was old, as were the families that tended to it. We walked along the river Vliet, the river which defined the border of Lord Arend's fief. Fishermen rowed up and down the river, casting nets from their fishing longboats. We saw the trade and transport longboats too and peasant women doing laundry in the water. Then there was the mill, a great building with a great big wheel in the water, turning with the current. Sluices diverted water from the river, allowing the millers to control the speed of the wheel. Almost as loud as the blacksmithy, the mill made an uncomfortable grinding noise — a necessary evil in the process of turning most of our grain into flour. Granted, none of us peasants would be eating this grain. It would all be either given to the Lady of Duivenvoorde and her castellans as tax, or sold off to the market of Leyden to be eaten by burghers. All the bread we ate was scooped out of our grain ark at home, ground by Mother in our quernstone, and kneaded by her on the grain ark's lid.

Upstream, we saw some of the free peasants from the free marshes across the river taking a bath. Free peasants had recently begun to come and drain the swamplands on the other side of the Vliet, called the Vlietlands by us Duivenvoorders, to turn the swamps into farmland. The free peasants used to be serfs and probably ran away or something. Lord Arend said that a group of burghers called the Water Board of the Rhineland had been chartered by the late Count Willem II in Hollant a while ago, which meant that they could come to create land wherever they pleased. We didn't know much about politics, but it sounded like more Germans coming to control the Low Countries. That usually wasn't a problem here in Hollant — Brabant and Gelrelant were usually tasked with keeping them at bay. We had Frisians and Englishmen to worry about. We saw the clothes and clogs of the free peasants cast aside by the riverbed on a patch of grass among the slippery, wet clay.

"We ought to put a toad in their clogs," said Maurits. He was always the one getting us in trouble. Thiel, the eldest, smacked him on the back of the head. We kept moving, we'd have to get started on our work anyway. As we walked, we looked out over the vast landscape.

Not a hill in sight, only flat land and trees adorned with apples, cherries, plums, and other sweet things. Villages off in the distance we marked by the tall church spires which protruded from the otherwise straight, unblemished horizon. Our village church was no different, made of bright red brick. Its spire sported a tall, wooden cross which signified to all travelers that they were welcome here. Roads between them could be noted by strings of light forests, often uncultivated as they sat on the border between two fiefs, or were left untouched such that nobles could hunt in them on their free time. Every now and then, on the horizon, you'd also see a windmill or two peek out of the landscape. Of all the buildings one could see on the horizon, the most impressive, by far, were the castles. They weren't as common as the others — perhaps one in every ten villages had one. Our village did. While most villages had a manor where a knight may look after them; we, instead, had our Baron, Heer Arend, who ruled out of Duivenvoorde Castle. It towered over the village, a three-story, brick donjon with a thick brick curtain wall that enclosed a subsidiary brick great hall and chapel. The castle was built atop a natural moat, situating itself on a small island in the middle of a swamp. Two bridges connected the main entrance to either side of the swamp. It made a crossroads of streams that connected to the sluices that irrigated the polders which formed our arable land. As we made our way to the fields, we looked on this arable land, the lands of Heer Arend, which were divided into four primary fields. One of them was a pasture where the cows and sheep grazed. We had far more cows than sheep, as we needed them to make cheese and butter. The sheep, on the other hand, grew cotton, which was to be sold to traveling merchants in exchange for textiles weaved in the towns. Three of them were for the crop rotation, a system that meant that we'd always have a field to harvest during harvesting season. That was the first field.

The second field was called the fallow field, and had been harvested with the spring barley. Thus, it was left to relax and rejuvenate. When the gong farmer came by, we sometimes bought manure from him to enrich this field and give it strength. The third field is where we had just planted the summer barley at the beginning of July. Now, in the rainier months, it was time to harvest the summer barley. Many of our neighbours had already gotten to work, bending over their selions and cultivating them in long strips. It was tiring work. The men, in our case Maurits and Sam, would have to cut each handful of barley by hand with their sickles, and lay them behind themselves for Yda to pick up and tie with a loose piece of grain. Once that selion was finished, they'd load all of the barley into a handcart and bring it to Thiel for threshing. From afar, all the peasants were so in-sync it almost looked like a dance, or like a race even. Their movements were skillful and exact — their muscles were trained to make these motions since birth. It was in their blood — they were people of the land. I watched in awe for a moment as my brothers and sisters split off to start their business. I, on the other hand, was to continue down to the blacksmithy. The smithy was located closer to the castle, with a bit of distance from the main cluster of houses that formed our village — nobody wanted to hear the constant pounding of the hammers, smell the smoke of the bellows, feel the heat of the forge, or see the light of the glowing hot iron as the smiths worked late into the night. As I approached the smiths, I could hear them well before I could see them. I saw Uncle Max and his journeymen working away at a scythe already in preparation for the rye harvest due in a few months. There were several smiths at the shop, including the brownsmith, the artisan who worked with copper and tin, and the farrier, the horseshoe maker. As well, a second blacksmith was working with an apprentice, who had taken on the role of a striker, essentially a second hammer in forging whatever it was they were making. Uncle Max had taught me a little bit about blacksmithing. He was Father's cousin, not his brother, but we called him Uncle Max regardless, as they had grown up together since they were boys. Uncle Max's parents had bought him an apprenticeship with a master blacksmith in Gouda, whereas Father stayed here in Duivenvoorde. As I approached, I held out my arms.

"Uncle Max!" I called out. Immediately, he had his journeymen pause what they were doing. He placed his hammer on the double-horn anvil and came to me.

"Piet!" he shouted. "Come here, you little man." He gave me a fat hug. He was a tall, muscular man, built like a bear, and almost as hairy. "How's your mother doing?" He ruffled my hair.

"She's well," I replied. "She asked me to have you repair this." I held out the sickle and a few groten.

"Ah, I see. The blade's warped. Keep the coins, boy, I'd never charge you for something as small as this. It'll be a few hours," he said. "When the church bells ring ten times, you come back here. Alright?"

I gave him a broad smile. "Okay!" Then I added, "Oh, and there's something else I wanted to ask." This was something I had been thinking about for a while — I wanted to help Mother, but sometimes she could be too proud for her own good. That's where we little people became useful.

"Go on, buddy." Uncle Max looked at me intently.

"Well, most blacksmiths take on an apprentice, and I couldn't help but notice you don't have any…"

"Oh, come on now lad, you're a little young for that…" Uncle Max started.

"Nay, not for me. For Sam. I know that he's always been interested in blacksmithing, and, well, Mother can be proud sometimes, so I know she wouldn't try to ask, but I think Sam and the others need something to make sure they'll be alright in the future," I said. "If you have space, Maurits could use a job too." Uncle Max knelt down to meet me eye to eye.

"Little man, what's all this about?" he asked.

"The grain ark has been light, Mother says," I told him. "A lord in Leyden told us that Maurits and Sam will have to escape to the city, and that Yda has to get married soon, and that little Filips will need to become a monk, and that…"

"It's alright Piet, don't worry. I'll talk to your mum about it, alright?" Uncle Max said, giving me a hug. "I'm glad you told me. You're right — your mother is as hard-working as an ox, but God save her if she ever needs to ask for help. You were smart coming to me for help — I'll see what I can do. I have to ask, what does your mother have in store for you then?"

"I have to become a page for the House of ver Heyen. They're nobles," I said with a sigh. Uncle Max laughed; he couldn't help himself. He put a beefy hand on my shoulder.

"You? A page?" he asked, giggling. "By God, you've been blessed, boy. Don't go around saying you *have* to do it, you should be honoured, little lad. You're gonna be a knight, eh?"

"That's what Lord Hillebrant said. That's who I'll be working for," I replied.

"Piet, that's a mighty achievement. You should be proud of yourself — most young men will never even see the inside of a noble's manor house. You'll be living in one." Uncle Max rose to his feet. At that moment, he became distracted, watching a set of riders in bright green colours off in the distance. Green as grass, they almost blended with the trees and pastures as they rode. "Hey, wait a minute. Isn't that the flag of House ver Heyen?" he asked, pointing to one of their banners. He was right! I saw the wolf hooks Lord Hillebrant had been speaking so much about. Startled, I looked at Uncle Max.

"It looks like you'd better run along now, Piet. I'll have this sickle fixed up for your mum, and I'll have one of these journeymen send it over. Best be on your way."

"Yes, Uncle Max," I said, starting to pick up my feet.

"Hey, make sure to come and visit often!" he called out. "If I don't see you, God speed and good luck!" he hollered as I ran. I looked back to smile at him, and clamoured my way along the dirt path to beat the riders. Oh wait, I'd almost forgotten. The fish traps! I made my way down to the river and began collecting the fish with haste. One of them slipped out of my hands — curses. I quickly shoved the other four into the basket, then slung it over my shoulder, and ran. As I did, one of my friends, Joost, hailed me over.

"Hey Piet, what fish did you catch at the river today?" he asked.

"Nay, I took my trap to the brothel, Joost," I replied. "You mistake a fish for your mother!" I said, laughing. Turnshoes and hosen soaked to the knee, I sprinted my way through the village as excited as ever. As I ran through, the riders briskly passed me, likely not realizing that I was, in fact, the boy they were searching for. As they passed, I got a good look at them. They were all mounted on palfries — riding horses. They were a far cry from the big, burly draught horses the peasants of Duivenvoorde used to push their ploughs during the planting season. Strung along behind the riders were some shorter pack horses, among them another unsaddled palfry. That must have been the horse waiting for me. I had never learned how to ride a horse — I never had any need to. We only ever travelled on foot, and horses were only for ploughing, and occasionally pulling karts; although we tended to pull the karts ourselves. We didn't own any horses, nor did any other serfs in Duivenvoorde. The stables were owned by Heer Arend and managed by his retainers. We were only granted the privilege of borrowing the horses for work and for the planting season.

In the front, of course, there was the round, blond-bearded figure of Hillebrant, as was to be expected, wrapped up in his travelling cloak although not lacking in fine jewelry.

Behind him were three armoured knights, each covered head to toe in chainmail, and each carrying variations of the ver Heyen heraldry on the shields slung upon their backs. The first knight bore the true arms, the simple two white wolf hooks on green side by side. On his person, he wore the same arms on the front and back of his surcoat, and a thin cervelliere helmet atop the chainmail coif. This man was the most aged of the four, with a silvering chinstrap beard descending down beyond the chin of his untied coif. The next man, younger than him, but still older than Hillebrant, bore the same arms on his shield, but with a white trim around it. His surcoat was not a surcoat at all, but an off-white coat of plates, and his goatee was as blond as Hillebrant's. His muscular physique and rugged features indicated that he was a man of the sword, far more than Hillebrant at the head of the column. The moustache of his goatee extended past the cheeks of his coif. Finally, of the three knights, was a man carrying the ver Heyen arms on his shield distinguished by a bright red heraldic label at the top. His angular physique and his clean-shaven face indicated that he was the youngest of all the noblemen. He would have been strikingly handsome if it weren't for a wrinkly, raspberry-pink skin mark that covered his left eye. He wore his chainmail coif down upon his shoulders so that his long, blond hair showed; fairly obviously catching the attention of many of the village's young maidens. Behind these four riders, there were another eight squires, each of whom was also armoured in chainmail and bearing the ver-heyen coat of arms on their shields. Swords hung at the sides of all the knights and squires, even that of Lord Hillebrant, his hanging alongside a deep orange buckler. They rode with serious faces.

In order to try and beat them to my home, I decided to take a shortcut. This route cut straight through the footpaths, requiring that I hop the fences of Mr. Witte and Mr. Maelkin. Luckily, nobody was tending to their market gardens, and their chickens didn't seem to mind me very much. It was only Ms. Lelien, Mr. Maelkin's wife, who noticed my foolishness and decided to speak her mind to me.

"Oh you no-good lout. Get your paws off of my chickens!" she called after me. I'd only caused a fuss in the coup — she didn't know I hadn't taken anything. Not that it would matter anyways. I would be gone from here by tonight, it seemed. All of my brothers and sisters looked at me as if this was something that could happen anytime now. They said kind words to me and taught me last lessons. Thiel told me that girls my age are like cheeses, they'll get better when they're older, but not too old. Yda, on the other hand, told me to always mind my manners and listen to my elders. But, it wasn't as if I wouldn't visit them. I would try my absolute best to.

I finally happened upon a tree that might give me a vantage point over the village to see whether or not they had already made it to the house. When I reached the top of the tall, prickly wall of branches, I decided to take a rest and catch my breath. From there, I peered out over the landscape, where I saw the party of green riders trotting their way through the streets. When I shifted my gaze to home, I soon realized why they had come armed. On the dirt road, blocking their path, standing in formation, was a contingent of the baroness's wapenknechten all clad in the Duivenvoorde black and yellow, as well as the baroness herself accompanied by several men-at-arms. They all bore the heraldry of House of van Duivenvoorde, the three black crescent moons on yellow. Beside the baroness stood a tall, fit boy on a destrier — a horse of war. He was the son of Heer Arend, young Floris. Floris was known to be a classy young man of perhaps fifteen years, taking after the chivalric ideals of bravery and courage from his father, while presenting himself in a more tempered light.

Many saw him as the most elegant noble to come from Castle Duivenvoorde, far more refined than his mother, Lady Mehaud van Duivenvoorde — a shrewd woman; she had denied even hearing Mother's plea to mortgage her crops. The reality was that she didn't understand the ways of peasants. She didn't understand the land — only court politics. Whenever any peasants appealed to her to settle disputes or exact the law, she was brutal and unforgiving, citing honour and chivalry and the word of God. She didn't have any empathy with us, and, as such, most peasants just resolved disputes on their own. Now, peasants were reluctant to take any dispute to her, in fear of losing their pinkie finger like Mrs. Suaneka, or an earlobe like Mr. Waldfridus. Now, she and her men stood menacingly on the road, likely having seen the green riders approach the village in armour. I scrambled my way closer to see what would happen when they met, climbing the thatches on Mr. Ramont's roof. A crowd of villagers had also come to see what the drama was about, although many also simply avoided the armed men, hoping to stay out of trouble. Upon bringing his mounted column in sight of the baroness, Lord Hillebrant called his men to a halt. He dismounted his horse, rotund belly jiggling as his shoes hit the earthen road. Baroness Mehaud did not dismount.

"Lord Hillebrant ver Heyen. To what do I owe the pleasure?" she asked with a sharp sarcasm in her voice. "Please, follow us into Duivenvoorde Castle where we might all take some rest and have a hearty lunch."

"I'm merely here to pick up my page boy, we will be on

our way back to Leyden soon," replied Lord Hillebrant. "There will be no need to go through such trouble." Floris gave a bold, echoing snort through the breaths of his charcoal-black greathelm. Lord Hillebrant reacted astutely to the insult with a raised eyebrow.

"And who might that be?" asked Lady Mehaud.

"The young Pieter, son of Lijsbet. One of your helpful villagers pointed us in the direction of their home. If it is no trouble, we may just get on our way there and…"

"You must be mistaken," Lady Mehaud replied. "Young Piet, as with all the villagers here, are serfs. They are tied to the land, and remain under the protection of my husband, Baron Arend van Duivevoorde."

"And where is your husband, Baroness?" Lord Hillebrant asked coyly.

"He has taken up the righteous cause of the Cross, Lord Hillebrant. He has travelled to Acre to protect Christian pilgrims on their path to Jerusalem. In the meantime, his lands and titles have befallen unto me, the Baroness regent of Duivenvoorde, and the representative of the greater Houses vander Wassenaer."

"I see. Quite fortunate, isn't it, that a girl from Utrecht might come to rule such an estate in Hollant?" Lord Hillebrant replied.

Insulted, Lady Mehaud riposted his comment. "Even more fortunate that a bookkeeper such as yourself would emerge from your townhouse to claim property of the vander Wassenaer lineage. The House of Duivenvoorde has stood proudly over this land for half a century, and its people have proudly farmed this land for hundreds of years. You would seek to rip this boy from his ancestral home?"

"I would seek to liberate him," Lord Hillebrant replied staunchly. "He is not your property, nor are Lijsbet nor any of her children."

Lady Mehaud smirked. "Is that so?" she asked. "They are my serfs, no?"

"They are no longer. Not since you rejected their crop mortgage," Lord Hillebrant said. Lady Mehaud looked puzzled and somewhat taken by surprise. Lord Hillebrant, without saying a word, pulled some scroll from his saddlebag — I couldn't see precisely what it was, but it was sealed; which meant it was an official document. "Upon discussing with the Count, your actions have been deemed unworthy of ownership, Baroness. Your ownership of Lijsbet and her children is hereby pronounced unlawful, and, as such, you hold no feudal claim to Pieter. As such, Mrs. Lijsbet and her children are now free peasants. What good is a liege lord who would let their people starve?" Lord Hillebrant's tone turned rhetorical with a little more volume than he had been speaking in before; no doubt to communicate his message to the peasants who had gathered around. Lady Mehaud's cheeks grew pink.

"You lawmen and your forked tongues. I will take this to court," she said with the anger and zeal of a warrior. "You will not pass here. If you lay your hands on that boy, my men will tear you and your horses in half."

"You would stand against the decree of the crown? That's treason," Lord Hillebrant said. "Your options are either to face arrest here and now, or hand over the boy."

"You would go through all this trouble for a page boy?" Lady Mehaud asked. Lord Hillebrant gave a coy smile.

"I'm a pragmatic man. I don't gamble. I only wanted to ensure that I would not leave your… charming estate empty-handed."

Lady Mehaud did not look pleased. "You lawyers are nothing but a nest of nepotist vipers. That is not law, that is an offense to the van Duivenvoorde name."

"May we pass?" Lord Hillebrant asked with cold rigidity. Lady Mehaud reluctantly shifted her horse to the side of the road, as did her men. However, Floris stood his ground, his horse growing restless as it was left alone in the street. Its bright yellow caparison became slightly muddled by the muck and clay tossed up by its restless hooves. The blackened steel links of his chainmail hauberk rustled loudly with every motion of his warhorse. Floris said nothing, only making eye contact through the eye slits of his greathelm. His glare was menacing, although his eyes were not visible beneath the veil of shadow.

"Nay," Floris spoke stalwartly in a voice high enough to startle the green riders.

"Follow your mother," Lord Hillebrant said, realizing he was only a boy.

Floris scoffed. "My mother is a lady, and as such, she holds no obligation to step in the path of armed intruders. I, on the other hand, do. My father has nobly taken up the Cross to join the ranks of the Knights Templar. As such, I am now the sworn defender of the House of Duivenvoorde, and I will stand my ground."

"You have too much life ahead of you, go home. You will be knighted one day for a feat of valour. That feat will not come today," Lord Hillebrant said. Floris did not reply, but reached out to his squire, a boy of merely fourteen years, for a glove. He took the glove high in his right hand and dropped it to the ground — the symbol was clear. "Do you take me for a fighting man?" Lord Hillebrant asked. "I will not duel you."

"You have dishonoured my family, my name, and my land. I will most certainly duel with you. If you don't have the gall, lawman, I suggest you present a champion to fight in your stead," the young knight said.

"Floris, this is foolish," interjected Lady Mehaud. "This is not how lords behave."

"I am a warrior," Floris retorted. "If I cannot protect my home, I have no worth."

"The law is the law. There is no shame in it, boy," Lord Hillebrant said.

"Your document could be a forgery. I would rather let God decide than your piece of paper. Let it be a trial by combat."

Lord Hillebrant rolled his eyes. "Trust me, boy. You don't want to do that."

"And why is that? Are you afraid no man of that grand retinue behind you can best me?"

"Have you taken a life before, Floris?" he asked bluntly.

"It's about time I took my first," Floris retorted.

"Boy, if we agree to this duel, you will end this day with

blood either on your sword or your burial shroud," Lord Hillebrant said.

"Then the fish in the Vliet will be salted with blood tonight," young Floris said. Lord Hillebrant, very clearly fed up with Floris, mounted his palfrey and trotted over to his retinue to discuss their course of action. As if on instinct, the three knights' squires brought over each of their greathelms in preparation for the duel. The eldest knight was brought a gilded greathelm, the second eldest an oakleaf-green one with a white cross on its face, and the youngest a greathelm with green mantling and a green and white torse. I saw the knights confer with one another, after which I saw Lord Hillebrant whisper into the ear of the youngest knight, while the other two sent away their squires. I don't know what precisely he said, but the young knight nodded in compliance. As Lord Hillebrant rode forth to meet Floris, the eldest knight embraced the younger, both still atop their horses. The elder knight must have been his father.

I heard Hillebrant say something along the lines of, "Lower your lance only when the time is right, son. Let God do the rest. If you win the joust, you've won the duel. The foot is no competition if you're still atop your horse."

Then Lord Hillebrant spoke to Floris in a voice far clearer. "We accept," was all he said.

"Let this feat of arms inspire our serfs," Floris said. His mother looked displeased with the whole thing, but she had evidently decided to stay out of it. The two parties formed two lines across each side of the road, ushering villagers to stay away from the carnage. We all couldn't help but keep a watchful eye on the duel. I saw young kids like myself even sticking their heads out of their huts' windows to get a glimpse of the action. The two young knights rode forth, supplied with lances by their squires, with their greathelms atop their heads and their shields in hand. The middle one of the three knights, the one with the goatee and coat of plates, rode his way into the centre of the field where the two knights stood ready for battle.

"Alright lads. Young Wollefram here wants to test his mettle. While I, personally, don't believe this to be the most tactful outcome of events, his father, my dear older brother, Lodewijk, here, believes that it'll put some confidence in the boy. As such, Lord Hillebrant has appointed young Sir Wollefram as his champion. What say you, Floris? Do you accept this battle?"

"I do," Floris replied.

The rugged knight turned to Sir Wollefram. "And you, Wolf? You aren't backing out now, are you?" he jested.

"Never," Sir Wollefram replied.

"Good," said the goateed knight. "I want a clean, honest fight. Remember, God's watching. He's the one pulling the strings here, but you've got to do the dirty work. That means keep it as clean as possible. Only one soul's getting damned today." Both of the knights nodded in agreement. "Alright then, boys. Take your places," the knight said.

Immediately, both of the young knights clasped their chainmail mittens with one another, and then spurred on their horses to take positions at either side of the road. Their squires stood awaiting them, each with multiple lances in reserve. Both knights took a lance, and the middle-aged knight exited the road. "Marks…" he called, raising his hand in the air.

"Charge!" he cried out, dropping his hand like a blade befalling an enemy. The two knights dug their spurs into their horses' flanks hoping to accelerate as quickly as possible. I swear I could feel the earth shaking beneath my feet. It was spectacular, the speed and vigor with which the two knights met in the middle.

The first pass was quick, both lowered their lances around the same time, smashing them on one another, before riding off to each other's squires for a second lance. All the while, both parties lining either side of the battleground shouted in favour of their own knights. Whether or not these words of encouragement could be heard behind their greathelms, I was unsure. Without a pause or hesitation, the two riders wheeled their horses around and went for a second pass, as if they were hoping to catch one another off guard. In this pass, Sir Wollefram managed to strike Floris on the cheek of his greathelm, sending him flying from his horse. He landed in the muck with a hard, crunching sound. As he struggled to his feet, it was clear that he had injured his left leg on the descent. However, undisturbed, Sir Wollefram came at him again with another lance. Bracing for the impact as much as he could, Floris held up his shield. Luckily, the lance head did not penetrate the shield. The lance simply broke as Floris was hurled backward into the muddy, earthen path. This time, he was much slower to get up, like a newborn calf. Seeing this, Sir Wollefram dropped his next lance, and dismounted from his horse, opting to honourably fight him on foot. As he approached the stationary Floris, he struck him once more to his helmet with the corner of his shield. Floris toppled over one last time. Laid flat on the ground, Floris tore off his greathelm to gasp for air, desperately struggling to slip his fingers out of his chainmail mittens. He pulled furiously at the buckles of the strap, but his ailettes were too big for him, mercilessly blocking his shoulders, leaving him writhing in the dirt like an animal to no avail. Seeing the poor knight desperately contorting himself in the muck, Sir Wollefram halted, giving him time, before threatening him with a menacing final blow. Lady Mehaud shrieked in agony as she saw the tip of his sword ascend high into the air.

Floris dropped his own sword and held up his unarmed right hand, pleading, "Mercy! Mercy! Have mercy, good sir!"

Sir Wollefram, having considered this plea for a moment, and having gauged the audience to ensure that this conclusion had been reached, buried the tip of his sword in the dirt right beside Floris's exposed face such that the sword stood upright, and then kicked the young Floris hard in his groin. Sir Wollefram then muttered something in French, something along the lines of *putain*, an insult by the tone of it. Having taken off his own greathelm, he spat in the dirt as a final insult, before, with his now free hand, helping Floris to his feet. He escorted his battered opponent to his horse, supporting him as his leg couldn't carry the weight of both the man and his armour. Lady Mehaud fell to her knees in prayer to thank God for sparing her son.

Lord Lodewijk made his way over to his son to congratulate him and was soon followed by his younger brother. The crowd of peasants was silent. It was shocking to see Floris beaten so badly. Lord Hillebrant finally made his way over to shake Sir Wollefram's hand and congratulate him dearly. Sir Wollefram reclaimed his sword and also fell to his knees, resting his hands on his sword in prayer.

Floris, seemingly struggling to keep conscious, was briskly awoken by a crisp slap to his cheek delivered by his mother. "Foolish boy!" she hollered. "What were you thinking? If that kind gentleman hadn't spared your life…" tears began to trickle down her cheeks. "Footmen," she snapped, "guide his horse to the barber-surgeon. He needs to be treated quickly before we send word for a doctor." She then turned to Lord Hillebrant. "I am indebted to your family," she said. "But the House of Wassenaer will hear of this."

"As they should," Lord Hillebrant said. "But has this dispute been laid to rest?"

"Indeed, it has. Take your boy and go. We don't want you here any longer," she replied. Lord Hillebrant turned around and made his way to his horse. Shortly after, Lady Mehaud did the same, following Floris's escort to the barber-surgeon.

The deed had been done, little blood had been spilled, and a conclusion had been reached. I was to go with Lord Hillebrant — not God nor Heer Arend could change that now.

Chapter 3. The Burner: Yda

Life on the farm was not the same without Piet. Every morning, the empty chair at the breakfast table was a stark reminder. A reminder that, not only was Piet gone, the rest of us would soon be as well. I don't know what that Hillebrant did, but he certainly aggravated Mehaud and her men. It wasn't safe for us anymore. He brought a purse of guilders to our mother, but I don't know if that was truly enough for any of us to go anywhere. I knew mother was sick, but surely there was some way. Just some way we could stick through it together. At night, when the rain would hit the hardest and my little sisters would cower from the thunder and lightning, I couldn't help but hold them and tell them it would be alright. That was before father slipped. Now, I didn't comfort them from the lightning, but from the soldiers. They looked at us like we were walking corpses. We had their attention now — I did, and I didn't like it. I avoided them, the tavern, the guard houses, everywhere a yellow-clad brute might be found. I tried my best.

Every night my sisters told tales of Piet in a castle and Piet rescuing young maidens as a knight. I feared the worst for him. I didn't believe much in those tales anymore—bards came and sang them to young boys who wanted to be knights and old peasant men who knew better. Mother had been more solemn too. I could tell, even more than she was before. Her silent tears watered every loaf of bread she baked, every bushel of barley she lifted, and every bedtime story she told the young ones. She had too much on her shoulders. I tried to help, to take on more, but she can be a stubborn woman.

At least she had taken to train me to be a wife—that way I could learn to take care of little Filips and manage Merin and Florie. The older boys, on the other hand, seemed to have gotten over it quickly. You'd often hear them making lewd jokes about Piet's conquests as a knight, and how he would have every village girl wrapped around his thumb by the time he was of age. I think, in reality, they were only joking to deal with it. We all loved him dearly. It had been a week since he'd left, more or less.

Too much thought for one night, I'd ought to get back to sleep. Like I told my sisters, if I stayed up, the house elf might bite me. They were fast asleep, faces planted against the rushes. I just couldn't. I slipped out of bed, still in my linen smock. I thought I'd better go for a walk to clear my head. I slipped into my kirtle gown, then buckled up my belt, and slipped into my surcoat. I put on my hose, tying them with garters, and hastily tied up my braids into a pretzel knot. Finally, I put on my fillet. If anyone was to catch me stalking about at night, I'd be caught looking put together. The last step was putting on my clogs. I decided I'd visit the spot where father fell. It's not like they had left him there—he had his proper burial by the church eventually. I suppose that was courtesy of Hillebrant's coin purse. I knew the spot on the riverbed by heart. This wasn't the first time I'd visited, and I wouldn't expect it to be the last. I hope it wouldn't be. Perhaps I'd be next to go. It felt as if we were all migrating away like sparrows. First Piet, then Sam, and now Thiel and Maurits had run off to…wherever they went.

I opened the door carefully so as to not awake anyone. Vlam, our cat, wide awake, came to follow me. Silently, I picked him up and gently petted him as I walked. My clogs moved quietly over the earth and floor rushes as I made my way outside. One foot after another, I walked down to the riverbank. The walk soon turned into a dance, as I found myself alone in the dark with little but fireflies and moonlight to light my path. Vlam's eyes glowed a bright yellow as they carefully stalked any movement in the darkness. In the distance, I could see the rising smoke of the charcoal burners working late into the night. Maarten was among them. He was a handsome boy. Hard-working, with big, strong hands. I think he liked me. At the spring harvest festival, when we danced the maypole, I saw him watching me. We'd also been talking for quite some time now. When he was in the village, he sometimes helped me with my chores. He'd carry heavy loads for me. Well, maybe he just distracted me. But he was a good boy; I liked him. He was a free peasant. He was with the men working to drain the swamp; he and his friends and brothers produced the charcoal for their encampment. They were going to build a village there, that's what he told me. *You know what? I should visit him,* I thought to myself. Carefully, through the dark, I made my way along the river where the bullfrogs were croaking and the grasshoppers were chirping. While not as pretty as birdsongs, I quite enjoyed their little chorus. It made me feel less alone in the dark. It was chilly, too, but the pillar of smoke promised the warmth of a great kiln. And the warmth of a friendly heart.

With every step, I felt warmer, as I approached the great fire. Its orange flames shone through the trees like the sun had been ripped out of the sky and brought to live among the trees. The closer I walked, the voices grew louder.

"Hendrik, help me with the spade," I heard one of them

say. And they joked and laughed as young men do. I hope they didn't mind me coming. Before I even approached the young burners, I heard my name from behind me.

"Yda?" the voice asked. It was distinctly Maarten's. Strong, but gentle. Calm but energetic. "What in the Heavens are you doing out here?" he asked, a pile of firewood in his arms. Vlam, just as startled as I was, let out a yelp, leaping from my arms to the earthen ground.

"Maarten!" I replied. "You snuck up on me."

"Hope I didn't scare you," he said, looking down at the frustrated, orange cat. "I was just collecting wood…"

"Nay, not at all. I'm actually here to see you."

"Me?"

"Yeah you."

"Why me?"

"I don't know. I just couldn't sleep and wanted to see you," I said with a smile. He replied with a broad smile of his own.

"Want to come and see the kiln?" he asked, extending one hand to me while desperately clutching the bundle of firewood in the other. Merrily, I took it. His grip was firm but gentle, like a reassurance that he was there to guide me. He stopped for a moment to look at Vlam. "Wanna come too?" he asked in a high voice, urging her to follow us. We made our way to the orange glow, taking great care not to rush. I could feel its warmth increasing.

Smoke thickened the air with every step. Maarten handed me a cloth. "Here, tie this around your mouth and nose," he said. "For the smoke." He handed it to me. I didn't tie it on, he knew what I really wanted. He took the rag and stood behind me, taking great care to tie it gently. Afterwards, we took a few more steps forward.

"You have one for yourself too, right?" I asked him, realising he hadn't pulled one out of his belt for himself.

"I've grown used to it," he replied, looking off into the trees. I reckoned he thought himself quite impressive for managing all that smoke and heat. Immediately, I slipped the mask off my face and onto his. However, by accident, what was supposed to be a mask became more of a blindfold for him, and the unaware Maarten nearly immediately found his foot in a marshy puddle up to his mid-calf. "Yda!" he cried out. Oh my. *Foolish girl, what have you done*, I thought to myself. To my relief, after a second of hesitation, he broke into uncontrollable laughter. I laughed with him, taking the fillet from my hair and wiping off what I could with it, squeezing it to dry and wiping again.

"What's all that commotion about out there?" asked a voice from the charcoal burners' camp. Maarten's head pricked up like a startled deer. "Maarten, what's holding up the wood, for Heaven's sake?" the voice asked.

"Don't you worry, I'll be there in a moment," Maarten replied. "Just slipped in a puddle."

"Oh, Christ, you haven't gotten the firewood wet, have you?" the voice asked. We both looked at the soaked logs, and then at one another, and couldn't help but chuckle. "Who's that with you Maarten, you sneaky bastard?" the man asked him. "Master Klaas, it's only Yda. From the village," Maarten replied.

"The girl you've been telling us about?" the voice asked. Maarten's cheeks grew red like hot iron. He tried to reply but he was lost for words. The voice was the one laughing now. "Get over here, you troublemakers. Both of you. No fooling around on the job." Wide-eyed, I couldn't help but look at Maarten's face in amusement. We both started to make our way to the clearing.

"So you've been talking about me?" I teased him.

"Oh, you know, I talk about all the people I meet. They'd ought to know what you crazy Duivenvoorders do."

"Mhm. And when you go to the alehouse after a long day's work, do you talk about those girls too?"

"Girls, what girls?"

"Oh, you know, the ale wenches?" I asked. Maarten grinned. "You've never been to an alehouse, have you?" he asked.

"What? Why do you say that?" I asked. I didn't know how he could be so certain—I thought that was a reasonable question.

"There won't be many *ale wenches* that are willing to do much more than give you a smile but in the towns. And in the towns, let me tell you, there's quite a grade of difference between those alehouses too. Now, the ale houses in the Rhineland are a good bit more wild than I should put to words..." he was clearly plucking memories from his mind, envisioning what exactly goes down in those sorts of places.

"Just about how well-traveled are you?" I asked. I'm not sure why, but I'd just assumed he'd been taken from some village or town and set to work. It hadn't crossed my mind that he'd been travelling around to many places, but, clearly, he had quite a few experiences to draw on. He spoke as if he'd seen the entire world. He hadn't time to respond.

"There you both are, emerging from the bush like bunnies. Maarten, you know what to do with the wood," a burly man said. This was my first time seeing the kiln and the camp in person. Maarten, as if controlled by a pulled lever, immediately dispatched himself and set off to drop his firwood. "You must be the famous Yda," the man said. "Be careful with that Maarten. He's as thick-headed as he's brawny." Realizing he hadn't introduced himself, he continued, "I'm Nicolaas. Klaas for short. I'm the man running this enterprise." After a slight pause, he said, "So, that begs the question, what are you up to this late? The night can be a dangerous place for a maiden such as yourself." He scanned the tree line as if fending off wolves with his gaze.

"Oh, don't mind me. Just had some trouble sleeping and figured I'd pay Maarten a visit," I said. "Don't worry, I won't be here for long. I'll have to milk the lord's cows in the morning so I'd ought to get a good night's sleep."

"Looks like you've missed that opportunity by a long shot," Klaas replied, scratching his gruff stubble. "You're welcome to hang around as long as you like. There's a barrel of ale and a few tankards in that hut over there. Feel free to grab a seat, and don't inhale too much of that bloody smoke, it'll have you coughing for days." I took a seat on a log that overlooked the kiln. It was a great mound filled with firwood that would burn for a whole day and night cycle—at least, that's what Maarten had taught me. The whole while it had to be tended by charcoal burners.

Not many people visited them. Not only were they associated with the free peasants draining the swamp, charcoal burners were just generally seen as untrustworthy people. In Voorschoten, for example, the village between Duivenvoorde and Leyden, also under Heer Arend, one of their charcoal burners was tried and convicted by the village aldermen for witchcraft. I never thought much of it… I mean, of course, I grew up believing that charcoal burners were mischievous people, but having met Maarten, I wasn't inclined to think that anymore. Klaas seemed alright too; hospitable at least.

Maarten, having done something to the kiln with a long pole, I was not sure what it was, came to join me with two tankards of fresh water from the Vliet. When he sat there, neither of us really knew what to say, so I just said a "Thank you," and stared at the flames.

It was warm and bright, like the centre of the universe in the dark and chill of the night. Through the rising smoke we could see a night sky full of stars. They twinkled, and almost seemed to dance for us.

"That one's the big bear," said Maarten, pointing to the sky. I had no idea what he was talking about.

"Excuse me?" I asked, confused.

"Those stars there. Those ones look like a bear, don't they? And her cub is right over there playing too." He pointed to a similar group of bright stars somewhere else.

"I don't know what you're talking about. They look like frying pans to me," I replied.

Maarten laughed. I liked the way he laughed. He had a handsome smile. "What?" I asked with a smile of my own, feigning confusion. He just looked at me, and lowered his mask, and kissed me on the cheek. The stars really were dancing now. I couldn't see it, but I felt my cheeks grow bright red. I didn't know what to think. We'd only talked up until now. As an instant reaction, I slapped him lightly. He just looked at me, confused. I didn't know what to do. So I kissed him back. On the lips. It was soft and light. His kiss was soft and light. He just looked at me. For a moment. And then we put our lips together again. The endearing moment was shattered by a, "No way!" from the kiln workers who'd dropped their tools to come see what was going on.

"I should go back," I said to him softly. "But I'll see you tomorrow night?"

"I'll meet you half way," he replied. "By the river."

+ Maarten +

As she danced off into the bush like a wood elf, I couldn't help but stop and stare at her. By God she was like a dream. Once she was out of sight, and more importantly out of earshot, I turned to my mates.

"Let's fucking go!" I hollered, met with a host of congratulations. I made the rounds like I'd just scored in a game of stone throwing.

"Pour the lad a tankard," Master Klaas said. "She's a fine girl ye picked. But stay focussed, yeah?" I cheered him with my tankard of ale. The burning was almost done. Usually we'd harvest the coals soon after, but tonight was for partying. The lads at the swamp could wait an hour or so, so could the town markets. My best friend, Kees, gave me a crisp clap on the back. He was a tall, brawny fellow, who always wore his characteristic linen coif.

"She kissed you, Maarten," he said a full volume, as was his usual talking pitch when he did talk.

"I know! And she was like, honey!" I replied. "If I'd have known she'd come tonight…"

"Lad," said Master Klaas, "my grandfather always used to tell me that the best things in life come as surprises. Three rascals on and I can't tell you he's right, but it might better apply to you." His sons, also burners, well, burners in training, I suppose, chuckled with us.

The next morning, I arose at the crack of dawn. Felix and Kees were already shovelling coals by the time I'd gotten dressed. All the boys were groggy; we'd only slept half a night. That's how it was on the days we had burning. Today was coal harvesting instead. From the early morning, after our bread and ale, we'd be shovelling out the old coals, taking it across the county, and bringing in more lumber. When Master Klaas said that somebody would have to take charcoal to the village blacksmith, I more than happily obliged, recruiting Kees as my assistant. I remembered Yda said she'd be milking cows early morning, so I figured we'd have some time to stop by the pasture beforehand. Carefully, we loaded up sacks of the black stuff into a handcart, and pushed it together. It wasn't long before we'd pushed our way past the trees and into the wide-open, flat country. Everywhere I'd been in the Low Countries was like this. I, myself, am actually Luxembourgish. I don't often tell folks, as people can have their views on outsiders. Nasty ones, at that. I suppose it doesn't help that I'm a charcoal burner either. But I've spent most of my life around the Low Countries, having worked for the Water Board of the Rhineland in Flanders, Zeelant, and now Hollant. Everywhere I've gone, I've come to adopt the local accent. It helps, really. I couldn't imagine now returning to Luxembourg speaking the Dutch I speak now. Not a soul would recognize a word, I'd say. I quite liked it here in Hollant. If Yda would have me, I wouldn't mind settling down here, starting a family, and keeping a small kiln here for good. But that wasn't the way of things. Master Klaas decided where we went; and we went where there was work. Despite my best efforts, I could only stay here as long as there were enough folks to buy our charcoal. If the swamp drainers went, we went too. The villagers had their own charcoal burners out somewhere near Wassenaer.

The village crept up on us quickly. By now we'd both gotten quite used to hauling our kart to and fro, delivering coals every which way and collecting supplies for the camp. I'd almost appropriated the role after having met Yda. Anything to stay near the village. We made our way up to the smithy with our coals and some tools that needed sharpening when I saw her. Gracefully, dancing about her daily tasks like the rosy petals that fall from spring flower trees. She was in the pasture with the cows, dutifully milking them, as she'd said, with the other milkmaids.

"Kees, stay here," I told him, leaving him to give the tools to the smith. I could do nothing but stare at Yda for a moment before heading back down the hill. As I took my first step, a beefy, "Hold it," echoed through my eardrums.

I turned around to find the blacksmith, an ox of a man, glaring at me, bigger than any of the tavern boys I'd seen in dankest alleys of Ghent. I only looked at him, unsure of precisely why his hey was tossed. A young apprentice behind him pointed at me and told him, "That's the one." The young boy had bright ginger hair and freckles, just like Yda.

"Which one of those maids are you looking at down there, pup?" the blacksmith asked.

"What's it to you?" I asked, calling his bluff.

"Young Sam here's seen you prancing around with my niece a couple o' times. Wouldn't think she'd take to a burner," he said, wiping his nose with a smithing rag. The rag left a dark mark on his face from the char. "Not exactly another log to toss in your kiln only to spew out a blackened husk, if you catch my meaning."

"Precisely sir," I replied, somewhat anxious. "I'm an honest man. My mate Kees here can tell you." I looked to Kees for some aid.

"Oh, uh jaja," Kees interjected upon meeting the smith eye to eye. "I've once seen this man tell a nobleman he's an idiot after he'd asked how long our coals last. Very honest." The smith just stared at him blankly. The silence was only cut by the incessant screeching of seagulls, as if chuckling to mock me, and finally the uncontrollable outburst of laughter from the smith himself. In fact, he was so big that, instead of leaning on one of the beams holding up the smithy's roof when he chuckled, he rested his hand on big Kees's shoulder instead.

"Right," he said, wiping his eyes with the rag he tucked back under his belt. "Best get a move on then before that last cow's dried out." With a smile, I picked my feet back up once more. I heard him call out behind me, "And if you do hurt her, you soot-shoveller, you'll find a piping iron under your pillow." I moved quite briskly down the hill, half to catch Yda before her work was done, and half to create as much distance between myself and that smith as possible. He must've been that Uncle Max she'd told me about. Since her father died, I was sure Mr. Max had taken it upon himself to look out for her and her brothers and sisters. As I headed down, I caught sight of another set of riders, different from those we'd seen two weeks ago. They were knights templar—crusaders of the highest order. They were all unarmoured, but loaded saddlebags hauled by their porters' rounceys indicated that armour and shields were well available should they need them. They each sported long beards which bounced and flowed with each stride of the horses, and on top of their clothing a bright, white surcoat with the scarlet templar cross over their hearts; and a long, light cloak, white as snow, with a red templar cross on their left shoulders. Their porters wore the same, with the exception that they sported black clothes as opposed to white. They were headed for the keep. It had appeared that Baron Arend had returned. No matter, Yda was only a few paces further. I called out to her with open arms, and she responded by nearly spilling all the milk from her cow's teat in response. With a smile, she came to meet me. Her fellow milk maids, on the other hand, also eagerly stopped their work for a moment to huddle and discuss my arrival in secret with giddy grins. Yda took me for a mellow walk to enjoy the summer breeze.

Chapter 4. The Declaration: Floris

I couldn't focus. The book in my hands did little to ease my boredom. My leg throbbed still, even after a whole two weeks. My linen sheets did little to ease the pain, although I was certainly glad that I had them. I felt frail. Useless, even. My walking cane stood leaning against the bed like I was some old man. I'm no old man. I'm a warrior. I'm a bloody warrior, damn it. And here I am, ashamed, embarrassed, and still recovering like an old dog. I scanned the surroundings of my solar. The white plastered walls, decorated with fictive masonry and adorned with a crescent moon motif, and the tile floors smothered in carpets, felt like a prison cell. I might well have believed I'd been in the deepest crevasse of the dungeon if I hadn't known any better. I sighed in boredom. My sword hung on the wall like some decorative piece. That's what it was, wasn't it? Not a scratch on it. Not a drop of blood. It hadn't even touched him. A heavy knock came on my chamber door.

"I'm reading," I said, index finger curling the next page of the book I held, turning it over to find out that I was, in fact, reading a manuscript titled *the Vita of Sir Ulrich von Liechtenstein.* I'd heard it was quite a funny book. Perhaps I should actually read it sometime. "What is it?" I asked.

"Riders are approaching, sir," said the voice of one of our wapenknechten. "They bare the cross of the temple order."

I felt my eyes light up. "Father's back!" I exclaimed. Hastily, I tore the linen sheets off of myself, grabbing my cane, and hobbling over to the door. My ankle was still swollen and my leg still felt week and painful, although it was nowhere near the agony of that day. The barber-surgeon had done a good job — he shifted the bone back into place. Now, although a little bent and an inch shorter than it was before, at least my shin had started to grow whole again. I opened the door and told the guardsman that he could already head out and greet my father, and that I'd meet him in due time. I'd need it.

I hobbled down the cylindrical stone staircase, taking great care not to slip and crack my skull on the fine masonry. Having successfully made my way down the keep to the curtain wall, I felt a gust of cool, damp, fresh air slap my cheeks. I shielded my eyes from the blinding sun. It felt liberating. I'd begun to spend most my days inside reading whatever was left on my shelf or playing my hurdy-gurdy. Occasionally, my little sister Agnes, only thirteen years old, would play chess with me. Much of my muscle, built up from hours of swordplay and riding and bowmanship, had now gone to waste, it felt. I felt limp as a lilly. My weaker leg dragging behind, I rushed out to look over the main gate where I saw the riders approaching. The gates had already been opened. There were two red and white striped gates, both equally large on either side — just wide enough to fit a horse-drawn cart, and tall enough to let in a mounted knight without his lance smacking the portcullis. The templars made their way into the castle, Father leading the way, followed by a chaplain, two other knights, what appeared to be a Saracen knight, and a set of porters of both Latin and Saracen descent. Slaavi perhaps. The whole castle was almost thrown into disarray at his arrival, as servants shouted orders at one another to fetch food and a basin of clean water and for the stableboys to come and tend to the horses. The chickens, on the other hand, waddling across the courtyard, didn't seem to notice their liege lord's arrival, only bowing, not to him, but to pick up grain.

"Father!" I shouted happily, making my way down the stone steps in the main guard tower to embrace him.

"Floris!" he shouted out. "It's been quite some time, hasn't it?" We embraced one another with crisp pats on the back, signifying that we were both men now.

"What have the maidens done to you?" he jested, noticing the cane in my hand and the limp in my leg.

"As the English say, *'tis but a scratch,*" I replied, not wanting to divulge the truth behind it here and now. Father gave some orders to the other men in French. I understood it well after my years of schooling. I suppose they must have been Frenchmen of some kind.

"Frenchmen?" I asked my father in Dutch.

"You wouldn't believe how many frogs there are in Acre," father replied with a smile.

It made his beard prick up — he hadn't worn one when he'd left.

"Mother's in her room," I said, realizing she hadn't come down to greet him. That was to be expected, in all honesty. They weren't the happiest in one another's company.

"Of course she is. We'll speak to the shrew later," he said. That was his pet name for her. It wasn't very flattering; it also wasn't meant to be. Switching to French, "Gentlemen, this is my one and only son, Lord Floris van Duivenvoorde," he said, "he's a strong, young man, and will almost certainly be a banneret one day. These men, Floris, are the lads who kept me alive in the Holy Land. This here is Sir Gaspard de Chinon, Sir Reynald d'Aurebac, and the mighty Sir Guillaume the Saracen. We also have here the holy chaplain, the Englishman Lord William fitz Roy."

"Pleasure to meet you gentlemen," I said, shaking each of their hands.

"Likewise," said William.

"That's quite a limp you've got there," Reynald said. "Hunting?"

"Nay, it was a duel," I replied.

"That's my son," father said. "Takes a leg for a life. A worthy trade I'd say."

"Not quite," I replied with hesitation. The men only looked at me to go on.

"Your idiot boy fell off his horse and wasn't worth killing!" screamed my mother out of a tower window. Of course. Perfect timing, Mother.

"I only challenged him to a duel because mother and all her men stood down while the bastards took one of our serfs," I retorted loud enough to ensure that Mother heard. Father leaned in to me.

"Don't beat yourself up, lad. You're a young man, you have a life ahead of you. You got lucky. And frankly, I don't know who these men were, and you'll tell me soon enough over a tankard of ale, but standing up to any man takes balls. Challenging them to a duel? That takes bigger balls than most knights have. Good on you. What happens after that is up to God." His words were like a cool sip of water after a long day's riding. It was quite nice to hear somebody come to my defence for a change.

Just as father said, the ale started flowing and a quick feast was mustered by the servants of the house. Pork sausage, eggs, cheeses, fish — we ate it all. The midday meal was filled with festivities now as the family, our wapenknechten, and our servants all enjoyed good food. Conversation was marked by riveting tales of the Orient from Father and his knights, and the many battles they had had with desert bandits. The Saracen knight, his Christian name being Guillaume, also told us the tale of how he converted to the true faith and served the templars as a turcopole, riding down heathen raiders and battling his former Muslim comrades among the dunes. Each and every one of their tales sounded glorious, marked with chivalry and honour. Once, father said, their wapenknechten had so many arrows lodged in their gambeson armour that, by the end of the day, they appeared more porcupine than man. Agnes laughed at that one in particular. She was more enthralled by the tales of knighthood than mother would have wanted her to be. It either meant she would soon be too little of a lady, or too much of one. I only smiled seeing the exchange of looks take place, and young Agnes sticking out her tongue at Mother only for her to roll her eyes in her classic, poised expression of shock. Agnes maintained a measure of vitality in the castle. Nay, *the* measure of vitality in the castle. She gave it life. She practised her French now, speaking to the grizzled crusaders. They were kind to her, speaking as one would to a child much younger than her. I suppose her limited French made her appear more immature than she was. She was a smart girl. Beat me in chess more times than I could count.

The flow of enthralling tales was dammed when Mother switched back to Dutch. "So tell me, husband dearest, what brings you back so early? Taken Jerusalem already?" she asked with daggers in her words.

"Believe me, when I realized I'd be coming back to you, I shook more than I ever had against Saracen raiders," Father replied. "Nearly pissed myself. But to satisfy your query, we recaptured Tripoli and crushed the Mahometan fleet. We secured peace in the Holy Land for ten years." His announcement was met with a round of cheers and tankards and fists knocked firmly against the wooden tables. "After that, Prince Edward of England, you know, they call him the Longshanks for his long legs, well, he left. He was the one man holding the war effort together, and we'd just signed a treaty, so the rest of us did too." Father recounted memories of glory and battle in his expression. Certainly more than he'd said. I burned with curiosity. "On my way back, I received word that the Count of Hollant has been issuing out a summons to his Barons. The Dutchmen in Acre have said that the time has come to take revenge on the Frisians." Upon hearing those words, the roar of the party began to dim. Everyone heeded Father's words closely. He turned to me. "Floris, you were too young to remember, but nearly a decade and a half ago, the great Graaf Willem II Gerulfing, King of the Romans and Count of Hollant, was torn off his horse, caught in a Frisian bog, and murdered by those savages. Our good Count, finally of age, has decided to take revenge on them and reclaim his father's body."

"Sounds like nonsense to me," Mother said. "Fighting a war just to get revenge? You lot are bloody children." She scoffed, wiping her fingers with her handkerchief aggressively. "Imagine the costs. Imagine what our lands will be like with half our men gone. Imagine the children! At least Duivenvoorde won't have half the armies in Hollant marching through it. Imagine the lords of the mark, over in Kenemerland and farther north. Imagine the hassle of having to accommodate hordes of unwashed, unruly soldiers. And soldiers themselves are known well to drink and whore their way to battle whether they're under the cross, the eagle, or any other banner. They're all the same. Rabble. Rabble I wouldn't want anywhere near our pristine town. We'll have our own funds to pay, thank you very much."

"Believe me, woman, if you ever met those raiders face to face, you would not believe that any expense should be spared. I would rather have a thousand armies brawl and party their way through Duivenvoorde than leave the mark under Frisian threat. They raid at sea and on land, taking good Christians as slaves like savages. Nobody is safe up north. Three more woolships from England were pirated, they said. One could barely call them Christian, those dogs. They have no lords, no laws, only gold and steel." Father was emphatic. He had been on campaign against them before — before he joined the Knights Templar. He had never forgotten the zeal with which they fought. He had never forgotten the Hollantic defeat. "We will ride once more into those marshlands and we will teach those Frisians a lesson. Count Willem's honour will be reclaimed." Father raised his tankard. The other men in the hall lifted theirs as well, and all drank to that.

Agnes spoke up. "But, Father, wasn't Hollant once part of Frieslant anyways?" Father smiled. In a much lighter, softer tone now, he spoke to young Agnes.

"That's true, my little bookkeeper. But, us Hollanters bravely fought for our independence hundreds of years ago, and formed a new county of our own. Now, it's time to rise up, many say, and uphold the legacy that those old Frisian kings left behind. You know, those Frisians don't have kings anymore?"

"Why not?" Agnes was curious, as always.

"Those heathens do not believe in God and the Holy Church," Father replied. I knew that this was wrong. They likely had more abbeys in Frielsand than the rest of the Low Countries combined. But, father had a point. They did not recognize the divine authority of nobility. They did not understand that we were born on this earth to rule. That we were appointed by God. That was something that nobody could take away from us, certainly not those scheming northerners. "That's why we must bring them under the authority of our great count, and our holy emperor," Father added, playing into the role of the lawful magistrate by the hyperbolic tone of his voice. He had truth to his words, though. It was a zeal that I saw burning behind his eyes.

"How long are you staying, then?" asked Agnes. It was clear that she wanted him to stay for a while — she had missed him more than anyone, in all honesty, though she held herself together better than I ever could. Father didn't look content with what he had to say.

"Only a fortnight." He sighed, picking at a herring bone in his teeth. "The journey has already taken longer than expected. We wait here and collect our knights and retainers for two weeks. We will meet up with my younger brother Hannes who will be waiting with the knights from Wassenaer, and the young Baron Gherrijt who will have his men from Raephorst." This piqued my interest. Gherrijt and

I were quite close with one another; although I hadn't seen him in some time. "Together we are to head to the tournament in Leyden where the Count's southern armies will be gathering. At the tourney we'll be linking up with our good friend Ghijsbrecht van Amstel," Father said. Now, he turned to me. "Can you ride?" Chills ran through my body. This is what I was born to do. I was to be a knight. Never before had I fought in battle. A real foe. Now was my chance to prove myself; that I wasn't some hot-headed incompetent. I am a fighter. I am to be a knight of House Duivenvoorde. I am to be a knight of the Wassenaer.

"Yes," I replied, contented with the fact that Father believed I could do good things.

Be a strong warrior. Be mighty. He put a faith in me that day. I would not let him down. Ever. "Good lad," Father said. Mother looked displeased. Mother didn't have a say in the matter. I bit deeply into my chicken.

+ Maarten +

The days were just as long, and the smoke from the kiln just as thick, as it was before, but both were made far more joyous knowing I'd have Yda's company in the afternoons.

She thought her mother had found out. If she had, it wouldn't be all that bad, because she hadn't forbidden the girl from seeing me yet. I sat now at the alehouse with Kees and Felix, the three of us cooling off after a hard day's work and before a long night of tending to the kiln. We had no more burning to do. Yda was off helping her mother sell an old hen in Leyden, which meant it was just us lads. Strange things had been happening the last few days. Yda said that some of the knights from out in the country and their men were all gathering at Duivenvoorde castle. I'd seen some of them ride in — that was true. Small bands of armed men from Voorschoten were marching in as well.

"Want to play dice?" Felix asked. Kees stayed out of it — that wasn't his sort of game.

He preferred wrestling or kicking the pig skin.

"I'm in," I said, putting a few groten on the table. He matched my bet. Felix was another contracted worker like myself. He, unlike me, was itching to get out of the trade. He hated the smoke, and what's worse, he didn't get along well with Master Klaas. It was something about Klaas calling him short once. In all fairness, he was a little impish, only a little. But he made up for it with the brawn of a coal shoveller — as did we all. He was a tricky fellow, in it for the coin, and always looking to get some more for as little effort as possible. Not against us, but against unsuspecting strangers in the alehouses of Leyden and Gravenhage, he'd swindle them out of their guilders with every roll of his dice. He had his weighted dice, his lucky dice, his normal dice, and his counterweighted dice, all of which he used to grab the extra stuiver.

We played for a while to pass the time. I'd thought he was using his regular dice, yet he still managed to beat me. Must have been lucky I guess. That's when a footman, or wapenknecht, as the nobles call them, approached us with his buddies. He was in bright yellow and black livery — a man sworn to the House of Duivenvoorde.

"Fun game you're having here?" he asked, clearly a few tankards in his belly already.

"Very fun," I replied. "How can we help you?"

"Oh just coming to say hi," he said with a grin. His mates offered toothy grins as well — I'm not sure what exactly they were smiling at. "You're burner, aren't you?" he asked.

"Me?" I replied. "I am." Felix looked disappointed with that answer.

"The lot of you?" the soldier asked. Kees nodded.

"You're a big fellow, aren't you?" said one of the men from behind, speaking to Kees.

Kees didn't look too pleased.

"Big where it counts," he replied. Felix had taught him that one back in Bruges. One of the soldiers snorted.

"Can I interest you gentlemen in a game?" Felix asked, gesturing to his dice. I looked at him, questioning his intentions. Did he really think that was a good idea? These boys were clearly out looking for trouble. His look seemed to reply that they'd found it. They grabbed a seat beside us and started to play. Sure enough, as the games went on, Felix started to win. He made it believable, of course, setting them up to win a little so they'd gamble more, and then slipping in the weighted dice. I was impressed he'd gotten that far. While they were playing, I figured I'd strike up some conversation with one of them. Maybe they weren't that bad after all — they seemed to be having a good time.

"How was the watch today?" I asked him.

"Oh, you know. Same old," he replied. "Tons of bastards coming in from the fiefs," he added. "It's becoming like a pig sty up in that castle."

"Actually, why are there so many soldiers coming in? I've just seen lads in that cloth armour and those chain shirts from all over the place."

"I suppose your burners don't get much news, do you?" he chuckled. "There's a war up north."

"A war?"

"Well, there has been for quite some time now. Those Frisians are always playing dirty tricks on us."

"Us?"

"Well," he said, eyeing me up and down, "us good Hollanters."

"Are you going to fight?"

"Aye, we'll all be. That's why we're here, smashed as a tart apple." He let off a hefty laugh. I gave Felix a side eye to stop what he was doing. I knew he was a trickster, but robbing men who were about to die — that seemed a little immoral.

"Ay, what's that?" one of the other two guards asked, raising a pouch from Felix's side of the bench. Too late.

"Boys, I can explain…" Felix said, already standing up and toes wiggling, ready to go. One of the footmen quickly rushed over to the alehouse door to lower the wooden beam and lock it.

"You bastard," one of them said. "I want my silver back."

Felix, sweating, replied, "Yes, fine, of course. Have it."

He gave it all back.

"Wait a minute," another said. "This little bastard thinks he can come here to our village and play his tricks on us? He's gotta answer to the law."

"Hold on," I interjected. "We don't need to get all handsy here. Just let him on his way and he'll dance right off back to the kiln, yeah? Are we good here?" The guards just looked at each other. The next thing I knew, I felt a leather glove and all four knuckles behind it slam into my cheek bone and send me across the table. From the ground, I saw Kees, now angry, tackle all three of them at once, wailing down on the guy that hit me. He had the strength of a bear compacted into his slightly more human-like hulk of a body. Felix tried to make a run for it, but his ankle was caught by one of the guards. They now started fist-fighting. Damn it. I had to get involved. I took a tankard and brought it down on one of their helmets, hoping to maybe just knock him out. It only made him angry.

"Bloody charcoal burners shaggin' each other in the woods. Doin' your pagan rituals. We don't want ye 'ere," he said. Kees, behind him, clearly triggered by his words, clapped both of his meaty hands on the guardsman's ears. He screamed out. His friend, now, terrified of Kees who hulked over him, drew his mace.

"No, no, no," I warned, but it was too late. One smack of the mace's head to Kees's forehead and he started bleeding profusely. If it had been a smaller man he'd have been out cold, or dead, but Kees's thick skull was just enough to keep him going. The studs tore through his skin like teeth.

"Are you crazy?" asked the soldier's comrade. "Do you have shit in your fuckin' 'ead, man?" The soldier, looking down at his bloodied mace, realized how far he'd escalated it. The two ale wenches and the landlady all found themselves packed into a corner to avoid the brawl. As the door was barred, they couldn't get out. But they'd seen it all.

"Oh God," was all he could mutter. "Jesus bloody Christ." He put a hand on his forehead. But, after a good second, I only noticed his grip tighten. "Nobody saw this," he said loudly, less as a statement and more as an order. His mates now drew their daggers. Kees, frightened at the sight of blood, and Felix now scrambling to fit his short body out of a window, I gripped my tankard and walked towards him. He tried to hit me with his mace just as he had hit Kees, but I expected it, letting it smash my tankard and, grabbing it from him, I yanked the weapon out of his hand and was about to strike him back when the alehouse door burst open.

"Halt! The lot of you, uncivilized bloody mongrels," a voice bellowed. It was a crusader, a tall one at that. He had a long beard which descended down to the red cross across his heart. "What in the name of God is going on here?" he said.

"That midget was trying to scam us," said one of the men in black and yellow livery, pointing to Felix, bum hanging halfway out of the window.

"Get him down," the crusader said. "You there." He pointed at me, "Drop your weapon." I was hesitant for a second, as the other guards still had their daggers drawn, but I dropped it begrudgingly. "Do you know who I am?" he asked.

"Nay," I replied. "I'm just a charcoal burner with the Water Board of the Rhineland, so I'm not from around here. My friends and I were just…"

"Quiet. We're not there yet," he said. "I am Heer Arend van Duivenvoorde, Baron of this village, and the one next door, and the castle between them. I just spent over two months travelling from the Holy Land to this rainy, boggy, wetland, and arrived four days ago, only to come back to you miserable louts causing a ruckus. Now, somebody get that big man some aid." Several of his retainers rushed to help Kees. He turned to the guards. "What happened here?" One of them spoke up.

"Like we said. That trickster with the dice tried to hoodwink us out of our wages," he said in a far more polite voice than he'd put on with us. I hadn't noticed it before but we had knocked out one of his teeth. Regardless, he continued. "So, when we asked for our guilders back, they attacked us."

"He's lying," I said.

"Quiet," Arend said.

"Don't give me orders, I'm not yours serf," I replied. He now turned to me, stone-faced.

"You have quite a mouth on you. You'd ought to know when to keep quiet. Serf or not, you'd ought to be one."

That's when I got an idea. One of my more brilliant ideas, actually. "Sir, I'd like to ask a favour of you. Well, a deal, really," I said. He sighed, giving up on trying to make me keep quiet. "What he said about my friend Felix here is true. But you have to understand that they started the fight.

And they hit my friend Kees here with a mace."

"He's just a charcoal burner," a guard interjected. "He's a bloody liar."

"Quiet," Arend said, this time to his guard. "I know all this already." I looked at him, puzzled. "They wouldn't have their helmets on nor their weapons with them if they weren't looking for trouble. I'm not daft. And I have nothing against charcoal burners; those are common superstitions. I'm no common man. And yes, you don't have to explain the obvious to me. That wound was most clearly inflicted by the stud of a wapenknecht's mace. One that *you* are holding." He pointed to the one in my hand, already wet with blood. "But I'm not foolish enough to believe that you'd hit your own friend, and that that man's baldric is empty." He gestured to one of his own men. "Now that that's laid out… um... What's your name?"

"Maarten," I said.

"Right. Maarten, what is your deal?" he asked.

"Um… well… it has occurred to me that, no matter what, my friend Felix here, and likely all of us, are subject to punishment."

"You'd be right in that assumption," Arend said. "Hanging, most likely. If not just your fingers." I felt myself swallow.

"Okay, well, all of us, well not Kees but he can join us, would benefit from staying here in Duivenvoorde and, well, staying in one piece as well."

"Go on."

"And you need men for your campaign."

"We have men. We've met our summons requirement already."

"You could do better with more…" I said.

"So you would like to serve in my retinue in exchange for homes here in Duivenvoorde?" he asked.

"Exactly," I replied. Kees and Felix both looked at me, shocked.

"What are you doing?" Felix mouthed to me as Arend began to stroke his beard to ponder by request.

"Shut up," I mouthed back. "I'm trying to help you."

"It's not every day that somebody asks to become one's peasant. I must say that this has caught me off guard," Arend said. "And you would work a full hide? Each of you? And pay all your dues to the castle?"

"Yes," I replied. He thought about it for a moment longer. He scanned us up and down, likely sizing us up to see whether or not we were good fighters.

"Have you fought before?"

"We did a decent job here," Felix interjected. Arend huffed, somewhat amused.

"If we can shovel coals all day, I'm sure we can hold a spear," I said with a more serious tone.

"Wapenknechten, get that poor elf down from the window," Arend ordered. "Lads, welcome to the retinue of the House of Duivenvoorde." He shook my hand. My eyes widened — I could not believe that my plan had actually worked. This meant that, so long as we survived, I'd get to live with Yda, Felix would get to leave the charcoal business behind, and Kees would, well, at least Kees wouldn't be tried as a felon. Frieslant, here we come.

Chapter 5. The Manor: Piet

Being a page was hard work. Better than life on the farm, but still hard work. It would have been a little more manageable if I'd seen Mother and my brothers and sisters, but it had been a long while since I'd seen them last. A month, I think. Not since I'd left. Whenever that was. I'd said my goodbyes, but I still missed them. I felt alone, especially at night. I was the only boy in the manor house of Lord Hillebrant. When they'd taken off with me, I'd thought I'd be living in some castle somewhere like in the stories that Father used to tell, but they told me that Castle Heyen was far away in Gelrelant. Of all of Lord Hillebrant's scribes and stewards, I was by far the youngest. I'd learned quite quickly to speak like the grownups and joke around with them. Ms. Filomena was perhaps the only one who treated me as a boy. The bookmen, the young men who helped Lord Hillebrant as apprentices and journeymen, saw me as more of a little brother. They didn't know my mother hadn't paid for my apprenticeship here, I don't think. Most of my days, I was made to learn about the world. I was taught all of the different coats of arms of local noble houses, and was given a world map to study the parts of Christendom and its borderlands. I spent most lessons watching the city kids playing on the street through the window. They played pig skin and tagand stone throwing — I wanted to be out there with them. Instead, I played chess with Lord Hillebrant in the evenings. Lord Hillebrant finished his work late most days. Afterwards he had some fine liquor made from a plum or something, and read a little bit while he ate dinner. After that, he'd come to me to play chess, and ask me about what I'd learned that day.

I was made to learn laws. There was the City Charter, which declared that Leyden was a city and thus was not a subject of the feudal state. I don't know why they needed a piece of paper to tell them that — they could've just looked at it. I never read the document, well not yet at least; it was all in Latin. And I couldn't read. Then there was the Count's law. Since Count Florens V Gerulfing was officially considered a sovereign prince within the Holy Roman Empire, he received semi-autonomy by the King of the Germans, who was also the Emperor of the Holy Roman Empire. I wasn't entirely sure what any of these words meant, but I knew for the last bit that Hollant was a County, within an Empire that barely held itself together. Right now, there was no King of the Germans. According to Lord Hillebrant, our own Count Willem was elected Emperor in 1248 anno domini, and ruled for eight years before he was killed by the Frisians, leaving his two-year-old son, Count Florens, behind. Then, the Germans elected a man named Richard of Cornwall, from Cornwall, a place Hillebrant said was in England. Mother used to tell me about England and France. She said that one ought never to trust a Frenchman with one's wife, and never to trust an Englishman with one's sheep.

Richard of Conrwall was a disgrace, Lord Hillebrant always said. He said we ought never to have an Englishman on the throne — we had enough languages to deal with already. But he died in April. Now, the Germans didn't know who their king was. Some wanted it to be a man named Ottokar of Bohemia, and others preferred Rudolf of

Habsburg. Some Germans preferred Ottokar because he won a big battle twelve years ago, and was a strong knight. Others preferred Rudolf, because, unlike Ottokar, he was actually German and not just pretending to be. Whenever I asked him about it, Lord Hillebrant said that he didn't care who'd win, as long as they took a long time to do it. He enjoyed that all the fighting gave Hollant and the other Low Countries more autonomy to make their own rules, build their cities, and trade with the German Hanse, the English, and everybody else. That was something else I learned, that Dutch cities were the centre of Western Christendom. They bought wool from English sheep and turned them into fine textiles, and bought goods from all across the North. In exchange, they sold goods down to the Alps and Lombardy, throughout France and Germany, and even shipped goods to the Teutonic Knights, German crusaders, over in Prussia and Livonia. This was all being done on Dutch ships, and all taking place in Dutch cities like Leyden. Leyden only became recognized as a city in 1266, and was only one of the cities in Hollant, along with the capital, Gravenhage, Alcmare, Delft, Haarlem, and only as of this year, 1272 anno domini, Gouda. Lord Hillebrant said that, of all the Dutch states, Hollant was late to the party, and that there was a lot of work to do. He said that we'd have to compete with the Flemings and the Brabanters if we wanted 'any coin from the game.'

Most days I helped Lord Hillebrant prepare his paper work for court and legal consultations. He said that he made sure that all the merchants and burghers and artisans were doing their work by the corpus of civil laws, to keep the city's economy a 'freshly greased mill'. In just my first month of working for him, I got to meet several of the city's aldermen, the men who create the city's legal codes and make decisions for the citizens. I also got to meet the Guildmaster of the Baker's Guild, Matts vander Oudekerke, and the delegate of the Hanseatic Trade League, Herr Albrecht von Köln, a close friend of Lord Hillebran. As much as I missed the farm, it was fascinating to learn about this whole new world. Lord Hillebrant was right in his speech to my mother on that rainy night that this truly is where a man can become anything. None of these men were noblemen — not a single one. They were all the children of shippers or goods pedlars or artisans or scholars. They'd all risen through the ranks, earning their place in society. I could see how much respect Lord Hillebrant had for them; and conversely, how little he had for landed and titled nobility. Of course he, himself was one, a fact which I watched him grapple with tactfully in conversation. But, no matter how much he loved his brothers, he saw them as no more than glorified soldiers. For his second eldest brother, still older than him, Renier, the man with the moustache and the coat of plates, if you can remember, this was somewhat true. Lord Hillebrant always called him the spare. I could see how this came to be his reputation among most people; he was born and raised to replace his elder brother, Lodewijk. However, Lodewijk had already gone and gotten himself an heir, a young man now by the name of Wollefram. Well, everybody called him Wolf. You know, the young knight who fought Floris van Duivenvoorde. That means that Renier's fate had been effectively sealed as a household knight under his older brother, Lodewijk, and later on his nephew, Wolf. I could see how this could aggravate any noble — I myself would hate to be in that position. Imagine taking orders from Sam? No way! Of course, Renier was a grown man now, a household knight, which meant that he'd grown to be content doing whatever he was up to over at the ver Heyen estate in Gelrelant.

Still, despite his distaste for the feudal heirarchy, Lord Hillebrant flew his own family colours proudly. Granted, one could consider him to be somewhat self-indulgent for it, but he did truly see himself as a defender of the freedom that the cities had to offer. He always wore his signet ring, his livery collar, and had a great heraldic weaponshield engraved and painted in bright green and white above the door to his manor house. That's where his office was as well — where I ate, slept, learned, and worked. My teacher, when it wasn't Lord Hillebrant, was one of his clerks, a man named Waleran vanden Ijssel. He was a scholar, trained in Cologne. He was old and grey, and was more preoccupied with books than anyone I'd ever met. Not even the interesting ones about knights and giants — he read ancient Greek and Roman texts. But he seemed to be happy — always coming to new conclusions about the nature of the world and our 'metaphysical reality'. He hadn't taught me what that meant yet. He had begun to teach me how to read and write. Not just in Dutch, but in French, Latin and German, although I wouldn't say I grew to be too proficient in any of them. All in all, my training here was training me to be a bookkeeper, a minister, a penman. I wasn't sure I'd be content with that. Since I was told I was going to be a page, I'd thought I'd be learning to use a sword and ride a horse. Lord Hillebrant said that it would only begin once I was fourteen, and would last until I was at least twenty-one. That was too far away. If I couldn't have home, I wanted adventure. It would seem as though there was none to be found here. But, at least a roof over my head and the guidance of Lord Hillebrant would have to do.

My day started as I woke up in the servant's dormitory. That's where I lived. They were fine living conditions; each of us got our own bed, and four sets of clean clothes. Lord Hillebrant was a wealthy man. There were twelve of us in all. Cooks, attendants, and bookkeepers of various professions. We all lived in the same quarters, slept in the same quarters, and ate in the same quarters as well. We ate in the buttery, a small set of tables beside the kitchen and the pantry down in the basement. Above us, in the manor, was the great hall, well, as great as one could make a hall within the crammed confines of a city.

Unlike the manor houses I'd seen out in the country, Lord Hillebrant's was tall, spanning four floors above ground. Thick, brick walls kept the cold out, and wooden shutters kept the wind out at night. Unlike the rushlights we'd use in our home in Duivenvoorde, everything in Lord Hillebrant's home was lit by candle. It was just enough for my nighttime reading. I practiced little by little, every night, to work on my letters. Lord Hillebrant only had books for adults; no adventures nor tales of elves and giants. Instead, most nights, I found myself working through a translation of the writings of a man names Pythagoras. It was boring, but Lord Hillebrant checked my bookmark each day and quizzed me on the pages I'd read — so I had to pay attention.

Every Sunday, we went to the Church of Saint Peter for mass, just as we had gone to the village church on Sundays too. The churches here in Leyden, however, were far larger. There were three of them, one for each section of the city, divided by a great canal which forked right at the city centre, seemingly splitting itself on the jagged edge of the central square. There were several small canals that branched out as well. The way the canals looked in a map of the city, stitched into a tapestry which hung on the wall of Lord Hillebrant's office, reminded me of the roots of a turnip.

This Sunday I'd have thought would be no different, but almost immediately after the wakeup bell was called, Lord Hillebrant, just out of bed, with his beard barely combed, came to me as we all made ready to break fast. Bread and ale, just as we had it in Duivenvoorde.

Well, bread and ale with some cheese or butter or pork or eggs. Quite a bit more flavour, although sometimes I found the sausage too spicy.

Lord Hillebrant called me aside.

"I have news," he said. "Before I announce it to everyone, I want to know who I can rely on for different tasks. There will be a tournament in Leyden very soon on the west field." I could feel my eyes grow large. I always heard of great tales of tournament knights fighting for chivalry and the honour of maidens. I heard of the pageantry and shining steel; the horsemanship, the swordsmanship, and the feasting. The food, oh, the food, it always sounded so delicious. Father always used to say there'd be jellies and fish and geese and animals from all over the known world. News that a tournament was coming to Leyden was like music to my ears. "The Count has called it in haste, it would seem. He was only twelve when he'd taken power from his regent and guardian, the late Otto van Wassenberg, Count of Gelrelant. Since then the Count's been raising forces across the county like a madman, levying troops, and summoning nobles to his cause. He's finally loosed his bow. He wants revenge on the Frisians, Piet. He wants blood. That's why they're all coming here. Armies of noblemen and their retainers will come and stay camped outside the city. Your friend, Floris of Duivenvoorde will likely be there. When they all come to meet, flying their colours and showing off to one another, they'll need a chance to test their mettle. They have to prove themselves, their worth. They have to show exactly what they're capable of, so that the count and the marshal and their men can decide who will take which command in battle. War is coming, Piet. And the bastards celebrate like barbarians." He scowled. I, on the other hand, was far from scowling. It was sport. It was a chance to see the knights in action, jousting with one another in their bright colours and asking for the favour of young maidens. Well, actually that part seemed kind of gross because sometimes they kissed after. But everyone says it's part of the festivities. "Piet, my nephew, Wollefram, needs a page. His squire was knighted by his own father like a golden donkey, which means that Wollefram's former page, a boy of fourteen now, became his new squire. So, I said that you were up to the task. It's only for the tournament. After that, you'll be back here with me. What do you say, boy? Your first taste of knighthood?" He placed his stout, bear-like hand on my shoulder, thinking that he was asking a favour of me.

"Yes!" I replied. "I mean, I would be happy to help."

"Good man," he said, ruffling my hair. "Break your fast,

young man. We'll go over the rules of etiquette afterwards."
Dutifully, I headed into the buttery to claim my bread and
ale and heard him call over my shoulder. "And not too much
ale, yeah? Have some milk with that."

+ Maarten +

Kees, Felix, and I only told Master Klaas about us
leaving the day before we were summoned to join the
baron's ranks. It was a hard conversation, but at least he had
his three sons to keep the kiln burning. He sent us off with a
few extra stuivers, and wished us luck.

The night before was a tougher farewell. I remember the
look in Yda's eyes when she said goodbye for the last time.
She'd known for a week already. That one week had been
the best week of my life. When times would get tough, as I
was sure they were about to, I had something warm and
happy to look back on. But the farewell didn't strike hard
until that night. It hardly seemed real, hardly material, that I
would be off, sword in hand, conquering lands and wearing
a livery. It only felt real that night — when I knew I'd have
to say goodbye to the one light that kept my kiln burning.
Never before had I felt at home. I was an orphan; I'd
travelled around my whole life, and now I finally had
something to come back to. Something beautiful. I
remember the crisp pain in my throat as I said it back to her.
I remember the kiss we shared. I suppose I had a good
enough reason to stay alive. No matter, I'd be back by Saint
Crispin's Day, surely. In that moment I couldn't tell if we
were fools for joining the lord's retinue. Were we dead men?
Before I left, Yda gave me a small, cross necklace, simple,
made of wood and rope. It meant the world to me. I quickly

91

put it on and stashed it below my shirt. This is what I was fighting for. I'd come back with a future in my hands. I was sure of it. I'd be marching out with memories of Yda, and dreams of who Yda might become. She'd keep me warm at night when the rain and snow bore down on us. She'd keep me on my feet and in formation when we faced a charge of angry Frisians. She'd put a smile on my face when I tried to fall asleep on the rocks and twigs below me. She gave me courage, because I knew that, if I made it out alive, that one week would become the rest of my life. I made a promise to her that I'd come back in one piece. I intended on keeping it.

The first time we mustered, they had us all meet on a green near the castle. The necklace was still new on me; I remember back then I used to fidget with it all the time, smoothing out the rough wooden edges. When we got there, there were a few of the Duivenvoorde soldiers, as well as several from Voorschoten and other smaller fiefs, but most of us were cooks, cleaners, horse groomers, foresters, farriers, and the like. Our banneret was to be Heer Arend, the Crusader. Whispers of a rumour quickly spread of his son's embarrassing defeat against a knight from Heyen. That was quite the introduction for him. I'd almost felt bad, almost — he could wipe his tears with his fine cloths and pearly-white beads. I had no idea whether or not they were true, so I stayed quiet. Felix, on the other hand, was quite enthralled by it, asking around whoever he thought might tell him more. I suppose it was quite the story for a small village such as this. That's one thing I'd noticed in all my travels — word travels the quickest in the smallest communities. Everybody was in each other's business.

Floris arrived late, with his father, riding in full armour

on their warhorses. I'll be honest, it was an impressive sight. If those Frisians had anything similar, I don't know what a horde of peasants like us would do against them. Those animals looked like they could plough through us like, well, a plough through muck. That's how we appeared in comparison — the bright colours of the soldiers and knights were a stark contrast to our dirt-laden drab. He had his men begin to distribute out some weapons and armour.

"Form a line, you sod-ridden worms," shouted an officer. Of course, he too was low born, but his station placed him ever so slightly above us now. "Single file. Wait your bloody turn." He wiped his nose between saying the words. When it was finally my turn, they gave me a thick padded jacket that went right up to my neck and down to my knees. It was a little warm and a little itchy, but I suppose it would be the only thing between myself and the tip of a spear. I accepted it graciously. Even so, I doubted what a few layers of padded cloth could truly do. It seemed a jest compared to the steel armour of the knights gleaming in the sun. Every foot soldier got something similar, whether it went over their hands, like mine, to their wrists, to their elbows, or sleeveless. Except for the crossbowmen who could have been armed as lightly or as heavily as they pleased, it seemed. They were told that they could purchase their own jacket at the war camp market once the armies had assembled. Similarly, they told us that we could buy chainmail in the same way. I don't suppose chainmail would be cheap. All those steel links — few of us could even dream of affording something like that. All of their soldiers already had chainmail, again either to their fingers, wrists, or elbows. Some of them even had a chainmail coif. That seemed unfair

— that we could die for simply not having enough coin. I suppose all this armour was quite expensive. Perhaps the Wassenaer coffers were not as bottomless as they seemed. Some of their footmen also had padded coifs or arming caps, and even padded hosen. All of the padded armour was a creamy, off-white, barley colour; the very colour God had dyed the fabric. No use in dyeing what would soon be red, I suppose.

It seemed that my doubts about all this padded fabric were not alone. I overheard others joking about Frisians being weaker than little girls if they couldn't puncture what a crone and a good sewing needle could. They were crass, but not wrong. That is, that's how I felt until they finally ordered our attention.

"Alright you whispering women, we hear you," said the same officer. He'd had a few of his men set up a tanning rack, but instead of a hide, they strung up one of these padded jackets. "You lot have the gall to doubt the word of our Count?" he asked. "His summons clearly stipulated that all men were to be armed in gambeson. And that is precisely what we have done. But for those of you who have hidden some yellow bellies under these padded jacks, I suggest you watch closely." He turned now to a crossbowman — a man of scrawny frame. "You there, Clais, loose a few bolts into this armour and see what you can do." The crossbowman said nothing and only saluted before priming his weapon. Carefully, he aimed the wooden instrument at the jacket hung across the field. Bolt after bolt he set off. To my surprise, not a single arrow went through. After a few, some of the soldiers began hooting and hollering, saying Clais was just a bad shot. Some of his comrades asked to take over but they had no luck either. It did alleviate my worries a little to see the armour catch each and every projectile — perhaps we were not dead men after all.

The next line was for the steel bits. I was issued a brimmed kettle helmet and a glaive.

Brim or no brim, not even every recruit got a helmet — some just wore their hoods and linen coifs like they normally would. Those lot were unlucky — the ones at the back of the line. All of us recruits got either a glaive or a voulge or some other polearm like a spear. Most of their household soldiers instead had two handed weapons, like two handed maces, falchions, badelaar swords, war picks, axes, or fauchards, or similar one handed weapons in addition to a round shield, or a triangular shield. It seemed like if there was any problem, they'd have at least one sort of weapon to deal with it. All the shields were painted with the Duivenvoorde coat of arms, or the coat of arms of the vassal knight they served. Each knight brought with him two wapenknechten, more or less, by the looks of it. They called that little unit a lance. They taught us that they wouldn't be sticking together on the battlefield, though. It was only for administration. Most of the trained soldiers had padded jackets, steel plates, or boiled leather jerkins over their armour. Finally, we were all given three sets of clothing each, all in the baron's colours.

"What are you lazy imps standing around for? Get dressing!" ordered the officer. We were expected to put on all our equipment at that moment. Clothes too. Most of us had hallowed braes; we were eager to try our fresh linens. But here? In front of everyone? I felt my face flush. I suppose it was a good way to make sure no Jews were hidden among us. It was also an easy way for the soldiers to inspect us to make sure we didn't carry any diseases on our skin we hadn't reported. No growths or red spots or devil's marks. It was somewhat embarrassing, really, to be changing out in an open field like that, but I suppose we'd be doing similar things over the course of our upcoming campaign. You never truly know a man until you've seen him in full, right? With a shrug, me, Kees, and Felix all stripped down to our braies and began equipping ourselves.

The soldiers looked ready, like they would be fighting tomorrow. They clutched their weapons like they knew what they were doing. I looked at Kees and Felix, who had been outfitted similarly to me (with the exception that Kees was in a skullcap and given a broad, two handed axe, and Felix was given a voulge and padded armour which only went down to his elbows). We didn't look like we knew what we were doing at all; nor did most of the other men assembled on the field. That's because we didn't. All we could do was emulate the professional soldiers. Frankly, we looked like a horde of filthy, unwashed peasants — just as the officers were eager to call us.

"Oy, you. You lot are the boys from the alehouse, yeah?" asked a booming voice from behind us. Godverdomme. It was that toothy cur from our little adventure a week ago. There he was, cronies behind him, all dressed up as I'd last remembered them — armoured to the teeth.

"Lots of lads visit the alehouse," I replied. "You'll have to be a little more specific than that."

"He's got a tongue," one of his mates chimed in.

"Save the jabbering," the soldier said. "No use in having an army that wants to tear itself apart." To my complete surprise, he extended out an arm for a handshake. Gladly, Kees took it, and we followed, fraternizing with the footmen. "But you, Felix is it? You don't play your tricks on us again or you're a dead man. Understood?"

"Yes… sir," Felix replied sheepishly, not knowing if they outranked us or not, and awkwardly dropping his voulge to give a salute. "You have my word."

"My name's Geerbrant," the soldier said to us. "We stick together, as a unit, we'll make it out alive."

"Have you seen a lot of battle?" I asked, intrigued as to where exactly he was speaking from.

"In all honesty, mostly bandit hunting and pit fighting. But, let me tell you, we once fought a skirmish a few years back with the Lords of Zoeterwoude over some fishing rights. You know how the highborn can be with their squabbles. But, let me tell you, if you've never seen battle before, it'll take you straight to Hell and back. And you won't do nothing on your own. You need good men beside you if you want to stand a chance. We're blessed they don't have no knights. Those bastards ride like iron-clad bloody bears; breaking through however many lads you put in front of them. They say they're trained from birth to swing a sword. I say they're trained from birth not to give a rat's piss about basic safety…"

The assemblage was interrupted by the young lord Floris. Proudly, he rode in front of the mass of soldiers, surveying the men as they readied themselves until all eyes were on him.

"Alright, gentlemen," he said in his coddled, silver-spooned, pricked up, boyish voice.

I was taken aback by how young he was. He was far from the height of a grown man. In honesty, his presence commanded little respect. I couldn't help but look down the line to see the reactions of the others; and I received the very same looks from most. "You are my wapenknechten. The House of Duivenvoorde has served the Counts of Hollant since their very emergence. We are an old house. An old lineage. And we hold a legacy of excellence.

Honour and glory, gentlemen. We expect perfection, and no less. Failure to stand your ground in battle, to follow orders, or to fulfill your assigned tasks, will be, quite frankly, unacceptable."

"You sure about that?" asked one of the men in a mocking tone. His comrade broke out into laughter. "Is it acceptable to piss yourself?"

"Who was that? Who asked me that?" Floris asked, riding around the small muster of men like a chicken with his head cut off. The laughter only became increasingly contagious, until even Kees and Felix were wiping their eyes.

"I heard the boy left the muck a little yellow after that ver Heyen payed us a visit!" shouted another man.

"Bloody boy thinks he's a knight!" shouted a third, again his identity shielded by the sheer number of men gathered. I watched as the young Floris rode about every which way, desperately trying to catch eyes on the culprits. Eventually, Arend, beard flowing, rode out in front of us, helmet in his right hand and shield slung over the other.

"Fall into shield wall formation," he called out in a far deeper, more grizzled tone. The laughs ceased in that instant. He had a way of catching our attention. Immediately, like a single organism, the professional soldiers formed up in front of him, with shield men in the front, and with other long weapons poking out over their heads and shoulders from behind them. The crossbowmen shuffled out in front of the shield line in a very loose, open formation. They made up about one-quarter of our footmen in total. All of the soldiers stood completely still and moved without speaking a single word, as if they'd practised this formation thousands of times. Arend turned to us. He took a moment to study us — all of us. "Alright you useless rats, join them," he instructed. We packed round them, forming a bulwark of what I could calculate to be nearly a hundred men. It was a much slower affair, with men shuffling to find their place and taking great care not to drop their weapons; something which had happened several times over the course of the full minute it took to set up. Last were the slingers, a handful of farm boys who knew how to use a sling, a skill used to ward off wolves and crows, who joined the crossbowmen in the front once they realized where they were supposed to be. Arend looked to Floris, who simply laughed.

"What incompetents," I heard him mutter. His voice sickened me. Arend then turned to us again with a sigh.

"Until today, none of you men would've considered yourselves fighters. None of you would have called yourselves wapenknechten, soldiers, men at arms, what have you. Today this changes. We don't have much time. The

Frisians muster their forces in the North, and by God, if we do not march to face them, they will come down here to face us." His eyes ranged over the men like flaring torches. "They will come down to face not only us, but our women, our children…" he changed his expression now, realizing the fear he was instilling in us, "…and those lady-boys I've seen some of you sneaking about with in the streets of Leyden." He managed to spark a laugh in the crowd. "Don't think I don't have eyes." He smiled. "But they will not do so." He shifted his tone again, and returned to his stern, serious nature. "You will not let them. You will be the impenetrable wall that will stop them in their tracks. You will be the anvil against which their hammer strikes. You will be lions. You will not waiver. You will not falter. You will not exude an ounce of cowardice. You are men of the crown. Men of the sword. You will live and die by it. You will camp together, eat together, train together, and fight together. You will be brothers in arms. A retinue. A unit. A brotherhood. And when the fateful day comes that you will make war with the enemy, you will make it well and true." He paused for a moment now. Despite his rousing speech he remained calm and collected. Not worked up. Not out of breath, but like he'd said these words a thousand times over. "When I'm done with you, you'll be marching into West Frieslant like a company of heroes. A unit of elite warriors, trained to strike and strike hard. You, gentlemen, are the last bastion against which the Frisians will charge. But you will hold your ground. You will think of Duivenvoorde. You will think of Hollant, of your families, your mothers and fathers. Think of the village girls. Lads, think of anything, so long as you know what you are fighting for and hold it deep within your hearts. The Counts of Hollant have strove to forge a new power in the Low Countries. Let not their efforts be in vain. Generations of Hollanters have heeded the call. It is now your turn. Will you let them down?"

A zealous "No!" was returned to him by all the soldiers.

"I asked, will you let them down?" he repeated.

"No!" we replied, with more and more zeal each time we spoke. I felt a fire burn in me, one that I saw emulated in Kees and even Felix as well. The words he spoke were true, they had to be. We would fight our way out of this, and we would build a new Hollant.

"And when those savages come at you screaming, axe in hand, will you falter?"

"No!"

"Will you let them pass?"

"No!"

"Will you watch them burn your villages?"

"No!"

"Will you watch them defile your women?"

"No!"

"We are Hollanters! We will stand strong! We will hold! Stand apart, weapons ready. Your training starts now."

+ Floris +

Great marching drums bellowed through the countryside as the Duivenvoorders marched. The army moved like a great serpent, unfurling itself at the first hour of sun, and recoiling itself at its new home, a vale of tents, winding and weaving its way through the forests and farmlands of the Wassenaer. My father, being the banneret, the commander of the retinue, held the honour of flying the great, golden banner bearing the three black crescents of House Duivenvoorde. It rippled and swayed in the cool, lowland wind, adorning the sky with an announcement that we were here, and we were ready to do battle.

Below it, our contingent was a colourful display of gambesons and chainmail and glistening, grey steel. Polearm behind polearm made the marching column resemble a porcupine, or a spiked serpent, weaving its way along the dykes. Aside from my father, his templars, and myself with my own squires and page, there were thirty riders in all — eight knights, sixteen squires, and eight pages, as well as another ninety Duivenvoorder and Voorschotener wapenknechten marching in formation behind us to the beat of a drummer boy.

My father led the column, proudly baring his black and white templar shield and red-crossed cloak and surcoat, as he had officially passed the right to bear the Duivenvoorde coat of arms to me. All of the nobles each brought with them two squires and a page. One squire held his lance, a long spear adorned with the knight's heraldic pennant. The other led the knight's warhorse — a mix of destriers for the members of the House of Duivenvoorde, and coursers, a less expensive alternative, all of which were barded and caparisoned. For travel, every rider seated themselves upon a palfrey. These horses took balanced, levelled passes with their hooves, as opposed to the up and down clopping of a warhorse. But I was happy to be mounted upon Galahad, my own trusty destrier; an iron-grey mare with long legs and a snow-white dapple. I'd grown quite fond of horses — riding was one of my favourite activities back in Duivenvoorde, particularly growing up. Most young noblemen were sent off to be a squire elsewhere in some other noble's court at the age of seven. But, with Father joining the order, Mother decided to keep me in Duivenvoorde Castle. She'd said she'd be too lonely without my company. That was a classic way for mother to be — she distrusted war and everything else at which father excelled. I'd always wished I had instead become a squire. I suppose it wasn't too late. It only made it easier to become a knight later on. I accepted my fate, though, to earn my knighthood through a feat of arms. That would be my destiny.

The column was marvelous to look at. Mighty in strength. It was a reminder of the true power we wielded as the lords of Duivenvoorde. It filled my stomach with a courage seldom else felt. On the horizon, around the small lake called Veen Watering, on the fields known as the horsts (hills) for the slightest trace of rolling hills one could find in the Low Countries, stood a grand military encampment. The banners of the House of Wassenaer, bearing three white crescent moons on red, and the House of Raephorst, bearing horizontal black and white stripes, flew prominently in the air, accented by several banners of smaller, vassal households.

The camp was like a town of its own — a town made of canvas and citizens made of warriors.

"Halt," my father called out. "We make camp on the southern side of the encampment." The men followed dutifully, guiding the pack horses and the draught horses which pulled two large karts filled with equipment and supplies. As we rode through the tents towards the centre where the barons would be, the scents of unhygienic animal keeping and poorly constructed latrines wafted through the air. To block out the pungent aroma, I fastened the mouth guard of my coif. I looked back to see the men setting up camp. A mangy group they seemed to be, only learning how to set up tents once they arrived. I turned to my father.

"How in God's name do we intend on turning these rats into warriors?" I asked. "They can barely stand in a line and pick up their feet for half a kilometer."

"We need all the hands we can get," Father replied. "We are lucky to have their service."

"I suppose they'll die honourably," I said. "A far better fate than they'd have on the farm or in the castle." Father turned to me in his saddle and looked at me with a gravity I had seldom seen since his arrival.

"It is your responsibility to make sure that their fate is met long after our campaign has finished. You will keep them alive until they are no longer your soldiers. Those are wapenknechten of House Duivenvoorde. They will not be torn to bits. We need them to push ploughs just as much as we need them to hold spears." There was a jagged sternness in his voice. I hadn't the confidence to respond. A stinging silence rang in my ears until we finally reached the command tent. It was a grand tent complex with canvas hallways leading to each commander's individual sleeping quarters. It was going to be pleasant to relax for a while after a long day's ride. We dismounted, handing off our horses to some stableboys turned wapenknechten, and made our way inside. As we swept aside the canvas flap and entered, we were met by a reception of old friends. Father and Uncle Jan embraced one another. Jan, Hannes, or Heer Johannes vander Wassenaer, was my father's younger brother. Grandfather, Heer Philips vander Wassenaer, decided to split his estates in two, as he had acquired Duivenvoorde over the course of his lifetime. As such, he gave his more prosperous barony, Duivenvoorde, to his eldest son, my father, Heer Arend, and he gave his less prosperous barony to Uncle Jan. Of course, Jan inherited the title of Wassenaer, which was still quite the source of pride for him. After all, we were all collectively known as the lords of the Wassenaer, not the lords of the Duivenvoorde.

"The crusader has returned!" Jan announced as they embraced one another. "Wench, pour out a flagon of wine for him," he ordered to a serving girl.

"By God it is good to see you brother," Father said with a smile.

"Likewise, Arend. You must tell us of your great battles in the Holy Land," Jan replied with a broad smile beneath his bushy moustache. Father then firmly shook hands with the young baron, Heer Gherrijt van Raephorst, my good friend. His father had passed when he was only five years old to an infected wound to his calf. He'd received it two years earlier when retreating from Frieslant after the death of Count Willem, and his health had only deteriorated since. Gherrijt was raised by his uncle, Dideric, in Gravenhage while his mother ruled in his stead. That is until he was sixteen, which was only three years ago. He was only slightly older than I was; we had played often together as boys.

"How goes the young baron?" he asked.

"More swimmingly than a herring," Gherrijt replied. "Yourself, Heer Arend?"

"Ageing like a fine wine," he said, bringing a smile to the lords' faces. I followed suit, shaking hands with Uncle Jan, Gherrijt, and few of their vassal knights whom I'd recognized. When the lords continued conversing and enjoying some candied fruits, pastries, and wine, Gherrijt pulled me aside.

"How've you been?" he asked. "It feel like it's been ages since I've seen you last."

"I've been well," I said. "Still out hunting for maidens?" A smile crept across his face, as if to say *you dog*.

"Of course," he said. "Only the finest."

"How are the girls in Raephorst? Because I can tell you, if you're in a drought, look no further than Duivenvoorde. The girls at home have the most golden hair and skin whiter than sugared snow. Lips like rosebuds too. And their behinds…"

"Believe me, friend, there is no thirst for girls over in Raephorst. The ale wenches, let me tell you, they get quite excited when a noble comes around."

"As they should," I said with a laugh.

"Well, I suppose it depends on which noble," he said with a grin.

"Yes, they all see the black and white stripes and grow husbands out of thin air," I replied. It made Gherrijt laugh.

"Believe me, a husband is no match for the mighty Gherrijt van Raephorst," he said, flexing a scrawny arm. "I've been lifting oxen to prepare for this war."

"Yes, when the Frisians see you they'll turn tail and run," I said with a sly grin creeping across my lips. "I am quite looking forward to gaining some experience in the field."

"I suppose so," replied Gherrijt. "But, in truth, I'd rather be under some tree somewhere writing music."

"Of course you would. If there's one thing any man should know about you, it would be that your sword is merely for the aesthetic."

"Just don't tell the girls that," he said. We both couldn't help but laugh. "You know, warring is no fortunate thing." He gave a somewhat serious groan. "I'd bet my own bollocks that half these knights here will come back dead or wounded."

"Well, it's what we do," I said with a shrug. "We're knights. I suppose we'd ought to act like it." Gherrijt pondered for a second.

"I mean, what precisely did the Frisians do? Have the men given you the slightest clue, because it's beyond me. Whenever I attempt to probe I'm met with tales of their savagery and offense unto God."

"They killed Count Willem," I said. "Haven't you heard the tales from all these elder knights who were on the Frisian campaign?"

"Bah, I suppose, but it's been sixteen years," Gherrijt replied. "It seems a little late. The Frisians we'll be up against won't even be…"

"What is this, Gherrijt? Why are you questioning this?"

"Well I figure we'd ought to do something about it if we're in the wrong. Imagine all the peasant villages we'll be tearing through…"

"Gherrijt they're Frisians. We can't even call them peasants. They're less than that. They reject nobility entirely." He didn't respond for a moment.

"Well," he began, "I suppose if I were them I would too…"

"But you're not! And you never would be," I said. "We're different from them, you know that. Sometimes you have these ideas, Gherrijt, which really shouldn't be…"

"Yes, we are different. Who are we to march in there and say that we have a claim to their lands? Their people?"

"Gherrijt, this is treason."

"Floris, you've known me since we were boys."

"And you've always been soft. It's time to toughen up, Gherrijt. It's time to show them all that you're a knight." I felt strange saying this — he was my elder of three years. He should be the one giving me this sort of advice.

"Like you did?"

"What's that supposed to mean."

"Word travels quite quickly, Floris."

"Word of what?"

"You and Wollefram? I can see you have a limp."

"What did you hear?"

"Nothing good. Only that you two had quite a run-in."

"I did, but…"

"And that you lost. Badly," he said with a laugh. I smacked him with my girded glove — amicably, of course.

"At least I fought," I said.

"Why did you?"

"They were stealing our peasant boy, what do you mean?"

"Wasn't he free?"

"Nay, he wasn't."

"The Count said he was."

"The Count wasn't there. Don't make assumptions about something you know nothing of." I felt myself grow angry now. A few moments after reconnecting and the conversation comes to this? By God I had embarrassed my whole damn lineage. And for what? I was right. It was the right thing to do.

"Floris I didn't mean to offend you, I…"

"You what?"

"I was just saying that perhaps blindly following chivalry is not productive."

"Excuse me? Chivalry is what put this tent over your bloody head. Chivalry is what put that wine in your cup. Chivalry put that sword at your side."

"A sword I would gladly forfeit for a lyre…"

"And chivalry put that lyre in your chambers as well. You think if we had no chivalry we would be happily making music and poetry and reading books? We would have anarchy. We would have chaos. How many brigands have you or your men hunted down in the past month?"

"Four bands."

"Exactly. Imagine how many more would be afoot if there were no knights to make safe our roads? No wapenknechten to keep peace in our alehouses?"

"But we are only knights on the labour of serfs."

"We are knights on the *recompense* of serfs. They provide us only with what we need to protect them. Don't be foolish, Gherrijt. I've known you for a long time, but these ideas are dangerous and foolish." I must have been looking at him like he was from a foreign land. "They work *our* lands. They eat *our* crops. They owe us their lives."

"And what makes all of those things ours?" Gherrijt asked, not done yet. The absolute fool — he loved to play the advocate for the Devil himself.

"Proclamation from the Count, the swords at our sides, and the right bestowed upon us by God," I said. Gherrijt snorted. I only rolled my eyes. "You've been speaking too often with the merchants in Gravenhage."

"You haven't enough," he replied. "You have a tongue

on you." He ruffled my hair. We exchanged words often like this — testing our rhetorical skills. Our tutors had recommended it; they said it forged learned knights, the backbone of any strong kingdom. Our conversation, if one could call it that, was interrupted by an announcement made by Father. His voice cut through the cacophony of rejoicing old friends.

"Gentlemen, we gather here not to socialize but to make war," Father said in a deep, stately tone. "There is much administration and logistics to settle. We will have to make haste to Leyden and grab up some mercenaries before the other lords have plucked the finest. But first, let's raise a glass to our fine warriors. The best of Hollant." He raised his own glass. The knights and barons all cheered for Father.

Chapter 6. The Streets: Thiel

The city was a nice place if you had money. We didn't. Maurits and I had applied to every bakery and snack shop in town. Not a single one accepted us. So much for that Hillebrant's word. We definitely couldn't head back to Duivenvoorde now — every knight and wapenknecht there would catch us and have us hanged. The image of the Count's justice loomed heavy over us every waking day; the pillory in the centre square was not too different from the gallows along the country roads. Brigands hung. Either that or they had their heads lobbed off. We'd be treated no differently — what was a runaway serf but a brigand in the making? Even if some fat man rode into our village and declared us free? The men with swords disagreed.

What was supposed to be our liberation became our nightmare. Cold, destitute, and enemies of the law, Maurits and I made a living performing in the market square. We were lucky that, of the few items Maurits brought with him, he brought his recorder. He could play it well, and we both knew all the peasant songs by heart, like *Mary's Wandering Eye, the Tale of Heer Halewijn,* and *The Farmer of Nederhage.* We found that the more lewd the better, so eventually we started to come up with our own music to please the audience. We found that a few more groten made a difference. It was not long before market-goers began to frequent our performances, but really, we were paid very little. Perhaps we could afford a couple of pies a day? On a good day.

Nights were worse. We weren't allowed to be out at

night — the city had a curfew to dissuade thievery and boisterous behaviour. As such, we spent our nights finding places the watchmen wouldn't go. Usually the city watch was lenient — unlike the district militias. They were a whole different beast; prodding and poking their way about at night to try and catch anyone who would make their own neighbourhood a little more filthy. We found that our best bets were along the banks of the canals, beneath the bridges. We weren't alone there — there was a good number of the destitute in the city. The city watch allowed us here, at least; they figured we wouldn't be up to too much trouble. City churches, confraternities, and Jewish brotherhoods made a habit of handing out old, mouldy bread and any bread that'd been left too long in the oven. We were grateful for it. But, it wasn't enough on its own. Work was the only way.

The hustle and bustle of the market kept us alert. We'd come to know who came on which days, both sellers and buyers, and who was there to pickpocket. There were a few boys in the business, a few young adults too. The older ones typically had a full scheme planned out, like an inquiry for directions or an accidental trip. They worked in packs too — hunting like wolves. The young ones, on the other hand, found no problem slipping their way through the crowds to snatch a coin purse off a belt every now and then. Little buggers. Never preyed on us, though. They knew who the ripe targets were. They went after the artisans, the burghers, the gentry, the merchants and of course the nobles. All of these sorts were clearly marked, like bright bull's-eyes, with their patterned cloth tunics, fancy hats, and their luxuriously flowing cloaks. They all wore fine jewelry too, as if they were trying to attract thieves. Gold and silver necklaces, rings, you name it. Of course, the nobles posed the trickiest targets I'd imagine, each of them with a sword and buckler at their side. There were more of them now that all the lords in Hollant were gathering here. Unless you'd been living under a rock, which Maurits and I nearly were, you'd have known that Hollant was marching to war. But word travels fast in the city. It marked the tone of the city now. What were once journeymen and artisans were now full-time militiamen, ready to march off to the beat of war drums. They drilled in the market square and in front of churches too. It used to be every Sunday. Now it was every day. We saw the night's watch and guildsmen training with their goedendags. Each unit marked themselves with liveries coloured with the same colour as their unit banner, each of which bore the symbol of their guild. The urban militiamen, for example, brandishing their spiked goedendags, carried a white banner with crossed red keys on it. It had come to be the symbol of Leyden, the keys to heaven, although the blue and gold striped shield was also carried often — the heraldry of the Lords of Leyden. While it may not be obvious, Leyden did, in fact, have its own liege lord, although not a very powerful one. In fact, there were considered to be forty of them, known as the Lord Fourty, but they mattered little in the politics and passings of day-to-day life. On the other hand, the keys were used as the city's symbol to embody the Church of Saint Peter, the church at the heart of the city. In fact, Leyden had come to be known as the key city. Thus, in times of war, the blue and gold stripes as well as the scarlet keys on white were to be flown side by side.

Other units had less dramatic emblems. The guilds only used symbols that described their trade overtopping a field of red. The badelaar swordsmen of the fishmonger's guild in their red and white-striped liveries, for example, flew a fish; the goedendagers of the baker's guild, garbed all in white, flew two crossed bread peels; the axemen of the butcher's guild with their red and yellow zigzag liveries flew a pig; and the spearmen of the textile cutter's guild, skipping the liveries altogether, flew a pair of sheers. Some of the confraternities were being called upon as well. The confraternity of Saint Sebastien, some of the kind men who'd been giving us bread at the start of the month, were now practicing with goedendags and spears and wearing red and white liveries beneath their red banner with five golden crosses. The Brotherhood of Saint George, on the other hand, had always been an archers' brotherhood. They would be practising with their longbows and crossbows anyway, even if there wasn't a war going on. Occasionally, during peacetime, they were hired to guard merchant caravans on the roads from the city down to Flanders and out into the countryside, known for their sigil the Saint George cross. They all wore their characteristic crimson, short sleeved liveries unlike the sleeveless surcoat-style liveries of the other units.

Maurits and I watched them train — rotating out which unit was practising when, but always with somebody calling out orders in the main square. They'd become a show too — attracting lots of the city's buyers to stop and watch their heroic sons and fathers and husbands training to march off to war. We cared nothing for it. It's not like they were gonna march us out. They stole the crowds. The first week here was our easiest. Each one since only got harder — although the new flood of nobles and soldiers helped us out a little. They donated the most, often not having less in their purses than a stuiver, but having to seem wealthy and charitable to impress their wives or fellow knights. But some of them were horrible. Our worst experience was only a few days before the tournament. It had started like any other. Maurits and I woke up with the sun, visited the church for some morning bread. It was charred to a crisp, but it was the best we'd get. We said out prayers, thanked our donors, and made our way to the market square after. We stopped by a well to get some water, before a militiaman started following us, noticing that we were not residents of that neighbourhood.

We'd gotten some good sips in before we were sent off on our way. It was a hard life. We were cold and miserable. In truth, I'm not sure if it was much better than starving back on the farm. By the time we'd run to the towns, our ribs were already showing. I know that little Piet and Filips would never have known how much we starved, but we did. Mother made sure to give them equal portions, feeding their fat little bellies. At least they'd have good lives now, at the monastery and in Hillebrant's home. We were left for the scraps.

The morning started with the brewer's guild practicing their goedendag drills under their blue tankard banner. Once they were done, the centre of the square was cleared out for a public execution. It wasn't the first one we'd seen since coming here, but they never got any prettier. Maurits still squirmed at the sight of hanging men. Today, they were two men who'd been caught sodomizing. Their sentence was read out by the bailiff — they were to be hanged. This was the common execution for someone low-born like them. Were they nobles, their sentence would be no less harsh, only culminating in the slice of the blade of an executioner's sword or axe. A priest came and blessed, not the sodomites, but the executioner, and the two men, fearful as anyone would be, were placed on blocks. For them, a few men from one of the local confraternities helped them say their prayers as a form of charity. Maurits, out of respect, stopped playing his recorder. I agreed with him — this was certainly not the time to be playing, despite the fact that the bustle of the city carried on throughout the execution as if there was little to be seen. Perhaps fifty people gathered around the gallows, aside from the petty thieves locked in the pillory who were forced to be there. Of course, this was a perfect moment for the pickpockets, who preyed upon the foreign war leaders.

At that moment, a knight rode in with a couple of squires and knights behind him, on a big, black, Frisian horse. It was a beast, let me tell you. Black as night, and hair wavy like the sea. I will never forget it. Atop the beast rode a slender nobleman. His shield, slung across his back, bore black and yellow horizontal stripes, overscored by a red and white chequered saltire. His eyes were a pale blue, and his hair was raven, matching his horse.

"Play for me, bard," he said, dropping several coins into the hood we'd laid out for collection. That was the most we'd ever gotten in one day. He never got off his horse. Maurits looked at me, he didn't know what to do.

"We would happily play for you, good lord, but there are two men being hanged over there. We will grace you with our music once they have gone to Saint Peter," I said, bowing down to him. Maurits did the same.

"Nonsense," the knight replied. "They are sinners. Mud-pushers, the both of them." I didn't know what to say.

Surely, he would still recognize that death is no trivial thing.

"Sir, we cannot play if they are about to be hanged. When they're dead they won't be able to hear us, and we will play on."

"Do you have the slightest idea of who I am?" the lord asked. Frankly, Maurits and I didn't. "I am Lord Ghijsbrecht van Amstel, vassal of the Prince-Bishop of Utrecht. My men and I have come for a fine tournament of adventure and festivity, and to serve *your* count, not mine, in his crusade against the Frisians. If I say play, you will play." I was tired of this nonsense. First, Mehaud takes our crops but offers nothing in return when we no longer have a father to help us work our fields. Next, Hillebrant steals Piet and frames it as charity, when he could have simply aided us with some coin. I was sick and tired of this.

"Nay," I said. "We will play when the execution is done." What was taking the executioner so long? You know what? Good. We had more time to make a point. Ghijsbrehct looked at us for a moment, until he said, "Squire, his flute." It was not a flute, it was a recorder. Regardless, his henchman of a squire dismounted and simply tore the wooden instrument from Maurits's hand, and snapped it over his knee.

"No!" Maurits called out. He would've hit the squire if I hadn't held him back. I could see tears forming in his eyes. We hadn't the strength or the energy to deal with this.

"Let me teach you a lesson, boys," the knight said, looking down on us menacingly from his great black destrier. "There will be many hands out in front of you. Some will aid you, clothe you, feed you, some will hit you, and some will rob you. Follow the hand that holds the sword. It is the only way to survive." Ghijsbrecht and his men simply rode on, as if it never even happened. The jingling of the chain links on the flail tucked into his belt still echoes in my mind. It was just a recorder, but there was something about the cavalier way he just… had it broken. Like he didn't even care. Like he didn't even stop to consider what profound impact it might have on us, on our livelihoods. He was supposed to be a man of honour. He was supposed to be a defender of the weak and defenceless. That was us now; and he just left us to die. Maurits knelt down, staring at his recorder.

"What are we going to do?" he asked, wiping tears off his face. He was hungry. So was I. We'd be even hungrier now that we'd have no more income. After the men were finally hung, and after several hours of trying to make a living by singing on our own to no avail, Maurits and I were ready to give in. We'd been defeated, and we had no recourse. We couldn't go to the militia. Even if we thought they wouldn't kick us out, they'd never believe our word against the word of a noble like that rancid Ghijsbrecht. Rotten luck. Simply rotten luck. And that bastard Ghijsbrecht just had to ride in and make things even worse.

At the end of the day, Maurits and I decided to ask for sanctuary in the church. We had no other option — perhaps they had a job for us. As we sat there, on the cobblestone, discussing what was in store for us, a figure emerged from the shadows, like an alley cat. It was a hooded figure, although hoods were certainly not uncommon. This figure was not tall, and shrouded in a heavy grey cloak which descended to the ankles. Behind it came some others, men all wearing normal street clothes, but all hooded, and most of them missing fingers, ear lobes, or even fingernails — all remnants of imperial justice. They also came with a couple of dogs — mangey things. They looked like they could tear a bite out of you with just a whistle or a word.

"Who are you?" Maurits asked, drawing his dagger.

"Well, well, well, the street cat has claws," said the figure in a woman's voice. "We saw what happened to you boys. It's a shame, really." I recognized her, she was one of the pickpockets. Now that I thought of it, some of the men behind her I recognized too.

They were around when the sodomites were being hanged.

"We don't have much money," I said. "You can take what we've got." I held out the hood. Maurits looked at me as if I was insane. Clearly, he hadn't thought it through, as per usual.

"We don't want your money, boy," the woman said, lowering her hood. She was a middle-aged woman, with a few more wrinkles than one might expect, and rugged features. She seemed tough as nails, though.

"Then what do you want?" I asked in return. The men started to surround us now. I felt a cold sweat trickle down my forehead. The sharp ringing of the curfew bell interrupted our conversation.

"I want you two to come with us," she said.

"We don't want no trouble," Maurits said, dagger still unsheathed, although I had no idea what he thought he was trying to do with it.

"You're street rats," she said. "Your whole life's gonna be trouble. I don't know where you came from or what you've done. I don't care. But you boys look like you can nick a few pouches if we train you right."

"Oh yeah? And why would you do that?" I asked. "More competition for you."

"Well, for our training, and our management, we'll skim a little off the top," she said. "Just a little."

"What if we don't want to?" I asked. Maybe that was stupid. The dogs looked hungry.

"What have you got to lose?"

"Safe passage to heaven," I said. "Our lives, too." The gang laughed at that.

"Boys, you forfeited both of those long ago," she replied. "Come with us." I suppose we didn't have much of an option. I heard my stomach grumble. Maurits gave me a shrug, so I led the way. We followed them down dark alleyways and side streets until we found ourselves in a rotten neighbourhood. The houses were all wood; if we could call it that. It was bleak. No shops or anything of the like, just people. Lots of homeless, actually. Most of them were ill with something, be it a bloody cough or lepers. They called it the pilgrim's disease, because pilgrims brought the bloody thing back from the Holy Land. Eventually, at the edge of the bank, we found our way back down to the ledge of a canal. There was a door there, made of a dark ash, one which would've seemed completely inconspicuous to someone who had no idea what was going on here. Through the door, they brought us down into what resembled a stone corridor. Ancient dankness festered in its air. The scent was rank. The sound was hollow, at first, until we descended upon the emerging cacophony of sticks beating sticks, and laughter, and conversation.

"What is this place?" I asked the woman.

"Keep walking and you'll find out," she replied. The stonework on the walls looked as ancient as time itself. It was all coarse, solid rock, not like the brick that painted the city red above. Every footstep echoed through the tunnel, from chamber to chamber. Finally, we reached it. It was a large, stone crypt, deep beneath the city. It had ancient runes carved into the masonry. In the chamber, there was a pit where two fighters were duelling with swords and bucklers — wooden ones. Around them, a number of criminal types were hooting and hollering for one side or the other.

"Break her face in!" one of them said.

"No, show him how it's done, Walpurga," said another, seeming to be coaching their fight.

"Where are we?" I asked.

"Welcome to the crypt," the woman said. "Your new home, if you're lucky." Maurits seemed to be just as stunned with the place as I was. "Long before Leyden Castle was built, the old pagans built a crypt here to bury their dead. To build the castle, the old knights made the hill from scratch, encasing this place in earth like a giant kiln or anthill. Soon after, it was forgotten. Well, until we found it."

"I did," interrupted one of the men on the sidelines — a slender man with a greying beard.

"Rolf did," the woman corrected herself. "Now, we sleep here, eat here, plan here. Really, we do everything here."

"And what exactly do you do?" I asked. Maurits seemed fixated on the fight now.

That muck-for-brains always focused on the wrong thing. "We steal. It's what we can do."

"Don't you think it's wrong to steal?"

"Why?" she asked me. I didn't think I'd have to be pondering an explanation for why theft was a sin.

"Well, because they earned that money."

"Did they? Do we really earn our lot in life?" the woman asked. "Today, you saw firsthand how cruel this world can be. Make it a little easier for yourself. Either that, or you go back to the market square tomorrow just to see his kind tenfold ignore you."

"She's got a point," Maurits said. The woman fighter in the pit, Walpurga her name was, smacked her opponent over the head. I saw how hopeful Maurits was in here. I suppose it was my fault that we were destitute. I was the older brother — it was my call to make whether we stayed in Duivenvoorde or left for Leyden. I suppose I'd had my fill of making bad calls.

"You want to join them?" I asked Maurits. He looked at me with an expression that yielded an emphatic yes. I turned to the woman. "We're in," I said. I held out my hand to shake hers. She gave me a firm handshake. In truth, I found her boyishness somewhat unsettling. I'd never seen a lady be so unladylike before; it was unnerving. But, she seemed to be running things alright. I'd bet having some women in the mix wouldn't hurt their slimy performances in the market square. Few nobles can resist helping a damsel in distress.

"My name's Swanneke," she said. "Call me Swan."

"You're gonna keep us alive, Swan?" I asked.

"I'm gonna teach you both how to keep yourselves alive," she said.

+ Maurits +

After an evening of training, the next morning, we were off to do our first mission.

Maurits & Thiel

Nothing complicated, Swan said. Me, Thiel, and Swan all made our way to the market square on the north side of the river Rijn. It was smaller than the usual one we went to on the South side near Saint Peter's Church. This time, we saw burghers and journeymen setting up decorations for the week of tournament festivities. In all honesty, I was excited for the tournament. I know that Thiel could be bleak and all. Well, I guess he had pretty good reason to be, but I still liked seeing the knights in shining armour facing off against each other. It was fun to root for one knight or the other, and tournaments didn't come too often. I guess this one would be different, though. We'd be thieving our way through it. Well, at least we'd get to buy some sweets. As we scanned the crowd, I couldn't help but keep my eyes on all the street foot vendors. There were so many delicious treats. Pies, pannekoeken, rolled wafers, pretzels, gingerbread, honey crispels, pepernoten, waffles, and cookies, they all smelled so good. The scent of honey and cake wafted through the air, straight up my nose, and I felt like I was flying whenever I passed by them. We had to get some coin.

"See that one, over there?" Swan asked. I got shaken out of my trance. I looked down at my belly. You know, I used to have some fat down there? It used to jiggle a little when I walked. No, I looked like a skeleton. Swan was pointing to a fat-looking merchant-type on the square scratching between the cheeks of his bottom hemisphere. Unaware, rich, perfect. Nothing as enticing as a fat purse, bulging with some precious mettles clanking around inside with each step. Thiel didn't know this, but I'd had a habit of nicking things from time to time in Duivenvoorde. Usually at the alehouse.

I'd seen one of Father's mates do it once, and, when I was little, I thought I'd give it a go. Granted, those were all drunken ploughmen late in the evening, but it surely wasn't too hard.

"What's the game plan?" Thiel asked.

"Shoelaces," Swan replied. We'd learned that one last night. Thiel, the bigger of the two of us, would stand behind the man's purse to block the crowd's sight. Then Swan would stand in front of him, blocking his path, and minding her own business. Finally, I'd bend down to tie my own shoe, and untie his. When Swan points it out, he bends over. Hopefully he rolls over, with that belly of his. Then, I nick the purse, he ties his laces, and we're out of there like mice. Simple.

We all got into formation, and I slipped off the leather lace on his turnshoe as smoothly as fresh-churned butter. Swan said the line, and, like a slippery alehouse magician, I plucked the purse from the man's belt.

"Thief!" we all heard from somewhere down the row. Shit. Immediately, the fats turned to look at us. The oaf hadn't even suspected Swan.

"You little pricks," he said in some foreign accent, lunging at us. We both dodged out of the way.

"This way!" Thiel said, leading the way to an alleyway away from the market square. We heard not one pair of studded turnshoes following us, but four. Oh God. I turned around to see, not the merchant, but four militiamen, each with a goedendag, ready to smash us in half. We reached a fork in the alley.

"The crypt," I said to Thiel as I split off. The chase was on. As expected, two of them kept coming after me, while two kept on after Thiel. I still had the purse firmly in the hand, by the way. Let's not forget about that. I rushed my way through a variety of different streets, thick and thin, dodging horse carts, handcarts, vendors, stalls of different kinds, snack bars, animals, babies, you name it. Eventually, having made my way past the textile street, you know, the one with all the tailors and weavers and textile cutters, I made my way towards the downwind part of town. The scent was foul here, even fouler than the shit streets. This was where all the tanners and the soap makers and the like worked. I figured they'd be less likely to follow me here, but lo and behold, they did. Damn it. They'd grown too tired by this point to call out for people to stop me, so really they just didn't. I suppose it was all that heavy padding they wore that must've worn them down. In all fairness, I was growing quite tired too — I'd been running on a few crumbs a day. As much as I wanted to hide in a tub of urine, I found my way out of the tanner's district towards the pub lane on the North side of town. Here, there were all the breweries. Quickly, turning corners, with the militiamen still hot on my heels, I snuck my way into the side entrance of a brewery without even the brewer noticing. She was a kind-looking old lady who was occupied serving customers at the front. I snuck my way through to all the barrels in the back and found a place to hide. At that moment, I heard the front door fly open.

"In… the… name... of… the… law," one man uttered, wheezing.

"There's a boy in here. A pickpocket. Where is he?" the

other asked briskly.

"Nay, no pickpockets in here," the woman replied. "Best keep your weapons at the door if you're stopping for a drink."

"No time. We have to look in the back," the militiaman said.

"I said nobody's back there, now are you drinking or leaving?" the woman replied. I heard her get shoved to the side of a table.

"Make way," he said, still short of breath. Jesus Christ! Why? Why did they have to know I was here? Rolling my eyes, I stood up, dusted off my trousers, and quickly dashed out the back door again, leaving a grote for the brewer for all the trouble. "There he is!" the man shouted. "Stop him!"

I had to think quickly. Right in front of me, a gong farmer was leading his cart out of the city. For those of you who don't know, it was a cart full of human excrement. Lord forgive me for what I was about to do. Thinking fast, I reversed my hood to cover my face and planted myself in the muck. I suppose human manure was still better than the noose. The cart made its way down the road until I realized that the sole of one of my turnshoes was exposed. Good God. I lay there, praying that the militiamen would not notice. Of course, they did. To my luck, I felt the cart make its way out over a canal bridge. It was now or never. I heard the militiamen running up to the slowly rolling cart. "Stop! Stop!" they cried. I rolled out into the water. Like a ghost, I was gone.

+ Thiel +

After Maurits split off, I led the men straight into a trap in an alley where I knew that some other pickpockets would be waiting. There, having seen around six of us all pull out our daggers, they just turned tail. It didn't feel good to steal. I didn't like it. I felt grimy, dirty even, like I'd lost some sense of morals. Could I really blame the world for this? Was this really justified by my hunger? Or by something else? Some deep-seated desire to steal.

To get revenge on all those who had done us wrong. When I was walking back, I decided to take the route along the walls; just to get some fresh air and clear my head. It had been quite some time since I'd looked out at the countryside. By God was I glad I did. I saw a sea of tents. Like a whole new city had been built beside this one, and it encompassed the entire city, stretching from one bank of the Rijn to the next. I watched out over it. I looked at the men, most of them muscular, some a little chubby even. And then I thought to myself. You know, they have to feed their fighting men if they want them to be any good. That means food. Money. Shelter. Maybe thieving isn't the only way. No, it can't have been. There was a better life than this. We had to learn to fight. Well, at least we had to look like we knew what we were doing.

I was relieved to find Maurits back at the crypt in one piece. At least that was one weight lifted off my chest. With the some of the coins he'd nicked, he bought us some rolled wafers. They tasted glorious. It was the first real food we'd had in a long time. The sweet dough, the crunchy outside, and the jam and honey on the inside were all so delicious; I thought I'd died and gone to heaven. It had been so, so long since we'd had a treat like this.

Not just since we came to the city, but since Father drowned. When I walked in, Maurits was hanging out with that Walpurga, the fighter. She was a young woman, around our age, but muscular, like a fighter. She still had long, curly blond hair, though.

"Hey Thiel, you know that Walpurga is Swan's daughter?" he asked.

"Really?"

"I am," she said. In all honesty, they looked nothing alike to me, but I certainly didn't have the guts to say it.

"Is that how you learned how to fight?" I asked.

"Nay, the lads trained me," she said. "Some of them used to be soldiers. They trained with clubs and bucklers most of the time." I felt a smile creep across my face.

"I've always wanted to know how to fight," I said.

"No you haven't," Maurits said with a snort. I gave him a sidelong glance. Oh, wait, I think I know what happened. I think he liked Walpurga. I tried my best to hide my smile; this was the first girl that Maurits took a fancy to. She seemed like she might've been a little older than him. You know what? Good for him. Aiming high.

"I sure have," I said. "Haven't you, too? I always see you watching the knights ride by…" I think he caught my meaning.

"Oh, jaja," Maurits said. "Fighting is so cool."

"I suppose I could show you boys a thing or two," Walpurga said.

"Here, Maurits, you go first," I said, shooing him forward, and seeing that there was only one set of practice weapons. I figured I could just learn by watching. She started by teaching him how to stand. I think she liked him too, because when he stood like a fool, as, of course, he would, she went to correct his stance herself. "Feet apart," she said. "Back straight, and bum out like a tavern wench." Maurits still looked like a jester when he did it, but Walpurga seemed like a true fighter. Then, she taught him the seven wards, or stances. She taught him the different variations of the sixth and seventh wards, and how to counter each one. And finally, she taught him her personal favourite stance. She called it the Walpurga stance. It was the simplest of the stances but the most practical. Eventually, I started to follow along on the sidelines with nothing in my hands but air. I still had to learn. Then, she taught Maurits the attacks and defences. The shield strike, the covers, the parries, you name it. By the end of it, he was moving like he knew what he was doing. Of course, being Maurits and all, he shifted his weight awkwardly from time to time, stumbling here and there, but overall, she really did turn him into a bit of a swordsman. "Did you wanna have a go?" she asked me.

"How about I fight Maurits?" I asked. She held out her sword.

"Go for it," she said with a smile. It felt different to actually hold the sword and shield in my hands. There was a heft to it. And a force. "Play on," she said. Maurits had clearly learned well, but I think I'd gotten the hang of it too by now. With every swing, I heard a tough *clack* as wood struck wood. If I actually got hit, it would hurt. We went back and forth for a bit until Maurits hit me on the fingers.

"Ow!" I let out as I dropped my sword.

"Pick it back up," Walpurga said. I just looked at her. My fingers really hurt. "Your enemy never waits. Pick it up." I listened to her, and picked up the sword, and we played again. This time, when Maurits's sword got caught in his hood when he put it back over his shoulder, I took advantage of the situation and poked him in the belly.

"That's not fair," he said. I just stuck out my tongue at him. He threw a big cut at me, which I managed to block with my buckler, but he seemed a little angry now. We kept fighting for a bit until we both got exhausted and needed a break for some water. As we sat there, drinking out of bowls on the crypt floor, I decided to tell Maurits my thoughts.

"You know, I think we should join the army," I said. He looked at me with a sceptical look.

"Which one?" he asked.

"I don't know. Really whichever lord wants to take us," I said. "The soldiers look well fed and well paid."

"You're not happy here?" Maurits asked.

"Well, it's not exactly what I had in mind when we came to the city."

"So you want to go to Frieslant instead?"

"Nay, I just don't want to live out my life as a thief."

"What's so bad about that? You make good money. You live in this crypt and learn how to fight." Maurits looked at Walpurga. "The people here are nice."

"Aren't there more honest ways to make a living?" I

asked him.

"We tried that," he replied. "You know we did. And what happened? Some nobleman comes and snaps my recorder in half and nobody bats an eye."

"Exactly, nobody bats an eye. But if *we* were to do it, we'd be running from the law. Just today, our first mission went horribly wrong. What makes you think we can earn a real living like this?" I asked.

"Because nobody batted an eye except for Swan. She came to us. She reached out to us."

"Maurits, she press-ganged us."

"She recruited us."

"Those are not the same thing," I said. "Would you really have followed her if you had a choice?"

"Maybe," Maurits replied. I didn't know what to say to that. My little brother choosing to be a thief?

"You really like it here?" I asked.

"I do," Maurits replied.

"Okay then. We stick together," I said. "And we should keep trying to find Piet." I figured the more of us, the better, although there was no way in Hell I'd pull the boy out of his new manor house to join us down here in the filth.

"What's that smell?" I asked, now realizing that something had been stinking pungently since I arrived.

"I had to hide in a gong cart," Maurits replied.

"You washed yourself off, right?" I asked.

"Yep. In the canal," he replied.

"Maurits!" I exclaimed. "That's disgusting! Go wash yourself off!"

Chapter 7. The Inauguration: Floris

When we finally marched out, nearly four hundred in all, our beat was thunderous.

The brummer boys, drumming synchronously, thumped hard on the snare drums, nearly masking the clopping of hooves and the rustling of chainmail. Our force was large — the largest I'd ever seen, and we were about to become larger. A hulking mass of chainmail, gambeson, and razor-sharp spearheads. All across the skyline in the distance, over the flat Lowland fields we saw the ocean of tents. Banners flew high over them, marking whose retinues were where, adorning the sky with lions and crescents and chevrons. It was miraculous, really, the mirage of reds and yellows and blues and blacks and whites. They coloured the sky as if the sky itself were marching to war with them. If not for the near constant threat of rain, the sky would have shone to match.

"Alright Floris," said Father. "Want to tell me whose coat of arms that white one is?" He pointed to one of the major banners.

"Jaja, those are the three scarlet hearts on white of Long Heer Wouter van den Kerckhove, the Knight of Hearts. He's the tallest knight in Zeelant," I replied. "Right hand of the Count there too."

"Very good," Father said. I was proud of that; give me any coat of arms in Hollant and I could almost certainly tell you to whom it belonged, and from where in Hollant it was. Zeelant had been a vassal state of Hollant since the reign of Count Willem the Great. He managed to wrestle it free from the Flemish and into the hands of the Hollanters.

Unfortunately, the Flemish never forgot, and had been feuding with us ever since. But they had the French to deal with — no use squabbling amongst other Dutchmen when Frisian raiders cruised the sea. "Okay, son, how about those red and yellow arms?"

"Those would be the red chevrons on gold of Heer Ecbert van Egmond, the Guardian of the North. The Baron of Egmond held out against Frisian raiders when his countryside burned, and drove them back to their side of the border."

"Prima! I'll give you three more. That golden lion with the billets?"

"Of course I know that one. That's another Zeelanter house. That's the gold lion on red with gold billets of Sir Jan van Renesse, Lord of Zerikzee. He's only, what is it, twenty-three now? His father lies ill on his deathbed."

"That is all correct," Father said. "I'm impressed. Okay, two more. The white stripe on black?"

"Heer Hendrik Wisse van Borselen and his son Wolfaert van Borselen. I think we dined with them once when I was little. From the tales I hear, Hendrik and his son are two entirely different creatures. Hendrik is noble and chivalrous, while his son is known to be more of a fox. On the battlefield too. At the tournament of Breda, he waited until midday to join the melee, whacking greathelms only once all the knights beneath them were tired and worn out. A close friend of Jan van Renesse."

"Yes, you are correct, son. That one was easy. Hmm,

how about that coat of arms with the blue label?"

"Ah, who could forget the mighty Heer Willem van Brederode? His symbol is the scarlet lion on gold, same as the Count, because they are family. He was the squire of Count Willem, and severed him in battle against the Frisians and the Rhinelanders, and became the Lord of Kennemerland."

"That is all correct, except you failed to mention that Count Florens has also decided to promote the Lord of Brederode to Marshal of the realm. He will be our commander," Father said. "He's a good man of great renown. Noble, honest, and chivalrous. A model knight, really." If father held him in high regard, so would I.

We arrived on one of the registration day of the tournament. Of course, it was always difficult to coordinate a meeting point with hundreds of knights, so the Count had set out a fairly wide range of dates in which war parties could arrive. We'd be jousting for a week before the final melee on the last day. This would by my first time competing. I was so excited that I could feel the worms gnawing at my belly already. I couldn't let myself have another embarrassment again. We scanned the tents for friendly heraldry. Most of the heraldic banners we'd expected were present. Of course, there was Father's old friend: Ghijsbrecht van Amstel and his retainers. We spotted the ver Heyens lurking on the opposite side of the camp as well. Neither of them were Hollantic houses. The Lords of Amstel were from Amstelland, in the Prince Bishopric of Utrecht, while the ver Heyens served the seventeen-year-old Graaf Reginald van Wassenberg, Count of Gelrelant. The Young Lion they called him, because he was known for his ambition and his haughtiness. They were warriors, the House of Wassenberg, with strong ties to the German nobility. His late father, Graaf Otto van Wassenberg, Count of Gelrelant had defeated our Graaf Florens' aunt and countess-regent, Lady Adelaide in battle, and claimed stewardship of Hollant until Count Florens was twelve years old. The barons of Hollant would never forget the disgrace of having a foreigner sit on our throne, even if only for three years. The ver Heyens, both Renier and Lodewijk, had fought alongside him at the Battle of Reimerswaal. My father served Lady Adelaide on the Hollanter side. He had not forgotten the defeat. I would not either.

It would seem that it was not just the Hollanters who were ready to hunt down some Frisian sea rats. In all honesty, I was somewhat perplexed by the vast size of the camp — I had only ever seen small-scale feudal wars and spates between noble houses. Certainly no grand campaigns of this stature. But this was something special; this was our young Count Florens' chance to make a name for himself. I'm certain it had been his dream all these years to take revenge on his father's murderers, and now that he had the throne, he had his chance. Of course, nobody liked to say it, myself least of all, but Frisians could also pose some financial burdens. They were pirates, mostly, and border reiving and banditry were not uncommon among their ranks either. Pious to the teeth, of course, but I'd never trust a Frisian with watering my horse. Say what you will about the common folk we have down here in Hollant, but they are trusty folk. For the most part.

We found a plot of land not too far from the city's gates

which seemed suitable. Father ordered the men to set up the encampment. The camp around the city was less of a war encampment than a mere appendage to the urban life of Leyden. Prostitutes from the city had been consistently streaming out to join the war parties. Similarly, so did tradesfolk who hadn't been called to arms. Blacksmiths, wood turners, butchers, rope makers, you name it. They all knew that there was a great market to be had in the camp — lords would pay high prices to see their men well-equipped, well-fed, and in fighting shape. Similarly, laymen and sellswords swarmed from lord to lord in the hopes that they were looking for more men to meet the quotas outlined in their summons. Not to mention the logistics of it all. That would be Father's role during the tournament; he wasn't looking to compete, so he'd spend his time commissioning surgeons, herbalists, and other sorts of camp followers, in addition to merchants who'd be willing to supply pork and grain along a string of captured Frisian settlements. It was a tough task, logistics. Each caravan had to be armed and armoured, racing rations from one holdfast to the next.

Gherrijt and I, on the other hand, rode up to the herald, and signed up for as many jousts as possible. Sure, I was only fifteen. Sure, my leg was still not what it was. But I'd been training on the quintain nearly every day back at home for years. And, of course, I wanted to redeem myself after my embarrassment. Unfortunately, I was only allowed to joust squires and wealthy burghers when signing up for the list, as I had yet to be knighted.

Gherrijt, on the other hand, being a Baron already, was allowed to fight real knights. Fair enough — I would send whatever squire who came my way flying. As I spoke to the herald, a large, muscly hand placed itself on my shoulder. I spun around.

"Uncle Ghijsbrecht!" I exclaimed, seeing my father's friend in the flesh after quite some time.

"Lord Floris," he replied. "Last time I saw you, you were this high." He placed his hand a little lower than I must've been. "I've brought you a gift," he said, cheerily. "Squire," he snapped, without even looking at the boy. The young squire scrambled to bring me a small pouch. "You see this here?" he asked. It was just a normal leather pouch. I nodded. "This pouch is filled with golden jewelry confiscated from moors in Italy. Here, take a look." He opened the pouch. They were quite beautiful. "Be careful with this pouch, boy. There are pickpockets about."

"Thank you so much!" I exclaimed. "It's beautiful."

"Aye. You can give them to some girl to woo her someday. Until then, guard it well. Boys, hear my words: girls don't come cheap. The older they get, the more expensive you'll come to find them, so don't hand it off so soon."

"Yes, Uncle," I replied. "How is life in Amstellant?"

"Oh, you know how it is. Ever since that Bishop Jan van Nassau came to power, he's been defecating all over the prince-bishopric and we've been cleaning up his mess. Let me tell you, the first time I met him, supposed man of the cloth, he had three whores accompanying him, all regained in church-funded emeralds and rubies. Some kind of ruler he is. When the autumn comes, I'm willing to bet his taxes will run out, and soon he'll start borrowing from your good

Count Florens." Ghijsbrecht let out a sarcastic laugh.

"That sounds terrible!" I said.

"It is, boy. It is. Anything to get away from that place, eh? You looking forward to skewering some Frisian barbarians?"

"Hopefully I'll be knighted," I said proudly. "It'll be good to get some experience."

"Slow down, boy. Usually squires make knights. And that's only once they've turned twenty-one."

"I'll be better," I replied. "Most squires squirm at the sight of blood."

"And you bathe in it?" His tone of sarcasm felt demeaning. "I got a pigeon a few weeks ago about your heroic attempt to hold onto that peasant boy," he said. My face grew red. Gherrijt looked at me sidelong. Did Mother send word to everyone we knew?

"Your father has asked me to oversee your performance in the lists. I'll be watching your every move, Floris. And, of course, I'll put in a good word for you with the maidens," he said with a wink. "I'd better enroll myself. Hang onto the pouch, and tell your father I'll come to speak with him shortly."

"He's looking for a logistics merchant with free riders," I said.

"Ah, he'll likely be near the market square. Well, I'd best not hold you up," he said before leading his men onwards to enlist. Uncle Ghijsbrecht was always a strange character to me. To myself and my family he always showed kindness. He always adorned my sister and me with gifts. But, to others, he always had a hint of assertiveness or entitlement in his voice.

To the herald, for example, I heard him say something along the lines of, "I don't like small talk so let's make it quick. My vassals and I will all be competing in both the joust and the melee..."

As we walked away, we realized that we had some time now to explore the city and grab a bite. I mounted up on my trusty destrier Galahad, and rode past the bakeries and snack shops, where the scent of fresh treats enticed me. I'll confess, we stopped more than once for some honey crispels. Their sweet, buttery scent was too alluring to resist. We also slowed more than once to check out the local maidens with their beautifully flowing braids and shapely kirtle gowns. Gherrijt tried to chat up one of them, but he was promptly rejected with an uninterested, "I'm already courting a knight," paired with an eye roll.

I quite liked the city — there was always something to do and something to see. The alehouses looked quite fun and lively, although I wasn't sure how they would react to two young noblemen entering and drinking on their own. We might become the target of the city's next robbery. We also watched the townsfolk practice their drills in the market square while sharing a nice chat and catching up on all we'd missed. I must say, that for commoners, they were disciplined in their movements. I wouldn't have minded having a few of them in my retinue. I know that Gherrijt would gladly have taken the whole lot. We rode past street musicians, magicians, artists and the like. The brick cobbles gave a unique ring to the clopping of Galahad's hooves. The stroll was soon interrupted by the distant rumble of marching feet and the blaring of buisine horns.

"That must be our great Count," Gherrijt said. Almost certainly. I raced Galahad against his palfrey over to the city walls to get a good look outside. A long procession of armed men wound their way through the streets of Leyden. Sure enough, great golden banners with the red lion rampant of House Gerufling flew, and a young Graaf Florens, clad in golden chainmail and a gilded helmet, with ailettes of solid gold, rode at the head of a very long cavalcade. It was quite the entrance. As Gherrijt astutely pointed out, there was zero chance that he'd ridden all this way from Gravenhage in full armour and on a warhorse.

Regardless of whatever political trick Gherrijt made it out to be, it caught my attention. His helmet bore a bright, scarlet lion rampant, seemingly sprawling out of the top, encased by a tall, outwards flaring golden crown. I huffed; the man thought himself royalty. I suppose, the way the Empire was, with no German to strongarm us lowlanders, he was the closest thing to it. In his hand was the golden sceptre denoting his right to rule. If there were two things that were clear about the Count, they were that he loved gold, and that the common folk loved him. They loved him more than his own nobles did, it seemed. They threw flowers at his feet, and flooded the streets to form an audience for him. Behind him rode his bodyguard, consisting of one-hundred-and-fifty knights, or so the people say. When I watched, the one-hundred-and-fifty shrunk to a couple dozen, accompanied by twice as many squires, but it was still quite impressive. Each and every one of them was garbed almost identically with the Gerulfing coat of arms, bearing bright yellow surcoats and red lions. Behind them marched a long column of what looked like two hundred wapenknechten, all wearing the Gerulfing coat of arms on their surcoats atop chainmail. Behind them marched another two hundred Brabantian mercenaries, pikemen all wearing leather surcoats over their chainmail hauberks and gambesons. Finally, some thirty mounted wapenknecht scouts formed his rear guard. It was a sight to behold. The drumming of drummer boys halted the entire city, as even children ceased playing kickball in order to make way and gaze upon the long procession. The Count made his way to the centre square in front of the Church of Saint Peter. Before him came his personal herald, a plump little man carrying the aura of a court jester.

"Hear ye, hear ye," he began, "I present to you the sworn protector of Hollant, the man encharged with your safety by the High Heavens, the son of Graaf Willem II Gerulfing van Hollant, hero of the people, the Red Lion, your Count, Graaf Florens V!" The crowd erupted into a long, drawn out applause to the tune of buisines and snare drums. The rattling of the drums sounded the count's approach in front of all. He took off his helmet, revealing a young, handsome face. He was eighteen years old. Eighteen, and a hero. Eighteen, and the Count of all of Hollant. In an unexpectedly soft, well-tempered voice, he began his speech.

"Good people of Leyden," he announced. "Nay, good people who have come from all across Hollant," he corrected himself, which in itself garnered applause. "I thank you all for your loyal service to the crown. You have all served me in my short term so far as Count. Your admiration for my father has truly resonated with me. He was a great man, although I never got to meet him. As such, I have called a war with Frisia in his honour. We will recover his remains, and return them to Gravenhage where he belongs!" he exclaimed. The crowd roared. He waited for the applause to die down before he continued. "Hundreds of noble knights have answered the call to arms. As we celebrate their loyalty this coming week with a tournament before we set out to do battle, I ask that you honour them, just as they honour you with their presence, and their boundless dedication." There was another roar of applause. Gherrijt rolled his eyes. To his credit, with all the applauding, this would take ages. "And for those of you who have volunteered, your sacrifice will never be forgotten. You will join your noble liege lords as defenders of the realm. Protectors of the faith. True men of courage and chivalry. So, with that, I say, let the games begin!"

+ Piet +

Lances splintered against shields as the festivities commenced. The streets were filled with tricksters, jugglers, acrobats, musicians, tall people walking on stilts, people with painted faces and jingling bells, every oddity you could possible imagine. The low humming and joyful tunes of bagpipes, hurdy-gurdies, and laughter laced the sweet, moist air. Children and young people danced their way through the streets, joyfully moving their feet to the minstrels' tunes, while all around, snack shops waved out their scents to attract customers, creating clouds of cinnamon and honey and raisins. It was truly marvelous. Lord Hillebrant, firmly clenching my hand to make sure that I kept up with him through the seeping crowds, was taking me to Sir Wollefram. I hadn't seen Wolf since the day I left

145

Duivenvoorde. The thought of him scared me a little, in all honesty, but if I got to wait around the jousting knights while I helped him, I'd happily cut his food for him, or whatever I was supposed to do. Honestly, I didn't really know. I tried to keep up with Lord Hillebrant and not get distracted, but a couple of mock jousters, peasants riding on each other's shoulders with broomsticks running through the streets, made that hard. They made funny noises too when they ran, like donkeys and pigs and sheep. I saw similar foolishness in the water too, as men, propelled by teams of rowboats, jousted one another in the canals. When one fell into the water, the crowds watching would erupt in laughter, and the team of rowers would all have to search for him in the water before he had sunk too deep.

Every now and then when making your way through the city, you'd hear the crash of a lance shattering against a shield or a helmet. I was so excited to see them. Everywhere you looked, you saw knights. They rode through the streets in their battle gear, making small talk with the ladies — the ones with their long, wavy hair showing that is. Only the most daring would go after a girl with a wimple, and even then, he'd never make a move while her husband was around. But everyone admired the knights when the tournament started — they were transformed from the men who had come to collect your liege's dues to magnificent heroes on bucking warhorses, draped in their heraldic colours. Each and every one of their helmets held a tall crest, most often displaying their house sigil, and they were all clothed displaying their coats of arms on their shields, surcoats, and even their horses' caparisons. Lord Hillebrant said that you could tell the German knights from the Dutch and French ones because their surcoats and caparisons would be colours or patterns that had nothing to do with their heraldry. I thought you could just tell them apart when they spoke German.

The jousting pitch was located just on the north side of the city; that's where the fields were the least wet. It was always a stark contrast when exiting the city limits. Travelling through the gates was like travelling through a portal to a new world; a wetter, dewier world. You could taste it, like the dew had been sitting there all morning. Stale. It was a sweet staleness — the kind you had back in Duivenvoorde every morning. The kind you smelled when you went to collect eggs or feed pigs. It reminded me of home. Lord Hillebrant seemed to catch how I was feeling by the expression on my face.

"Oh, chin up, little man," he said. "It must be hard. But think about everyone here. Ms. Filomena and the boys. You've got a whole other family here now." It didn't feel like it. The water in the city moat was murky and barely spat my image back at me. Even so, it did it with an insincerity that seemingly mocked me. My short, chubby features. My curly bush of red hair. My plump, chestnut eyes. I felt a little bit useless. And a little bit betrayed. I had since I was given away — Mother didn't even need a night to think about it. Then and there, gone I was. Like the wind. Like father. When Lord Hillebrant came for me with coin, she hugged me and squashed me, sure, but she gladly took the coin too. Could we really not have just tended to the crops as usual? I couldn't help but wonder. I loved Mother. She meant the world to me. But the mother that gave me away was a little different from the one that raised me. At first, before I left, I was convinced that Lord Hillebrant was handing me a ticket straight to the top. That I'd be living like a king. But this didn't seem like the life that was promised, was it? In all fairness, I didn't see any other boys or girls lounging around. No, my mother wasn't taken for a fool. She must've known. She knew how the city works. How the nobles think and live. And Lord Hillebrant, he was kind to me. He called me 'little man' and ruffled my hair and played games with me. And Filomena, she fed me well, always saying I was a growing boy. I couldn't tell what had happened behind all the bartering and trading, but I felt like I was more than a commodity. I'd ought to have been. Wasn't I? Seeing that my mood hadn't changed much, Lord Hillebrant took me to one side.

"Alright little lad, you're about to enter the war camp. You've never been in one before. It's completely normal to be frightened or disgusted even, just stick with me and you'll be alright. Don't go wandering off all by yourself, understand?" I nodded. As we strolled through the camp, most of the soldiers just looked busy. Chopping wood, sharpening things, polishing things, it looked like everyone had something to do. So did the women. When we passed by them, Lord Hillebrant shielded my eyes with the palm of his hand. We were looking for the green banner. Lord Hillebrant affectionately called his nephew the Green Knight, like Sir Bertilack in the tale of Sir Gawain. It was because green was a rare colour for knights to have on their heraldry — far rarer than the blacks and reds and blues, all complimented with either a white or yellow. And the little green that was there was used minimally, like the three green water lilies on white of House van Scalmen, or the green blacksmithing billets on white of the Lords of Pendrecht.

When we made our way through the camp, Lord Hillebrant leading the way because I couldn't see over most things, I saw the Duivenvoorders training in the field. I quickly stopped Lord Hillebrant to see if I'd recognize any. Sure enough, I did! There was Mr. Arnulf, the barber-surgeon, and tall Mr. Nicolaas with his two sons. And I also noticed that boy that Yda had been going on and on about. Maarten, his name was. She used to tell me about him, just me, because she was worried that any of the others might tell Mother. Mother ended up finding out anyways, but I don't think she ever did anything about it. Other than the fact that he was a charcoal burner, he seemed friendly enough. If you could get past the strong stench of soot and smoke. I let go of Lord Hillebrant's hand. I wanted to go ask him about Yda and the others.

"Maarten! Maarten!" I called out, moving as quickly as my legs could take me. I saw him swing his head over to look at me, at which point the man behind him in the formatting bonked him on the helmet with a spear shaft.

"Ow, you lout," he told him. I ran up to him; it felt like I was barely half his height. He pulled me aside, saying "excuse me" to the man telling them what to do. "You're Yda's brother, aren't you?" Maarten asked.

"I am," I replied. "How is she? Do you know about Mother and my other brothers and sisters too?"

"She was fine last I saw her. Happy. She misses you a lot, lad," he said, kneeling down to talk with me. "And your mother, last I saw, was in one piece, going about her business as per usual. Your brother Sam's working for the blacksmith."

"Uncle Max!" I said with a smile. "Sam always wanted to be a smith!"

"Well, he's going to be," Maarten said with a warm smile of his own. "Your little brother, Phillips, has gone to a monastery somewhere. And your sisters Merin and Florie are going to be nuns."

"We're all spreading apart?" I asked. A slap of sadness struck me over the head. "That's okay, at least Thiel and Maurits will take care of Mother," I said.

"Don't you worry, lad," Maarten said. "Your mother's doing her best. On another note, how've you been? Eating well?" He patted my tummy. I suppose it was a little bigger than it was in Duivenvoorde.

"I get pork and eggs with my breakfast," I said.

Maarten smiled. "As you should. You're a growing boy."

"Am I going to be as big as you one day?" I asked, curious. I wanted to be, well, maybe not *that* big, but big enough to joust in a tournament.

"Bigger," he said. "But only if they keep shoveling that pork into you." Lord Hillebrant came, finally realizing I was gone. Out of breath, belly heaving, his chubby fingers extended to greet Maarten.

"My name is Lord Hillebrant ver Heyen," he said. "I am the guardian of this boy."

"Maarten," Maarten replied. "Wait a minute…you're working for a lord?" he asked me. I nodded my head. "Then you'd ought to be as big as me. You'll be fighting dragons soon."

"Piet, do you know this man?" Lord Hillebrant placed a hand on my shoulder.

"He's Yda's friend," I replied. "I think they're courting." Maarten turned a little pink.

"Ah, pleased to meet you, Maarten," Lord Hillebrant said.

"Likewise," Maarten replied. "Look, I have to get back to training or else I'll be cut rations, but we'll chat sometime, eh? I'll show you around the camp?"

"Okay," I said, cheeks stretched in a big smile. He seemed strong and courageous. I wouldn't mind being like him one day.

"Come, Piet," Lord Hillebrant said, taking me by the arm. "You see that green banner there? The boys are over there." When we made it to the tent, I found the three ver Heyen men with their squires and a few retainers around them. They wouldn't have brought their retainers if they were just here for the tournament — they didn't bring them when they fetched me from Duivenvoorde.

"Are you going to war?" I asked when we arrived.

"Ah, the young man is here," said Wolf, coming to greet me. "Yes, we certainly are. Our dearest brother, Lord Hillebrant here still owes service. We're here in his stead."

"How've you been finding old Hille?" asked Renier. Lord Hillebrant was already in the process of greeting and embracing all three of them.

"I like it here," I said. "Lord Hillebrant is good to me. But he makes me read."

Wolf laughed. "I bet he does," he said. "Those books will make you a fine scholar one day, just like Hillebrant."

"But I don't want to sort through papers all the time. I want to ride a horse and joust."

Wolf said, "When I was your age, I was reading just like you. Although I reckon I wasn't half as quick as you. But now, I have to know my languages and my geography and my arts. How else will I throw insults at the Frenchmen during the melee?" Renier and Lodewijk gave a hearty laugh to that one. Lord Hillebrant, on the other hand, was far from amused.

"We'll leave you to it," Lord Hillebrant said, collecting Lodewijk and Renier. "We'll be in the city. Perhaps in the marketplace."

"By that he means the alehouse," Renier said with a smile. The three men left. Wolf then went on to explain the duties of a squire and what exactly I'd have to do for the week. Rule one, of course, was that nobody had to know that I was not of noble birth. He said I should avoid the question, or make up some German name. I think we agreed upon Dinklesburg or Oberunterbrugen or something like that. Next, I'd have my basic taste for the day. I had to polish up all of his armour and clean his clothes after each joust. That seemed simple enough — I sometimes used to see Mother doing the washing, or Yda sometimes too, and polishing was as simple as it got. I'd also have to run messages for him; luckily I'd come to know most parts of the city by heart. At the end of each day, Wolf promised that he'd give me a sword fighting lesson.

"Practice makes perfect," he said. That's why he never wasted a moment, practicing every hour he had free. He wanted to be the best knight alive. Oh, and I'd accompany Wolf and his squires at each joust; the best part. I would get to watch the jousts up close, see the action and the drama, watch the knights in their shining steel and bright colours charge at one another at full speed.

When the courier came to summon Wolf to the lists, his squires were nowhere to be seen.

"Godverdomme, they're off buying replacement lances. Piet, you're going to have to arm me," he said.

I looked up from polishing his greathelm. "I don't know how to," I said.

"It's time to learn. Come." He set up a stool for me to stand on. First came his chainmail chausses — leggings, essentially hosen, but made out of riveted maille links. Then came his padded arming jacket, a padded shirt that he wore over his linen tunic. It didn't look as chubby as the ones the soldiers wore, but it felt like a pillow a little bit. He said that this was to keep his bones from rattling. After that came his hauberk, a shirt of chainmail that went all the way over his fingers. He bragged to me about how each of his fingers were individually tailored and woven separately, whereas most knights wore it like a mitten instead. Luckily for him, there were also slashes in the hand protection to let him keep his hands out of the mittens until it was time to fight. He told me that his hands would've wrinkled like dried plums after the joust if he had to keep them in the chainmail the whole time. Regardless, when I did look at his hands, they were callused and veiny. I think it's because he trained with his sword every single day without gloves. On top of his mail shirt came the coat of plates, a leather vest that held together numerous interlocking steel plates.

He said that if their lance missed, this is what would keep him alive. He said that, if anything, the chainmail was almost for show in the joust. I suppose it might keep the splinters out.

Next, Wolf slipped into his padded poleyns on his own — padded armour that covered his thigh, with a stitched-in knee cop made of steel. Wolf told me about how he was also saving up to buy steel knee cops to protect his knees, because he was tired of taking blows to them with only chainmail to protect them. Over the torso, I helped him slip into his surcoat, a bright green surcoat with the twin white wolf hooks of the ver Heyen family. On his shoulders, I fastened his ailettes — leather rectangles to guard his shoulders and bear his heraldry. Over his head came his arming cap and chainmail coif — a hood of riveted maille links. Finally, he placed his great helm on before riding out to mask the pink mark over his eye. His helm was adorned with a tall pair of green and white dragon wings over green mantling and a green and white torse. Wolf looked every inch a knight.

"You know how I got that scar?" he asked me. I shook my head. "I was out hunting once. With your guardian and my father. We found this beautiful stag, tall and slender, great rack of antlers. My father tried to spear it once the dogs caught it. He failed, only brushing its tail. The thing sprang up again as if it was never hurt and kept bounding forwards. Then Uncle Hillebrant had a turn missing the thing entirely.

When it was my turn, I speared it square between its leg and it's belly, but it was like it never even noticed. Not wanting to let it get away, I held on, even when the beast ripped me from my own horse. Eventually, the smart thing, it bounded over our campfire, and dragged my face right through it. But I never let go. We got it, and now its antlers are hung above our mantelpiece back in Heyen. Moral of the story? I don't lose." He didn't even wait for my reaction before mounting up.

When he rode out, he slung his heater shield over his back. It also bore his arms, with a scarlet heraldic label over the sigil to indicate that he was the successor to the true Lord of Heyen, his father, Lodewijk. His horse was barded in a forest green heraldic caparison to match. I could certainly see why Lord Hillebrant called him the green knight now — every inch of him was green. Green and steel.

The lists were long, far long than I imagined, encased completely by two rows of bleachers on either side, extended and enwrapped by hordes of standing commoners, only barred from the field by a thin wooden fence. In the centre of it all, high above the rest, sat the count in luxuriously flowing robes. Beside him sat his favourite barons, among them Willem van Brederode, the Marshal. When we arrived at the lists, Wolf's squires finally showed up, lances in hand. They were each painted in varying stripes of green and white. "I'm sorry, my lord. There was just a long line at the…"

"We speak after," he said. He unslung his shield and slipped his left arm through the straps. His squires hurried over to tie the chin strap. Across the field, a menacing figure came to face him. He was clad in black and yellow, with a red and white chequered saltire over his shield. His red and white painted helm bore a crest resembling a chain mail-clad armour holding a flail; the mail instead made of black and yellow entwined rope. Most notable about him was his horse — a great, black Frisian horse.

The crowd's volume died down to the rolling beat of drums, bisected with the sharp twang of buisine horns. They only halted when the Count's herald stepped forward. He unfurled a long armorial scroll used to map the tournament.

"Lords and Ladies, Maidens and Gentlemen, Damsels and Knights of the Realm…"

"And all the other fine folk here!" interjected the young Count Florens. The crowd erupted in laughter. The herald continued.

"I present before you two haughty opponents, one from Gelrelant, and the other from Utrecht. From Gelrelant, we have the young knight, the green knight, the hero of the East, the feller of men and the wetter of maidens, Meneer Wollefram ver Heyen!" The crowd erupted in applause. I wasn't sure if they had ever heard of them before, but clearly they wanted to see Wolf joust. "And his opponent, harkening from the river lands of Amstel, known for his prowess on the battlefield, we have Heer Ghijsbrecht van Amstel!" The crowd cheered again. "Gentlemen, pick your ladies," the herald said. Wolf scanned the bleachers for the fairest maiden of them all. After considering for a moment, he decided to tilt his lance towards the twelve-year-old daughter of Willem van Brederode. Willem's bushy eyebrows cracked into a smile — luckily for Wolf he took it in good faith. An almost exaggerated "Awwww" swept the crowd. After asking for her father's consent, young Aeidis tied her handkerchief around Wolf's lance. Wolf raised it in the air towards her, garnering applause. Ghijsbrecht, on the other hand, extended his lance out to his wife, who tied her handkerchief around his lance as well. After both knights had received favour they returned to their ends of the field. It was an open pitch, no fence, no barriers, nothing. Just two knights, one in front of the other.

"Without further ado, let us begin." Both knights centered their horses. Wolf's squires made sure that I wasn't standing too close, backing away themselves. I heard utter silence; only the grunts of horses, and their hooves anxiously pawing against the dirt. "On your marks," the herald said, raising a glove. "Play on." The glove dropped. Immediately, like a lightning strike, both horses surged forward. It was a pass like any other; both knights missed, and they circled back to collect another lance.

"Quickly! Quickly!" I heard Wolf mutter through the breaths of his helm. His finger grabbed about in the air for a new lance; he couldn't see through the sides of his helm. His squires placed them in his hands, one after another. Crash. Both lances broke. They rode back for another round. This third time, they both broke their lances again on one another's shields. One of Wolf's squires accidentally knocked the lances over. Ghijsbrecht came charging again, hoof and dirt, the whinnies of horses. I could hear Wolf's heart pounding. Still no lance. He grabbed about in the air. Still no lance. Ghijsbrect was close now. There was no time. When the lance was finally presented to him, his horse grew restless. Shuffling to the side, away from danger. Wolf spurred it on. No lance. Ghijsbrecht, realizing now that Wolf had come to his right side instead of his left, tried to raise his lance again. No avail. Wolf spurred his horse at the last second. With the palm of his mailled glove, he grabbed Ghijsbrecht by the face of his helm, tearing him from his saddle. Like a hay doll he flung from his horse and hit the dirt. The crowd roared. The fallen knight screamed. He stood up, and threw his helm to the ground.

"He cheated!" he exclaimed. Wolf took off his helm as well.

"It was a fair pass," he said. The herald turned to the Count. The crowd fell silent. The Count whispered something in the herald's ear.

"The Count has proclaimed that you shall both continue. It was dishonourable of you, Ghijsbrecht, to charge Wollefram while he lacked a lance. Just as it was less than fair to smack Ghijsbrecht with your glove, Wollefram," he announced.

"Horseshit. It was that ugly bastard's squire's fault," muttered Ghijsbrecht. "You call my honour into question?"

"The Count has made his verdict. Mount up, gentlemen," the herald replied.

Reluctantly, both competitors returned to either side of the field, re-strapping their helms. "Best of luck to both of you, knights."

"Don't do that again," said Wollefram to his squire. He turned to the other one. "You. You and Piet will now hand me lances." I wasn't having fun anymore. The air had got thicker. There was a tension to it; I could taste it. It smelled of more than just horse dung and sweat; it smelled of fear and anger. "Lance." I took the lance, holding the heave pole up as best I could. Wolf snatched it from me. The glove dropped once more. Wolf spurred his horse forward. Ghijsbrecht did as well. The pass went as per usual; two lances hit, neither broke. They rode again. No hit. A third time. Both hit, Ghijsbrecht's broke. Their horses were seemingly getting tired. Every pass was a sprint. Every hit was a shock. Wolf's horse panted like a warm dog. It whinnied. But it kept galloping. As they rode, a young girl from the crowd started crying. Her parents tried to hush her and take her away, but that was enough to trigger Ghijsbrecht's tired Frisian. The beast staggered up in the air. Wolf's, tired, kept riding. They were in each other's way. Both knights raised their lances. I heard a startled "Shit!" bellow out from one of their helms before a large crash.

The horses smacked into one another, sending both riders to the ground. Wolf rolled, his crest smashing into pieces. His horse twisted its leg. The other, the Frisian, I saw a bone jut out of its knee. Thick, hot bouts of blood spewed from it. Right in front of me. I couldn't control myself. Overcome with fear and repulsion, I ran off to the side of the lists — somewhere that I couldn't see them, and threw up my entire breakfast. Nobody saw me. Nobody watched. They all raced over to the knights and their horses. The crowd erupted in a panicked roar. It was horrendous. It was so jarring I could scarcely believe it. It was disgusting. I was afraid. Lord Hillebrant emerged from some shadow somewhere to comfort me, but I could feel my heart racing and my lungs pumping out air faster than it was pumped in. Good God. God God. What in God's name? What in the deepest Hell? I tried to come to grips with myself. With a handkerchief, Lord Hillebrant wiped the orange acid off my cheeks.

"Shhh, it's okay," he said, holding me tight. "It's going to be okay. It'll all be okay." I heard the horses still crying out. Then I heard somebody call for an axe. I hated tournaments.

Chapter 8. The Contest: Floris

"Alright Floris. Let's see what you can do," Father said, drawing his sword. He was covered head to toe in chain mail. So was I, but I still anticipated the crunching pain of a sword blow. I got into my fighting stance, left hand behind my back, sword hand forward, in a two-dimensional bracing stance. "Feet out," Father said. "Good, now lean forward." He came to correct my posture by hand. "Who taught you to put your hand back there? I sure as Hell didn't." He took the left hand from my back and put it out in front of my chest as if I were holding a shield in it.

"Master Alwar, the fencing master taught me to," I said.

"Master Alwar is a wet lily pad," Father replied. "Hold it how you would a lance, fingers forward, not like how you hold a wood axe. Not that you ever have, you pampered rabbit." I corrected my grip. Lastly, he shifted my torso to face forwards, not to the side. "Very good. Let's fight," he said, knocking my blade to one side. His white cloak and his long beard began to flow in the cool, sea wind. I threw a cut which he blocked. Then another. He swept it aside like it was nothing. I lunged at him, hoping to catch him in the chest, but it was no use. He swatted it aside. I had shifted so much weight into it that I nearly fell over. I threw one more from above, which he caught on the chain mail links on his forearm, and threw a cut down from the same angle of his own, slicing me right where my neck met my shoulders. It was hard. It stung. If not for my hauberk that would have been my last practice. "Ow," I let out. "That hurt."

"That didn't hurt, it was uncomfortable," Father replied. "You know the difference between pain and discomfort?"

"What?"

"Can you keep fighting?" he asked. "Jaja."

"Then you are only uncomfortable. Pain is when you've been skewered with so many arrows you can't move. Pain is when a scimitar has sliced you across the belly and you don't know which way is up. That is not pain. That bruise tomorrow will be uncomfortable."

"I'll be jousting later," I said.

"And that'll be a lot more uncomfortable," Father replied. "Look, you have a lion within you. I've seen you roar. I've seen you let it out. But never ever let it whimper. The moment your foe sees you as a cub, you have already lost."

"When I stood before the ver Heyens, I stood like a lion."

"In the body of a boy."

"But I roared."

"Have you ever heard of a lion fighting a dragon? No. Because the dragon will always defeat the lion. It is not the lion's fault. He doesn't waste his time with dragons, and chases after unicorns instead. Be the lion. Know when to fight."

"When do I fight?"

"Nobody can tell you that but yourself. But, if you want to pick more fights that you can win, you must practice and improve. One day you will live up to your roar, son. But for now, get back in fighting stance."

"I know how to fight," I said. "Master Alwar taught me when you weren't there." Father didn't look pleased at that comment. I suppose that wasn't fair of me.

"Clearly not well enough," Father replied. "You will relearn."

"Don't I need a shield?" I asked.

"To hide behind it?"

"Nay, but in battle I'll have a shield."

"In battle, you'll have a lance and horse, too."

"In a siege?"

"Please don't tell me you were planning on storming castles with that dainty thing. A mace or an axe will do best there."

"Then why should I know how to use a sword?"

"You must know how to fight," Father replied. "You must know how to keep distance. How to manage it. How to control your space, your body, your movements. You don't learn weapons, you learn war." I didn't know what he meant, but I nodded in agreement. "Let's start with the basics. Your stance is good. Well, better now. Time to do arms. You have three guards. The Holy Trinity." He came and placed my hand right above my head, sword fanning out behind me.

"Where should the blade be pointing?" I asked, unsure of how to hold it.

"Who cares?" he replied. "Do you know where it is?" I

nodded. "Good, that's the only person who needs to. This position is called the Father. Give me a strike." I struck him from above. Of course, he caught it with his blade. "Very good. Next one." He brought my sword down to my right hip, facing forwards. "This one's called the Son."

"Which foot forward?" I asked him. He shrugged.

"Whichever one's forward when they come at you. Learn to fight from both," he replied. "Now, give me a thrust." I did as he told me, and he swatted it aside. "Good. When you thrust, make sure not to telegraph it. Be quick and sharp with your movements. Last one." He brought my sword hand to my other hip. "As if you're unsheathing the bloody thing," he said. "Same thing, either foot in front. This one's the Holy Ghost. Give me an underhand cut." I obliged. "Very good. Father." I snapped into position. "Son." I did so again. "Holy Ghost." I moved to position. "Again, faster. Father. Son. Holy Ghost." I followed. "Faster. Father. Son. Holy Ghost. Very good. Now give me strikes. Father." I sent one crashing down. "Son." Again, a heavy thrust and a quick recoil. "Holy Ghost." An upwards cut bringing me back to "Father, Son, Holy Ghost. Father, Son, Holy Ghost." Then, Father switched it up. "Back to guard stances," he said. "Father." When I raised my sword, he threw a cut down on me. I blocked it with my sword—the whole thing vibrated and gave in so quickly that I could barely keep control of it. He cut through my stance easily, tapping my chain mail coif with the razor-sharp tip of his blade.

"I'm not strong enough," I said, dropping the sword. "Will all the knights in the melee be as strong as you?"

"I've seen forty-five summers," Father said. "They'll be

stronger." I felt my frown grow. "Pick up your sword," he said.

"There's no use."

"I said pick it up. Are you going to become a knight?"

"Not at this rate. Not if I die in the melee," I said. Father sighed. I could see he was disappointed.

"You won't. You'll be faster. Smarter. More disciplined. They fight like you do. I'll teach you to be better," Father said. "Pick it up." I wanted that. That's all I'd ever wanted. To be better. No, not even that. To be enough. I trusted Father. I picked it up. "Next lesson. Never block a blade with your own. Throw a cut." I launched one at him in the best form I could. He swatted it away like it was nothing. "See what I did there?" I didn't quite catch it. It looked like he was just doing what I was, but better. "Again." I threw an underhand this time. He sent it right back down to whence it came.

"You're just beating my cuts with cuts of your own," I said. "But how can I do that if I'm not as strong as you are?"

"It's not about strength," Father said. "Whoever cuts second, wins."

"How does that work?" I asked.

"It's simple. Your goal is to hit me. Mine isn't to hit you. Not now, at least. So I don't have to cut through your cut and send it back to you, I only need to stop yours. Match it with enough force to keep it away from me. To send it somewhere else. To the side. Out of the way. You try." He launched a swing at me, which I did manage to counter with a swing of my own. "You see? Strength doesn't matter. And best of all, send me a thrust." When the tip of my sword almost hit his torso, he managed to not only redirect it completely, but also shoved the quillon of his sword firmly into my gut.

"Ouch!" I said.

"Discomfort," he said. "But see? Thrusts are the most direct, but they're also the easiest to block. I don't have to catch your blade mid-swing. I only have to hit it anywhere along the blade and it'll bugger off. Try it." He sent me a thrust of his own, and like he had said, I managed to parry it. "Prima!" he said. "You'll be a fine swordsman. Don't you worry." I gave him a smile. He was quite different than my mother. He made me feel like a man. He put in me the will to improve which I couldn't find at home. I almost wanted to thank him for it. "Practice these guards. Practice your cuts, and your parries, and your balancing. Footwork too. Face as many ghosts as you like. I'll see you here later." Father sheathed his sword firmly and mounted up to do something elsewhere.

Diligently I stood there in the field, following his words to the finest syllable. *Father,*

Son, Holy Ghost, I thought to myself, as I went through the motions. It was peaceful; the wide open field with nobody but myself, my sword, and Gallahad peacefully grazing off in my periphery. It was liberating, really. Even as a charging horde of grey clouds thundered across the sky and let loose drops and then buckets of rain, I stood my ground and practised. *Father, Son, Holy Ghost. Father, Son, Holy Ghost. Holy Ghost, Son, Father.* I imagined I had a buckler in my hand. How would my technique change then? What if I had a heater shield? What if I was facing two men, not just one? Parrying then striking. Striking then parrying. I picked some trees to be my targets along a line of uncultivated land. By the time I saw a glimpse of the sun again through what had mellowed to a drizzle, most of the bark had been hacked off. My blade was undamaged. Not a single warp or chip. It stood just as true as I did. *Father, Son, Holy Ghost.*

It was not long before I heard a galloping horse. When I looked to see who it was, it was not Father, but Gherrijt. His clothes were soaked through.

"Come from the lists?" I asked.

"Yeah, some meathead called Rodolf van Oudart sent me off my horse," he said.

"Arms?"

"Three crows on white."

"I'll look out for him," I said. Gherrijt gave me a smile.

"What are you doing out here all by yourself?" he asked. "Playing knights and dragons?"

"I'm practising," I replied.

"For what?" he asked. "You planning on sword fighting anyone soon? In armour no less?"

"Father said I need to learn how to fight."

"So he set you up with some trees," Gherrijt replied with a chuckle. "Take off the chain mail and show me what you can do." I shrugged. Fair enough—it wouldn't hurt. Gherrijt set his bucket hat by the stump of the tree.

"I'm a little tired, though," I said. "I've been at it all morning." I pointed to the stripped tree, filled with ruthless gashes.

"I face-planted in the dirt not moments ago. My whole body aches." Gherrijt let off a half-joking laugh, showing me a large bruise on his shin. It looked like it hurt.

"This'll take your mind off it," I said. We crossed swords. I got into my fighting stance and threw out a slow, controlled cut. Father was completely right. Gherrijt went to block it instead of redirecting the cut. "Father said that if you swat the cuts away with cuts of your own, you'll have a little more success," I said.

"Is your father any good?" Gherrijt asked.

"He's a Templar," I replied. They were known for being fearsome warriors.

"Fair enough," Gherrijt said. "Here, show me then." He swung at me, and I used the *Holy Ghost* stance to redirect his sword and face my blade towards his chest as if to say 'got you'. Gherrijt looked impressed. I taught him the three stances, and really everything that Father had taught me, save the hefty, emotional speeches. Gherrijt became quite good at it. Better than me, even. He had four years on me. But, the fights were not imbalances. We manoeuvred and tried our hardest, making sure not to actually cut either of each other. That was the hard part, harder than fighting. Actually controlling the blade. I heard hooves again, and in the distance I saw Father.

All he said to me was, "Saddle up, lad. You've been

called to the lists." I knew who I was to face—it was some squire from Zeelant. Something like Meyner or Mouriin van Reimerswaal. I only remembered his house because that was where Otto van Wassenberg beat the Hollanters. You know, many Zeelanter houses joined him. I wouldn't be surprised if the van Reaimerswaals were one of them.

Anyways, when we made it to the lists, I was unsurprised to find a snivelling, scrawny young squire. Typical. His voice was high and raspy too—he sounded like the offspring of a sheep and a seagull. His coat of arms, crossed swords on red, was barely on him. It was on his shield. Although his shield could certainly have been of higher quality, but his horse was completely unbarded. No caparison or anything. He didn't even have a crest upon his helmet. When he put it on his head, it looked almost like it was a bucket that had a single eyehole hacked out by a broad axe.

"Lance," he said in his unbearable voice. I had come all dressed up—a proud swan emerged out of my blackened greathelm as my crest. And he came with that old bucket. As you can imagine, the joust itself was no competition. Untrained. I was able to force him into surrendering quite quickly, before he was even off his horse. Most of the week passed along those lines for me. Opponents of little repute, victories of even less repute. I would never make a name for myself this way. For most of them, the Count wasn't even present.

When the squires tilted, that was his moment to empty his bladder or grab a bite or enjoy the street performers. At least some of the maidens in the stands were watching. But they never went out to the alehouses—they were too young to be allowed to. At least I was winning, I suppose. A slight confidence boost to be able to joust with men my age and pull some victories.

Well, that was until they let me joust the real men. On the fifth day of the tourney, two days before the melee, they decided to let me have a go at real knights. This went far less smoothly. The first man, the Black Lion of Alcmare, struck me to the ground without even a contest. The Son of the Baron of Drongelen, a blue knight with a white wheel and a black heraldic label as his sigil, took the fight to me on foot. I tried to fight him with my sword and use some of the new tactics that father had shown me, but it was nothing compared to van Drongelen's great, two-handed mace. As if that wasn't enough beating, they also set me up against Guillaume of Oudshoorn, a Frenchman in the Count's court. That one went a little differently. At least I used my shield this time to block his falchion, but eventually that very same falchion knocked the sword right out of my hands.

I don't know what it was, but I felt myself tense up when facing all of them. It was a fear that clenched me, although I'd never admit it. To admit fear was like emptying one's own entrails in the world of chivalry. Father attended my first few until he got bored. Gherrijt too. When I faced the knights, none of them were there but Ghijsbrecht, watching me closely like a hawk. It was better that way; minimal damage. But I felt as though it were all for nothing. No chance at winning. No glorious prize at the end. Only bumps and bruises and the fear I would face tenfold of what I was facing now, on the final day. I looked forward to it, though. The melee was always my favourite event to watch—when all the knights took to the field for an entire day, garbed in their houses' heraldries and bearing their great crests upon their heads, simulating real battle. It was as real as it got. If you were unlucky enough, you could be seriously wounded, or killed. Of course, nobody was out searching to kill one another; however, until sundown, it was completely legal. Frankly, once an unfortunate knight had been trampled beneath hundreds of hooves. Who could be blamed? The aim was to capture as many knights as you could, forcing them to give you their warhorse and a little ransom on top. If you succeeded, you were to offer mercy, which would come at that price. If they rejected it, well, you fought on. Few knights were likely to reject, however, when a mace was ready to rain down on their helmet for the thirtieth time, or when a dagger was held to their eye slit. It always sounded like much fun, or valuable experience. The two teams of the battle were to be made up of the real bannerets who would be leading their conrois of knights into Frisia. The bannerets were knights picked to command a retinue of roughly twenty to thirty, and would fly their pennant high on their lance to indicate where they were at all times. Gherrijt, Ghijsbrecht, and Uncle Jan would all be bannerets. There were to be eighty bannerets in all—fifty Hollanters, ten Zeelanters, and twenty from everywhere else all mashed together. That meant there would be around one thousand knights, five hundred on each side, charging at one another. It would be amazing. And, Father said that I could partake. Usually knights are not supposed to take their squires into the melee, but, since I was not a squire; although not a knight either, Father decided to let me join.

The morning of the melee came early. I remember the

scent of dew as I woke up on the tent grass. It was crisp, not just cool, just as most mornings were in the camp. It would take a while for the sun to climb higher in the sky and heat up the ground. For now a cloak over my linen nightgown would have to do. I grabbed a fresh drink from the Rijn and let it trickle coolly down my throat. The sun shone bright this morning. Clear skies, dry earth, what more could we ask for? I went to go take a leak out at the edge of camp.

"Morning," I heard from behind me as a groggy Uncle Jan came beside me to take a piss of his own. "Beautiful day, isn't it?"

"A good day for the melee," I said.

"Morning chill getting to you or are you nervous?" Uncle Jan asked. Embarrassed, I dried off and quickly tucked myself back into my braies. "When the horns sound and we're all off, make sure that you stick with your father, yeah? Wouldn't want that leg of yours getting any worse." Jan gave me a crisp clap on the back with his piss hand before heading back to the tents. I could smell the scent of ale on his breath. Once he'd left, I was so angry that I pulled out my sword and started hacking at the rushes. Godverdomme if I have to hear another jape or jest. It was one mistake. One. I felt like screaming. The whole week, no, even before that, everyone had just been constantly poking fun at me. Like I was some incompetent fool. I defeated all those squires in the lists. I stood up for my house. Just one damn duel. Ugh. I picked up a rock and threw it into the Rijn. Then another.

"What's the matter, boy?" The deceptively colder, harsh voice belonged to Ghijsbrecht.

"Nothing," I said. I almost stormed off at which point he held his hand out to stop me.

"Come here," he said. "Today, there's no room for folly. One wrong move, and not only is your life in danger, but your whole company." Not another lecture. I rolled my eyes. "Hey!" he barked. "I'm talking to you." I looked in his dead, blue eyes.

"I'm sorry," I said. "Just had a rough start to the day."

"Rough start to the day? It's just begun. What, did a bullfrog jump up and nip at your rookworst?" he asked. I laughed—that one was original at least. "All I'm saying is that you have to make sure that you focus. No distractions."

"Everybody thinks I'm going to mess up."

"Who?" Ghijsbrecht asked, as if he was going to seek them out and smash them in with his flail.

"Oh just Uncle Jan and most of the knights," I said. Ghijsbrecht put his hand on my shoulder.

"Look, respect isn't something that's given. It's earned. It'll take time for you to win back their praise, but let me tell you, once you have it, it'll be glorious. I saw you win every one of those jousts against all the other boys your age," he said. "You're a dragon in the lists. Unleash that in the melee, yeah? I've already told your father about how well you did."

"And you told him about how every knight stomped me to pieces after?"

"Who cares? Those are grown men. You're still a boy. You'll grow to beat every single one of them," Ghijsbrecht replied. "Your father said he's proud of you. Very." I felt the

173

sparks of a smile ignite my face.

"Really?"

"Yes," Ghijsbrecht said. "You wouldn't be fighting today if he wasn't. Look, the only advice I'll give is to stay sharp, keep that helmet on no matter how uncomfortable it gets, and stay on that bloody horse. The thing will be your saviour when you're too tired to even raise your sword. Once you're on foot, you're done," Ghijsbrecht said. I nodded. We were soon joined by Father, who had also come to water the bushes.

"Morning," he said to both of us with a nod. We replied in kind. I could see the bags under his eyes.

"Nice weather, isn't it?" Gherrijt said.

"Perfect for some bloodletting," Father replied. "Floris, I've been looking for you," he added.

"What for?" I asked.

"There's something I want to give you before the melee."

"Give me?" I asked, my eyebrows prancing up like an unbridled pony.

"Yes, a gift," Father said, tucking himself away and turning to face me. It was then I noted that he carried two swords on his belt. I knew exactly what this was, and I nearly melted.

"Why are you carrying Great-Grandfather's sword?" I asked with a broad, childish grin.

"I don't see any sword that belongs to your great-grandfather. Only one that belongs to you." I felt my eyes light up. "A young man's first melee is no small thing. As such, he must carry with him a trusted sword with which to do battle and give nothing but steel and valour to his enemy." Father unsheathed the blade. It was unusually slender for a sword of its kind, using the leftover weight to forge a long, Pietcing blade two palms longer than any other sword I'd seen; perfect for long reach on horseback. Its brass hilt was beautifully decorated with a lion's head on the end of each quillon; well, what was supposed to look like the head of a lion, although admittedly it resembled far more the bearded visage of a wild man. The handle was wrapped in a fine, black cord—a restored version of its original umber leather. The hilt was capped with a fishtail pommel. Most notably, the blade itself was etched with the three crescent moons of the Wassenaer lineage. My proud family. Father held the sword out in front of me with two hands. Eagerly, I grabbed the sword and began carefully waving it around, measuring its point of balance, checking its edge alignment, testing its sharpness, and so on. It was a perfect sword, even after seventy years of use. It had travelled to the Holy Land, England, and France with Great-Grandfather, it went to Hungary, Bohemia and Prussia with Grandfather, it went to Frisia with Father, and now I would take it to Frisia once more to reignite its flame and reclaim the honour of Hollant.

"A fine blade!" exclaimed Ghijsbrecht in astonishment.

"I know," I said with a smile.

"Lucky young man," he said.

"Do you remember what Grandfather called it?" asked Father.

"Stonesplitter, he called it," I said. "Because this was the sword with which he pledged fealty to the Count, and founded the House of Wassenaer. When he knelt to swear his oaths, the tip of Stonesplitter sank straight through the stone tiles of the Count's court," I added to give Ghijsbrecht some context. I had heard that story since I was a boy—it was an old jest that ran down through the family. Whether or not it was true, only God knew, but God forbid should you question it in front of Father. I suppose it should give me a bit of confidence; what good would chain mail do against a sword like this if it slipped straight through stone? I brandished the steel in my hand, making mock cuts through the air, practising the three stances. It was light and nicely balanced. Straight as an arrow, and long as a walking stick. "Very good," Father said. "Keep it well, son. And don't lose it today." He chuckled with a heavy clap on my arm. I laughed with him but that was definitely something I'd be afraid to do. No matter, I'd hold it tight, and treasure it.

"May the Lord and his angels give you a thousand blessings," said one of the monks traversing the long line of knights, making cruciform movements with his hands. Seeing the conrois of knights all in formation, all garbed in their heraldic colours with lances in hand and swords at their side, the sight was magnificent. It was all I'd dreamt of really; to ride alongside men like these and make battle. Father, Gherrijt, Ghijsbrecht, and Uncle Jan all had their companies align next to one another. Each and every one of us had a white cloth tied around our right forearm to denote which side we were on. Our left was covered by our shields. On the other side, they all wore white cloths. Including the Count himself. While I would have preferred to be fighting alongside him, at least we would now be able to prove our valour to him by defeating him in battle. But he would be the target of most companies—he would be able to pay up the most ransom for his captivity. As such, every knight this side of the field would be hunting the red lion rampant. And only one knight would catch him.

The herald rode to the edge of the field and shouted.

"When the horns sound three times, the melee will begin! Remember the rules; your aim is to capture, not kill. May God favour you all, and may the most valiant be victorious!" The crowds of onlookers, fenced off far from the action, roared in excitement. I felt my breath reverberate back to me as it hit the face plate of my great helm. Through my claustrophobic, narrow eye slits, I scanned the enemy wall of horse and rider, scouting out banners and shields bearing arms I recognized. Of course, I spotted the ver Heyens, stalwartly making ready in the enemy centre. The ground was still slick from the previous rainfalls. Surely nothing would come of that. I gripped my lance tightly.

The first buisine horn sounded. The horses heard it and grew restless. An array of snorts and grunts arrayed the battle line. I watched the flowing white star of eight points on black of the Wateringen company. Second buisine sounded. Galahad stomped her front hoof against the dirt, pawing it like an angry bull. All riders were knee to knee—a hulking mass of horse and steel. It would be mayhem with the third buisine signal. I looked to the other side of the field, time slowing, only hearing my breath and my heartbeat. *Follow the banner*, I thought to myself. I looked over to my left to see the gold, Duivenoorder banner. Third buisine. We were off. A trot, then a canter, then a gallop. I had no control. No say. Galahad just followed what every other horse was doing. And every other horse followed each other.

"Crailingen!" I heard one of the companies cry out, followed by a "Drongelen!" and a "Woerdt!" Soon enough everyone was shouting their battle cry. "Raephorst!"; "Amstel!"; "Wassenaer!"

"Duivenvoorde!" We shouted as we raised our lances in the air. I tucked my lance under my arm. The slick mud squelched and sploshed below our hooves. Our crests bobbed our helms left and right, mantles flowing in the wind. There they came. This was it. I held my breath. A smash of lance and shield, and shield and horse, and horse and rider, happening all at once where the two lines met. Cracks and shatters were all I heard through the thick bucket of a helmet that I wore. Was I hit? God knew. All I knew was that I had to keep riding. I had to make it out to the other side. I took a breath. We were out. I frantically looked from side to side as the horses spread out, checking to make sure that all of our knights were there. They were. Mostly. One of our men, Sir Robrant, had fallen from his horse already. We saw him swat around with his handaxe as though he were warding off a swarm of giant, heavily armoured bees. It wasn't long before one horse toppled him over, and another knight came to capture him. The melee ensued. Horse and rider rode about the field in chaos, as I frantically tried to follow the yellow banner. The arm bands did little to tell friend from foe—foes quickly became those who tried to attack you, and friends were those who minded their own business. Like a swarm of flies we rode about, dodging fallen horse and rider, striking knights with our swords and axes and maces. I unsheathed

Stonesplitter. She was a good sword, perfect for bringing down blows on other knights.

Then, we saw him. Like an angel from the heavens, it was the golden helm of Count Florens himself.

"To the Count!" Father shouted, waving his banner furiously. He lowered his banner, aiming straight for the Count with the point of his lance. I saw the Count's horse trapped in a blockage of horse and ride, trying to wheel him out, but there was no escape. Crack. The ver Heyens flanked us, wiping out Father completely. His horse staggered, and Father fell to the ground.

"Get back up!" I shouted, chasing after the ver Heyens. They were mine. I wanted vengeance. I was hungry. Hungry for ver Heyen blood.

"After Floris!" I heard one of our knights shouting.

"No, shield Heer Arend," another shouted. Ugh, I was on my own. I recognized the stature of the younger ver Heyen. With my sword from behind, I battered him on his helm, tearing off his winged crest and slicing right down onto one of his ailettes. He wheeled his horse around to do battle, letting his compatriots ride off. Shouting, he struck me with his flanged mace, but I blocked it with my shield. Our horses rode off, but we both wheeled around for another pass. It felt as if the world had melted away—there were only two of us, only one enemy. Galahad, jumping over a wounded, fallen horse, brought me straight to him. He tried to block Stonesplitter with his mace, but he misjudged the distancing, and received another blow to his helm. We both rode in circles now, blocking with our shields, and striking with our weapons, until Long Heer Wouter van den

Kerckhove, the Knight of Hearts, rode through us both, swinging around his double-balled flail like a madman. After that, I don't know where the young ver Heyen scampered off to, until I saw him doing battle with Ghijsbrecht. I wanted to follow, but Father rode in front of me.

"Stay with us or go back to camp," he shouted sternly through the breaths of his greathelm. I complied. I followed Father around as we chased after some other knight. I didn't recognize him, but he bore two red fish on yellow. When we caught up with him, we all surrounded him. He surrendered quite easily. Father had two of our knights take him back to camp. Then I saw the middle ver Heyen brother with his white coat of plates. Godverdomme. I wouldn't give chase; Father told me not to. But it was so enticing. No, I couldn't. I saw them again. And again and again. Each time I saw them battling different opponents, riding different knights off the field. They were successful. Too successful. The young ver Heyen especially. I watched him take at least three knights with him already. "With me!" Father shouted, riding us to do battle with another company. Begrudgingly I rode off. I had to prove my valour. All of us held our ground—we all rode about picking fights with their knights and circling around each other's formations. By now, it had seemed that already perhaps a quarter of the men were gone from the field. It felt like a stalemate. A slog. We kept fighting until, like a white hart, the young ver Heyen rode near us again. Alone this time. And seemingly wounded by the looks of it. You know what? I rode after him. I doubt Father even noticed.

"Get back here!" I cried after the ver Heyen. He turned his head just in time for me to bring a blow down on his shoulder with my sword, managing to ruffle a few riveted rings. He replied with a heavy swing from his mace. I nearly grew dizzy from the blow. We exchanged back and forth, again and again. When he tried to strike back at me with his mace, I caught it on my shield and swung again. I let the lion awake in me. I gave a battle roar as I rode beside him, hacking and slashing at him the whole time, driving him towards a tree line. *Father, Son, Holy Ghost,* I thought to myself as I parried his blows and sent blows of my own. Father was right—it wasn't the stances themselves but the distancing, the pacing, and the counters that mattered. I was winning. I was beating him. Even when his mace came crashing down over my head. My helmet rang like a bell. There were three of him now. No, it was the three ver Heyens. Damn. I was so close. I would have beaten him on my own. "Father! Father!" I called out reluctantly. Nobody. They rode me off the field, I tried to block their hits, but there was little I could do.

Until I heard the war cry, "Raephorst! Raephorst!" and out from the shadows like a pack of wolves, the black and white-striped Gherrijt and his men fell upon the ver Heyens, smashing all three until each of them were off their horses. We had them. We bloody had them. I took the reins of the youngest. He tried to resist, flailing his mace around like a mad man, until he took a still axe blow to the back of his coat plates. He tried to jump from his horse, but got caught in the stirrups. The animal pulled him along the dirt, coating the poor knight in mud. I slowed the animal and got off my horse, holding Stonesplitter to his eye slit.

"Yield," I said. He frantically looked around, only to find his father and uncle already captured.

"I yield," he said, dropping his mace and lying in the mud as if he were making mud angels. I expended my arm and helped him to his feet. Gherrijt rode over to me.

"We ride them back together? All of us?"

"I could do with some water," I panted.

"The young guy is yours," Gherrijt said. "You dismounted him."

"But I…"

"You dismounted him," he insisted. "And he yielded to you." He couldn't see it but I smiled within my helmet. When we returned the men to the camp, I intentionally rode past Father and his knights who were off taking a rest to catch their breaths. I'll forever remember the hearty applaud I received. Respect—it's not something that's given; it's earned.

Chapter 9. The Beginning: Maarten

The march northwards was harsh. It was only supposed to be one week's march, and we'd besiege the town of Enkhuizen and send the Frisians back across the Ijsselmeer to the Sealands. Regardless, thousands of men drinking and whoring their way through Hollant was no joke. We partied our way from town to town with minstrels at every stop eagerly playing for us in hopes of a tip. Who did they think we were? Nobles? We were soldiers, levies most of us; the only coin we had was for bread and ale. On our second day of marching, we were to cross the Zaan river at the small fishing village of Amsterdam. We managed to push through the marshes with our clogs, but the packhorses and the wagons had a harder time.

Some got stuck in places, or slipped off the dykes into the wetlands. We weren't even in Frisian territory yet.

"So what do these bastards look like, anyways?" asked Felix, carefully balancing his voulge on his palm as he marched.

"I reckon they're big as oxen, from the sounds of it," I replied. "Any of you lot seen one of them?"

"Aye," Geerbrant said. "Big bastards they are."

One of his comrades said, "I heard they jump across the marshes with their spears."

"I heard they fight naked," said another.

"Now why would anybody do that?" Kees asked, his planted skullcap lopsided as usual on his untied coif.

"They must think it scares us," Geerbrant said.

"I'm not scared of nothing," Felix said. We all laughed at that.

"I tell you what boys, how about we scare them?" I said.

"Oh yeah, and how are we gonna do that?" Felix asked.

"We strip down to our bollocks as well," I said with a grin. The march was filled with laughter and chuckling — it filled the time up quite nicely and distracted us from our aching feet.

"Got any more water?" Kees asked.

"Damn it, Kees. The day's just started," Felix said.

"Here," I said, handing him mine. "Only a sip, yeah?"

"Jaja," Kees said, proceeding to empty the flask into his gaping gullet. Of course he did.

"Can't wait to reach the bridge," Felix said.

"Oh, yeah? Why's that?" I asked.

"Well, for one thing, they'll make us stop walking," he said, looking at his already tearing turnshoes.

"It'll take some time to get those wagons across," Geerbrant said. "All those horses wheeling about. The nobles won't like having them all on at once."

"What's that to you?" I asked.

"A warm fire," he said with a smile. "Have a seat for a few hours while they explain to the beasts that there's a carrot on the other side. Maybe play my flute or have a nap."

"You know Arend doesn't like us napping," I said. "The whole week in Leyden he had us practising."

"Practising's good for you, boy. It'll keep you alive."

"Well you're pretty good with that mace of yours. Why don't you teach us a trick or two?"

"Nay, it's all in the teamwork of it. A wall of Frisian sheep-lovers runs at you hooting and hollering. What are you gonna do? You're sure as Hell not gonna wave that glaive around. Nay, you're gonna get in formation with the rest of us and hold tight until it's all over."

"I can fight," I said. "I could pick up a mace or a sword."

"You can hold that glaive and look pretty," Geerbrant replied. "Me and the Baron's boys have been training our whole lives for this. Most of us were mercenaries before, you know?"

"Mercenaries? Who did you fight for?"

"Just knights and lords, whomever could pay. We mostly hunted bandits," Geerbrant said. "When I was a boy, before I became a fighter, I was part of the baggage train that went to Westkapelle under Count Willem, God rest his soul. A damn slaughter that was. I never saw the battle; but I knew men that didn't come back to the camp that night. I was to treat wounds. Men came to the camp screaming in pain, thick, hot blood everywhere, coming out of everywhere, going everywhere."

"Sounds like it must've been horrible," I said.

"It was," Geerbrant said. "And it will be again."

"Come now," said Felix, "we're just putting down some raiders."

"We're marching out in thousands," Geerbrant snapped. "We're in for a fight, alright."

"Then train us," I said. "Make us better. Make us strong enough to come back in one piece. The only blood will be theirs."

Geerbrant smirked. The column came to a halt. "It looks like you picked a perfect time," he said.

We heard the faint voice of a man issuing orders to the troops as he rode up and down the line. We could see

Amsterdam off in the distance — a small village with thatched roofs and wattle and daub architecture.

"We've reached Amsterdam," the voice called out, galloping up and down the line. "Unpack here and stay put." The sun was on the cusp of making contact with the tips of the farthest trees, like the yolk of an egg as it is about to hit the pot. Geerbrant seemed quite excited — he'd voiced how he'd wanted to see Amsterdam for quite some time now.

"Do you think I'll make it through the gate?" asked Geerbrant, of course referencing the fact that the gate would close after dark, but the baggage train seemed to wind and coil so far back we might not make it in time. Naturally, Kees didn't understand.

"To be sure, you will; a cartload of hay gets through, why shouldn't you?" he said. "What? What are you talking about, Kees?" Geerbrant asked.

"He's calling you fat, you dumb bastard," Felix said with a laugh. That brought a chuckle out of me too.

"Alright boys, the two of you," Geerbrant said, pointing to me and Felix, "you're gonna stay behind the shields no matter what. There's no use having some lad with nothing but a spear up in the front rank catching all the blows. The big lad," pointing to Kees, "you'll be up front with me."

"I don't have a shield," Kees said with a shrug.

"Well what did you think you were gonna do with that axe of yours? Get your beauty sleep while the rest of us are up fighting?" Kees shrugged again. We all got in position.

"Alright now when we move, we all move together,"

Geerbrant said. "On my mark, take a big step forward. Now." We all moved, bumping into one another. "Not *that* big a step," he said. "Again. Now. Good. Left. Right. Good." Geerbrant now turned to a few boys who were all sharing a bit of bread. "Fat asses. Get up and come join us." As a bigger unit now we practiced our movement. After a bit of time, I think we got the hang of it.

"What about fighting?" I asked. Geerbrant just looked at us puzzled. "What you want me to hit you with this?"

"Nay, I don't know, maybe we can get some sticks or something."

"And play with sticks in the woods like little boys?" Geerbrant said mockingly.

"Yeah, I want to practice fighting," Felix added, coming to my support. Geerbrant looked at us for a moment, eyeing us up and down.

"Alright, listen up," he called out to everyone nearby. A whole bunch of soldiers raised their heads from their instruments, their conversation, their pissing to look at him. "All of you get a stick that looks like the weapon you carry. Whoever tears the necklace from Maarten's chest gets half his ration tonight." He found a long stick for me. "Good luck," he said with a wink. I don't know why, but I felt a grin sneak across my face.

"You boys in?" I asked Felix and Kees. "Are you mad?" asked Felix.

"More for me, I guess," I said. It wasn't long before I was swatting and prodding at excited soldiers, all of whom looked forward to the booze part of the ration. But there was no way in Hell I'd let them have this necklace. Not a chance. I managed to back my way into the treeline where I managed to find a tight gap only wide enough for a man and a half. I suppose this is where I'd hold my ground — it was just like Roncesvalles Pass in the tales of Karel's Paladins. I managed to jab at a few of them, taking care not to poke out an eye but still bringing my stick down on their helmets with enough force to ward them back. They were a little more rough than I'd have hoped — my fingers were smacked more than a few times under the weight of bludgeons.

"Halt!" a stately voice called, accompanied by the clipping of hooves. Damn it. The worst possible timing. Heer Arend called out, "Break it up, break it up." And then he saw me. "You! You can't get that fight out of you boy, can you? Please don't tell me it was a mistake bringing you here. We must save our scrapping for the enemy."

"It's no fight sir, it's practice."

"Practice? All these men against you?" he asked with a raised eyebrow.

"Yes, sir. Whomever takes my crucifix gets half my ration," I said. Lord Arend stroked his long, Templar beard.

"It won't do to have you go hungry," he said. "Any man who takes the crucifix, and gives it back, will receive double ration from the baggage train. None of young Maarten's." He remembered my name? "Good initiative, boy. Don't die," he added. "Carry on." Immediately, the men surged forth like a horde of hungry wolves. I was in for it for quite some time.

The infirmary did a good job of patching up my scrapes

and embalming my bruises in a healing salve. Of course, the cauterization was unpleasant. It had taken three grown men to hold me down, and a hard twig to bite down on.

The great, white tent was calming — there were few injuries yet. I clutched the necklace tightly in my hands with a smile. Kees and Felix came to meet me once the commotion was done.

"Have you heard the news?" Felix asked.

I shook my head. "Nay. What's up?"

"Those silver-spooned morons brought carts too wide for the bridge. They don't want to wait here and widen it, so they're sending half the army around the river through Kennemerland with a new target of Alcmare."

"Alcmare? That capital?"

"They're saying we have enough men."

"By God. So who's going?"

"Take a guess," Felix said.

"Boys, we'll get to see Brederode."

"Lads we've seen half the Low Countries already."

"Not like this," Kees said. "They say that Frieslant is wetter and darker than anything you've seen before. Wetter than a maiden's…" Felix swatted him over his thick head.

"Language, Kees. There are nurses here," he said with a chuckle.

"Why don't they keep the army all together?" I asked.

"Because half of it's already on the other side!" Felix

said. "They didn't even check first." He laughed. I did too. These incompetent fools — sounds about right. In all my time as a burner, everywhere I'd worked, the nobility all had one thing in common — none of them lived up to their role. Drunkards, tyrants, children in the bodies of men; few of them could live up to the commanding presence of Heer Arend. At least we were following him into battle and not some peacock-plumed milksop. Like his son.

After camping around Amsterdam for the night, our battalion set course to Brederode Castle — the house of the Count's Marshal and the seat of power over all of Kennemerland.

Three years ago, or so Heer Arend told us, Heer Willem van Brederode was chosen to be the Lord of Kennemerland to try and quell the raiding and slaving. Some good he's done — they're all at it again.

After a long day of marching, the castle was a welcome sight. It's tall, brick towers and deep moat were formidable, to be sure, but what came to our avail was the town surrounding it.

"Boys, when we unpack I'm headed straight to the alehouse, I don't know about you," Geerbrant said.

"Yeah it'll be good to get a few drinks in me," I replied.

"Company, halt," Heer Arend called out. "We pitch our tents here," he said. "Enjoy Brederode, boys. It's the last stop before Hell." That it was — it sat right on the border between Hollant and Westfrieslant. Every step here on out would have to be taken with severe caution.

After unpacking everything, our unit decided to grab

some drinks at the alehouse.

Naturally, the place was teeming with men, most of whom had never seen the village before. Of course that did not stop them from acting as if they were the ale wenches' lovers. A few unsavoury grabs and whistles would make anyone uncomfortable, let alone someone locked in a room with dozens of armed and armoured fighting men. While Felix went about scamming boys from other companies, Kees placed his heavy arm on the ashwood alehouse table to challenge any unfortunate soul to an arm wrestle. Of course, more than a few men with more than a few pints in them obliged, and, needless to say, Kees did not need to be a tradesman to make much coin that night. I, on the other hand, while watching everything unfold, listened to Geerbrant tell stories of his mercenary company and their battles with bandits. He told them to a crowd of us like he was some sort of minstrel — the real troubadours, on that note, had been drowned out by the hooting and hollering of us positively plastered bears in the shape of men. With every tankard Geerbrant's words slurred, and with every tankard I laughed a little more at his crude jokes. When the night was done, and the sun had shattered into a thousand stars, we wobbled our way back out to the war camp.

"You know mates," Felix said, barely keeping his ale down, "I love you all."

"We love you too," I said, making sure the poor bastard didn't trip over himself. Of course, it wasn't long before he was yacking up whatever he washed down at the alehouse in some alley behind some poor, unsuspecting villager's home. Of course, Kees had to make it a little worse by taking a leak right beside him. "Lads, this isn't the best idea," I said.

I was only met by a "Shhhhh" come from Kees's lips shielded by his fat pointer finger. And then I heard an arrow twang in the darkness. And then another. And then a shout.

"To arms! To arms, men!" I heard some knight call out. There was a commotion in the alehouse, and the streets, they were alight with hundreds, no, the patter of thousands of turnshoes.

"Back to camp, boys," I said. They followed. "Quickly now. We need our weapons." Through the darkness, we snuck our way out of the village to the camp where it seemed as though not a soul knew what was afoot. Then a rider came, storming through.

"Frisians!" he shouted. "Frisians!" With that, the camp awoke like a sleeping dragon. Knights shouted orders. Instantly, as if a gift from God, I felt more alert than ever. My heart pumped. This was it. I would fight or I would die. Soldiers hurriedly slipped into their gambesons and their chainmail and grabbed whatever weapons they could find. Horns blew and drummer boys rolled their drums, sounding the ready. We snatched our arms from the camp where we ran into Geerbrant.

"Just like I taught you lot. With me," he said, mace and shield in hand and chainmail armour jingling like a pouch full of coins. We charged back into the village, and there, in the light of the moon and a flurry of flashing torches, we saw them. Big men, like beasts. Unarmoured, most of them. Some even shirtless. Hollering and shouting war cries, and pelting us with bows and sling staffs from all directions. Their warriors fought with large and small centre-grip round shields and long spears, or whatever they could find. Some rushed at us with sickles and scythes refashioned for war, others clutching simple wood axes or threshing flails. They were not warriors, but not mere men either. Whatever they were, they were blood-curdling. The fighting was chaotic. I'd never seen anything like this before. It wasn't like the melee that we'd all watched — here men were being hacked into pieces, blood staining everything and everyone. Civilians from the village ran to safety, only to be caught and slaughtered by men of either side. Some held the line. Some didn't. Some charged. Some didn't. Some knights ordered a retreat. Some ordered us to torch the village.

Heer Ghijsbrecht rode in, swinging his flail above his great helm, shouting, "No mercy! Death to the heathen! Kill all before you! Leave not one standing!" as he rode his way through their ranks, leaving a trail of blood behind him.

My mates and I tried our very best to hold formation, thrusting at the oncoming wild men and looking away so as not to think about who we were truly fighting. They had dogs too; black and white water hounds that viciously tore at soldiers' legs. All the while, arrows and stones came from windows, alleyways, rooftops, everywhere. It took some time before we hurled back arrows and bolts of our own. Some homes did indeed get torched. And then I saw a child. Good God, the children. There were children here! I felt a deep rage. There was a burning ferocity in me — the image of a child surrounded by this carnage.

"Pull back," I told Kees and Felix.

"We can't abandon the fight! We'll be hung as traitors!" Felix said.

"We need to get the villagers to safety," I said. Kees gave a look of approval, and Felix caved in as well. I first went to one of the children who stood in shock on the side of the road, picking her up in my right arm while hauling my glaive in another. Kees and Felix saw some more, whom they ushered my way. I tried to lead them to safety, away from the carnage, to the tall rye crops. When we managed to get them to safety, we darted back to find more. Instead we found a group corralled by our own men. Duivenvoorders. Shameful.

"Traitors!" they cried. We intervened swiftly. Kees tackled one of their men, and Felix and I told the others to get back to the fight. After a moment, they relented, and we managed to free up the captives and set them free in the rye field. We continued on, until we heard some voices in the dark. From a treeline, we heard what was unmistakably Frisian.

"Quiet," said Felix. "We need to sneak up on them." He tightened his grip on his voulge. It wasn't like him to show bollocks like this. I was proud of him. With a hand, he waved us forward. We snuck through the rye field until we managed to find them, a group of maybe seven Frisian warriors, all with swords and round shields. They were big men with the sides of their heads shaven clean. I don't know what got into him — even I was second guessing attacking, but with his fingers he gestured, "3, 2, 1," and then we fell upon them as quickly as we could, Felix and I impaling two with our polearms instantaneously, while Kees smashed his way through two of them, leaving us a fair fight. They must have thought there were more of us, because one of them simply ran away, and we were left with two.

"Hollânske hûnen!" he cursed. "God ferdomme dy!" We didn't need a translation for that. We closed in on him, and quickly Kees split his shield with his axe, and tore it from his hands, sending it flying. With only a sword left, he dropped it and surrendered, falling to his knees. Felix was in the process of unbuckling his belt to tie him up when I just told him, "Run." He understood, and ran faster than a palfrey. Felix and Kees didn't question it.

We just headed back to the village where the fighting was still going on. Flames painted bright strips of orange in the black sky. We rejoined the fight finding that our men were pushing them back. We fought them through every street, every nook, every cranny, every space there was where a man could have been. The whole village was one gargantuan mess of body against body — shoving more than fighting. Blood stained everything. Weapons, armour, men. It was everywhere. And it was from everyone. Frisians, Wapenknechten, innocents. They were all subject to the blade. Behind the line, men transported soldiers on stretchers back to the camp. Only wounded Hollanters — wounded Frisians were instead finished off. With the blow of some animal horn, the Frisian raiders retreated back into the blackness as quickly as they came — our solid formation gladly letting them run off into the moonlight. Bare chested and bare footed, they scampered off like game animals.

+ Floris +

The scent of death accompanied every corpse down every street. Death and ash.

Death and victory. I sheathed Stonesplitter after cleaning the Frisian blood off its blade.

"Savages. All of them," I muttered as I watched the dead being cleared off and buried in mass graves out near the village graveyard. The men and I all beaded through our rosaries and said our Hail Marys and all the other prayers we could think of for our fallen brothers. This night was blacker than all others.

"Sir, you want to see this," a soldier warned me. It was that Geerbrant whom Father had spoken to me about.

"What is it?" I asked.

"Follow me, my Lord," he said, leading the way. What he brought me to was an abomination. A crime against honour itself. The alehouse, where so many stewards of the Crown of Hollant, faithful servants of the Count, had been locked in and baked like cookies beneath the burning thatches of its roof. Good God, how could men behave like this? Honourless brigands they were. I knelt before the burned-down edifice, made the sign of the cross over my chest, and prayed for their souls. They were good men, all of them. Boisterous and simple, but good and valiant servants. Marshal Willem rode in, his mount's yellow caparison fluttering in the cool, nighttime breeze, followed by his lackey, Lord Wouter de Vriese, the Bailiff of Kennemerland.

"I want every man, woman, and child interrogated. We must know how they did this. How they knew we were here, and how they slipped past our scouts," he ordered. "You, soldier," he addressed Geerbrant, "you are to round them all up. For any who seem suspicious, you may do whatever you like to them. I care not."

"Heer Willem, they are innocent…"

"For all we know, these rabble aided the Frisians in giving them our whereabouts. For that matter, every man who was on patrol tonight shall be flogged," Willem ordered. "These barbarians will pay for this." At the same moment, Ghijsbrecht, bloodied from battle, returned with his knights from pursuing the raiders. He was carrying the head of one, still leaking blood, and dropped it before Willem.

"Their leader," he sneered.

"What questioning did you get from him?" Willem asked, temper clearly still raging.

"We put him to the sword as soon as we found him," Ghijsbrecht replied with a toothy grin. I'd never seen this side of him before. His black and yellow surcoat was stained with dark red Frisian blood. His flail was as well.

"You're saying your lapdogs executed him without questioning?" Willem asked.

"As I ordered them to," Ghijsbrecht replied.

"Come here," Willem ushered him. Ghijsbrecht dismounted, tearing off his greathelm and combing back his chainmail coif to free his head. He was met with a hard and brutal slap across the cheek from Willem's chainmail gauntlet. Ghijsbrecht spat blood onto the earthen road. "You imbecile. You animal. You are like a pack of hounds!" Willem shouted. Angrily, he threw his own greathelm into the dirt and rode off back to his castle. Everyone was stressed. Everyone could still feel the blood rushing through their veins and their stomachs churning. "Floris, you did well," Ghijsbrecht said. "I saw you fighting. Good work, lad." He gave me a pat on the shoulder, his mouth still bloody. "I'm gonna go get this fixed up. Make sure that soldier of yours does what Willem ordered, alright?"

"Yes, of course," I replied.

"Good man," he said, mounting and riding off. I turned to Geerbrant.

"No mercy," I said. "You owe nothing to these people."

"Come on, they're just farmers," Geerbrant said.

"Are you disobeying orders?" I asked. He didn't respond. I felt a rush of empathy for him — it had been a long night. We all needed rest.

"Look, rest up, get your wits about you in the morning," I said. "Do what you have to do. But these are Heer Willem's people. The Kennemers belong to him, and he can do with them as he likes. It's just the nature of things. Iron fist, Geerbrant. I'm entrusting this to you. You're a Duivenvoorder; don't make Father and me look bad." He gave me a solemn nod. "I'm off to sleep."

"Be careful," he said. "Don't sleep too deeply. We're in the shit now."

The next morning, every man, woman, and child in the village was lined up in front of Geerbrant and the rest of my Duivenvoorders. Tears still in their eyes from the violence and from seeing their loved ones slain, many had barely the heart to even speak to him. Half-heartedly, for I knew he was a man of principle, he asked questions such as, "Was anyone here involved with the skirmish last night?" or "You, you there, what do you know about [so and so other villager]?" Of course, it was to no avail, and I only watched as Marshal

Willem grew impatient. Of course, the success of this branch rested on his shoulders, but these were his own people. His own Kennemers. Did he not trust them? I suppose he had only been their baron for three years now, and he was only stationed here for their Frisian sympathies, but still. It felt… off. The questioning continued until Marshal Willem abruptly threw a baton at Geerbrant's feet.

"Enough," he said. "If they won't answer, beat it out of them. At the very least, one of them must have hid them." There was a stark silence among the crowd. Geerbrant, contemplating his next move carefully, never picked up the baton. "No," he said. "They're innocent."

"No? They slaughtered a hundred men. They are your enemy. Beat them, or you'll be beaten."

"No," Geerbrant said stalwartly. "I won't do it. It's done, Marshal. We can just march on…"

"Mercenaries," Marshal Willem ordered. Summoned, a number of Brabantian mercenary pikemen, all clad in their leather jerkins over their chainmail armour, stepped forward. "Flog this man. And then flog any villager who claims to know nothing," he said. Of course, the gold-seeking lapdogs that they were, they followed their orders to a tee. They grabbed Geerbrant and were about to carry him off, when Willem bid them to do it publicly for all to see the price of disobedience. Gherrijt, the fool he was, rode forth.

"Stop it, you madman," he said. "I've had enough of this nonsense."

"Who are you, boy?" asked Marshal Willem.

"I am Heer Gherrijt van Raephorst."

"A baron, huh? What did your daddy run swimming in the brothels?"

"My father died at the hands of Frisians," Gherrijt said. "And, under his command, I would bet that you all will too. If I cannot put a stop to this madness, I will take no part in this."

"Take no part? Bold words from such an insolent brat," Marshal Willem said.

"Forgive him, Sir," Ghijsbrecht said, now entering the fold. "He knows not what he says. He will ride with us." I looked to Father, what did he make of all this? He only stood watching, unreactive, as if he'd seen this tale a thousand times. I leaned over to him.

"Why do you not say anything?" I whispered.

In a hushed tone, Father said, "Gherrijt can do what he wills. We, on the other hand, will stay true to our vows. We have a task to complete. We must not stop until it is done."

"He is free to go," Marshal Willem said. "But, boy, answer me this. What exactly do you think you are?"

"I am a knight of Hollant," he said. "That means that I am a protector of the people. All the people."

"Nay. You are a knight of the Count of Hollant. A baron, actually. A landholder. You are no better than any of us."

"I do not beat my people."

"If they slaughter your men you will," Willem replied. Gherrijt spat on the floor out of disrespect. Willem added, "Where is your composure, boy? You're a damn knight. Act like one."

"If being a knight means to be a tyrant like you, I will have none of it."

"Do you think we are fools, boy? Do you think we are children playing with sticks? We do not ride out because it is fun. We do not ride out because we hold some strange fascination with swords or blood. We ride out because there are dangers in this world that no man can face alone. There are bandits around every corner, lurking, hailing Satan and preying on their fellow man. There are rapists and murderers. There are robber barons and raiders and foreign invaders. Saracens and Mongols and other barbarians. We are the shield against it all. We are what allows them to harvest their crops and tend to their bloody chickens. You don't get damn chickens when everyone in the whole world is at each other's throat. You can bet your arse that if there were a dragon to lurk about Hollant tomorrow, there would be hundreds of knights willing to brave its flame for the honour of protecting the realm. This campaign is no different, boy. Frisians are monsters. Those Frisians capture good, Christian girls and force them into their beds. Those monsters terrorise the waves and slaughter man, woman, and child alike. They steal precious wool and costly ships. They raid and pillage—pirates they are. Believe me, boy, I would wish no more than to sit here with my pork and mead and grow a fat belly, but my honour dictates otherwise. My duty dictates otherwise. It's my knight's fee. So is it yours. So quit your sulking and get on your horse. We have a long day of riding to do. Are you a knight, or a pile of logs, you lily-livered excuse for a warrior?"

"I am the Baron of Raephorst. Not whatever hand of cruelty you want me to be," Gherrijt said, wheeling his horse around. Finally, Father intervened.

"Gherrijt, be careful."

"What, will you side with this disgrace?" Gherrijt asked. "You have been given orders by your liege."

"He is not my liege, I answer only to the Count."

"Count Florens has entrusted his will to Marshal Willem," Father said gravely. "He has authority here."

"I should not be here," Gherrijt said. "This is not my place."

"You are a knight," Father replied. "The battlefield is your only place. Turn your horse around, son. No need to be drawn and quartered before the day is done."

"Would you rather have me die with the blood of innocents running down my fuller?"

"I would rather have you die a warrior's death. Or, live a hero's life. You have a long life ahead of you."

"Perhaps not."

"Perhaps Saint Peter will commend your loyalty," Father said. Gherrijt looked to the earth beneath his horse's hooves.

"Lord Arend speaks true," the shrill voice of Bailiff Wouter de Vriese interjected. "You could be hung for this. Your family too. Stripped of your lands and titles at the very least."

"I am willing to forget your…outburst, boy," Marshal Willem said. Gherrijt, pensive for a brief moment, eyes still fixated on a puddle of what one could only assume was a concoction of blood, soil, and rainwater, finally uttered his capitulation.

"Wise," said Father. "We will need all the swords we can."

"All the bodies?" Gherrijt asked.

"Your tongue is sharp, boy," the Bailiff said. "Make sure your blade is sharper."

"Fear not, Bailiff," Gherrijt said. "It is sharp enough for any man."

The Bailiff meekly rode behind the Marshal as if he was a trained dog. Behind me, I heard the first strike land. Then another, and then another. Poor Geerbrant kept his composure through it all. I didn't want to see it. In truth, I would never admit it, but I couldn't stomach it. But I would not break my oath. I heard him fall to the mud as he was finally released, and his friends rushing to his aid. One more for the infirmary.

Chapter 10. The Mercenary: Piet

After the tournament, life went more or less back to normal. Well, as normal as it could be, I suppose. Some nights, I fell asleep to haunting images of shattered horses and fuming riders. I heard Wollefram barking at his squires to pop his shoulder back into place and Ghijsbrecht cursing and hacking at his poor Frisian, calling it a dumb beast and a waste of money. On other nights, I couldn't sleep at all. Books kept me company, for the most part, when I was supposed to be sleeping. I'd sneak one from the shelf, mostly maths or politics books, and I'd bring it up to where the candles still flickered and just read. Lord Hillebrant caught me a few times. Sometimes, he ushered me back to bed, but after enough sleepless evenings, he let me come and read with him while he worked late in his office. Before then, I had never truly grasped how hardworking he was — but he really spent most nights up late, scribbling down notes and letters and records, you name it, in those big parchment books of his. Once he was done, he'd always dust off his work with ash from the chimney to let the ink dry. That would be my signal to go off to bed.

To break through the monotony of it all, I spent my days watching out the windows and listening to the other kids play, while I attended my duties. Fetching records and practising my letters was far from a fun time. On the other hand, I found myself lost imagining what it would be like to play again with other boys and girls, play kickball or tag, or pull pranks on one another. But my friends were back in Duivenvoorde. Gone, like Mother, like my brothers and sisters, like the very world itself. Instead, I was stuck in here, in this cell of a manor house. That is, until they caught sight of me once. I heard them speak among themselves in confusion and then call out to me to ask my why they never saw me. I was writing a note on Archimedes' Stomachion—I had no time to play. But, of course, their voices repeated themselves, luring me in like sirens. Those were the mermaids in the Greek legends—I read most of them. Before I knew it, I felt my bushy red hair flop out the window of the second floor.

"Hi there," I said. They looked at me.

"Who are you?" one of them asked. She was a short and chubby girl; well, I suppose they all were a little squat, but she was chubbier than the rest.

"My name's Piet," I said.

"My name's Halene. Everyone calls me Heile. My father's the merchant down over there," she said, pointing to one of the more affluent residential areas."

"How about the rest of you?" I asked. I was soon hit with a wash of Beatrices and Willems and Alenes. "How did you all meet?" I asked.

"School," Heile said. I heard a creek out the halfway door behind me.

"I don't go to a school," I said. "My guardian has me schooled in here."

"We go to the grammar school," she said. "Do you want to play with us?" she asked.

"I have to write notes," I said.

"That sounds boring," she said.

"It is."

"What happens if you don't?"

"I'll get caught by my teacher," I said. "Master Waleran will spank me if he finds me missing."

"He won't find you if you're missing," said Heile. I couldn't help but laugh. "We are going to go play hide and seek in the market square." That sounded like fun, loads of fun.

What was I doing locked up in here? It was a beautiful day out—no rain, not even puddles or mud. After that tournament, I didn't want to be a knight anyway. So what was it all for?

"Okay," I said. "I'll come. Just give me one second," I said. I quickly locked the door to the study, and climbed out the window, grasping the holes between bricks where wooden beams had once sat and rotted away. I was down to the street in no time. We moved as a group, taking our sweet time, laughing and playing—it was like a dream. I felt myself soaring with joy as I ran after my new friends, looking in each and every corridor to find them, and hiding among the most inconspicuous of places, such as beneath vegetable carts or behind oxen. Hacko, a taller boy with lanky arms and spidery fingers, would always be the fastest.

His long legs raced across the cobblestones whenever he was it. I, on the other hand, was not the runner I'd hoped I'd be, frequently stumbling and stopping to catch my breath. I was having fun, and loads of it. I felt my eyes crinkly, and my smile widened with every 'gotcha' and every 'there you are'. And then the church bells tolled. Six chimes.

"Oh no, I'll be late for supper!" I exclaimed, kicking my feet to push my body as fast as they could go. "I'll see you all tomorrow?" I asked.

"We'll be here," they said. "Right after school." I quickly raced back to the manor, scrambling up the side wall when I was certain that nobody was peeping out at me and making it just in time for a hefty knock on the door.

"Pieter? Are you in there?" asked Master Waleran in his thick, elderly Franconian German accent. He always called me Pieter—he said it was improper to call anyone but their given name. So I called him Tom when he wasn't around.

"Jaja!" I said. "Just finishing up." I scribbled down a couple of words to finish the sentence I was working on when I'd left, and I haphazardly collected my papers, adjusting them by tapping on the table to get the alignment. I then quickly unlocked the door to find a hunched old man looking down at me.

"What did I say about locking the door?" he asked, stroking his wizard-like beard.

"The wind kept opening and shutting it, which made a lot of noise. I couldn't focus," I said.

"Hmm, we should get that looked at. Tell me, what did you think about our old friend, Archimedes?" he asked me.

I didn't know what to say, I'd only read the first part, but I suppose I was able to fill in the rest from what I'd read of his teacher, Euclid.

"Ah, well, it seems like a natural development of

Euclidean geometric axes," I replied, fishing for whatever jargon my memory could muster.

"Did you have fun practising any of the puzzles?" Master Waleran asked.

"Puzzles? What puzzles? I prefer to work with numbers," I said with a smile. Master Waleran cracked a smile of his own.

"Run off to dinner now. I'll review your work this evening," he said. Merrily, I did as he bade me, content with having gotten away with my day of mischief. I supposed tomorrow would be no different. Of course, Master Waleran was naturally unimpressed with the little work I'd done, but I'd remedy that with some swift maneuvering tomorrow morning to ensure that I'd have my studies done before the school was released, and I'd be able to play once more with the burgher children in the square. And so that happened, and it happened again and again, day after day of rapid learning and boisterous play, weaving our way through the city, taking great care not to work our way into the more shady parts of town. At some points, I thought I saw Maurits and Thiel, but they turned out to be two common pickpockets instead. Life in Leyden was turning out to be much more fun than I'd anticipated.

As the days turned into weeks, my friendship with Heile and the other children deepened. We became an inseparable group, exploring every nook and cranny of Leyden. We climbed trees, played in the river, and even ventured into the outskirts of the city, where we discovered hidden meadows and secret hideouts.

In the midst of our adventures, I couldn't help but

wonder about my life before. The memories of Duivenvoorde and my family felt distant, like fragments of a dream. Leyden had become my new reality, filled with laughter, companionship, and the thrill of exploration. I no longer yearned for the knighthood or the grandeur of tournaments. All that mattered now were the shared moments of joy and camaraderie.

As time went on, the whispers of the city reached our ears. Stories of the war in the North, of unrest and tension, became more frequent. The adults spoke in hushed tones, worried about the future. But as children, we were shielded from the weight of those concerns. We lived in a bubble of innocence, cherishing each day as it came.

Yet, beneath the surface, there was an awareness that our carefree days might not last forever. We knew that change loomed on the horizon, and the idyllic world we had created could be shattered at any moment. But for now, we continued to play, to laugh, and to savor the freedom we found in each other's company. We treasured the time.

One day, as the sun cast its golden glow upon the city, Heile approached me with a mischievous glint in her eyes. "Piet, I have an idea," she whispered, her voice filled with excitement. "There's a treasure hidden in the abandoned windmill on the outskirts of town, down by the Rijn. We should go and find it!"

My heart raced at the thought of a thrilling adventure. The allure of hidden treasure was certainly resistable, but the thought of venturing out with my friends, laughing, playing, sounded just as great as it always had.

"Are you sure it's safe?" I asked, my voice betraying a

mix of curiosity and caution. Lord Hillebrant had told me never to leave the city without him or another close adult, but, in all fairness, we'd been exploring meadows and pastures this whole time. The windmill, though, was another case. It was an old, broken-down windmill that hadn't been used for decades. Who knows what, or who resided there now? Heile grinned mischievously.

"Of course, it'll be an unforgettable adventure! Besides, what's life without a little risk?" Her words echoed in my mind, and I found myself nodding eagerly. She was right. If the tournament had taught me one thing, it was that life is short. I should make the most of it.

The prospect of breaking free from the routine and the confines of the manor was exhilarating. With our hearts pounding in sync, we gathered the rest of our friends and set off on our quest for the fabled treasure.

As we ventured through the outskirts of Leyden, the city's grandeur faded away, replaced by the rugged charm of nature. Tall grasses swayed in the gentle breeze, and the sound of chirping birds serenaded our steps. The abandoned windmill stood before us like a forgotten relic, its weathered walls whispering stories of times long gone.

With each creaking step, we explored the mill's dark corners and climbed its dilapidated staircases, our excitement fueling our bravery. Finally, amidst piles of forgotten debris, beneath cracked wooden beams and stone, we heard a whimpering. It wasn't treasure, that's for sure. It was something else, something living.

"Who's gonna see what it is?" asked Heile.

"I'll do it," said Hacko, bravely stepping forward. Fleet-footed, he approached the pile of dust and wreckage with caution. Fingers trembling, he poked at the lump, and then it moved. A beam slammed to the floor as it was dislodged. It caught Hacko's foot. He screamed out in fear and pain and then began to cry. Panicked, Heile and other kids started frantically crowding him, asking if his foot was okay, and so on. Of course, I felt for him as well, but I was still curious about what our hidden beast was. I approached the pile while all were around Hacko, carefully unwrapping the dust-covered gift. Out of the debris came a wide-eyed puppy, panting, a little scrawny, and covered in dust.

"It's a puppy!" I exclaimed, dusting the poor thing off with my hand and holding it up for everyone.

"A puppy?" they all asked, coming now around me to see the fluffy friend. Even Hacko, limping a little, stood up to see it. The little thing cowered, trying to wriggle itself free from my hands.

"You're scaring it," said Heile. "Everyone, back off." Of course, if Heile said it, they all did it.

"Here, Hacko, you should have it," I said. "You paid the price for it." Hacko happily picked it up.

"I can't take it home with me," he said. "If my parents find out…"

"You should have it," said Heile with a bright smile. "You found it."

"Me? I don't know…"

"Why not?" asked Hacko. "You know what? I could do

with a companion at the manor. Besides, what food I couldn't finish, I'm sure he'd probably enjoy."

"Okay," I said. "I guess." I took the puppy back into my own arms and looked at him.

His little, droopy ears. His orangy-brown coat reminded me a little of Vlam. "I'm gonna name you Pythagoras."

After washing him off in the river, we headed back to the city. It would be dinnertime soon, and if I were to return with a companion, I ought not be late. As we made our way back to the city, Pythagoras nestled in my arms, I couldn't help but feel a newfound sense of warmth and joy. The puppy's soft fur tickled my skin, and his wagging tail was a testament to the trust he had placed in me.

As we reached the manor, I hesitated at the door, unsure of how Master Waleran would react to the addition of a furry companion. Taking a deep breath, I pushed the door open, revealing the flickering candles and the scent of roasted pork and sauerkraut wafting through the air.

I quickly headed down to the kitchen, where I found Filomena chopping some apples. She glanced up from chopping apples, her eyes widening at the sight of Pythagoras in my arms. Her stern expression softened, and a smile tugged at the corners of his lips.

"Well, well, it seems you've found a little friend," she remarked, her voice tinged with a touch of amusement. I nodded eagerly, a grin spreading across my face.

"Yes, Ms. Filomena. This is Pythagoras. He needed a home, and I couldn't leave him behind." I replied, gently setting the puppy down on the kitchen floor. Filomena knelt down and extended a hand towards Pythagoras, who sniffed it tentatively before wagging his tail and licking her fingers. Her smile widened as "My my, my silly boy, where's you get that name?" she asked.

"He wrote one of the books Lord Hillebrant had me read," I replied. "I like him the most of the authors. He's a mathematician! Can I keep him?" I asked.

"Well, I'm sure Lord Hillebrant won't mind a learned little house guest, and besides," Filomena chuckled and wiped her hands on her apron. "I suppose we can't turn away such a brave adventurer and his loyal companion. But remember, Piet, a pet is not just for play. It's a responsibility. You'll have to take care of him, feed him, and make sure he gets the exercise he needs. Now change out of your clothes; they're filthy, you little piglet, and race back for supper, it'll be six in a few minutes," she said with a warmth that embraced me.

Dinner was interrupted when we all heard the anger that burst from Lord Hillebrant as he entered the front door.

"Godverdomde carpenters!" he cried out as the door shut behind us. Down in the servants' quarters, none of us spoke as we ate our meals; we only heard the rage burn up above us. And then his steel-studded turn shoes made their way downstairs. Each step was louder than the last, and a ruby-red Lord Hillebrant, trying his best to keep his cool, took a deep breath in, a deep breath out, and a seat without saying anything.

"Cool water for you?" Filomena asked. He nodded. He never drank, a far cry from his gluttonous brother, Jan. "Pork pottage?" He nodded again, saying nothing. And then, at the worst possible moment, little Archimedes trotted out from below the table, paws lightly tapping the floor.

"Whose rat is this?" Lord Hillebrant asked. "Last I checked, we didn't have a vermin problem." Pale with fear, I said nothing, meekly sipping my pottage. "Well, if none of you speak up. He'll be out with the wastewater," he said.

"Come now, my Lord, he's just a pup," said Filomena. "He's mine," I said, ashamed and trembling.

"He's yours?" Lord Hillebrant asked. I said nothing. "You found him when you were studying your books?"

"I…"

"Speak carefully, boy. I know where you've been — the city talks. And now those merchant cubs of yours have sent you back with another mouth for me to feed. Splendid."

"Lord Hillebrant, I can explain…"

"No, enough. You never lock your doors again. You work in my study with me. And as for the hairy pig you brought a bag, you'll feed it, wash it, and keep it in your bed. Understood?"

"Yes, Lord Hillebrant."

"Come on, my Lord, he's just a boy," said Filomena. "Boys ought to play."

"Do you think I was playing when I was his age? No, I was working—day in, day out. This boy's been handed an opportunity for a better life on a silver platter, and what does he do with it? He risks it all by running off with the street rabble."

"My Lord, he's been taken from his home."

"He's been rescued. He's been rescued, Filomena."

"He's right there," Filomena replied. What didn't she want to be said in front of me?

Whatever it was, Lord Hillebrant took his seat again and quietly ate his pork pottage. He finished quickly, wolfing it down.

"Piet, when you're done, you're to take the Carpenter's Guild files from my bookshelf and bring them to my study. We'll get to work soon," he said. We? What did he mean? I didn't know.

By the time I got there, it was dark out, and only candles and rushlights lit the home. Archimedes, following me everywhere all day, scampered up the stairs with me. I petted him and told him to wait outside. What good that would do, I wasn't sure. Lord Hillebrant's study smelled of old wood and older parchment. I knocked on the door.

"Come in," he said, studying his accounts with his hood on his head for warmth.

"Take a seat," he said, gesturing to one of the chairs in front of his desk. "Oh, and close the door behind you." I did as I was asked, and I placed the files he requested on his desk. I took a seat across from Lord Hillebrant, feeling a mixture of apprehension and curiosity. The dim lighting cast long shadows on the walls. Lord Hillebrant removed his hood, revealing a tired expression on his face, lines etched deep with the weight of responsibility. "Piet," he began, his voice softer than I had anticipated. "I want you to understand something. The world we live in is not always fair or kind.

It can be harsh and unforgiving, especially for those who have not been born into privilege. I know that you long for adventure, for freedom outside these walls," Lord Hillebrant continued, his gaze focused on the files before him. "And I understand the allure of such escapades, especially for someone your age. However, you must also recognize the importance of the opportunities that have been presented to you. Now, all that set aside, I summoned you here because I want to apologize for my conduct earlier. I was not in my wits, and I conducted myself indecently to you. So I want you to know that I'm not angry at you. Not even disappointed, either."

That took an unexpected turn. Surprised, and somewhat relieved, I leaned in closer. "I demanded too much of you. I wanted to shape you into a bureaucrat and the best one that ever lived, for that matter. But I realize that you must decide your own fate. You're a young man, a very young man, so I propose this. We continue your studies so that you will gain the skills necessary to traverse the world of city charters and legal counselling. But, on your twelfth birthday, should you see fit, I will send you off to work as a knight's page, where you will be fast-tracked into a squire position. Does that sound reasonable?"

"Nay, Lord Hillebrant, I don't want to be a knight. I've come to like my studies, really. I only felt a little, well, lonely here. There's nobody in the manor my age. Nobody to talk to or to play with."

"You don't like chess?"

"I do, but sometimes I want to just stop using my head for a second."

"I understand." Lord Hillebrant said. "Where's your noble steed?" he asked. As if understanding his words, Archimedes trotted into the study, yawned, and lay down on the floor. Lord Hillebrant chuckled. "Good boy," he said with a grin.

"What's his name?" Lord Hillebrant asked.

"Archimedes," I said. Lord Hillebrant laughed at that. As the laughter filled the study, I couldn't help but join in, the tension that had been hanging in the air dissipating like smoke. Lord Hillebrant's genuine smile was a rare sight, and it warmed my heart to see him share a moment of joy. Archimedes wagged his tail, clearly pleased with the positive attention.

"Seems like Archimedes has found a place in your heart." Lord Hillebrant remarked, his tone softer than usual. "Perhaps having a loyal companion will make your days here at the manor a little brighter. And a little less lonely." I smiled. Lord Hillebrant leaned back in his chair, studying me intently. "Piet, I must admit, you have surprised me. I did not anticipate this turn of events, but I see the joy and determination in your eyes. You have a spark within you, a thirst for knowledge and experiences that cannot be extinguished easily." I felt a surge of pride swell within me, knowing that Lord Hillebrant had recognized my passion.

"Thank you, my Lord. I am grateful for the opportunities you have given me, and I promise to make the most of them." He nodded, a solemn expression on his face.

"I believe you, Piet. You have shown resilience and a thirst for knowledge that I haven't seen in many young minds. You have the potential to accomplish great things."

With those words, a renewed sense of purpose washed over me. I realized that I had found my place at the manor, not as a burden or a servant, but as a student and a companion to Lord Hillebrant. "Tomorrow, you will not be studying books; instead, you will take a flagon of wine to the market. I received it as a gift from a client today, a client who was absolutely not supposed to be giving gifts, if you catch my meaning. You are most certainly not to drink it, young man, nor are your friends. But, of course, you may have fun with them once the wine has been sold. It should go for six stuivers, or I suppose you could accept twelve Flemish groten or eighteen Brabantine groten. It's a red from the Loire. That's in France, which means it should be expensive. Only accept coin, no papers or contracts or anything silly. Understood?"

"Yes, Lord Hillebrant, I said."

"Good, good. Would you like to bring up a book and read with me here?" he asked.

I nodded. "Come, Archimedes," I said.

The next morning, I rose up and got myself dressed bright and early. There was no time to lose—the sooner I had this flagon sold, the sooner I'd be able to play with my friends. It was a Sunday today, which meant that if I didn't have it sold by morning mass, I'd have to wait until after the sermon and the prayer and what have you before I could head back out into the market, and by then, all my friends would surely be out and about, up to mischief in the streets.

With my canine escort, I hauled the flagon, taking great care not to stumble over the cobblestones or let the vessel slip from my fingers. The market was alive and bustling.

Every which way, vendors were hollering heroic epithets for their goods, applying adjectives which really didn't need to be applied.

"Sweet, slippery clams!" one vendor called. "The finest, sturdiest wood on this side of the Rijn!" announced another. It wasn't clear to me how he would know that—it was likely false like most of the other claims one heard here. The only auguries one could truly trust here were their own senses. If something were rotten, not a soul would tell you—you'd be the one to sniff it out yourself. Nevertheless, there was the occasional buyer with deep pockets and some left over to waste who would heed the sellers' remarks. Those would be my targets. The ladies in their tall hats. The men with their shimmering silvers. I'd simply have to find a way to explain why I, a boy of few years, would be selling a flagon half my height. A simple believable story, that would be quick and easy. I sat by the wayside, pondering for a moment. I saw the wastewater trickle through the gutters—calming the rank as it was, and it helped me to think. It was like a tiny river after the night of heavy rainfall we had. The stone felt moist and smooth and slippery, like that guy's clams. I looked up at the houses surrounding the market square—each one had sculpted figures decorating its wooden beams, ranging from beautiful maidens to scowling funny faces. A symbol of wealth. Merchant homes, no doubt. That's where I had to go—not here among the crowds, but up close and personal with the money.

A few knocks here and there, and finally, I'd found someone willing to listen. An older gentleman with furling eyebrows and a heavy set of gold rings on his fingers, he let me into his home. It was a lovely place inside, with a braided rush carpet and a deliciously smelling pottage cooking on the firepit. It was a far cry from the foul-smelling streets right outside. All was in the main room—a draped bed, chests, tables, everything. His bed looked thick like it was stuffed with down or something of that sort. His hat was a broad chaperon of fine material. He was rich.

"Welcome, take a seat," he said, gesturing to the chair across from him on the small, ornately decorated table. "My name is Lauerens. Pleased to meet you."

"I'm Floris," I said, making sure to conceal my real name lest it be tracked back to lord Hillebrant.

"I'll tell you what," Lauerens said.

"I'll give you four stuivers for it, and you tell me where you got it," he said. "And, of course, a bowl of pottage for your trouble."

"My master said eight stuivers, and I won't be telling you nothing. I don't need your pottage, but thank you," I replied.

"Suit yourself," he said, pouring himself a bowl.

"It's a pungent red. From France," I said, accounting for what I could remember of Lord Hillebrant's description.

"Jaja, that'd fetch you a good coin. I reckon it would be a little tough selling from door to door, though," said Lauerens. "How's five?" he asked, fetching his coin purse.

"How about six and a delivery fee? You didn't have to fetch it from the market yourself," I bargained.

"Not a truer word, but I had to do more; I'm hosting a wily lad in my own home," he replied. "That'd ought to earn me a solid stuiver, I'd say."

"Tell me, mister, why do you wear those rings on your fingers?" I asked.

"Well, I suppose they're insurance," he said. "If I ever find myself swindled by young merchants such as yourself, I can always turn to a good barter."

"But in your own home?" I asked. "Did you have them on before I knocked?"

"Nay, I suppose I didn't. It's a part of dressing oneself, making oneself feel presentable."

"To display your wealth."

"You mean my fine taste?"

"Either or. See the wine the same way. You aren't paying for the taste of the grapes but the impression it gives. Don't drink it all yourself. Bring it out for a party, for guests of high esteem. I promise you on the grave of Saint Maarten that those extra stuivers will be well worth it," I said. He smiled.

"You have a tongue on you, boy. Who's your master?"

"He wishes to remain anonymous," I replied.

"You must have been educated quite well," he said. "As well as I'd ought to be, I suppose," I replied.

"You say the wine is worth eight stuivers?"

"No truer price."

"Tell me, how come you're out and about, door to door, instead of at a stall in the market?"

"I figured I'd have better luck this way."

"Better luck in fetching a fair price or dodging lawmen?" he asked, placing his dagger on the table. "I suggest you leave the wine here now, boy, and run. That or you may find yourself in more trouble than you'd be so willing." Oh no. Oh no, oh no, oh no. I had to think quickly.

"Wait," I said. "Fine, how's seven?"

"How's none?"

"I know where you live."

"So I should gut you right now?" I felt my face flush with fear. I had to think of something quickly.

"I'll scream."

"The market's loud."

"I'll be louder."

"You're just a pup."

"God is watching."

"God knows I've been good enough."

"What do you trade in? How can you be a merchant and so vile?"

"Who said I was a merchant?" Lauerens asked. "I'm a sellsword, boy. A cutthroat. I'm the man that maketh corpses and widows. I'm the bogeyman that nibbles on your feetsies when you sleep. I'm the dragon that hunts for gold."

"I can see you've got a lot of it."

"I'm good at what I do."

"Can I make you a deal?" I asked. "I can do a favour for you."

"So you can keep your wine?"

"And my head."

"What sort of favour did you have in mind?"

"What do you need?"

"Well, I suppose you could run a message for me. I'll keep your wine safe and sound until you return."

"But you'll just drink it."

"Then we've come to an impasse."

"Why are you not fighting in Frisia if you're a mercenary?"

"We're the Company of the Vermillion Boar—we prefer local business."

"So you're small-scale?"

"Nay, just selective."

"What happens when conflicts run out?"

"They won't."

"Why not?"

"There's always something to war about. Land, taxes, cattle, you name it."

"My master told me that when mercenaries don't get paid, they turn to thieving."

"Jaja, that or worse. What's it to you?"

"Have you ever done that?"

"There's a fine line between a mercenary and a brigand."

"So?"

"I suppose you could say I have," Lauerens said with a grin. "I'd ought to lock you in a chest and sell you off to the Greeks."

"I'm going to take my wine now," I said. "Who said you could do that?"

"If you stop me, I'll tell the militia where you are."

"You think they don't know?"

"I think they don't know who you really are," I said. The man looked slyly at me, trying to gauge my thoughts. I was gambling at this point—grasping at straws.

"And if I cut you right now, you runt?"

"I scream. They'll be sure to come looking whether I'm alive or dead. Then we both lose," I said. The man sighed.

"This wine, you got it below the table?" Lauerens asked. I didn't respond. "I'll tell you what, I'll only give you six, and you get out of my hair. Alright?" I nodded. "You've got a quick wit. Be careful with that tongue, lad." He handed me the stuivers, and I was off like a jackrabbit.

Chapter 11. The Advance: Maarten

The campaign had felt long and hard. The Hollanters raided village after village, the spoils of war granted to them freely, from fine cutlery, to coin, to women. A trail of death and destruction followed the column wherever it marched. The men grew tired and restless, the looming threat of Frisians behind every tree, every hill, every bend in the road. Downpours only worsened the conditions, masking the sounds of Frisian raiders in the night who were ready to pick off sentries or any men unfortunate enough to relieve themselves near the wrong tree. It was hell, well, it was close enough to it. Eventually, after nearly a week spent raiding and subduing the local Frisians, Count Florens decided to have his marching columns converge on Alcmare where they would meet to consider the next steps. Death and disease plagued the camps. The infirmaries were full—one could only imagine what horror would come of a real battle. Marching in constant terror of ambushes and raids was arguably even worse. The Hollanters felt like lambs to the slaughter, that is, until they were the raiders, the pillagers, the desecrators of churches, and the executors of praying martyrs. Fire filled the skies of Frieslant, and blood watered its dykes.

+ Floris +

The tent flap opened with a gust of summer wind. Behind it, I saw the entire command of the Eastern army, under Count Florens. There were his headsmen, Simon van Teylingen, his son Dirk, Werenbolt and his son Aelbrecht, the Lords of Gravenhage, and Gherit van Hermalen. Father stepped in before me, led by the Marshal himself. We were all here—battered knights, ready to report the wave of carnage we'd brought to Frieslant.

"What news of the West?" asked the young Count in his golden hauberk. Marshal Willem stepped forward to give his response.

"A sweeping string of victories, my Lord," he said with a bow. "The lands of your loyal vassal, the Baron of Egmond, have been liberated, and all the lands from Ijmuiden to Bergen are yours. The people cheer for your return."

"Do they? That's far from the welcome I received. We must do better—I want Frisia under Hollant and fully garissoned by autumn. What of losses?"

"They have taken their toll, my Lord."

"No matter, I expected as much. That is why I have decided to conjoin the army."

"Excellent strategy, my Lord," said the Marshal, stroking the hairs on his chin. It wasn't; we were winning. If it wasn't fast enough, I would have suggested that the count to exercise some more patience. But, he was our liege, and what he said was ordained by the heavens, was it not?

"From Alcmare, we shall march North to Rekere river where my father, God rest his glorious soul, began work on a dam."

"A dam, my Lord?"

"Yes, a dam. It was a project he was quite proud of, or so I am told. This campaign is in his legacy, is it not?"

"Of course, my Lord."

"We shall repair this dam—the Baron of Egmond has informed me that it is no longer what it was. We shall return it to its former glory. On that note, what news of the search for my father's remains?"

"No avail, my Lord. Few Frisians seem to have heard of it—even after some convincing."

"No matter—we will have all the time in the world once this collection of bogs and marshes is finally in our hands," Count Florens replied. "And your command, is it strong?" I felt Marshal Willem hesitate for a second longer than he should have.

"Willem is a fine commander," I said, speaking for him.

"Not a single knight or any other man under his command would dare to speak ill of him," Count Florens smiled.

"Splendid," he said. "The valiant protector of my father is now the valiant protector of me. I am honoured," he said. I felt ill to hear those words. Not to this man.

"My Lord, I am humbled by your majesty. May I ask, how long would you expect these repairs to take?" asked the Marshal.

"My engineers estimate three weeks," Count Florens replied. "Three weeks? But my Lord…"

"A mere moment in comparison to the honour it will bring to my father's legacy," the count replied.

"How would you suggest we populate our new lands?" asked a gruff voice from behind the Count. It was Simon van

Teylingen, another influential noble. "Dams, dykes, poulders—those are what bring us arable land, Willem," he said. "Those populated the Low Countries. Those feed our people, and bring more to become our people."

"And what of the Frisians?"

"What of them?" he asked, taking over the conversation now on behalf of the Count. "It would appear, at this rate anyways, that there will be few of them left once we're done here. Dams create land—irrigated land. Land attracts Germans."

"If there's one thing about Germans, it's that there are too many of them," said Lord Werenbolt with a sinister laugh. "They're sending their excess peasants and their second sons to Prussia."

"We figure we could use them instead," said Simon.

"Here? In Frieslant?" asked Willem.

"Here, in North Hollant," said the Count with a determined look on his face. "We do this for God."

"They're Christians here, my Lord," said Willem. "They would serve you well enough."

"They're Frisian," said Simon in retort. "They've grown too accustomed to freedom."

"You've seen what's happened in the towns," said Werenbolt. "Just look at Gravenhage. No nobles, just men with gold and godlessness. It's anarchy."

"They threaten our way of life," added Simon. "If we can't strike at the towns, we strike at the Frisians. Gain momentum. Return to order."

"Land for the landed," said Werenbolt with a sharp smile.

"Land for my loyal vassals," said the Count.

"I see," said Willem. "That's what this is truly about? Lands? Titles?"

"It is about order, Willem. I know you to be quite the proponent of it, judging by how you've run Brederode and the Kennemers," said the Count. "We must simply resture the balance of things,"

"A victory in Frieslant will not subdue the towns," Willem said.

"No, but it will subdue the Frisians," the Count replied. "Come now, we must march out at once," he ordered. It was the will of the count—it was to be done. It was quite the conversation to take in. That's what this all was—a bid at restoring power to the nobility. Were they right? Would the burghers and the Frisians soon come for the rural lands of Hollant? I suppose this was an ugly truth of it. If the time came, and the people sought to overthrow their lords—my own family, I know that I would meet them in the field with steel and blood. This was no different. I understood it now— Graaf Florens would not stop until the Low Countries were feudal in their entirety. I suppose that was a banner I could rally under.

+ Maarten +

Geerbrant's wounds did not heal well. Long, black bruises stained his back from the shafts of the cudgels they laid on him. Every ounce of plunder I nicked, coins, chalices, tools, I gave a bit to him. So did Kees and Felix. He, on the other hand, spent his days in the infirmary. The Marshal's justice was not to be trifled with. It was swift and brutal. The Frisians suffered no less—not one of them, man, woman, nor child, was spared from the wrath of the Hollanters. We did what we could to mitigate the violence. We sheltered children, helped young girls flee to the woods, but it was a plague that could not be stopped. Wherever we marched, we stained the dirt paths red. The hot, August sun did little to dry that much blood. It was red until we marched, only crispened by the flames descending from the blazing thatched roofs we left behind us. All under the orders of the knights. Of course, the Marshal, the Bailiff, Heer Arend, they all told us to only hack combatants to pieces. Leave civilians unscathed, they said. They also told us to take what we willed. To burn homes and churches alike. Most of the men with us were levied. They were the worst—they were undisciplined compared to the wapenknechten like Geerbrant and his boys. Team building, the knights called it. Having their retainers pin down Frisian warriors to be slaughtered by boys my age, or younger. An initiation, they said it was. It was a disgrace. The rain did not wash away the blood on their hands. The charred altars would provide them no solace. They were murderers now. The only solace I found was in the belief that the Heavens would judge them when their time came—sooner or later.

It would come sooner or later. When we left each village, we transformed from predator to prey. We transformed from death dealers to lambs for the slaughter. Every tree, every bush, every grassy bog could be hiding a horde of Frisian warriors. They moved swiftly, traversing the marshes by vaulting on their pikes. They were one step ahead of us at all times, picking us off like chicken feed. They took reprisals for each civilian we ran through with out polearms. Each Frisian with his arms in the air and weapons on the ground impaled with crossbow bolts. They were merciless, like a spirit of vengeance. Nowhere was to be trusted. Patrols around our camp at night became more deadly than our raids themselves. The night was not to be trusted. The dark hid many forms of death, all of them unwavering.

What killed most of us was not Frisian blades nor even the hunger that bit down to our ribs, but disease. It ravaged our ranks—only made worse by the toll long marches took on our feet and the damp, wet nights we spent below patched-up tents. Herbalists in the infirmary were completely overrun. So were the priests. There were too many dead to be each granted their own service. Mass graves adorned the poulders wherever we marched. We came across them, and equally left them behind us.

"Don't get too comfortable, boys," said Heer Arend, riding back with his retinue of templar bodyguard from Alcmare. "We march out with haste."

"Where's His Highness sending us this time?" asked Heer Gherrijt.

"We are to repair a dam at the Rekere just north of here," Arend replied.

"A dam?"

"Yes, no greater symbol of Dutch glory," he said. "Should be no longer than a fortnight and a half." I noticed a good portion of the men prick up now. Another three weeks of this nonsense? Now all crowded around some building project like ducks in a pond? I could tell they were not pleased.

"Do we even have enough bread to last us that long?" asked Felix. Arend gave a grave look.

"The Eastern cotingent has established a supply line from Amsterdam. We will have enough to get by. But don't worry, lads, the ale will still flow."

"These Frisian rivers run with pisswater," said one of the levies.

"Riddled with disease, too," said another.

"Fresh kegs are coming from home, lads, don't you worry," said Heer Ghijsbrecht, riding to Arend's side.

"And after we patch up this dam?" asked Gherrijt. "What then?"

"We play it by ear," said Arend. "We are winning, boys. We should be celebrating." I looked around, it certainly did not look like it. I was ready to march home, I'm sure we all were. "We bring victory to Hollant," he said. "Honour, glory…"

"Riches," said a wapenkecht, chuckling with his mates.

"Fanny pox," joked another. Served them right, I suppose, for fraternising with the camp girls. Kees, Felix, and I knew to stay far from them unless you wanted to feel the fires of hell when you pissed.

"What a joke," Felix said to me. "There's a war going on, and the Count wants to plug a dam? Ridiculous."

"Remember why we're here," I said. "We never came because we agreed with them. We came to earn our freedom."

"We were free."

"We were despised. And we would have been convicts or amputees."

"Sounds like a better life."

"Only three more weeks," I said. "We patch the dam, and by then, I'm sure the lords will have had enough of this place. Enough of this damp muck beneath our feet."

"Their feet don't touch the ground," said Kees. "They only touch stirrups." He couldn't have been more right.

Work on the dam was more like what we were used to. I actually preferred it—we felt like the freemen draining the marshes back in Duivenvoorde. It was hard work, under the hot, summer sun. Sweat soaked through our gambesons to the point we laboured down to our braies.

It was more dangerous this way—bare flesh does little to stop a Frisian arrow whistling from the foliage, but in truth, we had little means to stop them as we worked. What would we do, rush at them with picks and spades to scare them off? It was up to our crossbowmen and archers to keep us secure with waves of arrows and bolts to drive them back while the rest of us toiled hard.

The mornings were silent, for the most part. They came early, and we were too tired to make conversation. We spent them filling the inside of the dam with straw and hay, tossing in great bundles with pitchforks looted from the countryside.

I wouldn't have engineered a dam this way, from what I knew of building kilns, but it was the greatest resource available to us.

By midday, we were allowed to break fast with a ration of whatever our light cavalry, wealthy burghers and landed gentry who could afford a horse but not the armour of a man-at-arms, could forage. They were our scouts, clearing the roads and running down fleeing Frisian raiders. They usually brought with them large carts of hay, that was, until the supply lines had been established. Then, we witnessed the army turn into a machine of war, well oiled, and well drilled. Every day, carts of barley from the harvest down south came in fresh for us to grind and retinue cooks to bake into bread. On Sundays, after mass, we were even given dill sausages or cheese, and on Fridays we got salt herring, just like back home.

Having been charcoal burners, we offered to build kilns far better than the ones the engineers and cooks designed, but we were no more than grunts to them. Arrow fodder. Cheap labour. The back-breaking labour was only mitigated by thoughts of Yda. Oh Yda, sweet Yda, the one thing keeping me going. If it wasn't for her, I might have deserted by now. But the thought of her face put me to sleep at night. And the thought of her being caught by a Frisian raid kept me fighting. Never would we let them push south. For all who we cared fro deeply, we would keep them in the North, and batter them into submission.

Labour was greater than sentry duty. Patrols around the camp were dangerous, even more dangerous than they had been before. We were no longer an army on the move, but a sedentary force ripe for the pruning. It wasn't unheard of for us to be called out to fight a skirmish near some outpost raided by the barbarians. It was easier to see them that way, barbarians, inhumans, savages. They weren't, but it easier on the mind to think that the man on the end of your glaive was no man at all, but some wild beast.

"Damn bastards are everywhere," said Felix one night as the three of us scouted out the woods near our camp. "It's been a fortnight and they just keep coming."

"I know," I said. "Just stand fast and stay vigilant."

"That's all we can do," he replied.

"Oy, what's that?" asked Kees after a few moments of silence.

"What is it?"

"Over there, that bush is rustling," he said. "Is it a Frieske?" I put my finger to my lips and gestured for them to follow me towards the rustling. It was not the first time we'd come across signs of a Frisian. Luckily, we'd never caught the beginnings of a raid ourselves—I don't think we'd have lived to tell the tale, but we'd certainly captured a handful of Frisians every now and then. I pointed for Felix to take a right, and Kees to take a left.

Careful to not make a sound, we stalked the bush, taking great care not to rustle too many leaves or step on any twigs. We could only hear the hot summer breeze blow against the trees—a rustling of leaves that masked our steps. Freeing my hand from my padded sleeve, I gestured 3, 2, 1, and at once we struck at the bush. Out of it came not a Frisian, but a small, hairy animal. A wild boar! It had been so long since we'd had pork—I immediately saw Kees lick his lips. The hog squealed as it dashed away from us.

"Quickly, catch the damn thing!" said Felix. Hurriedly, we rushed after it, following over roots and even under logs, chasing it through the forest. The fact that we were able to keep up with it amazed me—it spoke to how much we craved its delicious flesh. At one point, Felix dove for it, launching his voulge forward, but he missed, planting himself in the mud. It ran into another bush, where we couldn't find it, but the sound of its cloven trotters ceased. It was hiding somewhere.

"Here, piggy piggy," said Kees, ushering it out. He began oinking like a pig. After a while, we gave up. It was gone. Damn, it would have tasted delicious over a campfire.

Disappointed, we began the march back. We made our way back through foliage, now registering that we'd have to march all the way back. That was until a stone was launched in our direction. It shattered the bark on a tree behind us.

"What in God's name was that?" asked Felix, ducking low. A scream from the bushes answered his question, and four big Frisians emerged from the greenery.

"Here, piggy piggy," one said with a toothy grin in the best Dutch accent he could put on. With his great round shield, he slammed his hulking mass into me, knocking me over. He would have finished me off with his sword if I had not been able to unsheath my utility dagger and gut him first like a fish. Two others, one with a side axe and the other with a threshing flail, took on Felix and Kees, screaming their hearts out, faces caked in dirt and grime. A fourth stood behind them with a sling staff, loading another stone. This time, I wouldn't let him lose it.

"Duivenvoorde!" I cried, echoed by felix and Kees and we charged into them.

Quickly, I managed to hack my glaive into his staff, nearly splitting it in half, before he unsheathed a crop sickle from his belt with which he slashed at me wildly. I heard Kees lift the man behind me over his head, dropping him against the stump of a broken tree, while Felix wrestled with the third man on the ground. I managed to shove the shaft of my glaive into his forehead, knocking him to the ground before he could land a hit on me, and I dropped down the head of my glaive to deliver the final blow. We had become warriors by now, trained in war, and ready to fight. We drilled the moves Geerbrant had taught us—they were instilled in us like the cogs in a watermill. We heard screams for aid erupt across different forest patrols—this was more than a few raiders—this was an assault. Felix, managing to knee the great barbarian on top of him in the bollocks, was aided by Kees' axe which tore through the raider's iron scale armour. We quickly cleaned ourselves off, and raced back to camp, from which we now heard the drums and trumpets of the muster sounding. That was the call to arms—this was a battle.

+ Floris +

"To arms, men! To arms!" Father cried out. I rushed out of my tent to see him on his horse, the beast restless, with his templar guardsmen, ready to do battle. I heard the drummers now rattling their snare drums, and the warhorns blaring. On the other side of the encampment, I heard the screaming of men, and the rustling of steel. Immediately, I awoke my squire, bidding him to arm me with haste. Confused, once completely armed, I rushed outside and mounted up. On the way, I found the Duivenvoorders sallying out to join the line.

"They came from the woods!" said a footman. "My mates and I got in a skirmish with them. They're everywhere!"

"With me, boys," I said, shouting as loud as I could through the breaths of my greathelm. Lance in hand, I led them forward to the front where I saw the chaos ensuing.

Half-dressed men fought hand-to-hand with the raiders, using campfire logs, knives, and anything they could get their hands on. The scene was chaos. The men of Wassenaer had already joined the fray. I saw my young cousin Jacobus vander Wassenaer, son of Uncle Jan, Jacob for short, lead a heroic charge. The white crescents on red streamed their way through the enemy ranks. I also caught sight of Gherrijt, dismounted, fighting alongside the wapenknechten of Raephorst to clear out some of the tent yards. Some had already been set ablaze, men in pitch-black gambesons and burning cloth frantically rolling about the battleground like pigs in the muck. I felt a mailed mitten clasp my shoulder. It was Ghijsbrecht's.

"Send your boys to the western flank," he said. "My men have formed a battleline there." I nodded, ordering my men to charge into the frey and reinforce the flank as I followed him and his riders into battle. The red banners of Wassenaer, meanwhile, had made their way across the field. That's when a second wave of fighters emerged—the famed Frisian pikemen, the defenders of the North, the men who used their pikes to vault the Frisian marshes and outmanouever their enemies. They were finally here, led by the Protestaat, the Frisian general himself. He was no extraordinary man, only he was armed like a man at arms of the rest of Christendom—covered head to toe in chainmail. He was distinguished by a gilded nasal helmet of the sort our grandfathers and greatgrandfathers wore. He was exposed it had to have been a mistake. The field was open between his retinue and the knights of Wassenaer.

"To the Protestaat!" called out Jacob eagerly, courageously spurring his mount onwards with his sword held high in the air. His lance had already shattered, and sword in hand he rode down Frisians left and right, slashing and stabbing all around him. His men were in a similar situation, ground to a halt quickly, bogged down by hordes of the brawny warriors, some even being pulled from their horses or their horses themselves being impaled by the long pikes.

"They're in trouble," I told Ghijsbrecht. "He's made a mistake. We need to ride after them."

"Nay, they're surrounded. We have to wait until the time is right," he said.

"They need our help," I insisted.

"They're knights—they'll fight and die with honour," he replied without emotion, riding off to command his men. I felt my eyes widen, and I spurred my horse onwards to aid poor Jacob alone. Beside me came a now-mounted Gherrijt, clad in his black and white, having successfully pushed the barbarians out of the Zeelanter sector of the camp. He was accompanied by several of his knights and their men-at-arms.

"Bastards came out of nowhere," he said to me, panting. "Like devils in the night," I replied. "No honour."

"We'll ride them down like dogs," he replied. "With me, men. Charge!" It was swift and heavy—like the thud of a brisk punch. I felt the weight of our charge crash into their block of massed infantry, sending five men each flying backward into the dirt, and running our lances through their unarmoured corpses. I drew Stonesplitter, hacking and slashing all around me, and Gherrijt did the same with a war hammer. Together, we successfully managed to ride our contingents out of the block and cycle in another charge, but by that time Ghijsbrecht had been proven right. Tragically, I saw Jacob torn from his own horse, piled on my Frisians each with dirks and dagger, finding all the weak points in his armour. This is what separated these barbarians from true Dutchmen—they gave no mercy. Any honourable man would have captured a knight of his rank and let his family buy his Ransome—not these cravens. In an instant, I saw a dagger in his eyeslit and another up his ventail. Limp, the poor, red knight sank back into the dirt.

"For Jacob!" I shouted. "For Jacob!" the riders around me echoed, riding over the infantrymen who butchered him and planting them all firmly into the damp, wet ground. What would I say to his father? What could I possibly say? He died with honour, that's it. That's all we could hope for in times like this. I must have gotten distracted by the men with axes and spears all around me, as a new unit of pikemen fell upon us out of the woods in a third wave. They simply kept on coming.

"Make for the treeline!" called out Gherrijt. I had no

idea which one he was referring to, or even where was safe—my eye slits revealed little. But, I managed to follow him. At least, as I scouted the battlefield, it looked as though we were winning, although the woods were no place for massed cavalry action. I saw Werenbolt of Gravenhaage and his son Aelbrecht and their riders get dismounted by a particularly fierce volley of arrows. I saw no more of what happened to them, but I knew that the chances of surviving battle after having been dismounted were slim. I also witnessed the Warband of Marshal Willem van Brederode and the Bailiff Wouter de Vriese lead a vanguard assault to try and break through the Frisian centre. Well, if we could even call it a centre, amidst the chaos of the broken lines. I felt no affection for them, and even perhaps a burst of joy when I saw Wouter ride himself into the head of a pike. I'm sure it only glanced off his coat of plates, but it must have been painful as he called out to his men to rescue him.

We rested by the treeline, surveying the battlefield. Gherrijt had picked a good position. You had to give it to him, no matter how little he respected knighthood, he was excellent at being a knight. Just as we thought we'd caught our breaths, we were sucked back into the chaos of battle as a volley of arrows whistled towards us.

"To the river!" shouted Gherrijt. "They're shooting from near the dam…" he was cut short. I heard only a choking sound. Nay, nay, nay. Shit, no. God, no. When I looked over to him, I saw only an arrow through his chest, right above his coat of plates and below his helm.

Perhaps a rib caught it? Perhaps his arming doublet was thick enough? He fell from his saddle, squirming in the dirt, unable to speak. I heard the blood clogging his throat. I felt Galahad stagger beneath me—she had already taken three arrows to her chest. She tossed me from her as she writhed backward in pain. I scrambled to unbuckle my helm and tear it off, ripping back my coif to scan my fallen friend.

"Godverdomme, Gherrijt. Not like this," I said, frantically tearing off my gloves from out of my maille mittens to stop the blood. It trickled out now. Gently, I lifted off his helmet to reveal his eyes and ease his breathing. I saw the fear in them—I heard his lungs struggle to pump air against his maille mouthpiece. Carefully, I untied it, revealing a pool of blood trickling from out of his mouth. "Breathe. Breathe, brother," I said, holding his hand in mine and his head in the other. I put my forehead against his. "Breathe, damn it. You're not leaving me here." I looked him in the eyes. "We've sent for help. The surgeons will get you. They get the arrowhead out of you. Just breathe," I told him. His men-at-arms had all dismounted now, those who didn't chase after the archers to charge them down.

"Fl… Floris…" he muttered, gouts of blood splattering from his lips, tainting the pale white of his black and white striped surcoat. "Tell my mother I died well," he managed to say. "I'll be with Father," he said, looking up. I could only imagine that he saw the angels beckoning him now. It was hard to imagine. Hard to take in. No, he was a warrior, a fighter, not like this.

"I will," I said solemnly. "I will avenge you, brother," I said, holding his head in my arms. "Surgeon!" I called out. "Surgeon." I looked at one of his riders. "Get me a bloody surgeon, damn it." His grip weakened. I felt my eyes running, and a teardrop trailed down my cheek. No, not like this. Not by an arrow. He wasn't given a chance. It wasn't fair. Not like this. He deserved better. He was a good man. I would make them pay. By B Saint Michael and Saint George, by all the Heavens, Lord hear me, I would make them pay for what they did to him—honourless brigands. They would come to fear the lion. They would come to fear the Wassenaer. They would hear vengeance in his name. I held Gherrijt in my arms, holding him close, careful not to touch the arrow sticking out of him. I felt my despair turn to a blazing, forge-hot rage. When I finally felt his soul slip, I closed his eyes and stood to take a glance at the battlefield, slipping my coif back on. "This blade will slay a hundred Frisians for what they did this day," I vowed, looking to Stonesplitter. "I will have my revenge." I turned to his riders. "One of you, pick up his corpse. He deserves a proper burial. Take his helm, too, I want his effigy to be accurate. The rest of you, mount up and follow me. We have a debt to settle," I said, fixing my chainmail over my chin and lips. "For Hollant."

Chapter 12. The Revelation: Piet

It was another one of those late nights in the study with nothing in the air but candlelight and the mutterings of two scholars. Lord Hillebrant was at work—he'd been working extra hard for days now, staying up even later than he usually would. At least it meant I could stay up with him. Today it was the *Art of the Banker*, by some old monk named Arnulf. It flowed better than the translations of the ancient texts, but the parchment was nowhere near the same quality, even with holes in it in some places. The illuminations in the margins kept me entertained after the grueling pages of Hollantic tax law. I reached chapter three tonight, an accomplishment I'm quite proud of. I scanned the decorated letters beginning each sub-chapter, running my fingers over the embossed ruling parchment. Some poor monk must have scribed this manuscript to the tune of his superior orating every word. Every bland, grey word about tithes and knights' fees and city charters. Before I knew it, I heard a snoring come from Lord Hillebrant's side of the table. I looked over to see his hooded visage planted flat on the table, his plump cheek and manicured silvering gold beard embedding itself in the grain of the ornamented, oak table. Usually, I'd just let him sleep there. Usually, he'd get up in the morning and be down for breakfast anyways. Usually, I wasn't this bored.

Stealthily, I tiptoed over to his desk. I was curious as to what he actually did when he was working. He always looked so busy and hard at work, but never did I understand what this work looked like. The book and scrolls in front of him all had long lists of payments and assets.

Ludolph the Tanner	3 Bbts Groten
Gerulf the Wood Cutter	4 Stuivers
Stemaers the Turner	1 Vlmg Grote

These lists ran from top to bottom of the scrolls, with dates occasionally included to demarcate which day of which year the payments were made. I scanned the documents looking for the biggest payments—it was interesting to look at these accounts. They were almost like a window into the lives of the buyers. Apparently, they'd made a loan of two pounds Flemish in the Jewish quarter—no further information about the lender was made.

More recently, I noticed, they'd bought a flagon of wine for precisely six stuivers—these must have been the people from whom Lord Hillebrant received the wine. I was hooked now, scrolling through the lists to find more interesting things. It was common to see large payments in the lists to other trading companies, and an annual fee to the Hanseatic League.

The words and numbers all danced around in my head as I crafted stories to explain the expenses. A daily expense to the baker? Perhaps they're having an affair? A bi-weekly expense at the market—what were they buying? Cheese and fish, or did they have an insatiable desire for sweet waffles?

And then I came across one large payment, twenty pounds flemish, made to a name that I recognized all too well—Lauerens of the Company of the Vermillion Boar. Similarly, there were unusual payments to abbeys, and artisanal guilds, and more payments to anonymous sellers in the Jewish quarter. What could these all mean? I heard him snort a little—just in case he was about to wake from his hibernation, I scrambled back to my chair.

"Huh? Oh, I must've fallen asleep." Lord Hillebrant said, making a wide yawn. "I'd best be off to bed."

"Lord Hillebrant," I asked, "What is it that you really do?"

"Well, you know that Piet, I'm a lawman. A lawyer—I make sure that my clients are represented well in court, and I make sure that those who have broken the law are held accountable."

"Well then, why are you always poring over books and scrolls when you only need to craft a story?"

"Ah, that's because these are the evidence. These records are submitted every year to the aldermen of Leyden, and using them they adjudicate which merchants must pay which taxes. And, if you don't seem to be telling the truth, they'll send spies to see what your finances are really like. All boring numbers, I suppose."

"Who says numbers have to be boring?" I asked. Lord Hillebrant met my question with a warm smile and a ruffling of my hair.

"Whose are those?" I asked.

"Those? Oh, those accounts belong to a company owned by a couple of wealthy burghers named Ludolf van Bilthoven and Stemaers the Deutser. The two of them have been giving the town quite a hard time."

"Why's that?"

"Well, usually when people cheat on their taxes, it's because they want to seem poorer than they are so that they can dodge paying. These fellows, on the other hand, seem to have made more than they actually have. Where is all this money going? I have no idea." Lord Hillebrant said with a set of wrinkles entrenched above his brow. "How can you solve a puzzle like that?" I asked.

"Usually, to get away with a false transaction, a company will keep the record of the transaction itself but simply lower the amount. Here, though, nothing seems out of place."

"Any strange transactions? Anything that their company wouldn't usually buy into?"

"Well, they're a shipping company. They bring wool from England and then guard the caravans that take the wool down to the Alps," he said. I pretended to glance at the page for a second.

"What's the company of the Vermillion Boar?" I asked, taking care to hide that I'd snuck a peek beforehand.

"I don't quite know." Lord Hillebrant said. "That's something I simply haven't been able to place my finger on. I've never heard of them."

"Could they be mercenaries? They sound like it," I said. The great crease in Lord Hillebrant's brown unfurled like a blown-up leather ball.

"Did you just guess that?" Lord Hillebrant asked. I felt myself involuntarily swallow.

"Yes," I replied.

"What makes you think it's a mercenary band?"

"I'm not sure, I think I heard some peasant boys talking about them back in Duivenvoorde. Why? You seem to have placed something…" Lord Hillebrant began to scour the paper again, carefully reading each over and writing down equations on scraps.

"There may be some things connected, Piet," he said. "You've helped me dearly." He grabbed a spare torch from a cabinet and lit it in one of the candles. "Please put out the lights before you're off to bed, I must run a message over immediately," he said, putting on his cloak. "I will be back before morning." I nodded. I heard him rush out the door. I obeyed as I was told. But, there was a spark of curiosity that I couldn't reject. It burrowed its way deep into my thoughts—I found myself fearful that Lord Hillebrant would not return. I decided to scramble out of the study window— my old escape route, stalking Lord Hillebrant through the shadows so that I wouldn't get in trouble. Fleet-footed, I managed to tail him. I made sure that not only was I cloaked in shadow, but that my own shadow was no more visible. The moonlight, embers from kitchen stoves, and solitary candles lit our path. Lord Hillebrant took great care not to run into the city watchmen—the curfew was no trivial law. I remember when I first arrived he told me that under no circumstances was I to leave the manor at night.

Now look at me—creeping about after him as he broke his own rule.

I watched as he snuck every which way, finally knocking on the door of another gated manor, one which I could only assume belonged to an important individual as a familial crest was carved proudly into the main doorframe. Six coins it appeared to be—the man must've been a burgher of some sort. I couldn't tell from his nightgown—although the fine cloth was still telling of his status. The man seemed surprised—perhaps startled. He offered to entertain Lord Hillebrant in his own home, but Lord Hilebrant insisted that he'd best make his way back home with haste. As the two men spoke, the man in the gown ushered a courier—a young boy a little older than I am, to run a message, giving him his signet ring as well. The boy ran off quickly. I quickly hid behind a corner so as to keep him from noticing me. Eventually, Lord Hillebrant broke off, making his way back now with a little less haste and a little more fatigue.

It was when we returned that I finally realized my mistake.

"Lord Hillebrant! There you are!" cried out Ms. Filomena. "Is Piet with you?"

"Piet? No, I left him in my study." Lord Hillebrant replied.

"He's not in the house." Ms. Filomena said. What had I done? Now, if I stepped out, they would hate me. They would be so disappointed in me for sending them into a frenesie like that. Surely, they would kick me out for good—and then where would I be? I would have disappointed Mother—oh surely they would tell Mother. I couldn't muster the courage to step out or to make a noise, I just stood there, frozen in the dark with no embrace but the warm, summer air. The fear gripped me like a ghost with its hand clasped firmly around my throat. Not a peep would come out of me even if I wanted it to.

"We have to look for him," Lord Hillebrant said. "He's probably off with his friends."

"Should I awake the others?" Ms. Filomena asked.

"Only Master Waleran," Lord Hillebrant said. "Let the boys sleep—they work hard." Oh no, not Master Waleran. He'd surely give me a spanking if he found me. I'd just follow Ms. Filomena. Perhaps if they separated I could talk to her alone? Maybe I could explain myself? She's the only one who might understand. She was always so comforting to me—oh but she would still have to kick me out. I felt a churning in my stomach. I'd failed as a ward. I hadn't fulfilled my duties. They decided to split up. Master Waleran went to the market square while Lord Hillebrant and Ms. Filomena decided to go to the abandoned windmill in search of me. They must've thought that I'd gone out with my friends. I found a seat behind a comfortable bush where I could watch their silhouettes moving in the moonlight. It was there that I heard a ribbit. Startled, I looked around in the crass, running my hands through it to feel for the little creature. Eventually, I found it—a pudgy little frog or toad or something like that. Unfazed, it just sat there, even as my fingers ran over it. I picked it up.

"Hello, little frog," I said in a hushed voice. "What are you doing out here?" I asked. I could barely make it out in the moonlight—but I believe it had a brown coat and bright yellow eyes. His chubby body was squishy and a little slimy to the touch. It didn't respond. "Are you hiding from anyone? Because I am. Maybe we can hide together. If you were in my situation, what would you do? I know, I know—I am foolish. I shouldn't have left the house. But I didn't know what would happen to him. You're right, now everyone is awake searching for me. Well, I want to tell them, but how can I? I feel like, even if I wanted to, I couldn't. Like something's stopping me from just popping out of this bush and hollering *hoopla I was with you the whole time.* What's worse is I saw him, too. Was I not supposed to see that? What would you do?"

"*Ribbit.*"

"Hush now, I think they're coming over this way. Let me readjust—that's better. You know, last time I was here, I picked up a small pet just like you. His name is Archimedes. When I brought him home, Lord Hillebrant wasn't happy with him. Ms. Filomena was nice to me, though."

"*Ribbit.*"

"I suppose you're right—he did change his mind. But I feel like, no matter what I do, I can't live up to what he wants from me. There's always another book or another task—I feel like he wants me to be better than I am. Smarter than I am. More hard working. And I'm just… not. I just don't know if I have it in me. I'm not even of noble blood."

"*Ribbit.*"

"Of course they're different—what do you mean? They walk around with swords and train to be knights—and they're born blessed by God. We're born to work the field while they are born to keep law and order."

"*Ribbit.*"

"I suppose they don't *look* all that different, well, they wouldn't if they were in our shoes. Or we wouldn't if we were in theirs. But come on, I can't just pretend to be noble—I've lived my whole life a serf."

"Ribbit."

"I know I'm only seven. You know what? You're right. I'm going to tell them. I'm going to put you down and tell them. I'm going to do it—I swear. I…"

"Piet, is that you?" Ms. Filomena asked—her voice slicing through the darkness and the chirping of cicadas. The little frog hopped away hastily. I stood up, rubbing the muck off the seat of my braies.

"Yes," I said, ashamed, looking at my feet. Ms. Filomena rushed to me with a blanket that wrapped around me with a warm hug.

"Stupid boy," she said, holding me tightly.

"Well, well, well, quite the rabbit we've caught, eh?" said Lord Hillebrant, coming towards me too now.

"What were you doing out here all by yourself?" Ms. Filomena asked. I didn't want to say anything.

"Spit it out, boy," said Lord Hillebrant, placing a chunky hand on my shoulder. "Lured out by those friends of yours?"

"Following you," I muttered, looking at my turnshoes still. When I looked up, I saw Lord Hilebrant's eyes widen.

"Since I left you in my study?" he asked. I nodded. "And you managed to stay out of sight the whole time," he said to himself.

"The boy's a fox," said Ms. Filomena.

"He's more than that," said Lord Hillebrant. "He's a little spy," he said. "How much did you see?"

"Everything, but I couldn't make out what you were saying," I said. They looked at one another.

"Do you have any idea of how much trouble you're in, young man?" Lord Hillebrant asked.

"Please don't send me back to Duivenvoorde," I said. I couldn't hold it back any longer—I felt my grimace turn into a long stream of tears. I couldn't even see them anymore aside from their fluttering silhouettes through the water welling in my eyes. I felt Ms. Filomena embraced me more firmly than she had before.

"Of course not, Piet," she said softly.

"Never," said Lord Hillebrant. "Never," he repeated. "You are my page, and I vowed to take you on and give you a better life—that is precisely what I intend to do." he knelt down. "And this idiocy is a far cry from an offence worth warranting such an action," he added.

"Come, let's go back home," said Ms. Filomena.

"Ms. Filomena, would you be so kind as to carry our young espion?" Lord Hillebrant asked.

"Gladly," she said, gently lifting me in her arms. I felt her run her fingers through my hair to calm me down. Lord Hillebrant, with a handkerchief, wiped the snot that now trickled from my nose. The way back was quiet. So quiet, in fact, that I dozed right off to sleep. The mellow rocking made me feel like I was in Mother's arms. I dreamt deep dreams of Mother and Duivenvoorde. A happy memory.

+ Floris +

The dead were piled high. No matter how hard the war

council tried, they couldn't escape the stench of blood and rotting flesh, the sight of dead men wrapped in blankets or buried as they were, or the cries of the wounded above the solemn preachings of the priests' mass eulogies. All parties were present, Father included, well, all left alive. In the moment, this appeared to be only the Western Command and the ver Heyen brothers. Eventually, the Count, and what were left of his headsmen arrived.

"Speak plainly, Brederode. How many have we lost today," he said in a solemn and ghastly voice, his throat trembling at the words. Marshal Willem took a moment to collect his thoughts before he spoke.

"Before I let the number of wounded known to you, let it be known that we drove the savages back."

"We bathe in blood, and you would seek to comfort me?"

"We won, my Lord."

"We have lost good Hollanters, Marshal," Florens corrected him. "Now speak or you will join the men you see rotting before you. I have no time for games, not now."

"Yes, my Lord." Willem conceded. "One third of our pedites stand dead or wounded." What a choice of words. *Pedites*, of course, being the official term for our infantry. Our rabble. The good Hollanters who died for this Count. And *stand*? Please, the only ones standing are the Frisian dogs who ran, pissing their fear out in the woods. No man was standing but those who were lucky.

"And of the nobility?" the Count asked.

"No exact numbers yet, my Lord, but we have word that

many of our high command have been slain. Doubtless their retinues fell valiantly with them, holding their ground to the last man."

"If I wished for honey with your words I would have marched this army to a monastery, not to a dam. Rinse your speech with water, Marshal. I wish to see through it as clearly as the Rijn. A full list, if you have names."

"The names of the fallen thus far are vast, my Lord. To name a few, there were the mighty father and son, Simon and Dirk van Teylingen. My personal vassal and trusted retainer, Sir Wouter de Vries, the bailiff of Kennemerland. Also your acclaimed father and son, Werenboult and Aelbrecht uter Haghe."

"May God rest their souls and pity their wife and mother," said the Count.

"There are more, my Lord. There was the young Lord Gherrijt van Raephorst," said Willem. I felt a deep throb engulf my throat. "His younger brother, Dideric, rests in the infirmary, with two arrows to his stomach." His brother? Oh God, young Dideric. I hadn't even known he had come. He must have crept in amongst Gherrijt's wapenknecheten. I had to ensure that he was safe. "There were the noble brothers in arms, Beernt uter Haghe and Gherit van Hermalen…"

"The entire Eastern Command has been lost?" asked Count Florens. Willem replied only with a nod. The Count, speechless, formed the sign of the cross upon his chest.

"May God help us," he said.

Before continuing, the Marshal looked to Uncle Jan,

who looked pensive. What had happened? I didn't even know, although the air felt thick. "And the courageous young Jacob vander Wassenaer, who fell leading a cavalry charge against the chief of those marauders." the Marshal said, spitting to the earth. "May he rest peacefully, and may Saint Peter welcome him with grace." Uncle Jan looked red, and defeated. The crease above his brow grew thick, veins popping, eyes bulging, tears forming. Even the Count's countenance shattered, with an empathetic visage emerging.

"Your son?" he asked. Jan could only look at him, holding his noble expression together just barely. "You have my thanks for his sacrifice and my utmost sympathy. He was a good boy. You are dismissed, Heer Johannes," he said. Jan nodded, and with his men left the party with haste. Father and I looked at one another with sympathy. It appeared that he already knew. My cousin Jacobus was slain too. Young lives were lost before their time—before he could even ascend the throne of Wassenaer. I felt my mailed fingers clench hard. A numbness coursed through my veins, breaking only at the pain in my heart and throat, and replacing itself with a rage that begged me to mount Galahad and return the fight to them. But I couldn't. Even Galahad was no more.

Like a harbinger of the apocalypse, a young scout rode in on a brisk rouncey.

"A message for the Count!" he called out. "A message for the Count!" Two burly men-at-ars clad in chainmail from the Count's bodyguard halted him in his tracks, grabbing a hold of his mount's reins.

"Let him through," the Count ordered. The young scout

slipped as soon as he dismounted. Hastily, he clambered to his feet, panting, and took off his plumed bycocket hat out of respect. He knelt before the Count and held a sealed scroll high in the air. The count took off his riding gloves and broke the seal with care. As he read in his mind, his eyes widened. "Council, what is left of it, at least, it is time to serve your purpose. I know not what to do."

"What is it, my Lord?" asked Father.

"Enveloped. We have been enveloped. Cut off."

"Give it here," said the Marshal, sceptical that the barbarians could be so cunning.

But, they were. As he read, the Marshal dropped the scroll. "They wish to draw us into battle."

"That means they must have many men with them," said Lodewijk ver Heyen. "We are dead men." trembled the Count.

"Heiloo," said Ghijsbrecht with a surprising assurance. "The last town we passed. Heiloo—it's our only choice."

"We have no food stores, we cannot settle in for a siege," said Willem. "We should focus on fighting our wait back to Hollant."

"Nay, the woods are their greatest ally," I interjected. All eyes now turned to me. I suppose it was not my place to speak, but I had to voice my thoughts. "I've seen it, first hand. You have, too. If they want to fight in the field, we should force them to fight in the town instead," I said. Marshal Willem was quick to reject my opinion in front of his liege.

"This is no time for…"

"My son speaks with the wisdom of a seasoned veteran," Father uttered sternly with the roar of a tempered and calm lion. "If they mount a siege, we break it," said Father.

"Agreed," said Renier ver Heyen. It felt as though he wished to extend a sort of olive branch between our houses. That man, the gruffest of the brothers, surprised me with his words. "We trap them—bait them into thinking they have us." No matter how little respect I had for those tricky ver Heyens, he was right—such tactics were our only hope at that moment. I'd had enough of honourable fighting. We'd lost enough men. "The pup has learned the art of battle well," he said, nodding towards me.

"And then crush their lines," added Wolf. "My men would be more than happy to lead the vanguard and spearhead the charge."

"Temper your courage, boy," said Lodewijk.

"If the young knight wishes to test his steel, so be it," said the Count. "Do we have the men?" he asked.

"We still have a handful of good knights," said Lodewijk. "Enough to scare off whatever rabble they send at us."

"And our footmen have yet to break," added Gherrijt. "Those boys are tough as "Then Heiloo it is," agreed Count Florens.

+ Maarten +

"Alright, alright, alright," said Geerbrant, sipping from

259

his flask. "I've got one for ye nails."

There's this meadow, right? It's a lovely little meadow with little bunny rabbits and poppies and all the like. So, first, a couple of nobles ride past it. It's a nobleman and his wife. He turns to her and he says, *Love of my life, fairest maiden of all, I would love nothing more than to make love to you in this beautiful field on this lovely Spring morning.* So they ride on, and a little later, a couple of burghers come by. One turns to the other and says, *My good man, I tell you we will sew this field and reap enough barley to earn us a fortune.* Of course, his mate turns back to him and goes, *Not if I do so first.*" This earned Geerbrant a chuckle from the others, but he wasn't done yet. He leaned in, taking care not to hurt his ribs too much. "Now get this, a couple of peasants are walking by after. What do you think they say?" he asked.

"It's a feast," said Felix, to an uproar of laughter. I couldn't help but crack a smile with them.

"Nay, nay, nay, lads you're thinking too hard. They don't say nothing—they just take a shit and leave," Geerbrant corrected. This one got me—I found myself crying out of laughter. Kees doubled over.

"It's good to see you back in fighting shape, Geerbrant," he said, giving Geerbrant a hardy pat on the back. I saw the poor man wince at the contact. He rolled his shoulder over a bit.

"Eh, it's not perfect but I'll be good enough," he said with a small smile. "I can't let you lot have all the fun." The four of us looked out over the makeshift barricade at the Frisian camp. Long lines of ditches and stakes and tents lined the village on all sides. We were promised a town, but what we got was really just a small settlement—a small settlement to a Hollanter, anyway.

"This will be a fun night," I said, scanning the campfires illuminating one after another as the sun settled westwards.

"That's one way to put it," said Felix. "Remind me again how I got dragged into this?"

"Because you're a loving and loyal friend," I said with a grin.

"Because we get to smash some Frisians," said Kees with a broader one.

"Vengeance," muttered Geerbrant under his breath. "We need a whole lot of it to heal these wounds."

"We'll get it," I said, looking him in the eyes. "Those bastards don't get to play the innocent card anymore," I said, scanning my friends. "While our army is battered and bruised they keep us trapped in this God-forsaken country like kenneled old dogs awaiting the farm-hand's mercy."

"You know what we do with trapped dogs?" asked Geerbrant.

"What?" asked Kees.

"We let them loose," said Felix with a smirk as he peered out to gain at their camp. "You know, Maarten, they didn't listen to you before when you offered your skills as a charcoal burner. What changed?"

"I guess men become a little more equal with a sword at their throats," I said.

"Those fools are the men that got us into this mess," said Geerbrant. I wanted to reassure him of the bravery we witnessed in battle when he was resting. I wanted to console him that the red lion of Hollant really did fly on the battlefield. But, that would hurt him too much. As valiantly as they fought among us, they were also the steel-clad titans that broke this poor man. The men who ordered the cudgels to hammer down on him. And while he took it like a damn anvil, I'm certain it hurt even more on the inside. To watch as his liege lord who he'd served so faithfully watched and did nothing.

"When we get out of here, we'll be rich men," I said to all of them. "We can be whoever we want to be with coin and loot like this," I said, brandishing my now-heavy coin purse.

"That's only *if* we get out of here, boy. Focus on what's lookin' ye in the eye." corrected Geerbrant. I nodded. "Alright lads, it's almost time. We take the tall grass."

The high reeds only hid us partially—it was the night and the lowland mist that did the heavy lifting. The mist was both a blessing and a curse that night. We found ourselves carefully calculating every step, taking great care to avail our boots from entrenching themselves too far into the wet sod. Geebrant raised a fist. We all halted. I was glad that we were lightly armed and armoured. No polearms tonight—just daggers and padded jacks.

Hoods, face covers, and mud wiped thoroughly over the visible bits of our faces helped to conceal us in the dark. When Geerbrant gave us the clear, we stalked onwards. We'd have to find ways to use the fire available to us. On Geerbrant's mark, we fanned out near one of the campfires on the edge of their camp. A few watchmen, absolutely hammered from stolen ale, stood guard. Their yawns and sunken eyelids told us all we needed to know. Their sleeping comrades were entirely unaware of the blood that trickled from their throats. Then came the fire. That was my job. I had a cloth wrapped in oiled cloth ready to go, which I dipped in the fire for just long enough to let it catch. I looked for the most flammable objects. Tents, lean-tos, hastily assembled thatched roofs, wagons: they all lit up without a hassle. The sleeping men had no idea—after all, the flames and the smoke only travel upwards. With every item that caught alight, I felt a burst of excitement released in me. It was as if I was a master of the craft, kindling all the wood around. It was beautiful. Glorious, even. The bright orange roared high into the night sky. Of course, we also quickly removed all the rocks from around the campfire and led a trail of extra hay from the fire elsewhere about the camp's edge. Before we heard any sort of alarm, we snuck out like thieves. Correction, we were thieves. In complete honesty, we nicked a few goods here and there off the dead men. After all, Saint Peter wouldn't care if they were missing an extra stuiver or an ornamented dagger—they were going straight to hell regardless. Bach into the tall grass, it wasn't long before we heard shouts in Frisian that vaguely resembled, "Fire! Fire!" and "Alarm!" These barbarians would have no sleep tonight. "We should do another," I said excitedly.

"It may be risky now that they're awake," replied Geerbrant.

"They're coming to look for us!" said Felix, pointing to search parties scrambling about, half asleep.

"The ditch," I said, nodding to the long trench filled with stakes pointing outwards to thwart any cavalry charges against them. Geerbrant ushered us to the ditch where the four of us hit, out of sight, completely invisible, one with the muck—one with the land. It was ironic, I suppose, that that's what I'd set out to do—become a serf. Who in their right mind would become a serf? I suppose it was better than the violence and blood of battle, although, on occasion, I wondered if I'd miss the excitement. But then I'd remember the showers of javelins and arrows that hailed us from the foliage of the Frisian woodland. Then I remember the screams of fallen brothers, and the neighing of horses, and the thunder of their gallop.

And of course, I remember the first man I killed. In fact, I think I remember them all. Not all of them had weapons in their hands. All of them were screaming, though. Whether it was a menacing, gut-wrenching war cry, or a cry of agony. A cry for mercy, perhaps? It was never clear if that meant for them to be spared or for them to be gotten rid of. I suppose there was no true difference there. I'd seen few captives among our ranks—Frisians were only worth small ransoms.

"Do you hear that?" asked Felix. I heard it. Footsteps slowly made their way towards us.

"Oy, Hollanters?" a voice asked to the darkness. I looked up, taking care not to move a muscle, as I saw a big Frisian warrior with shaven sides of his head, shirtless, and with a menacingly long sword in his hand. I reckon it was so big it would take two of mine. "I hear you," he said. When I looked at my comrades, Felix was gone. Frantically, I looked around. I didn't want to assume that he had fled, but what other choice did I have? The man was sneaky enough to slither off into the darkness without a word. The Frisian stood above us for a few more moments, looking out at the fields and the swaying banners of the Hollanter camp. "I know you're there, you Dutch dogs," he said. "You cowards do nothin' but run and hide.

Honourless asses you are. You come as thieves, to steal our lands and slaughter our kin. You think yourself clever, skulking in the night with your fires? Some say you're like ghosts," he said as a spat down on us. "I say you're like stray cats. You don't like your home and you come here. You want ours instead. Bastards. You don't like our freedom. Cowards, the lot of you.

Show your faces like men."

"I'm right here." I heard the voice of a quick-tongued Felix utter as I raised my head to find the man run through by my good friend. Felix' face was exposed as he had very intentionally lowered his mask, and he looked the warrior in the eye. He was half the man's width, and a good two heads shorter than him. But, Felix' dagger had the man right in his gut, and then again through his ribs, and then again and again, and finally through his shoulder until the beast of a man was on his knees, lifeless. Felix, quite proud of his achievement, looked to us.

"Let no man call me a coward," he said. "I'm practical," he added with a smile. He then looked back to other bands of warriors coming, marking their great round shields in the orange light. "Let's get out of here," he said. With a clasp of his hand, he helped me out of the ditch. When we heard more coming, we were already engulfed in the tall reeds, lost to the mist, indeed like strays in the night. When we looked back on the great illumination we painted, I felt nothing but pride. Pride and a deep, deep longing for home. I didn't know where home was, exactly, but at least I knew what she looked like.

Chapter 13. The Abduction: Piet

A thunderous knock pounded on the front door.

"Who's that?" I asked Lord Hillebrant. He lowered his reading glasses to listen more carefully. Again, we heard the knock.

"I haven't the slightest clue, Piet," he replied. "Keep to your books; I'll be back shortly." He stood up, sliding his belly out from between the chair and the table. I heard him make his way down the stairs. Curious, I decided to scramble over to the ledge to peek out at the door, peeking over like a squirrel in a tree. When he opened it, just a crack, I heard the rain more clearly now, and a gust of cool night air filled the main hall. Hidden, I spied on the old master.

"Who is it, pray tell?" he asked the empty slit between the door and its frame.

"Night Watch," the man replied in a gruff voice. "Open up," he said. What could they possibly want here? Lord Hillebrant opened the door fully.

"Heavens, who bid you come here at this hour of late? I half thought you were brigands or cutthroats," he said. Of course, he remained diplomatic as always, but I could sense a keen note of suspicion in his intonation.

"Lord Hillebrant ver Heyen, I presume?" the watchman said. Three men stepped in behind him, unbidden, dirtying the wooden floorboards with their wet, muck-ridden turn shoes.

"Jaja, that's me. What can I do for you gentlemen?"

Lord Hillebrant asked.

"You are to come with us. You will be tried by the burgher council shorty." the watchman said.

"I… I don't know what to say. This is completely unfounded," Lord Hillebrant replied. Then, when a watchman rested the butt of his goedendag on the wooden slats, Lord Hillebrant changed his tone with a, "Alright, gentlemen. No need to have your laces crossed—I'll be right out. Let me just grab my cloak and inform my servants…"

"You will comply with this instance, traitor," one of the Night Watch captain's men said with a crooked sneer.

"Traitor?" Lord Hillebrant asked with shock. "You take me for some… some Ganelon? I will let you know that we ver Heyens, take great pride in our loyalty. I have served the Count and this town for decades…"

"Lord Hillebrant, you are to be tried for embezzlement and the unlawful support of treacherous, unholy upstarts."

"Unholy wh…"

"Don't play the fool, Lord Hillebrant. Coffers of guilders have been sent to Kennemerland--guilders which belonged to the town."

"I don't even have access to town funds!"

"Save that for the burghermeisters," the watchman captain said. He then nodded to one of his men, who proceeded to tie lord Hillebrand's wrists together.

"Unhand me," he said. "Is this truly necessary?"

"Just following orders." the captain said with a chuckle.

"Let's go, boys," he said, ordering his men out. They had almost left the front door ajar until one reluctantly returned to slam it shut.

+ Merin +

Merin & Florie

"What brings you to the convent?" Mother Roos asked, ushering me to put down my broom and come to her side. The slender old man dismounted from his horse.

"I bring word of the war from the Abbot of Egmond," he replied, handing Mother Roos a scroll.

"Sister Merin, lead his horse to the stables where

269

yourself and sister Florie can groom it. And fetch it some water," Mother Roos ordered. "And be quick about it." I curtsied and did as I was told. But, as I found myself fiddling with the mare's reins, I listened intently to the words of the messenger. He spoke in a hushed tone to Mother Roos, but he spoke of great battles in Frieslant, and brave knights fighting wildmen and giants. He spoke as if they were battling the fairies and the dryads in the trees themselves—the land appeared to be the enemy just as much as the people who lived on it. Also, he spoke of rowdy peasants, serfs, most of them ungrateful for the protection of their liege lord, causing chaos and violence in Kennemerland. War loomed ever around us, it felt. The war was much of what we talked of these days. Life in the convent was insular, and isolated, and there was little to do but chat.

Of course, one had to pick the right words, the right phrases, or the Mother Abbess will certainly, teach you a lesson. Florie was the only person I could really talk to. Since we were sent from Duivenvoorde, life has been full of work, chores, and scriptures. It was lonely, too. Yda was gone, and my brothers. The only fun we had was when we snuck out or played with the critters that snuck into the cloister. We'd draw pictures of rabbits and snails—some of whom found their way into the illuminations in the scriptorium. As boring as it was, it was a peaceful life. It was filled with beautiful music and serene speech, accompanied by the feel of calm breezes through the colonnades and the lovely architecture of the convent itself. I suppose it was a place of respite for many of the older girls; it was just so boring!

Today, my chores for the day were mostly in the chapel.

I liked those the most, as I got to hear the sisters of the chorus practice their music. I never learned how to read it—that would only begin if I were to be granted studies with the nuns as a reward for my work. But, I had seen those ink-laden pages, filled with dots and lines and scrobbles, complex and foreign. I don't know how people figured out writing, but it sure wasn't created by a peasant like me. God helped me to figure out how to spell, and we left that to the scholars. I couldn't help but feel a growing sense of curiosity as each day; I worked with a different set of sisters in their respective workrooms. There were the alchemists, the scribes, the illuminators, the musicians, the gardeners, the cooks, the educators, and, of course, the theologians. They were the most devout of all of us—their ranks often filled by the most senior sisters. They spent all their daylight hours studying the Bible and other holy texts, re-reading the words until they were engraved in their minds like the face of a close friend or the smell of a meal your mother used to make. Of course, all the sisters joined each other for our silent meals in the refectory. Silent, of course, aside from our orator, a sister chose to read a passage from the Bible to ensure that all hours of our days were spent learning. I rarely got to eat in the refractory—that was only for the learned sisters. The lay sisters, or servi, or ancillae, whatever you wish to call us, lived in separate quarters. We were all sisters who served in some way or another, helping to tend to the Abbey's demesne, cooking, cleaning, washing dishes, hauling goods, and other things of that sort. We interacted much more with the land outside the Abbey. Just like the Lords of Duivenvoorde, the Abbess had her own serfs and free peasants working her land, her own demesne, her own village, and her own three fields. Simply put, the Abbey was as much a castle as it was a place of worship. There were wapenknechten loyal to both the Count of Hollant as well as the Bishop of Utrecht and the Pope. In addition, many Templars, Hospitallers, and Teutonic brethren passed through the Abbey, making it their place of refuge on their long travels across Christendom. The world outside sounded more and more horrible while I stayed here. Men came from all corners of the world, travellers, merchants, crusaders, and all other sorts, each of whom had news of the infidels in the Holy Land, or the pagan savages on the Baltic coast, or the wildmen of the woods of Ireland and Wales, or the Frisian barbarians at our doorstep. To add to the chaos, now there was word of rebellion. It all seemed like too much—I was quite content here, on second thought. Bored, but safe.

The traveller's horse was a beautiful, dapple-grey mare with a mane as white as snow.

She came easily behind me as I led her.

"Good girl," I said as I unbuckled the bridle that separated her jaws. "What's your name?" Of course, I received nothing in return but a snort, but that was enough for me. There were only a handful of horses in the stables these days—the Count's men had come to collect many of them in exchange for a knight's fee, as we had no fighters on the land but a few wapenknechten lay brothers. The horses that remained were big, tough horses—perfect for ploughing fields and drawing carts, but not for riding. The mare that I gently led was the smallest among them. I led her to her stall. It had the name *Guus* written on it—the name of one of the wild stallions that lived here before and now trotted his way through the North. Now, it was her resting place until her master decided to leave. I brought her a trough. She must've been thirsty, because she indulged in the water with great haste, sending it all straight up that long, furry neck of hers. While she drank, I brought her a bushel of hay—cut yestermorn, a part of the midsummer harvest, resting in the shed that overlooked the scythe-swinging serfs that reaped it. Hungrily, she began to tear the bushel apart bit by bit, munching happily. As she was merrily distracted, I began to pick her hooves. One by one, I lifted each leg, taking great care to secure her leg in place as I first scooped out all the muck from the wet, muddy, Dutch roads, and then brushed furiously at it until the hoof was cleaner than my own two feet. Then came the next, and the next, and the next. Next, I brushed her fur, running my brush all over her, dusting off all the loose hairs caught in her coat, followed by her mane and tail. Once it was all done, I decided to wash her off with a rag dipped in some water I fetched from the well. It was quite hot out—I'd wished I could bathe myself too - but that could not be until my chores were complete.

"I'm going to call you Marjolein," I said with a smile, petting her nose. Before I would leave her to attend to my daily cleaning, I ran off to the orchard to pick her a fresh apple. My smile broadened at the orchard when, to my surprise, I saw Sister Florie beneath an apple tree munching away and practicing her letters on a piece of birch bark. Either that, or she was making funny drawings as she loved to do.

"Look at this one!" she said, showing me the bark scroll. "It's a cat dressed up as a girl!" she said with a broad smile. I laughed—I had never seen a cat dressed as a girl and the deep, misshapen lines made it all the more amusing.

"One day, you'll be drawing like an illuminator," I said to Florie.

"And you'll be singing like the sister of the choir," she said to me.

"I will be *in* the choir," I replied with a grin. "And you can watch from the pews as I sing my hours nocturns."

"You'd be lucky if you grow up to be a recluse," she said with a teasing smile.

"Finally, I'd have some peace and quiet," I replied. "How come you get to lounge around while I'm hard at work?"

"I finished my morning chores," she said, sticking out her tongue. "The latrines are all prim and proper."

"No fair," I said.

"What are you up to today?" she asked me. I picked up a bright apple from the dirt. "A man came today with a beautiful horse. I get to take care of her."

"Can I see her?" Florie asked, already letting her piece of birch fly away in the breeze. "Come with me," I said, taking her hand as we quickly made our way towards the stables, half skipping and half running. Marjolein loved the apple—she loved it so much that we decided to go back and fill a whole sack of them for her. It was when we were filling that sack that Mother Roos approached us.

"What are you two girls doing?" she asked. "Thieving apples from the orchard?"

"The rider's horse wanted apples, that's all, and…" Florie began to say.

"It was all my idea," I added. "I'm so sorry, Mother Abbess."

"I'd ought to bring you both to the chapter house," she said to us sternly. "The judicial sisters would have a word for you." She had a change of expression, though, which permitted me to exhale the breath I hadn't realized I was holding in. "Nay, I'd ought better to feed you both to a gryllus, or ship you off to the lands of Africa where the blemmyes might eat you alive." It was clear that she was making a joke now as the wrinkles about the corners of her eyes perked up ever so slightly. "It is nearly the day of the Assumption of the Blessed Virgin Mary, not to mention 'tis the season of the Saint Lawrence Feast, so I suppose I'd have mercy on you two delinquents. However, you must understand the workings of the convert. The fine man to whom this horse belongs will ride for Leyden on the morrow, accompanied by several of our lay brothers who will take our wares and goods, including the apples which you have not yet consumed, to the market. It's a faire day, and the merchants will all be there—buyers and sellers alike are bound to get hungry. You will be present, and you will observe how the sale of these goods is important to us here. *And,* you will write a report to me of your wrongdoing and how sorry you both are by the next morning. Understood?"

"Yes, Mother Abbess," we both replied in unison.

"Hand me the sack and tend to the horse, sisters," she said.

+ Florie +

Our morning barley porridge tasted stale. It might well have been the scraps from the previous harvest being finished on us lay sisters. At the very least it was something—Christ did provide, but it might well have been nicer to enjoy our breakfast from home, the warm freshly-baked bread and cheese and salt herring. But, porridge it was. Porridge and silence. Thoughts were the only thing that passed the time, really. The orator wet on and on about her parables and the natural order of things. Men are better than women, women better than beasts, beasts better than birds, and so on. My mind instead drifted to better thinks, merrier things, things to come. We would see the town today. Merin looked quite content. I was far more excited than she was, I think. With my spoon, I drew a funny face in the porridge. It had become a habit to try to make Merin laugh during mealtimes—to get her in trouble. But, today she only looked at it, and smiled at me, and continued to smile away. She really must've been excited.

The gates of the city were tall and looming, just like the gates to the convent. Across the bridge, great oaken doors crested with the crossed keys welcomed us. Through them, we were greeted by the men of the watch and a bustling, vibrant community about its day. Men, women, and children all hurriedly made their way through the streets with a cacophony of sound—a far cry from the tranquil existence of the convent.

"Come with me," the man said, leading us and the entourage of lay brothers through the streets. He was a quiet man, gaunt, aged, and thin as a skeleton. A man of the cloth, no doubt. His tonsure made that evident. His habit was a raven black, and his mantle a plain white. He must've been a Carmelite. The nuns preferred colourful gowns. That was except for their wimples, which were all a deep black, as were their cloaks. We, on the other hand, were too young to wear wimples, and as such our hair was freely plaited into a shape like a pretzel.

It had been so long since we'd been to town. Mother always used to take the boys, but never us.

"Do you smell that, Florie?" asked Merin. "It smells so sweet!"

"Those must be pannekoeken," I replied, looking at the great frying pans with sizzling pancakes on top. Burghers lined up, each waiting their turn to enjoy the delicious treat. I felt my stomach growl in envy. I tugged on the man's habit.

"Can we have a snack? Please?" I asked him.

"I'm so hungry!" said Merin. He looked at us with an expressionless face.

"Just as Saint Benedict teaches us, a life of gluttony is a life of sin. These people here are all sinners, girls. You'd best take not so you don't join their ranks," he said. How could he not like pancakes?

The market square was alive most of all. It was the week of the annual faire, when merchants from across the Low Countries and all over Christendom would come to sell their wares. The streets were filled with performers too. Street musicians played for crowds of passersby, and magic men played tricks on unassuming onlookers. Dice tables, riddlers, sooth sayers, entertainers of all sorts conglomerated here. Our place in the market was small, but it was enough to fit the apples, textiles, and other goods produced at the convent.

"Now you girls sit here and watch, and don't go anywhere until the day is done. Understood?" asked the man. We nodded our heads. There was enough to see here—the platform in the main square still held all the important performances by travelling bards and minstrels and troubadours all looking to make a name for themselves through enthralling stories, folk songs, and lewd jokes. There were also, of course, criers, announcing the news of the world and of the war. Many brave knights rode to their deaths, it seems. What a terrible way to spend one's life— training and obsessing over the prectice of taking someone's else's. Absolutely disgusting, and boring too.

I picked up a rock from the ground and began to draw on the brick building behind us.

It wasn't lost before the rock which I'd thought I'd been guiding was soon guiding me, drawing my hand this way and that, etching out funny creatures and plants and animals. I drew the bards in the square and the apple trees from the orchard and the mangey cats walking by. Merin played with one of them, but in all honesty it looked a little gross to me with all the city dirt on it.

We watched as all sorts passed by. I tried my best to draw the different types I saw, sometimes asking the churchman who they were. There were the Jews with their tall, yellow hats. He said they'd all come running to the Low Countries because nobody wants them anywhere else, but I've heard of merchants telling of Jews in cities all over Christendom. Then there were the nobles all in fine, beautiful textiles. The burghers were hard to distinguish from them, in honesty, although they never wore any swords on them. Of course free peasants of all status walked about, labourers carrying things, artisans peddling their wares, fieldmen or city-dwellers buying those wares—all sorts. Then there were the serfs.

Much like the peasants, of course, you can't tell a serf from a peasant just by looking at them, but some accompanied their liege lords as bondsmen. They walked behind them, following their orders. The sisters of the convent always preached about the savagery of the Frisian slavers, but, looking at these serfs, and looking back on my life in the fief, I could only pick out a handful of differences.

I found myself sketching one interesting man in particular. I'm not sure if he was supposed to be part of the festivities—it certainly didn't seem like it. After one performance in the centre square, he proudly announced himself as a 'speaker of the people.'

"I speak to you all of the events in Frisia, and in Kennemerland, and in your own yards!" he announced. "Count Florens has forsaken his domain. His people starve! You all feel its effects—bread has doubled in its price, the grain to make it too! Our yield this year was scant, not just here, but across the country. The Lord is punishing us! Shame! Shame!

Our nobles ride to war and take our young men with them! For shame! They will feel the wrath of God! They, like tyrants, burn the country on their way up and back! Foreign knights come to savage our girls while on the campaign! Shame! Frisian slavers against unholy tyrants— but who will fight for Heaven? Who will fight for Earth? Shame!" he preached. He went on and on, most people paying little heed to him, until he was eventually arrested by a set of town watch goedendagers and beaten bloody for heresy and treason. They left him a pile of bones and bruises on the streets, where he was pickpocketed and left for scant until a barber-surgeon and his journeyman came with a stretcher to fetch him. Of course, most of the while, the churchman told Merin and me to avert our gaze, which we did, on occasion. People simply wanted to ignore him—paying him no heed so that they could enjoy their day at the faire. The churchman said he was mad and a fool and that he was the one forsaken by God for past wrongs or a stain on his soul. But I still drew him, folding the paper and tucking it tight into the belt that clenched tightly to my kirtle gown.

Even though there was a faire, just like any day, the criminals of the town were put in the stocks for all to see. Today, two hooded boys, young by the looks of it, were led up to the central podium. An alderman read out their sentences—three days in the stocks for both of them on the grounds of pickpocketing and illegal fighting. This sentencing was overseen by the Lord of Leyden, Heer Walraven—a short man who proudly bore his blue and gold heraldic surcoat with no armour underneath nor sword at his belt. I suppose he didn't need it with a set of town watchmen following him wherever he went with sharp-looking goedendags and crossbows in their hands and badelaars at their hips.

"Look away, girls." the churchman said to us, physically turning us around when the criminals were brought up for all to see. "The guild-masters' justice is no sight for you younglings," he said. Merin obliged, returning to her new-found feline friend. I, on the other hand, was not content.

Without him knowing, I turned around to watch the ceremony. I had never seen a public punishment before—I had heard that they were quite common in the city. In Duivenvoorde, while it happened, it was quite rare, and where they happened was off-limits for me and my sisters.

"These boys need to learn to respect their fellow man," announced Lord Walraven.

"As such, the court has deemed them worthy of the stocks. The court sees this punishment to be merciful. Let it be known to anyone who would seek to rob and thieve in this city that they will be treated with the harshest fist the aldermen and guildmasters have to offer. These boys own nothing now. Their coin has been returned to the people of Leyden. Do not attempt to do the same, or you will be caught, and, mark my words, you will be hung."

"Alright, alright, Heer Walraven." interjected an older-looking man in long, flowing clothes and a funny hat. "Nobody will be hung for thieving, unless you thieve enough. To any pickpockets out there, lurking in the crowds, we will indeed find you. But, to the rest of you lovely, God-fearing people, have an excellent faire."

"Who is he?" I asked the churchman.

"What's it to you, nunling?" he asked.

"He seems important. If you tell me I'll go back to my drawings."

"If you must know, that is the alderman Reyncken the Long."

"The Long?"

"Because of how tall he is," the churchman said. I hadn't noticed it before, but now as the man climbed the steps and stood himself next to the little lord, he did, in fact, seem nearly twice his height.

"I suppose, he is quite long," I said.

"Impressive for a man of that age. The Lord has blessed him well."

"I think he drank a lot of milk," I replied.

"Milk?"

"Mother always said to drink our milk when we were young so that we'd grow fair and tall," I said. The churchman gave me a warm smile—the first kind expression I'd seen from him.

"Your mother was indeed right," he said. "Our Heavenly Father created the cow and the milk to grow us tall and strong to craft us into better servants of his will."

"Amen," said one of the lay brothers managing the apples who'd overheard our conversation. I was quickly distracted from the conversation when I, in the corner of my eye, saw who the boys were when their hoods were unveiled.

"The boys Maurits and Thiel of Duivenvoorde are to serve three days in the stocks and will soon thereafter be returned to their rightful lord in Duivenvoorde," the alderman spoke.

+ Maurits +

Even in the darkest nights, under the most frigid rain, Thiel managed to crack jokes. "Alright, here's one Father's mates used to say at the alehouse. So, in Gent, a young

282

woman was on the point of delivering a baby. She had long been enduring acute pain, and the midwife, candle in hand, inspected her secret area, to see if the child was coming. You know what she says? *Look also on the other side, my husband has sometimes taken that road,"* he cracked with a broad smile. I know not what that meant, but I'm sure it was quite funny so I gave him a laugh.

"My turn, my turn," I said to him, biting through the cold and the hunger. "Why are the Flemish kids on Tanner Street so fat?" I asked.

"I don't know, why?" asked Thiel.

"The reason is simple," I said. "Dutchmen work alone at manufacturing their kids, but when Flemings are away at sea, they have quite a number of assistants in the making of theirs."

"Oh, that's a good one," he said, laughing as hard as he could without knocking his head against the stockade. "You remember farmer Cornelis? Remember how he kept asking around about his wife? Well, I heard that he emasculated himself with his own hands." That was too funny.

"Now," I mocked, *"if my wife becomes pregnant, she will not be able to hide that she's the village honey crispel."* It sent Thiel squealing. As he laughed, I saw the misty downpour part in the darkness. A figure was there. No, two. Short ones—not Walpurga and her boys.

"Maurits? Thiel? Is that you?" asked the voice of a young girl from the darkness. I was shocked. I looked at Thiel.

"You hear this?" I whispered.

"It's not just me?" he replied.

"Florie?! Merin?" I replied to the shadows. The next thing I felt, before I could even make them out, was a warm hug from small hands.

"I'm so happy to see you both!" exclaimed Thiel, wriggling around in the stocks to try and hug them back but to no avail.

"You have to get us out of here," I said. Merin fiddled around with the lock. "We can't; we need a key. We have bread, though," she said, pulling a warm, sweet-smelling loaf from an old rag.

"And apples!" added Florie, dropping a sack full of them before us. I didn't care that they were covered in muck—they looked delicious, and I was hungry. While Merin tore chunks of the loaf to feed Thiel, Florie shoved the apple in mine like I was a feast pork.

"Ow!" I hollered, muffled by the juicy, red fruit. I felt its juices trickle down my chin.

"I can see your ribs!" exclaimed Florie. "You're so bony! Like skeletons!"

"There hasn't been much to eat," I replied.

"No, you just only eat waffles which cost a whole guilder more than a loaf, you fatty," jested Thiel. I saw a light flickering through the streets.

"The town watch," I said. "Hide."

"Why?" asked Merin, looking at me confused as always.

"We're in the stocks, Merin. You can't be caught feeding us!" I exclaimed.

"But the sisters in the convent teach us charity and to care for the sick and…"

"Enough, go now or else they'll catch you both!" I said. "You can come back later if nobody's around."

"Wait," said Thiel, "If you don't find us again…"

"Why wouldn't we find you again?"

"No matter, if you don't, know that Piet is in the city. We saw him."

"How was he?"

"Better than us," I said with a smile. Thiel kicked my shin with the studs of his turnshoe. "Ow!"

"Knock it off, the watch will hear," he hissed at me. "Piet looked good—plump as always, and growing. Last I saw him he stood to about my shoulders."

"But that's because you're an imp," I said. Thiel chuckled.

"Go now, and find Piet in the morning if you can. I'm sure he'll be happy to see you."

Thiel said. Merin stuffed some final pieces of bread in our mouths before the two of them scampered off into the dark.

Chapter 14. The Butchery: Maarten

"I don't want to see none of you louts yacking before the enemy," announced Geerbrant, waving his mace around like a sceptre. "So get it all out now. You're not recruits no more—you're veterans. We stand, or we die, so if I see any of you mangy rats gettin' weak in the knees, I'll smash 'em in for ye free of charge." As he spoke, we heard the Frisians chanting. They were all around us, on all sides, beating their shields with their spears, raising their pikes high in the air, and chanting in their ancient tongue. The thickness in the air could be felt in the hair on our hands. Our anticipation grew as the Frisians' chants grew louder. The echo was ominously around us. Our village was on the brink of a bloody confrontation.

It was not night. It was not an ambush or a raid or some sort of clandestine attack. They had mustered to do battle. I'll admit fear shook me to my core. Everywhere you looked or raised an ear, you'd hear their brutal voices on the wind.

"What are we waiting for?" asked Kees, impatient and eager. "Let's go out there and get 'em."

"They outnumber us, Kees," I said. "We have a better chance in here than out there."

"We're gonna die," said Felix. "I know it, we're gonna die."

"If you die, then die like a man," said Geerbrant. "On your own two feet and with a weapon in your hand," he said, shoving Felix's voulge into his hands.

After several hours of standing all lined up in formation and listening to the chants, my knees had grown tired. We'd begun to hollar our own chants back at them—singing the *Tale of Saint Dagobert, The Goode and Fyne Yellow Sheep,* and the *Lady of Doordrecht.* But they weren't to intimidate the enemy—no they were to keep our boys on their toes. To keep them sharp, and to keep them together. Felix did not look happy. Even Kees looked stressed at what was to come. We had become hardened warriors, sure, but this—this is not an experience any man should face. The devils across the marsh stared at us hauntingly. The flat, wet, field was ripe for the Frisians to march across. Our country boys, spears in hand, and the goedendagers from the cities, plugged every street, every road leading into the village.

Houses were barricaded and turned into infirmaries. Traps were lain across the field, hidden deep in the mud, and through the streets if you knew where to look. Knights, men-at-arms, and wapenknechten all fought among us, often forming the first line of shining steel maille and bright heraldic colours. Heer Arend dismounted to fight among us as well; his black and white templar shield out in front of him and his white surcoat with the red cross over his heart marking his piety.

"Today is the day of Saint Philibert," he announced to us, marching up and down our ranks, greathelm in hand so that we could actually hear him. The men of the Wassenaer had all compiled into one unit now. At our head, behind Heer Arend, were his son, Floris, his brother, Heer Jan, the new Baron of Raephorst, young Dideric, limping, and their old family friend, who had brought the most men with him of all, Heer Ghijsbrecht van Amstel. "Now, you may know little of this man, and for that, I blame you not; it was only through my education as a templar that I learned of him. What he did does not matter to you on this day. What does matter is that when the Northmen came to France to pillage their lands and take their people, just as the Frisians do to us now, it was the relics of Saint Philibert that protected so many monks from slaughter and enslavement. Similarly, on this blessed day, we stand to face the heathen, and when they finally muster the courage to fall upon us, we will send them straight to Hell!" His speech was met with loud cheers from our men. I cheered as well—who could blame them? We needed something to give us the courage to fight. Something to tell us that we would make it out alive. And then Jan stepped forward.

"Gentlemen, warriors all. I address you today not only as your rightful lord, not only as a knight, a man of steel and blood but as a father. A father who lost his only son. They took my boy Jacob from me. But think not of Jacob; think of the many others they have seen fit to end before you. Think of your comrades. Think of every brother in arms who has since been pelted with arrows, or every farmhand with whom you used to till who now rests on the end of a pike. Some say that these men fight only for their homes. Nay, these men are harbingers of death. Devils, they are. They fight with no honour, hiding in the forests, strafing across the bogs like phantoms. I will have none of it. They trespass upon us. They enslave our people. They pirate our ships. They steal our cattle. Most importantly, they slew our great Count and Emperor Willem. We now bring them vengeance! We now bring them death!"

"Hurrah! Hurrah! Hurrah!" the men cried.

"Death to the heathen!" shouted Heer Arend.

"Death to the barbarians!" echoed young Floris. What had happened to him? He was once a pompous, stuck up nobleboy. Now, he spake like a full man, hardened by war and by loss. He looked different now—new creases shot across his face. He stood taller now, and his steps had more weight to them.

The cheering continued for quite some time. Some men even put down their weapons to run out, stick up their middle fingers at the Frisians, hurl insults, and show off their manlihoods. The excitement only built throughout the day—standings and waiting. Priests made their way from unit to unit to say grace and hand out bread as communion. We were starving, so the hunks we got were truly blessed indeed.

Around midday, I finally watched as a team of Frisian outriders with crosses decorated on their round shields looking to be guarding an emissary, and leading heavily bloodied and beaten prisoners of war with ropes bound to their hands, came forth to speak with our Count. I watched as a party full of knights, with the Count at the head, met them in the centre of the field.

+ Floris +

"Good boy," I said to my horse. It was a courser—after Galahad was slain, I couldn't find any other destriers. But, if a courser was good enough for the Count's men-at-arms, he was good enough for me. His yellow trapper had been stained bloody by Frisians and Hollanters alike. My retainers hadn't gotten a chance to clean it off, what with all the defensive preparations and foraging and the like. Our food stores were running out—it was a good day to die.

289

"Good day, gentlemen," said the Frisian spokesman in a surprisingly highborn Dutch.

Of course, like all foreigners, he still spoke with a thick accent. The Count said nothing in response, but opened his gilded chainmail coif so as to ready his mouth to speak. "I represent the Protestaat of the West Frisians."

"Who are you?" the Count asked.

"I am his chosen emissary, Lord Florens."

"That is Count Florens V."

"Yes, my Lord."

"Yes, Count Florens V. Say it."

"Yes, Count Florens V," the man echoed sheepishly. Then, Florens relieved his hand of his gilded chainmail mitten, revealing a ring on his third finger with the heraldic seal of Hollant. He extended it to the man wordlessly. Afraid of misstepping, the man dismounted his steed and kissed the ring.

"Good," said Count Florens. "Now we can speak as honourable and honest men." The man then handed the Count a scroll with a bright scarlet wax seal. "What is this?"

"The Protestaat's terms," the messenger replied. The Count sneered.

"This is a joke. This must be," he replied. He hadn't even broken the seal before he tossed it to the muddy sod. "That is not how this works."

"My Lord…"

"*Count.*"

"Count Florens, I suggest you consider his terms," the man said, retrieving the scroll from the dirt.

"He places a seal as if he has the authority to plant his own bollocks crest on anything. Your Protestaat is no noble. He is no lord; he is common," evidently disgruntled, the man replied. "Our Heavenly Father made all men in his image," he said, handing the scroll to the Count once more. The Count spat to the mud.

"Clearly not," he said with a laugh. "You dare speak to me as if you were a learned man? You Frisians, always so entitled. You dare see yourselves as your own masters—God will strike you down. You give me terms? Nay, I give you ours. We will never surrender to the likes of you, scum. Hollant will not give an inch to the barbarian horde—just as Karel once stood mightily against the Saracen, and our people nobly stood against the Northmen."

"Please, Count Florens, I urge you to reconsider. Every one of your men will be put to the sword. You would be too—those were the Protestaat's orders. He ordered every man to bring him your head on a plate."

"Enough! Insolent wretch. You are nothing. Nobody. You dare give me counsel? You are the shit that slips beneath my gold-plated maille chausses."

"Count Florens…" interjected Father.

"What?" the Count replied tersely.

"It pains me to admit this, but he is right," Father said. "We can avoid the bloodshed if we at least hear their terms."

"These savages are not to be trusted," said the Count.

He turned now to the spokesman. "Tell your master that the Hollanters will not give an inch. And that if he seeks to drive us from his land, he should do so with haste, lest God think he a sluggard." The Count wheeled his horse around, and began to trot back to Heiloo. Father and I followed him.

Soon that trot turned into a canter, and then a gallop.

"To arms!" the Count shouted. "To arms, men of Hollant. The heathen wishes to make war, and we shall meet their desires with blood and steel!"

As I looked back to the surrounding battleline, I noted the Frisians raising great crosses made of wood above them—an appeal to a false god. They then knelt to pray.

As they did so, the Count decided it was best to ride up and down the lines, swinging his sword and shouting, "For Hollant! For the Crown! For God! We will bring the scum to their knees! We will show them how true Dutchmen fight! When they come to you, hold your goedendags and your spears and swords firmly, and strike hard and true. Saint Michael and Saint George fight alongside us this day! Show courage, men, and they shall lead you to victory!"

He was met with great cheers. Say what you will about his disdain for the lower echelons; he knew how to get them excited. The soldiers loved him, cheering loudly as he passed on his horse. Young boys even clamoured forth through the lines to catch a glimpse of their Count in golden armour. To them, he might as well have been a king or the Emperor of Rome himself, so spare God. Loud, bellowing, *hurrahs* filled the air. It was only eventually cut short when the first wave emerged from the enemy line. To screen their advancing infantry, the Frisians sent out skirmishers first. Lightly armed, with bows and javelins and slings, they begin to unload a barrage onto our men. Of course, it was not enough to do anything significant, but it was enough to pin them all in place and instill what fear they could.

I spurred on my horse to quickly carry me back to the men of the Wassenaer with my Father. It wasn't long before the men of Hollant replied with missiles of their own, sending out the schutterij—urban militia watchmen—and rural crossbowmen to respond with volleys of bolts. Some shepherd boys armed with slings joined them, as did the levied burghers of the longbow shooting clubs and the mercenary English longbow company of the High Weald. It wasn't long before the two parties were exchanging projectiles, filling the air with bits of steel and stone zipping about like a beaten hornet's nest.

"Stay firm, men!" ordered Father. "Keep your shields up and your heads down. The bastards can't hurt you as long as you don't run."

I wish he was right. Surely enough, shields caught most of the projectiles, and I noticed the occasional arrow getting stuck in a gambeson or a stone glanding off a helmet, but some men were hit, and when they were hit it was gruesome. Not unlike the wounds that struck Gherrijt. It took every ounce of will I could muster not to order a charge to cut all of them down. Of course, knowing those dogs, they lacked all forms of honour—it was to be expected that they would rather murder their foe from afar than strike at them close like men. But nay, they fought seldom like men—more often akin to little girls, running at the first sight of blood, only making sure they'd done their dirty work.

This time was different, though. They hadn't come to ambush us, or sneakily slaughter us in the night. They hadn't come to launch missiles at use down from the edge of a ravine, or strike at us from the woods. Nay, they had come to do battle—true, Christian battle. They too caught many bolts and arrows on their shields, emerging across the wetland like a wall of porcupines. But, our traps had done their work. Caltrops, buried deep in the mud and pools of rainwater, pierced through their feet like a knife through fine butter.

To make matters worse for them, while we took refuge behind barricades and buildings, they advanced, bogged down in the mud, soaking arrows like a depressed game boar. And yet, as an unrelenting wall of bristling spears and shields, they advanced. Behind them, we could see the tall shafts of an even stronger foe—the Frisian pikemen. Like a moving forest of birch trees, they advanced behind their shielded brothers in arms, ready to confront the Brabantian pikemen and feudal levy in a push of pike. But we had planned for them.

Hidden in the streets behind us were two more contingents: one from Arnemuiden and the other the men of Wateringen. At the perfect moment, just as the Frisian battle line made its way into the village, Father gave the order.

"Charge!" he shouted. With a surge of courage, our men hurled ourselves at the enemy. Myself in the frontline alongside the other knights and wapenkechten, supported by our levies who hurled jabs between us with their polearms, we smashed into the enemy.

Meanwhile, the men of Arnemuiden and Wateringen

flooded the streets from the sides. With nowhere to maneuver or form their pike wall, the Frisian pikemen had been pinned in place and caught off guard, dropping their long pikes to reach for more wieldable weapons in the ensuing brawl. Ours was the first retinue to make contact with the enemy. Soon after, we heard fighting erupt on all sides of the village, as the Frisians slowly attempted to push their way to the centre and envelope the other retinues. The air was filled with hollars of "For Hollant! For Zeelant! For Utrecht! For den Haghe!" and so on. I couldn't help but shout my own, "For Duivenvoorde! For the Wassenaer!" I hurled my shield over my shoulder, letting it dangle on my back, wielding Stonesplitter in two hands. I felt a rush come over me. Left, right, and centre, I hacked and slashed at the enemy, felling them one by one as their blows fruitlessly smashed into my chainmail hauberk. It wasn't long before their horns of retreat began to sound.

"Chase them out!" cried Ghijsbrecht, swinging his flail about—splintering shield and bone alike. As the raiders routed, we chased after them, cutting them down as they tripped over one another, attempting to escape.

+ Maarten +

Kees, Felix, Geerbrant, and I were running as fast as we could—chasing after the Frisians with weapon in hand.

"Piss off ye damn bastards!" Geerbrant cried. The stuffy horde of human mass quickly dispersed as we poured out of the streets and into the field—fresh air. The soil was already wet, and now beneath the feet of hundreds of warriors the ground became slippery and coated in mud. Each man quickly became brown as we wrestled and stumbled on the field—dagger came out to finish the job. Men suffocated beneath the weight of all the fighters. After some time, we found that there were no Frisians left to kill—only writhing about in the muck to try and find Dutchmen.

"Hit the others from the flanks," ordered Heer Jan.

"Reform the line!" shouted Heer Arend. The brothers, now standing side-by-side, led the charge. We hit a second Frisian contingent from the rear—encircling them and boxing them into the crammed street completely. I heard a young Count Florens shouting,

"Drop your weapons and you'll live! Drop your weapons, and you'll live!" Nobody responded, until his herald said the same words in Frisian, but those who did were too few to discern. The fighting slowed.

"To Hell with it, kill them all," said Ghijsbrecht. "No quarter for the craven."

"No quarter for the craven!" men shouted in echo as they descended on their enemy. "No quarter! Not one, many left!" I saw Arend take hold of Ghijsbrecht.

"That is not honourable. We should spare the rest," he shouted, not out of anger but out of sheer necessity to communicate over the shouting and chaos.

"They have no noblemen among them. They are scarcely Christians. Mercy has no place here," replied Ghijsbrecht with a sneer. "God knows his own—let Him sort them out."

"The men you slay will be on my conscience and mine alone!" ordered Count Florens. "God sees not your sins, only mine!" he exclaimed. "And by God, I will take the godverdomde day," he muttered to himself.

The chaos raged on, only finally breaking when a wave of men shouted, "Arrows! Take cover!" swept over the battlefield. Godverdomme—it had been a trap.

Our new exposed rear was the perfect target for Frisian skirmishers who took complete advantage of the situation. The gambeson-clad infantrymen at the rear fell like row after row of autumn leaves. Panicking, the nobility shouted conflicting orders.

"Sally out! Get them on the run!" ordered Arend.

"Form a shield wall!" ordered Jan. Ghijsbrecht said nothing but had his personal retinue of men-at-arms fetch horses from the village centre to mount a cavalry charge. Of course, there were too few of them. Wait a minute, he was launching no charge at all. Digging deeply, he spurred his horse onwards away from the field, finding the nearest place of foliage and bolting straight for it. The coward.

"Forward, boys!" shouted young Floris, now taking command. "With me!" he said, retrieving his shield and leading a retinue of men towards the barrage of javelins and arrows and sling stones.

"With Floris," Geerbrant commanded, pointing to him with his mace before a stray arrow sent him straight to the ground.

"Good God, Geebrant's taken an arrow!" cried Felix. Quickly, I scanned his body for it—it had hit him straight in the collar bone, snapping through and puncturing deep into his chest. He couldn't speak—only coughing and wriggling about in pain. I held him, as did Kees. The arrows kept coming. I took a hold of his shield and raised it above him to protect us.

"We do this for Geerbrant," said Felix. "We follow Floris." Kees just shouted angrily. Hastily, we joined the advancing battleline. We advanced across the field, determined to deal a crushing blow to their men. Like rabbits, they routed immediately, sprawling about the fields to avoid contact at all costs. They ran to the trees, to the camp, and some even would rather jump into the river than confront us. And then came one final blow—more of them, as if they were an endless wave, emerged from the camp. They had a second battleline in store, ready to come and kick our teeth in. No orders were shouted—at this point, it had become routine. We simply turned and braced.

+ Floris +

Somehow, there were more of them. These, clad in scale armour, some shirtless, all with shaven sides of their heads, were the elite of the Frisian army. The rearguard. The trained fighters. Like wild animals, they charged, shouting and screaming as they smashed into us. I could not see how many they had. I unstrapped my greathelm and tore it off my head—I needed to breathe. Silently, I muttered a prayer to myself as I saw them approach. Frankly, what precisely I was saying did not register—the words of the prayer had become muscle memory at this point. Faster than I could vocalize, I mouthed the words, going through the motions, but training my eyes keenly on the enemy.

"Grant me, I beseech Thee, almighty and most merciful God, fervently to desire, wisely to search out, and perfectly to fulfill, all that is well-pleasing unto Thee. Order Thou my worldly condition to the glory of Thy name; and, of all that Thou requirest me to do, grant me the knowledge, the desire, and the ability, that I may so fulfill it as I ought, and may my path to Thee, I pray, be safe, straightforward, and perfect to the end. Give me, oh Lord, a steadfast heart, which no unworthy affection may drag downwards; give me an unconquered heart, which no tribulation can wear out; give me an upright heart, which no unworthy purpose may tempt aside. Bestow upon me also, oh Lord my God, understanding to know Thee, diligence to seek Thee, wisdom to find Thee, and a faithfulness that may finally embrace Thee. Amen."

"We welcome death, boys!" shouted Uncle Jan. "For the Crown! For Hollant!"

"For Hollant!" the men echoed as we advanced to meet the Frisians in kind. This was death. This was the endless horde that would slay me. But, like Raoul de Cambrai or Roland or Arthur, I would die on my feet, a sword in one hand and a shield in the other. We heard their battle cry.

"Fryslan! Fryslan! Fryslan!" they shouted in unison.

"Come and take it!" I replied. The lines smashed. Spears and swords and axes hacked and bit at us. I raised my shield over my visage to offer it some defense as I recklessly slashed at all that was in front of me. It wasn't long before I saw my brothers fall around me. Dutchmen, Hollanters, fell all around, giving way to the Frisian horde. "Stand your ground!" I shouted. "Give them not a single inch!" And then, like Saint Michael himself, Father, leading a contingent of riders, swept the field. The Frisians, so focused on beating us back, had no idea of their advance. Like phantoms, with

Father at the helm with his flowing, templar cloak behind him, shattered Frisians with their lances, impaling them, stacking them like pork skewers, some three men deep.

"We bring death!" shouted Father. "Death to the enemy!" When he got to me, he swung off of his horse, sending it off to the tree line. "We stand and fight together," he told me. I could barely hold my sword. I had grown tired, and weak. I was wounded, I realized, bruised and broken all over. But Father stepped in the way. His snow-white templar surcoat flashed about as he slaughtered Frisians in droves. I helped him as much as I could. I had never seen him fight this way—taking on ten men at once like a paladin of the tales. "Run," he told me when he looked back.

"Nay, I stay and fight with you."

"Run!" he insisted. I didn't respond; I only kept fighting. And then, an axe caught me from behind. They were all around us now. I was dragged to the much. I felt three men pin me down, and I saw a dagger plunge towards my exposed visage. And then I saw an arming sword slice the hand off. Then, the man's head. Father came in again, taking all three before he then took a spear to the back of his leg.

"No!" I shouted. I wanted to stand up and fight, but I just couldn't. I felt the energy surge through me but to no avail. My hauberk weighed me down. I felt myself being dragged through the muck. They were Father's retainers from France.

"Nay! No! Non! Non!" I shouted, struggling to free myself, but it was too late.

"God and Glory," I heard father mutter as he took three Frisians with him. Finally, a spear pierced his hauberk from behind, and then a sword slipped up his coif. He fell to the floor, limp like meat.

I couldn't believe it. I watched him fall, and the world around me seemed to have slowed down. My father was now lifeless, sprawled in the mud. One day he was alive, and well, and we were training together and laughing together. We rode with each other and played games. He sang his merry tunes. And now, he lay dead. Gone. I would never get another moment. It was over too soon. Too quickly. I wanted to go back. Just one more hour with him. One more minute. Please. I had to be near him. I had to…

Chapter 15. The Insurrection: Piet

"You know, Piet," said Master Waleran, "I once met a man. His name was Willem van Rubruck. A friar—one of the Franciscans."

"Yeah?" I asked, watching the pea soup fall off my spoon and back into the bowl again over and over. The soup made a small splash every time, but no ripple. It just tore through the ever-growing layer of pea film, which now encased the surface since it had been poured and began to cool. I watched each spoonful join its compatriots, or I suppose its body, however, one might think of it.

"Are you listening, Piet?" Waleran asked in a surprisingly gentle tone. I let the spoon slip comfortably into the bowl, resting its grip on the rim. I nodded my head and sat up. "He was an adventurer. He went all over the world."

"Did he find the end of it?"

"No. Not *that* far," said Master Waleran with a smile. We joked. I suppose I hadn't put much thought into it when in Duivenvoorde, but here, with my studies, I had become much more knowledgeable. I knew that the earth was round now, like a ball, and that our side of it was divided into three by the Mediterranean, the Hellespont, and the Nile, into Europa, Asia, and Africa. We Europeans derive from Japheth, Master Waleran says. Shem received Asia, and Ham received Africa. Master Waleran also warned me that, though many churchmen would have me believe of Ham's curse, it is the heat of the sun and the height of the sky that darken the folk of Africa, he says it's because they are of a low geographic clime, and so the sun's rays darken them. He also taught me about the blemmyes and long-eared men of Africa and the cynocephali of the North—the same land where the pagans came from in the times of Karel. Master Waleran always taught me things. He was no Lord Hillebrant, of course, but he was, at least, a good storyteller. "This van Rubruck fellow, quite a smart man the last I spoke to him, travelled all the way through the Middle Orient to the lands of the Khan."

"The Khan?"

"Yes, the Khan!" he said. "And there, among the pagan Tatars, he found another society of Christians."

"Living with the pagans?"

"High up in the mountains," said Master Waleran. "Willem's writings say they shaved their heads completely, unlike any monk in the vicinity of Rome's light, and they wear yellow robes," he said. "And hey fight, just as ours do too in the Holy Land," he said. I smiled—he knew I loved hearing about valiant crusaders. He was trying to cheer me up; I could feel it.

"Now, you'd better eat your pea soup before we return to your books." I looked at my bowl woefully. "Come now, it's not that bad. It's all in your head."

"When will Lord Hillebrant come back?" I asked him. That's what was really on my mind. Lord Hillebrant always said that to speak your mind is to be honest to oneself. He said it was a sign of respect—no matter how rude it might seem. Master Waleran always told me that folks don't like it when people do that in Germany, and in France, and in

England. I told him it's good that we're in the Low Countries.

"I don't know, Piet," he said to me with a sad expression on his face. I handed Pythagoras a hunk of bread—his furry belly plopped on my feet. "Once he has been put on trial?"

"When will that be?"

"It should be any day now. They must be waiting for some information before they proceed."

"What could they be waiting on?"

"Any number of things. You know how the Aldermen can be—slow and lazy. Perhaps they need some sort of record as proof of their conviction."

"Proof? What proof could there be if he is not guilty?"

"Lord Hillebrant is a cautious man—he doesn't play dice. I'm sure if there was proof of anything, he'd have a way to fight it."

"Will you watch the trial?"

"The aldermen have asked Lord Hillebrant to present himself twelve-handed. I will be one of his witnesses."

"What does twelve-handed mean?" I asked him.

"Ah, yes, this is good for you to know. When a court summons you, they may need witnesses to attest to your moral character and your presence in society. If they call you six-handed, they need six witnesses. Twelve-handed? Then twelve."

"And you can call upon just anyone?"

"Anyone who cares about you," Waleran said. "I suppose you could pick up a random wayfarer off the street, but I don't suppose you'd get very far with that sort of representation in a court."

"In the fief, when Lady Mehaud van Duivenvoorde held court, everyone was expected to watch. Even I did! There was never much of a trial, though—it was always more of a conversation. Lots of arguing."

"I don't suppose it might be much different here," said Waleran. "These lawmen think they're high and mighty because they have power—but really, they're playing with men's lives. Whatever they decide is true will inform what they do to Lord Hillebrant."

"Will they fine him?" I asked.

"They could," replied Waleran. "They could do worse things to him too. Like cutting off a finger. I suppose that would be better for him," he joked. "Let's not think about it—no use worrying over something we have no control over." I suppose he was right, but then… a spark flickered in my mind. Wait a minute; perhaps there was something we could do.

"Master Waleran, what if we surveyed Lord Hillebrant's records?" I asked.

"I'm sorry?"

"They accused him of sending money to somebody in Kennemerland, right?"

"Jaja. So?"

"So, if we can account for every grote that's traveled

through his purse, we can prove to the council that he is innocent!" Master Waleran began to stroke his beard.

"The Aldermen may not believe us, but if we have this all worked out before the trial, you're right. We might just be able to convince them to have their own record-keepers or mathematicians to look through it themselves. I just haven't a clue where to begin—I've never touched any of Lord Hillebrant's records."

"They're in his study—I can show you!" I said with a growing grin.

"Smart lad," said Master Waleran. "You really do take after your master," he said.

"Well then, drink up the rest of that soup or hand it to your pup—we have some work to do."

+ Maarten +

He was a good-looking young man with a square jaw, scrawny, and long brown hair that drooped over his eyes as he limped. In his heft hand was a collection of coin purses stuffed into a sack barely holding at the seams. With his right, he searched the dead, patting them down for anything that might feet his sack or that he might tuck into his belt, just like the bronze dagger he'd found off a Frisian. I watched him intently. I couldn't move. Honestly, I couldn't feel a thing. If you had told me the doctor was prying apart my musculature to find the last shard of a shattered iron bodkin arrowhead, I wouldn't have believed you. And yet, if I'd dared to look down, that's what I'd have seen. That, and blood. Horrible, excessive amounts of blood. Enough to stuff into a year's worth of sausages. And not all of it I could take ownership of. On my person, I noted the splatters of Frisian sap running its deep current through my linens.

"Of all the bastards this side of the Rijn, why in Hell did God decide to spare you?" joked Felix.

"Fate is a cruel gambler," I replied, letting the surgeon open me up like a herring. "I wish we could say the same for Geerbrant."

"With a wound like that, you'll be lucky if you keep the leg," said Felix.

"I don't need it; I already have two more," I said with a smile. Kees erupted in laughter when the joke finally dawned on him. "Any good loot?"

"Enough coin to keep us rich men for a year," said Felix.

"Lots of shiny stuff," said Kees. "Rings, earrings, metal teeth," he said, reaching into his pouch.

"Keep it in there, friend," I replied. The whole place reeked of blood and guts. I suppose there was not much that smelled nice on the campaign. The soft scent of Yda's hair felt like a distant memory now. It hadn't been particularly long, but we felt like different men. Real men, I suppose. We now joked about death, even when it was imminent, not softening to the fear of impending peril. Fear felt like nothing now—we fought, and we destroyed; that's how it was. In the aftermath of the battle, the lands felt calmer and stiller. Of course, the trees remained unsafe, with watchful eyes hidden in every crevice, but the truth was that danger felt disparate. We were hardened. There was not much more that would yellow our bellies—our spots in Hell were neatly reserved. Of course, I was not doing much fighting, what with a thigh torn apart like a shredded ham. The locals we interacted with told me that bogwater would help to cure it. It certainly did something—growing gangrene in the worst of places. The sight was unholy. I will not describe it further for fear of wetting the pages of your book. The lords had commanded us to garrison the North. The Frisians now belonged to us, as they put it. Under the maille chausses of the Empire, of the Count, and of all Dutchmen. Revenge, they called it. The subjugation of an inferior people. The scarlet lion flew high above us wherever we marched. Roaring with the wind. Triumphant. Our command, on the other hand, was shattered. A boy, his second-fiddle uncle, and their sadistic family friend were the triumvirate at our head. Floris' mind had gone from green to red to black now. He said little, ate little, and withered, seemingly wishing to join his father in the peat. Heer Arend had died a hero. A true defender of the faith, falling the only way a knight templar should—with a sword in hand and another through his chest.

The people were surprisingly friendly. I don't know if they were simply unaware of the horrible trespasses we made upon their kinsmen. Or, perhaps, they survive as the rat does, scurrying about the cat, unthreateningly, amiably, even, so as to avoid the fateful hour when the cat chooses its next meal. The women, in particular, varied in their response to us. The men, of course, either ignored us, spat at us in the wake of a harsh beating, or drank with us as men embracing fellow men. The women, on the other hand, either tightened as if they'd seen an army of ghosts or loosened as if we came as saviours returning to our faithful wives. Some of the boys had their fun. Others had their fun with the other girls. Many of us gagged when they did it. And looked away. And prayed for his soul. And prayed for her life.

We'd all thought that once the fighting was done' we'd be able to return home. We'd expected our owners to let slip our leeches. But we were bound with far more tenacity than ever we'd hoped. Men clad in maille ordered us about daily. And men padded in gambeson obeyed their command. At first, the rule was brutal and unforgiving. Frisians were beaten, abused, taxed, and humiliated publically. Then, even us soldiers had slowly had enough. The knights saw no honour in it. The nobles saw the whole ordeal as filthy. And we were left to make the decisions, calling the shots on the streets, in the alehouses, down every alley.

Enforcing curfews just like at home and calling the farmers out to work. New lordships were established. Every day the image of a life in the Wassenaer, in Duivenvoorde, seemed to fade. I'm not sure why—presumably, we'd be able to return at some point. But, of course, this new profession was life and death. Every week, Dutch soldiers were taken as reprisals for slaid Frisians. And in response, the Hollanter command would have us exact a toll on the people tenfold. In this environment, how could one possibly envision a life beyond tomorrow? The morrow was all we lived for. Our brothers in arms. Our ale. And admittedly, I found my eye slipping from Yda onto others. She was just an image in my head, a sensation in the palm of my hand, a memory. She wasn't real. These Frisian women were. And the looks they gave—even those who would not regularly consort with a Hollanter, I found emotion, depth behind their eyes. Every interaction charged with... something else. Perhaps I read too much into things. Other soldiers seemed to have no problem grabbing women and hoisting them onto their laps like household pets. And those women, usually, never seemed to fuss. But was it real? Was it ever real? When we were the invaders in their land, could they truly look into us, into our souls, and find what they were looking for? Or is it all an illusion? A game of power? Of soldiers hoping to have a fun night and girls looking to survive or provide for their families on Hollanter coin.

One night at the alehouse, where Kees, Felix, and I usually went after finishing our watch, the mood was of particularly high spirits.

"Did you hear the news, Maarten?" asked Kees as we entered.

"Jaja, of course he has," snapped Felix. "Freedom!"

"I've been out on watch all day," I replied. "What's got you boys smiling like that?"

"Some of us are going home," Kees said with a broad grin. "The Kennemers have had enough."

"You didn't hear it from me," said Felix, "But word is that Castle Heemskerk and Castle Old Haarlem have gone up in flames."

"Did the Frisians do this?" I asked, processing what he'd just told me. This was war, not in Frisia, but down south in Hollant. We'd brought the fight to Hollant. What evil had we unleashed?

"Nay, the Kennemers in Brederode. I suppose if I had to keep hauling ale carts to and fro across the country while a garrison of these bastards," he said, nodding to the rest of the company partying rowdily, "watched over my family, I'd have a thing or two to say as well."

"This is bad news, boys. What if it spreads down to the Wassenaer? To Duivenvoorde?"

"So what?" asked Felix. "Master Klaas and his boys will surely be out of there the moment they smell trouble."

"And what of Yda?" asked Kees to Felix. It warmed me a little to feel his empathy.

"Yda this, Yda that, you'll find yourself another Yda," said Felix. "Look around; there are Ydas all over the alehouse, not to mention this godverdomde land."

"Take that back, Felix. She's the reason we're here…"

"Nay, *you* got us into this mess. You are the one who got us bonded to a lord who now lies dead in a field somewhere. You had us throw our whole lives away. We had lives, Maarten. We were burners."

"I did this to save your bloody hides!" I exclaimed.

"So how exactly does Yda factor in, Maarten? You're a young man. There'll be plenty of women coming your way."

"I made a promise…"

"You don't owe her anything. You could've died on the campaign. Do you know how many soldiers make promises and then go off to fight somewhere else? Look around you. Look at these Frieske girls and their big, strong Hollanter boys."

"It's not the same thing."

"No? Does she know you're not even a Hollanter? No family here? Nothing to tie you down? You owe these people nothing, Maarten." He was right. I was Luxembourgish, no matter how concealed that could be. It meant little to me—it never came out in any way, but the fact I'd never told her… Come to think of it, there were so many things I'd never told her. Of my childhood. Of my past. Perhaps with more time? But did she even know who I was?

"I love you, Felix, but I've had enough of your schijt. I'm gonna get some air," I said, slamming my tankard down on the table. Kees got up to go with me. "Keep him company, Kees," I said.

The air was crisp. I looked out over the village's small dock—it was a fishing village on the coast of the North Sea. The sea breeze rushed against my face as I watched out over the crashing waves. Coated in nearly ashen white sand, the beach felt good on my feet. The grains nestled between my toes burrowed under my arches and splayed my muscles like a massage as I walked. I kept my hosen, turnshoes, and kettle hat in one hand and my glaive in the other. The water, though cold as a fresh tankard, enticed me. I dipped my feet in and looked down at my reflection as it shifted and stretched against the moving tide. Every time the water rushed against my shins, it felt a little less cold, like an embrace from a stranger who you know won't be for much longer. The silence was broken. There was never silence to begin with— the frogs and seagulls stained the air, but as if by a siren, I heard a voice carry its way over the salty wind. Faint. It reminded me of Yda's. But the words, the close I found myself, sounded like Frisian. Feet sinking farther and father into the sand, I made my way up the beach to where I heard it from. A voice to pierce even the darkest of nights—more beautiful than the moonlight, and more graceful than a swallow. And the girl who sang, doing her washing so late into the evening, singing all alone, I recognized her. I'd seen her around the village before—she'd caught the eye of many of the soldiers. I'd seen her give them looks, too, perhaps a few words, but I'd never heard of her giving anything more.

"Hallo?" she asked into the dark. My damn limp must've given me away.

"Sorry, I don't mean to frighten you," I replied, setting down my weapon and helmet and even taking off my gambeson to show I meant no harm. "I just heard your voice, and I had to see who could possibly make such music."

"You like it?" she asked, continuing to tend to her washing. "It reminds me of home," I replied.

"And where is that?" she asked. "Somewhere I haven't seen yet."

"Very mysterious," she said with a smirk. "Well, if you'd like, I'd be happy to have an audience. Washing can be quite boring without company."

"I can help," I said, rolling up my sleeves.

"That's quite kind of you," she said. "But no need; I'm sure you have better things to do. Besides, you don't get paid to stand around doing our washing, Dutchman."

"No, really, I don't need anything for it," I said. "Only to hear your song." She gave me a smile.

"It's an old Frisian song. We call it the song in the North Wind. It's a song of a mighty warrior, Redbad," she said as she continued to sing. I heard her now change the words into Dutch, so that I could understand. I couldn't help but grin. It was a testament to Frisian freedom. The song sang of resisting even the mighty King Karel in the name of freedom for all Frisians. It sang of a land where all were equal, without lords or kings, and where men chose their leaders in agreement with one another, without swords, only words. It sounded nice—liberating even. It also sounded like a far cry from the land we came across. A far cry from the blood-infested bogs through which we marched—the fierce warrior people who tore Hollanters apart with their bare hands. When her song came to an end, I had a question to ask her that lingered in my mind.

"Do you wish to see a Fryslan that is free again?" I asked.

"You ask as if I am your equal," she replied, looking at the dagger on my belt. I handed her the now clean fabrics.

"You are," I replied. She smiled.

"It'll take more convincing than that," she said. "Meet me here tomorrow—if you aren't taken back home to your kinsmen."

"Tomorrow it is," I said with a grin. "Can I walk you back home?"

"To see me walking at night with a little Hollanter boy would do me more harm than good, brave knight," she said in jest. "Goodnight," she said.

"Goodnight," I replied. I didn't feel either of our feet move in the sand. They felt no urgency to. A kiss on my cheek broke the silence, leaving me grinning like a fool in the dark as I then watched her trod off over the sand bank to her home across the village. I looked over the water to the moon's reflection. Godverdomme, man. Felix was right.

+ Floris +

"Nay, nay, nay, I will not have it!" screamed Florens at the top of his lungs. I watched from my seat in the corner of the hall. The great hall of Alcmare, quaint and rustic as it was, was no comparison to the great castles that existed in the South. I watched as he threw over his own planning table, and his near council simply watched—unable to act in their weakness. "Those Kennemer bastards will taste the wrath of my blade. I want every knight we can muster to take to the field at once. I want mercenaries, men from across the Low Countries, everyone who would rally to our banner. I will not have our glorious victory over these barbarians tainted by some unhappy peasants."

"My Lord, they are more than that," said Uncle Jan sheepishly.

"Hundreds of civilians have poured into Haarlem for refuge," said Lodewijk ver Heyen. The three ver Heyens stood proudly at the side of the Count, having managed to survive the Frisian threat. They, along with a handful of other nobles, managed to cling to the station of command.

"So, what do you suggest, gentlemen?" asked the Count. Ghijsbrecht stepped forth. "The Amstellanter wishes to speak."

"If the Count of Hollant will hear what he has to say," the Baron replied with a sly look on his visage.

"Speak, Utregter."

"My Lord, I suggest you retreat your garrisons from

315

Frieslant entirely." Swiftly, the Count launched a chalice towards his head, narrowly missing, which Heer Ghijsbrecht weathered unflinchingly. The vessel clanked on the floor, rolling to my feet where it silenced. "I will not let the sacrifice of good men, including your good friend Heer Arend van Duivenvoorde, be wasted. What will we have possibly accomplished?"

"You, my Lord, will forever be remembered as the count who subdued the Frisians."

"And then let them go? Nonsense," said Florens.

"Perhaps listen to the Baron," counselled another counsellor, Heer Harmant van Woerden, the knight of three scarlet diamonds on gold.

"A vote may help signify the sentiments of the room," added Heer Zweder van Abcoude, baring the three alabaster pillars on scarlet. The Count took a moment to pause. "I will not have my authority challenged by the will of my counsellors," he said dismissively. "Ghijsbrecht van Amstel, you have a brother, yes?"

"Yes, my Lord, his name is Arnoud. He is acting castellan until I return to Amstellant."

"Good. Have him raise an army of local levies and mercenaries, on the coin of Hollant, of course, and meet us at Castle Vredelant."

"Yes, my Lord," replied Ghijsbrecht, turning about to leave the hall with haste.

"And you two, Harmant and Zweder, fetch him an Utregter pigeon and ride out with him. We will collect men from the North and meet you there within the fortnight," the Count added. The two men bowed and followed their orders. As he exited the hall, Ghijsbrecht, gestured subtly for me to join him. Inconspicuously, I made my way out of the hall to join them.

"Chaos is coming," he said as we walked out into the yard. There was nobody around now, but the four of us.

"Will you write to your brother?"

"Nay," he said with the confidence of an ox. "I will ride to him, and I will bring back an army with him at my right-hand side. I suggest you do the same—collect your men from the coast; we must march South to meet the threat head-on."

"Why not wait for the Hollanter army?"

"Where there is victory, there is glory," he said with a smile. The two other men, Harmant and Zweder, agreed with him.

"Anarchy breeds the most excellent knights," said Zweder.

"I was a friend to your father," said Ghijsbrecht. "I will be a friend to you as well. We will meet not at Vredelant but in Waterlant. I have friends in Zeelant who will link up with us. Our time is now, Floris. The ashes of the old world will furnace the bricks of the new."

"But Uncle Ghijsbrecht, you will be abandoning orders…"

"The Count is only as powerful as his army, and so long as he clings to the Frieslant, he has none. His army is drinking and whoring in the towns while his own people tear each other apart—I will not wait for such a milksop of a boy to give me the order to attack."

"We must restore order to the county," said Harmant.

"Agreed," said Zweder.

"Look at me," said Ghijsbrecht, planting his maille mitten on my shoulder, "Your father was not killed by Frisians. This campaign should never have come to that. Your father was killed by the fools in that hall. Your father was killed by the Count."

"Chivalry teaches loyalty…"

"Chivalry is for deadmen and lapdogs," retorted Ghijsbrecht abruptly. "Now ride out, boy. Collect your men and ride. And we will see you in one week's time." I nodded... I felt empty inside. This was… something. I felt no duty to the crown, or to Ghijsbrecht. I only felt a duty to honour my father, Gherrijt, and cousin Jacobus—all of them. If Ghijsbrecht was right, if it was truly the Count's fault, then I would take it out on him. I craved vengeance. I craved something, anything, to feel whole again. Anything to pull me out of this pit I'd landed myself in. But he was right— now was the time for action.

+ Piet +

The night was long. The scent of candlewax filled the air of the study. I found my eyes drifting close and then back open again whenever I remembered what was at stake. Page after page after page of records, scanning, noting anything that could possibly be related to Lord Hillebrant sending off money to the peasant uprising. The news had reached the town by now of the chaos happening in the North. They made a rhyme out of it.

In Brederode, the peasants rose,

Their spirits as fierce as the crows,

With pitchforks and might.

The challenged the knights--

The Kennemer Opstand still grows.

Against the Marshal they stand,

In rebellious Northern lands. With passions ablaze,

They seek better days.

Here's a toast to the grand Opstand!

As you can see, in Leyden, as with most of the towns, the people tended to like the idea of the peasants taking up arms to feed themselves. Of course, Master Waleran says that in the countryside no lord would have it, and that the lords would hang anyone caught singing the tune. The lords feared any tune that stirred unrest and rebellion. But here, you hear people whistling the tune in the streets. The burghers don't seem to mind either. My friend Coppijn said that his dad, one of the burghers, actually likes the song because he's always arguing with the nobles.

"Piet, I think we have something," Master Waleran said between yawns. "What is it?"

"It says here that Lord Hillebrant has, indeed been sending funds to a mercenary company."

"A mercenary company?"

"Yes, to a man named Lauerens of the Company of the

Vermillion Boar," I remembered that name well. When I'd asked Lord Hillebrant about them he denied ever knowing who they were.

"I know where he lives," I told Master Waleran. "Is that so? And how is that?"

"I encountered him once, when I was selling wine for Lord Hillebrant."

"Selling wine for Lord Hilllebrant? What in the heavens are you on about, boy?"

"Yes, I sold a vessel of wine for him because he said he needed to get rid of it, and wanted a good coin for it," I replied.

"Are you sure?" he asked me with a piercing skepticism. "I am!" I said. "And I met Lauerens."

"Now is not the time for games, Piet."

"I'm not playing—I'm serious." Master Waleran considered for a moment.

"In that case, there is no time to lose. You will have to take me to him. And we must maintain a disposition of the utmost secrecy. Do you understand?" I nodded my head up and down.

"What will you do when you meet him?"

"I will ask him, for his sake and for Hillebrant's, what precisely was the nature of their contract."

"Will he tell you? He's not a nice man."

"We have little choice. Perhaps it is better, then, that I go alone. And with coin."

"And a sword?"

"There is little a man of my trade can do with a sword, Piet. But I suppose you're right—it never hurt the sheep to have horns," Waleran said with a grim undertone in his voice.

The dark mist illuminated the white clouds of our breaths. Each breath cool, more congested than the last. The night was calm, with little noise but the street cats stirring - hunting for their furry little prey. The rats scattered about as we passed like the water rippling from a droplet in a pond, or a raindrop in a puddle. Many of those would be coming soon - we'd have to be quick about it. The market square was empty, for the most part, aside from a couple of undiscernable young men trapped in the stocks. I made no effort to approach them, only watching as we passed by on our way to the sellsword's home. Three knocks from Waleran's gloved hand was enough to throw the relatively empty house into disarray—I heard a cacophony of feet erupt on the floorboards. Master Waleran scanned about and found an empty barrel.

"Here, Piet, stay in here; it will protect you from the rain until I come back out again. God forgive me for how I must stow away this poor boy," he said. I followed his instructions, but there was little time. I had only pulled the lid over myself when the door opened. I saw nothing but darkness inside and smelled nothing but grain. The door seemed to have only creaked open a little.

"Who is it?" asked a recognisable voice from inside. Lauerens—it must have been him.

"My name is Waleran vanden Ijssel. I am a scholar in

the patronage of Heer Hillebrant ver Heyen. I believe you two are associates?" The door opened further and then slammed shut. Barrels are boring. It wasn't long before I hopped out—they would take a while anyway. I supposed that if I'd stay away from the flickering torches that marched about well enough, nobody would catch me, so I did.

I started by hopping in the puddles. My hosen were already soaked through to my braies, so it didn't make much difference to how wet I was. It was fun work, jumping in the puddles, making my way down the street from one to another. Then I saw a cat. It reminded me of the one that was perched up by the window the night Lord Hillebrant adopted me. I looked at it curiously, and it at me, as if we were both frozen in time, neither of us wanting to move a muscle. And then I couldn't hold my position anymore, so I fell over, and my friend was gone—off into the shadows from whence it came. But I heard its paws scamper about on the wet cobblestone.

"Here, kitty," I said to it. "Here, kitty. Push, push, push." It didn't come back out to greet me, but I heard its paws playing in the water. It was strange—I'd thought that cats and water were not friends. But this cat didn't seem to mind the rain, unlike its comrades who, as far as I'd seen, curled up in window sills and under the hangouts of the thatched and tiled roofs. Into the darkness, I went, intent on finding wherever the cat appeared to be guiding me—deep into the chilly night. I think the cat was playing with me—it never went faster than I could follow.

Or, perhaps, I am simply more nimble and fast than a cat.

The pursuit lasted for some time—I scarcely knew how to return to where I had started until I realized that the fur ball had simply taken me in a great loop around parts of the town, bringing me right back to the market square. And there, in the moonlight, I saw the cat. And as it walked towards the centre of the square, without shelter, weathering the rain, I understood precisely what the cat wished to show me. The two young men, clamped tightly in the stocks, shivering in the cold, were all too familiar. The rain, now pouring, stuck their hair to their faces. They were skinny and gaunt.

"Maurits? Thiel?" I asked, feeling the cold air tighten my throat. A pair of weak, limp heads lifted to catch sight of me. And then smiles. Broad smiles.

"Come here, you street rat," said Thiel affectionately. I rushed to embrace them both.

"Where the Heavens have you been?" Maurits asked.

"Living like a little king, I bet," said Thiel. "I bet they feed you ham and butter every day," he said with a smile.

"They do on most days!" I said with a grin. "Why are you both in the stocks?" I asked, dazed and confused. Thiel looked to Maurits and then spoke.

"Oh, you know, it's not easy for us. Nicking a coin or two kept us eating."

"Yeah, but the watch found out," Maurits added. "And that got us here."

"We need you to help us, Piet. If morning comes, we'll be sent back to Duivenvoorde."

"And Lady Mehaud will not be kind. That woman looks as though she's got a tally stick up her."

"Yeah, she's not known for her mercy. Remember the gallows at the edge of town, down by the river?"

"She won't send you there, will she?" I asked. That seemed hardly fair for pinching a few purses.

"Even if she doesn't, we'll be working her demesne till we die," said Thiel.

"Okay, what do I have to do? It's locked." I replied.

"Piet, you're an expert climber. You're like a damn squirrel," said Maurits. "We need you to fetch the keys—or something that can break the lock."

"Like a hammer?" I asked.

"Yeah, like that," said Thiel. "Or a saw."

"Or a mace," said Maurits. A mace—that's a weapon, as far as I could remember.

Perhaps Lauerens would have one.

"I know where to look," I said. "I will be back before sunup."

"God speed, little man," said Maurits.

"And don't get caught, yeah? Last thing we need is you here with us," added Thiel.

Chapter 16. The Sea: Maarten

"Farewell, mates," I said with a broad grin on my face as I knew the prompt would herald an onslaught of inquisition.

"Where are you off to, you knave bastard?" asked Felix.

"It's a mystery," I said with a smile, finishing my last sip of ale.

"Maarten's got himself another girl," Kees said with a laugh.

"We've been in this godverdomde village for a week, and you've managed to find another princess? I've got to drink what you've been on, brother," said Felix in jest. "Keep yourself from harm, yeah? The Frieske lurk in every shadow."

"Of course," I replied. "I'm a mighty warrior."

"Yeah, a true war hero," Felix said, rolling his eyes. "You're going to teach me your sorcery when you get back later."

"If by later you mean tomorrow morning, sure thing," I replied.

The call of seagulls echoed through the empty streets—it had appeared as if the village had all gathered in the alehouse or the comfort of their own homes, well, I suppose they had. On my way, I noticed a few purple heathers sprouting out from a small patch of grass. They reminded me of the time I'd spent working in the Veluwe in the Bishopric of Utrecht, where the vast plains of deforested land had sprouted a violet meadow of purple heathers. I decided to pick them and bring them with me—I suppose it never hurt anyone to bring a gift.

As I had hoped, I was met with the same angelic voice I was beholden to last night, faintly, masked by the tide swelling its way over the salt-white sand. Merrily, I took off my turnshoes and hosen, again marching only in my braies and tunic to find the mysterious, unnamed Frisian lilly.

Merrily, I climbed down to the sand bank, where I found her. She'd stopped singing.

An arm planted itself firmly around my neck while another set of hands ripped the glaive from my own. Then came a punch to the face. It crashed against my bone, sending my face to the sand. And then came down on me a cudgel of some sort. Perhaps it was a plank of wood—it all happened too quickly. I later found out that it had been a great threshing flail. They'd started by beating my stomach, but it was coated in my padded gambeson, so they instead turned their attention to my leg. Seeing the bandaged thigh, they proceeded to kick it—perhaps four of them. Another tore my kettle hat from my head, and it proceeded to receive blows as well. All I could do was tuck my head under my padded middens and pray for the mercy of God. The sand beneath my face grew wet, with the blood trickling down from my nose. I cried out every time they kicked my leg. Every time, they stomped on it, some dignity of mine stripped away. It was a flurry of pain. I heard cracks in all the places you'd fear to hear them. And the whole time, I heard deep voices shouting in Frisian.

"Stupid Hollanter," one said to me in the best Dutch he could muster.

"Not for much longer," another said with a chuckle. And I watched as my Lilly simply walked off into the night. Heathen wench. Snake of the lowest order. Eventually, the beating ceased. I was too battered to move. They would do with me what they will. One of them rolled me over, slicing the straps to my gambeson and pulling it off of me. Another bound my hands together behind my back—a third kicked sand into my eyes. No help came. Despite my cries, no help came. I was a deadman.

"You're ours now," said a man who'd planted his boot firmly on my back. "You belong to me. I am Roan the Raven, captain of the Saint Nicolaas. You are my slave, Dutchman." It had happened so quickly. There was nothing I could do. Damn it. Damn, damn, damn it. For the first time in a very long time, I felt tears trickle down my eyes. I could say nothing, nor would I. The last shred of dignity I could hold onto was my tongue. I tried my best to understand their communications in Frisian. "Load him on the ship with the others. They're headed for Schiermonnikoog. And then wherever the Lord has in store." One of his goons knelt down beside me—a big man with cream-coloured hair and a brine-smelling beard.

"If you scream, I'll gut you like a fish," he said with a grin. I couldn't lift my head—my neck was too sore. They escorted me to a rowboat. All I saw were their puttees in the sand and the loose ends of their plaid mantles. That, and the droplets from my busted lip hitting the sand, tainting it.

The trip was uncomfortable. I spent the whole while

praying—it was all I could muster the sense to do. I was nothing now. I was nobody. I knew that seeing Kees and Felix again would hardly be a possibility. I'd try to run. I'd try to fight, but I couldn't. There was simply no possibility—they had already broken me. In those few minutes of carnage, they had broken me. I could hardly believe it, and yet so it was. Seawater occasionally spilled over the edge of the boat onto my face. And when I finally mustered the strength to raise my head, there I saw it. It must've been the Saint Nicolaas—a towering cog ship concealed by the dark of night, lined with menacingly colourful shields and manned with what looked like at least twenty hardy sailors. Twenty sailors and another ten bound men. The Frisians stood tall in the night with their bows and sling staffs and javelins.

"It's the captain," announced on of the men on the rowboat. A bowman relayed the information to the others, who all scrambled to put down their weapons and ready a rope ladder.

"Welcome to your new home," said the briney henchman, ruffling my hair.

"We've got the last one," said the captain. "Let's get out of here before the Dutchies catch onto us."

+ Floris +

"That's another one of ours missing," said the captain. "What would you like us to do, my lord?"

"We have no time for this; we must march south at once. Respond swiftly and brutally," I replied.

"March south? My lord, we are the only retinue

garrisoning the village. If we leave…"

"And the other retinues are soon to follow. But we have a deadline to meet, captain. Butcher the lot of them, make them fear the sable crescents of Duivenvoorde, and then muster the men," I said to him, wheeling my horse about. "No time to waste." The captain saluted in compliance.

"Your father was a fiercely loyal man," said Sir Guillaume the Saracen. "He would have died for the Count. You throw this all away for Lord Ghijsbrecht?" I appreciated his use of French, despite him having picked up a fair bit of Dutch throughout the campaign, as it kept his statements from reaching the ears of my inferiors. My father's bodyguard of templars had since become my own bodyguard of sorts, perhaps hoping to coax me to become a man of the cloth as well. That was not an aspiration of mine, but the men had served my father well, and in the short time since his passing, they have served me faithfully and loyally as well.

Guillaume was the most straightforward with me; perhaps it was his Saracen temperance.

Gaspard de Chinon, William fitz Roy, and Reynald d'Aurebac instead tended to converse in French with one another, failing to master Dutch in the same way. At least William was able to understand the Frisians, acting as a translator—English was practically the same language. "My father was also loyal to his friends. Ghijsbrecht is like an uncle to me. I trust his judgement." But even as I said it, doubt gnawed at me.

"Remember, this is the man who would slay innocent women and children at the command of Marshal Willem van Brederode. I see a snake in his eyes," he said. I knew that he was only being honest with me, and I hadn't the energy to put him in his place, but I could not resist taking offense at such blatantly taunting language.

"You would do well to remember that I could just as easily see those serpentine eyes in your skull, Guillaume."

"I know that the passing of your father has taken its toll on you."

"I will do what I must to lead. I will seek out the best possible options for Duivenvoorde."

"I see you so easily willing to turn on your brothers."

"My brothers?"

"Your fellow Hollanters."

"What's it to you, Saracen?"

"Those are men who you fought and bled alongside, and you would risk doing battle with them for what?"

"For a chance at glory. For a chance to build a better future for the Wassenaer, even if the Count would run all of Hollant into the dirt."

"Then why have you not spoken to your uncle Jan?" Sir Guillaume asked. I felt his logic drive a dagger into my mind. He was right. I hadn't even considered it. I just obeyed Ghijsbrecht and left without a trace, like a Lilly-livered rabbit.

"He would not have accepted the decision."

"And you think it is wise to divide the Wassenaer?"

"He need not stand in our way."

"He will be compelled to if he is to obey his liege lord."

"Then I will meet him on the field, and we will pass by one another as kinsmen." I jested. "You are under my command. You have not sworn vassalage to me—you are all here in service to my father. You are free men. Freelances. Seek fortune, or the mercy of God, or whatever it is you wish to find."

"We have decided that we wish to stay in service to the House of Duivenvoorde," Guillaume replied. The others now joined the conversation.

"We swore to your father that, in the case of his death, we would not let any harm befall Lady Mehaud nor yourself," said Reynald. "Our swords are yours."

"You wish to follow a man you scarcely know? On your own will?" I asked.

"You may not see as much value in loyalty, but our oaths are binding. Our swords are yours," said William.

"That is very chivalrous of all of you, but I cannot promise honour in the road ahead. It is uncertain."

"We ride into the fire," said Gaspard. "Of course, there will be flames."

"What makes a man is not the storms through which he sails, but the courage with which he sails them, not knowing how long they will last nor how mightily they will rage," added Guillaume. "Your uncle Ghijsbrecht said it himself— we ride to remedy the chaos, at whatever cost that may ensue. What is nobler than to restore order and justice to God's earth?"

"Then you will support my order to march south?"

"We do so out of loyalty to you," said Guillaume. I felt a faint warmth glow in my heart where there had not been for weeks. For once, I felt a little less lonely. The breach in the walls my father left had been filled in, even if but slightly, by these boulders who stood before me.

"Then I place you all at the head of my command. I need loyal men—men who understand the task at hand. And I ask that, only in this capacity, you swear and oath of fealty to me. Only insofar as the road takes us, that we are bonded by oath before God." Each man dismounted from their warhorses and took a knee, pressing their cops against the earthen path. Heads held low; my blade gently rested atop their shoulders as they spoke.

"Wise words," said the Englishman. "I do hereby pledge my sword in vassalage to the young Baron Floris of Duivenvoorde, heir to the late Baron Arend of Duivenvoorde, a hero to us all. May my blade never falter until the fighting is done and peace is restored to the Wassenaer, and to the Low Countries."

"I, too, pledge my blade," said Reynald. "I promise on my faith that I will be faithful to Heer Floris van Duivenvoorde, never cause him harm, and will observe my homage to him completely against all persons in good faith and without deceit."

"With God as my witness," began Gaspard. "This man shall heed the call of arms to the Lord Floris van Duivenvoorde without rest and will, insofar as his mortal shell enables, exact his will." Finally, there was Guillaume.

"Just as I have bonded myself to your father, I bond myself now to you, Baron Floris. Before God, I swear it that, unto death, I shall ensure that no harm befalls you, and until the struggle has been mended, I will serve you, Floris, faithfully, without deceit, and without malintent." The ceremony was more than simply a set of words or actions; and it was transcendental. The force of the heavens reverberated through the flat of my blade onto their bodies. A new confidence in their fidelity radiated through me.

"Rise, gentlemen. We have much work to do. We will be the liberators of Hollant. We will not rest until justice is restored and peace graces the endless fields once more."

Autumn was on the horizon. The march south was welcome but colder and wetter than it had been northwards. The increasing number of windmills in the countryside was a joyous sight, to be sure. I couldn't help but feel one with the grey all around me. The dark skies, cold air, wet earth— it resonated with me. My maille hauberk weighed me down. I hadn't the energy nor motivation to even lift my arm, on occasion, when discussing directions. In retrospect, the memory of the entire journey is a blur in my mind—one of deep, deep pain. The road gave me too much time to reflect and reach within myself. Of course, the marching songs told me the men were in good spirits—how could they not be? For all they knew, they were returning home. I knew more. I knew worse. I knew the vile nature of this profession of ours.

"Cheer up, lad." Guillaume once said to me on the road, rearing his white Arabian stallion next to my own destrier. "You have a long life ahead of you. You must not spend it in this despair."

"My father was a good man. So was Gherrijt. You know, when we were far younger, we'd made plans that I'd marry my sister off to him such that we'd live in the same castle. He was a good man."

"Death comes to all men," said Guillaume. "Your father walked the path of the Warrior. He also died by it—a fate which comes far earlier than most." His words were harsh but surprisingly comforting. "But those passed look down upon us and watch everything we do—so if you wish to honour their legacy, and show them how much they mean to you, act how they would have you act. Act how they, themselves, would act. There is no greater honour for a man than for his life to make such an impression on the world." I was right, I suppose.

"Tell me, in Araby, do Saracen knights live and die by the sword as they do here?"

"Many things are different about the Holy Land, but many things stay the same no matter where you go. A knight, such as myself, is known as a faris. But we are not nobles. Some faris are free men who choose to enter the world of farusiyya; others are bonded to their masters, such as myself. We are called ghulams, and we are the most powerful cavalry on earth."

"Not powerful enough to defeat the crusaders," I retorted.

"Many of us *are* crusaders. Perhaps that is what your romances do not teach you," he said with a smile. "In all my travels from Hispania to Constantinople, I have not found a land in which there are no knights. They find different names, different faces, clothes, and what have you, but the soul of the knight lives across the world. It is a mantle of responsibility, bravery, loyalty, and, as you rightly point out, violence. Where we ride, blood follows."

"Then what is the point? Why fight if we will never achieve peace?"

"We are the arm of peace. We are both the sword that cuts the man but also the blade that parries—and it is up to us, *you*, which blade we will become. Which one we will be remembered as."

"But you are a man of faith. How do you contend with all this spilling of blood? God commands that we are not to kill a fellow man. He said to turn the other cheek."

"And the priests would say that we are not to kill a fellow Christian. But perhaps we sacrifice our place in heaven for those more deserving—those we protect."

"Or perhaps God makes exceptions," I replied. Guillaume smiled. "Perhaps he does."

"If you are called a Faris in the Orient, do you have an Arabian name as well?"

"My name at birth was Zayn ad-Din Abu Hassan. But I was since baptized and received a Frankish name by the grace of God."

I liked Guillaume. He made me think about things beyond the world I could see and feel, but he led my mind to greater questions. I would not hesitate to call him a philosopher. He reminded me of my tutors back in Duivenvoorde. That was a place I found myself longing for increasingly. My mind drifted to a time when I was enchanted by tales of chivalry and noble deeds—unscarred by the loss of comrades and the brutality of it all. I longed to return to those days. But I also took pride in what I had become. War built me into a man—someone I could only aspire to be before. Loss strengthened me. The things I had seen and done replayed in my mind when I slept. Over and over, the Frisians wailed beneath the hooves of Galahad. And I was above them. I survived, tempered like a freshly quenched blade. I was sharpened, hardened, and ready for whatever dragons lay ahead in need of slaying.

+ Piet +

The candlelight in Lauerens' apartment flickered shadows across the street through the cracks in the wooden window panes. The conversation sounded civil. Low, hushed voices and Master Waleran's staple throat clearing. I hadn't a clue what to do, but I knew that time was of the essence, so I decided to do what made the most sense to me.

"Did you hear that?"

"Yes, I think somebody with very small, weak hands is knocking," replied Master Waleran. The door opened to a Lauerens in his nightgown and a Master Waleran sitting at the table with a hunk of bread and pottage in front of him.

"Can I have some?" I asked.

"I know you," said Lauerens. "You're the wine boy." He turned to Master Lauerens. "Sharp wit this one has. The tongue of a grown man."

"I know, if it weren't for his stubby little size, I'd think him one," replied Waleran with a laugh. "Come, Piet, join me," he said. He turned to Lauerens. "If he may, of course."

"You think me the sort of man to leave a young boy in the cold of night? While it is raining out?"

"I think you the sort of man who'd do it for tupece."

"You'd be right about that, but I don't see you paying up," Lauerens replied, ushering me in.

"I see you two are well acquainted," said Master Waleran. I'd already told him anything—I think this was Waleran's way of finding out how Lauerens knew me without revealing that I'd told on him.

"Yes," said Lauerens. "And that French red was delicious. The party guests were quite impressed," he said with a smile. The smile appeared genuine—was he being kind to me?

"Sorry for frightening you, boy. It's a habit of the trade."

"Yes, I'm sure you lot find yourselves intimidating many young children," said Waleran sarcastically. "Had enough of the rain, Piet?"

"I came because I need something," I said. "I wouldn't've come otherwise. But it's urgent."

"What could you possibly need at the moment, Piet? Haven't we more important mysteries to solve?" asked Master Waleran. I turned to Lauerens.

"Can I have a mace? Or an axe?" I asked. Lauerens erupted in laughter. As did Waleran.

"Usually the cutthroats aren't quite so brazen in their wording," Laurens said with a grin. "What possibly for, you stout halfling? If there be trouble about it's best a real man do the fighting."

"I need to break the pillory in the market square," I said. "My brothers are locked in, and tomorrow morning, they'll be sent back to Duivenvoorde." I heard a very loud sigh come from Waleran.

"For what were they arrested, Piet?" he asked.

"Only pickpocketing. They were hungry," I said.

"Oh, give the boys a break," said Lauerens. "I could use young men like that—particularly if they have the wit of their brother."

"Perhaps they ought to learn to deal with the consequences of their actions?" asked Waleran.

"Now's not the time for a lesson," said Lauerens, already donning his braies beneath his gown.

"You would stalk about in the night to free two boys you do not know?" asked Waleran.

"I've done worse. Besides, I fear I must provide Piet here with some recompense after our last interaction—I certainly hadn't known his affiliation with the esteemed Hillebrant." Lauerens replied. I looked to Waleran. He replied with a look of *I'll tell you later*. I suppose his quest was successful. "Right, an axe or a mace, you said?"

"Only to break the locks," I replied. Out from a chest, Lauerens pulled a fully-sized goedendag.

"This ought to do the trick," he said. He turned to Waleran. "Mischief excites me," he said giddily.

With a few hard blows, the locks smashed against the wooden platform. Maurits and Thiel were free. Thiel immediately stretched his back.

"Pietie, you did it," he said with a broad smile. Maurits

picked me up. "You beautiful little bastard," he said.

"And thank you, sirs," added Thiel to the aged Lauerens and Waleran. "Remember the price at which this comes," said Lauerens.

"A welcome one, sir," said Maurits. "Adventure calls."

"So does a warm meal," added Thiel.

"Two seasons and your work will be done—if you wish it to be," Lauerens said, shaking both of their hands in agreement.

"What now?" I asked.

"Now we get a good night's rest," replied Master Waleran. "Tomorrow will require quite a bit of energy. I suppose your brothers will require lodgings for the night?"

"There's always the bridge," said Maurits with a look of embarrassment on his visage. "We would appreciate any space you can spare," said Thiel.

"I'm sure Lord Hillebrant wouldn't mind a couple of new guard dogs in his absence," Waleran said. "Let's get you gentlemen cleaned up. And thank you, Mister Lauerens. For your kind deed tonight and for the invaluable information you have provided."

"Godspeed, Waleran. It was a pleasure to make your acquaintance. May we meet again soon."

"I certainly hope not," said Waleran with both a broad smile and a look of forewarning. Come now, gents, we'd best be off before the watch catches us out and about at this hour.

Chapter 17. The Betrayal: Floris

The black and gold stripes of Amstelland flew high in the grey sky as we finally arrived at Ghijsbrecht's camp in Waterlant. It was a relief, to be sure—my bones had grown stiff, and my legs tired from the long days of riding. It was finally time to coil the great snake of men we led through the northern forests. With a smile, I ordered the herald to sound the halt. I turned to my bodyguard of Knights of the Temple.

"Ready the men to make camp. Let them rest their weary feet," I said. This was the first time I'd smiled in days, I'd reckon. Rest was a welcome reward. Rest, and the sweet smell of manure and sea air. The air of the Zuiderzee, enriched with Dutch sea breeze. A tall, slender, dark-haired man with piercing sapphire eyes rode to us with a feathered bycocket upon his head. Upon his arm was a hawk, blindfolded, upon a thick, leather glove.

"Look who decided to show up?" he asked with a grin.

"Uncle Ghijsbrecht," I replied, riding glove outstretched to shake his. The prefix 'uncle' flowed from my tongue nearly effortlessly. Nearly. It simply seemed appropriate now.

"Just in time for a bit of sport," he said. Over the glade, among the colourful weeds, came finely dressed retainers with boar spears and hunting hounds in hand. Some of the dogs were greyhounds, ready to chase down small game. There were also scent hounds and sight hounds, constantly in search of the beasts' trail. Others were short-muzzled biting things, mastiffs and alaunts, capable of tearing down moose if they had to. We were lucky that they were bred and trained by the best trainers in the Low Countries. With them rode a few more nobles, some carrying falcons and others with falconers beside them and a few men with crossbows in case all else failed. Among the lords were Harmant van Woerden and Zweder van Abcoude, whom you have already met. I had the privilege of meeting, or perhaps reconnecting in fear of omitting long-passed childhood memories, Ghijsbrecht's younger brother Arnoud van Amstel and Gerard van Velsen, the youngest man of the five, and up-and-coming young lord of the northern marches. He was a devout young man, taking up the Agnus Dei of gold on a field of blue as his arms.

"Out for a hunt?" I asked, with the answer obvious.

"Splendid weather, isn't it?" asked Zweder teasingly. "Come, bring those templars of yours to bless the meal before it's been shot, and join us."

"And get out of that haubergeon of yours—the peasants are far from us," added Ghijsbrecht. It was freeing to ride without armour for a while—I felt much lighter. It was freeing, I suppose, not being encased in steel and leather. I felt my linens flying off behind me in the wind as I rode. Our horses splashed about on the moist soil, making their way into the woods. They were teeming with life—squirrels and rabbits everywhere set off the dogs, whom their masters were tasked with holding back, mustering all their strength. "Nothing smaller than a hare, gentlemen."

"If we don't find a stag today, there'll be an ox from the country waiting on your trencher. Don't you worry, boys," added Harmant.

"With the luck we've been having, we'll be spotting a white hare today," said Ghijsbrecht.

"Is that so?" I asked, hoping to be filled in on the details thus far.

"Out men are stretched thin—the damn rabble are everywhere." Ghijsbrecht explained. "But they don't know how to fight—that is certain."

"I've tasked each gleve, sworn to the house of Woerden, to bring back ten heads," said Harmant. Each gleve was made up of a knight and two retainers of varying sorts, perhaps a squire and another man-at-arms, or two squires, perhaps even a squire and a page. Regardless, for each three-man team to return with ten dead was quite the task.

"And have they been successful?" I asked. Harmant looked at me.

"With Ghijsbrecht at the helm, success is the only option," he replied. Ghijsbrecht's expression did not change—his eyes were fixed on the trail. He was scouting for game. I was not surprised by what I heard—he always struck me as a man menacing to his enemies. I knew that mercy was not among his nobler traits.

"I take it my men are late to the party then?" I asked.

"Those mud-stained pigs keep coming," said Ghijsbrecht. "We need all the men we can muster. Besides— we must always claim victory with overwhelming force—be that in horses or in men." There was the mind of the tactician my father knew well. After all, that was Father's reasoning for bringing him along. And he was right—this man would bring death to his enemies.

"I don't suppose they are much like an expected foe—they are the very people we seek to rule," I replied.

"We have no claim to these dung farmers," said Zweder. "Their lords are dead or riding for with the Count."

"Has the Count replied to our… initiative?" I asked. The men fell silent.

"No word yet," said Ghijsbrecht. He was distracted. He lifted his fist to signal the halt. Our horses dug their hooves deep into the muck. Ghijsbrecht pointed to a small shape beyond the treeline.

"There," he said in a whisper.

There it was—a massive, beastly little rumb of a hare—a Flemish hare. It was the size of two dogs put together, the little monster. I noted now that the scent hounds had been hot on its trail, and the sight hounds were now rearing to go.

"Dogs, sir?" asked one of the retainers.

"No, no," said Ghijsbrecht. "Let loose the birds. I want to see it run."

"Sire, no falcon nor hawk can pick up a Flemish hare. It will only stare at it," advised Zweder. Ghijsbrecht turned to him, nearly expressionless.

"Where's the game in letting the birds have all the fun? We will make the furry little thing run before us. The birds will give it a head start. Then we ride it down."

"Shall we place a wager?" asked Harmant.

"Two guilders from each of us to the man who brings us the hare," said Ghijsbrecht. "I'm not much of a gambling man," said Gerard.

"Then become one, you stiff-lipped boy," said Ghijsbrecht. "Live a little—or have you no faith in your spear?" Gerard grabbed a boar spear from one of his retainers.

"My aim is truer than any man here," he replied, rearing his horse about. Ghijsbrecht was impressed.

"Good, that's the warrior spirit we need. Gold and scarlet, gentlemen," said Ghijsbrecht.

"Gold and Scarlet?" I asked.

"The gold of the banner of Hollant and the scarlet of the lion Gerulfing," said Gerard. "Nay, nay, nay, the gold of the guilder that lines his purse, and the scarlet of the blood he spills. Such is what truly makes a knight," said Ghijsbrecht.

"You mean the noble blood in his veins," said Zweder as a correction.

"Nay, I learned it the old blood of his forefathers that binds his oaths," said Harmant. "I believe it be his own scarlet blood he spills in the name of his lord," said Arnoud. "His lord? Or his Lord?" asked Zweder with a smile to the templars.

"Whatever it be, it be blood, and blood a bright scarlet," said Ghijsbrecht. "

"Then I say we wager more than the gold," said Zweder. "To the victor goes the heart of the hare."

"You wish to have the blood of a lilly-livered hare in you, you flower?" asked Harmant.

"Nay, but the cunning," replied Zweder.

"Prima," said Ghijsbrecht. "That is what we truly need in this hour. And that's what many of you men-of-steel lack. For the gold and the scarlet!" he cried, removing the cap that sat over his falcon's eyes.

"The gold and the scarlet!" echoed the lords, myself included. The birds were off. The race had begun. I grabbed the lance of one of the men as I rode past—I'm sure he cared little. Now was more than simply a game—it was a chance to prove myself. I knew my uncle, and I knew that if there was one thing he praised more than anything, it was results. A cunning and cruel man he was—he wanted to see the hare bleed. And I would make the thing do so as painlessly as I could. And as quickly. And I skillfully. I spurred my horse on now.

I'd switched to a different mount so as to provide my destrier a bit of rest. This courses was far faster than I was used to—I liked it. It had been long since I'd felt the wind in my hair this way. It had been long since I'd shaved too, or cut my hair. Granted, my face still only bore the fuzz of a trimmed mare upon my upper lip and nowhere else. The wet ground made rough terrain through which to ride—the air was a much faster vessel for the birds to chase the poor thing down.

Briskly, it ran, springing about, rushing toward the nearest bushes. But the birds were ruthless. Ghijsbrecht certainly had the stomach of a warrior. If I had known what this sight would have resembled, I would not have made this order. The poor thing was being picked apart. I would put it out of its misery. Beside me came Gerard and Arnoud, riding fast on their horses, riding out every bump and grotto hard on their thighs. Arnoud held his lance like a knight, Gerard like a hunter. I was never much of a fan of hunting—I couched mine like Arnoud had. I felt it in my hand—far lighter than any lance of war or even a jousting lance, but shorter, too. The aim would have to be more precise. I would have less time to think.

"Where even is the Godverdomde thing?" shouted Harmant.

"The bushes!" shouted Arnoud. "I saw them move." He gestured with the head of his spear to the rusting foliage. I spurred my courser onwards into the green, piercing the wall of leaves like I was riding through an enemy line or a palisade. It was easy to forget I wasn't coated in steel links— the branches left a few scratches.

"Look at the young lord go!" shouted Zweder in praise.

"The boy will ride himself into a tree like that!" said Harmant.

"God helps those who help themselves," said Ghijsbrecht. "Let the boy prove his spurs."

My horse whinnied and then staggered. It was a riding horse, unknown to the danger of combat. It still had fear in its heart, and it was spooked. I'd seen this look on a horse before—there must've been something else among the trees.

"Keep chasing after it; we'll find another way around the thicket!" Ghijsbrecht shouted.

I suppose I had my orders. I dusted myself off. I was bleeding, but nothing too serious had been done. There I stood, just myself and my winged spear, alone in the glade.

And there I saw it. The poor thing had been torn apart already. The birds had all scattered. Something far more terrible had come upon us—wolves. At least four of them, all tearing apart the fluffy thing. I could've hidden or tried to run. Perhaps my chances wouldn't have been terrible. But this was a chance to prove that I was capable of more than just surviving.

That was our hare. I would have it. I would have its heart.

Now, I had the surprise of the animals. While they were occupied, I stalked my way closer to them. I made sure not to even make a sound. I rolled my sleeves, masked my scent in muck, and crept through the tall grass. I wouldn't have much time before the others arrived and scared them off. I'd have one of the beasts before nightfall.

From the grasses, I sent one strong thrust. The hungry animals were taken straight through the stomach.

Immediately, as if possessed by a single entity, the others now lunged upon me. Thank God for the wings of the spear, as I was able to pull the thing out in just enough time to catch the jaws of one of the wolves with the shaft. Another, I managed to slice its paw with the blade. The third, I let land on the head of the spear as it came upon me. Drawing my sword, I then slashed at the remaining wolf, spilling its blood in the mushy ground. Finally, the limping one, lying on the ground, I hacked at as it sprawled towards me.

It felt no different than ending Frisians. They were not

Frisians, though. They were sent by God. He made them to be part of this land. This was their land. They were no more.

I had defeated them. I had overcome them. And I would not relent. They chose to gnash their teeth at me, and they laid the price. I would survive.

Stonesplitter ran red with blood. Scarlet, I thought to myself with a smile. I did, too. I wiped it off on one of their pelts before placing it back in its scabbard.

My dagger was an excellent tool for claiming a tooth as a trophy.

I would not wish to be a braggart, and so I won't. Suffice it to say the men were pleased. Very pleased. I had successfully earned the respect of the men I knew scantly, and for the one I knew well, I saw the flame of ambition flicker in his gaze. He had made the right choice in recruiting me to his cause.

My trencher was bloodied by the hare's heart. It was perhaps half the size of my fist. The thing was fleshy, and a little tough, like beef that'd been overly salted. Floris the Hare they began calling me, and Floris the Hunter. That was the toast made in my honour by Uncle Ghijsbrecht.

He kept his camp disciplined. Although it was a feast, he gave no credence to partying or drinking. It was a serious affair, in his opinion. He told me that decisions could be made at any time, and there was always a game to be played. That's why he didn't even touch the wine that was poured before us. As the feast went on, and the commanders were happily conversely over delicious hare's meat and pork for the rest, Ghijsbrecht leant in close to me. "You see these men?" he asked. "Look at them all, fattening, gorging on the products of their soldiers' labour."

"Do we not do the same?" I asked. Ghijsbrecht eyed me up and down.

"I see the way you treat your men. You treat them as you should, with discipline."

"Justice and discipline. These men know only to take."

"Why are you telling me this?"

"I'm giving you advice, boy. The pig loves the farmer, even though the farmer will happily send him to the slaughter once he is fat. These men are much the same. They will die for me. Each and every one of them. It is because, without the farmer, the pig would have no food. No scraps on which to indulge." Ghijsbrecht gestured with his hand to the camp women and then to the troubadours playing their instruments. "I give them food, drink, and entertainment. And they love me for it. A noble's claim to his land doesn't lie in the oaths their families have sworn, but in what he can provide." he placed his hand on my shoulder and looked me in the eye. "Remember this, boy. The day your coffers run dry, your men will leave you. Until that day, make sure they want for nothing, and they will give you everything."

"I will, Uncle," I said with a nod.

"And remember your father, always. He was a good man. He lived like a man and died like one. You must do the same." I lifted my glass to that. No matter how cruel or ruthless Ghijsbrecht was, he was always loyal to Father. I respected him for that. The feast went on, with great tales of the hunt fresh on the lips of all the noble hunters.

A messenger arrived at one point to hand a note to Lord Ghijsbrecht. Upon reading it, expressionless as always, he excused himself. I'd thought nothing of it. I suppose there would always be something to attend to in his world. He had much to manage—even as we spoke, his men raided hamlets and villages and battled peasants hiding in trees and bushes across the land. The Kennemer scurge had completely drained the land of all life, or so it was said. I could feel the tension, even as the party grew in its roar.

"Are you alright?" asked Guillaume, resting his hand on the pommel of his scimitar.

"I'm fine," I said. "Just thinking."

"That's a fine stunt you pulled today," he said. "I'm impressed—if a boy were to slay four wolves where I grew up, he would be a hero."

"Uncle wants me to prove my courage. I have to earn the respect of the other men at this table."

"You have certainly done so. But, remember, you are young. You have a long life to live. Do not throw it away so easily."

"I threw nothing," I said, looking at him now. "You could have been torn apart."

"But I wasn't," I replied. "I knew I could defeat them."

"Did you?" he asked with a cynicism I did not appreciate.

"How could you know? When I rode through the thicket, you weren't there behind me. You rode about the green with the others."

"Remember what is important to you, Floris. Do not become another tool of your uncle." I could have chastised him as a Saracen. I could have asserted my rank. But, Father told me, *the lion who chooses not to bite is the strongest of them all.*

"Why do you say this?"

"I am pledged to you, not him," said Guillaume. "You must make your own decisions."

"Then I swear to you that I will," I replied. "And if you believe my uncle would not have the best intentions of mine in mind, you must report to me. But, I also ask that, when I do act, my actions remain unquestioningly followed. You are sworn to me."

"You have my word," said Guillaume. He looked at the unfinished organ on my trencher. "How's the heart?"

"Tough," I said with a smile. "Would you like some?"

"Nay, that is yours to enjoy," he said. "You earned it, wolf slayer."

Ghijsbrecht never returned to his place at the table. Once the eating and drinking were done, I decided to check in on him to see for what reason he was gone. He was not in his tent. I found his squire nearby, doing his washing.

"Excuse me, might I ask where your master is?" I asked. "Perhaps he didn't recognize me."

"What do you want, boy?" he asked.

"Have you no idea who I am?" I asked.

"I am Heer Floris van Duivenvoorde, knight of the three

crescents.”

“Not a knight yet,” he said.

“You have a tongue on you, you pancake,” I said. “I could have you flogged.”

“But you won’t,” he said. He simply looked at me.

“No? Just wait until Ghijsbrecht hears…”

“Of course, you will run to him. He will do the dirty work, and you will report to him like a good puppy. The son he never had,” he said with a smile.

“You would speak of your master this way? You are his squire!”

“He flogged me earlier. What difference would it be if he did it again?”

“What for?” I asked.

“I don’t know. He came out of the feast mad as an ox,” said the squire. “If you really want to see him, go at your own risk. He has his flail with him.”

“Where is he?”

“In the wood, that way,” said the squire, gesturing in a direction. What a strange set of events. I took my horse and rode off toward him. The night was dark. The cool air brushed against my brow as I rode. I could see my breath as I left it behind me in the air. The closer I rode, the louder the sound grew. It was a hacking of sorts. It sounded like someone was felling a tree. As I approached, I then saw him alone, down to his braies, sweat garbing his body, hacking at a log with his sword. Splinters flew off in every direction as he struck it.

And every time, he cried out. It was a rageful cry. He sounded like a lion. I slowed my horse. He didn't even notice my approach—he was too busy hacking at the log. He ended up breaking the whole thing in half, at which point he found another to tear apart.

"Calm, uncle! Lest you dull your blade," I shouted over his cries. Panting, he looked at me and dropped his sword. He pounded at the earth with his bare fists. "Calm now," I said, rushing to pick him up off the ground, dismounting from my saddle. "What has thrown you into this disarray?" He simply handed me the message. It was long—I hadn't read words for some time—certainly not such a fine script. I looked at him.

"The Prince-Bishop has come to aid Florens," he said.

"This is good news, is it not? The men of Utrecht will come to our aid! Your brothers!" I said, attempting to lift him. He refused to erect himself.

"Nay. I have been disinherited. As have you," he said. "Prince-Bishop Jan has decided that our venture disregarded orders." He looked at me. "He said we are disloyal. They march toward us."

"This is ridiculous," I said. "It can't be."

"There's more," he said. "My informants have reported more." Resting on his sword, he rose to his feet. He was still breathing heavily. "Those ver Heyens of yours have poisoned the Count's ear. They have vowed to claim our heads." This made me flush with rage. The bastards. We ride out to save the land, and they take their opportunity to get rid of us. Even after all we had done together—the war we fought together. I felt light-headed.

"Those traitors," I muttered. He nodded.

"We will meet them with fire and sword," he said.

"We will have to deal with these peasants first. Perhaps we can speak with the Count and the Prince-Bishop? They must listen to reason."

"It may be too late."

"They will not waste their men on us. Not if we capitulate."

"Capitulate? I expected more of you, boy," he said. He sounded feral, like a wild animal. "Are you not the same lad who slayed wolves in the woods? Are you not the butcher of barbarians?"

"I am," I said.

"Then act like it," he told me. My stomach churned. "Do you wish to do battle with them?" I asked.

"We have been betrayed," he replied. "No mend will return us to our place. The shattered vase cannot be mended perfectly."

"And you wish to cast it away," I replied.

"Yes," he said. "If they would so easily label us traitors, there is no world in which I would accept their rule once more." How, in God's name, could the Count have so grievously mistaken our intention? There was devil's work at play. I was sure of it. Those ver Heyen serpents were venomous. I had known it all along. I should have slain

Wolfram all those weeks ago on the green of Duivenvoorde. I shouldn't have let him disgrace me. I would have my chance again. I would have my vengeance. I felt the fishtail pommel of Stonesplitter with my left hand. By God, this blade would run through all three of them. I would show no mercy. They made the choice to disinherit us—we had nothing to lose now.

"I suppose we'd ought to make a plan," I said. His expression changed. The snarling bear I saw in him now returned to the man I knew.

"You are right," he replied. He seemed somewhat embarrassed. "You are completely right." He grabbed a piece of linen to wipe the sweat off his brow. "Summon the lords; I will wash off."

+ Maarten +

"The winds are slow today, lads. You know what that means!" the captain barked with a toothy grin. "Get your arses down to the oars. We'd best get rowing." I knew what that meant—another still day at sea. The captain had deadlines to meet, and he wouldn't tolerate a bunch of slaves sitting on his ship, eating his food for too long.

"Row boys, row!" shouted the overseer. A hardy Frisian rowing song kept our pace. The oars were heavy. The more you rowed, the heavier they became. I'd thought that my life as a charcoal burner had made me hardy and strong—I had nothing that prepared me for this. There were eighteen oars in all—mixing the slaves with the sailors. Of course, if the sailors left slack, they'd face little compared to the beating a slave might endure.

"Keep the pace up, Slamander!" shouted the overseer. The shipmen came to call me Salamander after one rough night at sea. Below deck, the captain had his candles lit, but one's wax grew weak and fell over in the storm. I remember the overseer ordering me to stamp it out with my bare feet. As all know, salamanders are invulnerable to fire, for they carry dragon's blood in them. As such, that came to be my name—miraculously, my feet had not become scorched. I say it was all the seawater that soaked into my soles. They said it was Saint Nicolaas guarding us, as he always did. They said there was hope for me yet, a sinner. I told them they were the heathens. I gained a black eye and a few purple ribs that night.

By the end of the third day, finally, solace came.

"We're out of the North Sea, lads," said the captain. They never told us where we were headed—the less we knew, the better. But, of course, I was able to track the position of the sun. It rose behind us and set before us, leading me to believe we were near France. France or England. Or somewhere else that was West—I didn't have an excellent knowledge of the lands that lay to the West. I'd always heard tales of giants and gryllies in the forests of Western islands from the Age of King Karel. We had yet to make port. I often felt my stomach grow ill, growing green against the rocking of the waves.

On deck, the shipmen had us take care of tasks. We'd be preparing meals, fishing, cleaning, and so on. In large part, we were given many of the same tasks with which the sailors were charged. But, of course, we knew that at the end of this journey, we would be sold off into some unknown fate, and the sailors would continue on with their lives as shipmen, merrily traversing the open waters.

I would not let them break me. No matter how little water I was given or how little food or rest, I would not let them break me. I spent most of my time looking out at the sea—the endless blue waters that housed the occasional ship or coastline off in the distance.

Eventually, we finally came to our first stop. It had a great castle overlooking the water. The chirping of seagulls filled the air. It was good to no longer be moving.

"Unload the cargo," the overseer ordered as he peaked below deck. "If any of you bastards intend on running away—know that none of the good people here speak Hollanter," he said with a grin. "We'll find you, and we'll cut you up into bits." Begrudgingly, we'd become accustomed to the routine hard labour. I looked down at myself—unwashed, filthy, and tired.

"Get those shoes on. We haven't got all day," said the captain. "We need all hands."

"You heard the man, let's get moving. And I don't want to see your braies—let's be decent for these fine folk," added the overseer. Us Hollanters, all men of fighting age, all garbed in what we'd last worn before capture, our tunics, and our hosen, all looked weary. I saw the gaunt expression on their faces. Stubble marked each man's face—those who did not already have a beard. "Move or I'll..." began the overseer, raising his flogging stick before the captain halted him.

"Not in sight of the port authorities," said the captain,

gesturing to a couple of padded men marching about with what looked to be a voulge and a fauchard, respectively. They were in blue livery. The port itself was bustling and alive. There were children playing, men unloading and loading cargo, merchants selling wares, buskers, fishmongers—if you can imagine it, they were probably there.

"Welcome, lads, to Cherbourg." The town itself was surrounded by massive walls that towered high into the sky—far above our small cog ship. Overlooking both the water and the town was an even taller castle—sturdy and tough. Atop the towers flew blue banners bearing three gold circles divided by a horizontal white line.

I recognized the language they spoke—the Language D'oeïl. They were French—I recognized it from the tongue the noble spoke in the Low Countries, and it was a language many travellers spoke growing up in Luxembourg.

"Get your arses moving," ordered the overseer. Ten crates of English wool, weaved in Flanders, were ready to be sold at various markets along the Western coasts of Christendom. In addition, one found a crate of craftsmanship, including Frisian jewelry and plaid mantles, and a few more crates of goods left over from Scandinavia, Prussia, and the Princes of the Rus. Much of what was sold was decorative—artistic in some form or another.

Many of the sailors turned out to be far more adept at trade than I'd have expected. Kapmonnen, they called themselves. Each kapmon found his own wealthy-looking buyer to sweet-talk in very, very broken French. Sometimes, the kapmonnen even turned to Latin when they needed to, flexing what they'd learned in mass to whoo their potential buyers.

All the while, we watched them hone their craft. For such merciless men, they had a way of befriending the wealthy men easily and sweet-talking the wealthy women. It appeared to be less about the value of the good but more about how well they could make their target feel special.

"Special price, double the deniers after the bells ring thrice" was one I heard quite a bit—that is, until it was past three and the time alluded to became progressively later. "Come, I have the perfect cloth, just for you; it will make your eyes shine" was one I heard fairly often as well—a young, muscular Frisian tended to use that one whenever he found the chance. Of course, there were also ways of alluding to our prices when no guardsmen were looking. "Are you in the business of buying hard-working hands?" one might ask. Or one might simply state "Should you know of any lords looking to populate their fiefs, look no further."

When it came to settling prices—this was in itself an art. A dutch cheese that might usually cost a few groten would go for a guilder here. Well, a livre, which I could only assume was of equal value. The kapmonnen would always begin with an absurdly high price. If their buyer would bargain low—they would match them near the middle. If they would bargain only a little lower, they'd say it was the best price they could offer. Of course, how willing they were to bargain was all dependent on how their buyer looked. If they appeared to be shrewd or knowledgeable about the goods, a far fairer price would befall them. And, of course, if they were another Frisian merchant, it was immediately half off.

We had set up a few tables as make-shift stalls, but there was still not enough room.

Some kapmonnen unfurled linens to keep the goods clean as they laid them out on the ground. Others instead carried them around in baskets as they made their way through the crowd to peddle their wares. Not too far, of course. I'm certain they remained weary of pickpockets and thugs.

At one point, a beautiful woman dressed in luxurious fabrics and a wimple as white as salt seemed to approach one of the kapmonnen after eyeing me up and down. I prayed to God she'd buy me—it would certainly be a much better life than anything I'd find at another port. But alas, it was not to be. I'm unsure of what they said to one another, but I believe she drove too hard a bargain. It was then that I wondered where they were taking us that the buyers might be so much more affluent. Wild thoughts of travelling to Rome or Aethiopia crossed my mind, but I quickly swatted them away for the flies they were. I let out a heavy sigh—I suppose my life would soon be found working some lord's fields, far from Kees and Felix, far from Master Klaas, and far from Yda. Oh, how I missed the prospect of returning to Duivenvoorde with a girl waiting for me now. What a fool I had been to throw that all away for some stupid temptress. And now, what would become of me? I felt my cheeks grow heavy. I looked to my grime-coated nails. My fate was to be among the lowest of all society. I would gladly take up the spade and axe once more as a charcoal burner to escape this destiny. But alas, I had no more choice. I had made poor decisions. The consequences would certainly find me, no matter where I fled.

"Oy, Salamander. Come over here," said the overseer. "This man would like to have a word with you." I looked up to find a wealthy-looking Frenchman in a gold and white patterned tunic looking at me. He ran his thumb along his chinstrap beard.

"Come here," he said in slow, simple French. I did as I was told. "Show me your hands." I did. "Good, strong, worker's hands. This man says you were a soldier. Is this true?"

"We all were..." I said. I was slapped on the back of the head immediately for that. "You will answer with a yes or no," said the overseer.

"Yes." I corrected myself begrudgingly.

"They all are?" asked the man to the overseer.

"This one put up the most fight," he replied. The man smiled.

"My master could use a fighting man," he said. That was an acceptable fate. I looked to the overseer to see his reply.

"Excellent, this man will do finely."

"Name your price," the man said.

"200 livres," said the overseer. The man looked shocked.

"You'll never get a sale for that sort of price here," he said. "You must not know the worth of a livre..."

"Perhaps you would prefer a more affordable option?"

the overseer asked. The man appeared grossly offended.

"Good day, sir," he said before storming off. I looked at the overseer. "What are you looking at, Salamander?"

"Are these prices not too high?" I asked.

"You wish to leave us so soon?" he mocked. "You'll fetch triple where we're sending you."

+ Floris +

Ghijsbrecht pounded on the table.

"Arnoud, what's your counsel on the matter?" he asked with a stern expectation of excellence.

"I suggest we return to Amstellant and fight a defensive war."

"Lock into a siege?"

"Yes, brother," said Arnoud. Ghijsbrecht considered the option. "How about you, Harmant?"

"I say we fight like men," said Harmant. "We need only to capture the Count and the Prince-Bishop—without them, the others will have no will to fight." Ghijsbrecht looked at him with disappointment.

"Harmant, answer me this…"

"Yes, Ghijsbrecht?"

"How much did you have to drink last night?" Ghijsbrecht asked. Zweder was the first to laugh. Ghisjbrecht snapped his gaze to Zweder. "Silence," he ordered. He returned his gaze to Harmant. "Answer me."

"Five goblets of wine, my lord," he said.

"I am not your lord," said Ghijsbrecht calmly. Then, his calm brewed into a tempest. "Your Godverdomde lord is a few days marching from here with an army of ten thousand men!" he shouted. "I have no time for children and mules in my tent." He turned now to Zweder. "Have you an idea that is worth our time?" Zweder paused for a moment.

"We have the advantage," said Zweder. "They are coming to us, meaning we can pick the field."

"So you would not have a siege?"

"Nay, Lord Ghijsbrecht."

"Is my brother an idiot?"

"Nay, Lord Ghijsbrecht."

"Then why do you not agree with him?"

"I believe his plan places traditional wisdom at the helm, but I believe, in the long run, a siege would be untenable."

"Why is that?"

"We have not stocked provisions. With the combined armies of Hollant and Utrecht at your door, there would be no way to feed this many men," said Zweder. Ghijsbrecht turned to Arnoud.

"I cannot deny that," said Arnoud. "But I cannot see a more sound military strategy. If we can bait them into attack…"

"If," said Ghijsbrecht.

"It would be a game of dice," said Zweder.

"One not in our favour," said Ghijsbrecht. "Where would you have them engage?" he now turned to Zweder.

"I say we take Vredelant Castle and mount a defense there," said Zweder. "And what makes Vredelant a more defensible location than Amstel?"

"They have already stocked for a siege," said Zweder. "They fear the Kennemers. They have stocked to hold in the castle but not mounted defenses to repel a well-equipped army." Ghijsbrecht smiled.

"Good," he said. "So we can die in a castle surrounded by Utrechters—just how I always wanted to be remembered. A coward and a traitor." He shifted his gaze now. "And what of these peasant rabble? I have heard many ways to defeat the Count and his men, but I will not march my army out only to be harassed at every brook and hamlet by this unwashed filth."

"We don't have time to finish them off first," said Arnoud.

"At least they will do the same against the Count," said Zweder.

"But will they?" asked Ghijsbrecht. "Now that we have become their executioners, the Count could just as easily ally with the bastards to reconcile this little kingdom of his."

"Then we move first," I said, asserting my place at the table. "We make the first move we open relations with the peasants." Ghijsbrecht looked to me like I was a fool. I felt my face flush with red, but I would not have it. "I'm serious; we ally ourselves with the peasants."

"We just slaughtered hundreds of them," said Zweder. "They hate us with every bone in their bodies."

"It's not against us they rebelled—it is against their masters. Those masters still pledge fealty to the man descending from the North to kick in our teeth." I replied.

"Peasants? Really?" asked Arnoud. "Are we descending to that level of desperation?"

"All is fair in war," said Ghijsbrecht, now seemingly coming to my aid. "How do you suggest we open relations?"

"We need to find their point of command and send an emissary. We need to treat them as an equal force." I replied. Zweder and Arnoud laughed. Harmant did as well. "If we do not, we risk sending each and every man in this camp six feet under."

"And you truly believe they would listen to us?" asked Ghijsbrecht. "There is no harm in trying," I replied.

"Oh, but there is," said Zweder. "If we appeal to them, it is a sign of weakness. They will only resurge against us tenfold."

"They will not care about us when they hear there is an army ten times out size descending from the North and West to encircle them like chickens in a pen," I replied. "This is nonsense," said Harmant. "Not only is this an offense to God, this is an offense to common sense. Even if we have as many peasants as there are fish in the sea, not a single one of them will stand in front of a cavalry charge."

"Then we train them," I said. "We give them goedendags and teach them how to fight."

"And what happens when they finally face a more experienced foe in the field?" asked Zweder. "Then where will be your Uncle's swift and ferocious victory?"

"Then we do not rest our fate on one engagement," said Ghijsbrecht. He appeared to be deep in thought. "We fight for every dyke and windmill. We make them pay for every fief. It will be long and bloody." He looked to his counsellors. "But what better have we to do?" he asked with a smile. I looked hard at the war table—the armorial rolls, the maps, the casualty records. "Gentlemen, it would appear that the wolf slayer has two more wolves in his sights." He turned to me. "Do not fail," he said slowly and sternly. "This is your plan. You will speak with them in person. Godspeed." I felt a grin creep across my jaw. "You are dismissed, gentlemen." He gave me one last remark. "You earned this. Forge your legacy."

Chapter 18. The Deal: Floris

"You, what's your name?" I asked as I surveyed all the Duivenvoorders standing at attention. This man stood out to me—he was tall, very tall, and very wide.

"His name is Kees, my lord," said a much scrawnier man beside him. "You speak for him?"

"He hasn't spoken since the disappearance of our good friend, Maarten," the man replied.

"Was this Maarten a man of the retinue?"

"Yes, my lord," replied the small man.

"Then his sacrifice will be well-remembered. What is your name?"

"Felix, my lord," he replied in his timid voice, which relaxed slightly now.

"Felix, your friend Kees, here, is a big man, scary, a true man of the land. Biggest man here, by all accounts. A fine son of Duivenvoorde. I would like him to escort me to the parlay. You are welcome to join—you can be his tongue."

"I would be honoured, my lord. Would you not prefer to bring with you knights?" asked Felix.

"If I am to make peace with these rebels, I must earn their respect. I fear men clad in fine steel may not meet this end," I replied.

The chosen meetingplace as a small village called Hooftdorp. It was one around which much of the fighting had taken place. The people there looked weary, like they'd seen Hell, and fearful, like they were staring straight at the Devil. I felt an involuntary sigh leave my lungs as I rode through—my work was cut out for me. We were first to arrive. We had agreed to meet in the village church—no weapons, all witnessed by God. It was a small, brick building with a thatched roof. I left a few men outside to keep safe our arms and horses. It reminded me much of the one for the commons of Duivenvoorde. It was a small place with simply painted walls—a faux masonry. The limewash was peeling off in places.

Hooves stamped about outdoors. They were here. They all made their crosses and bowed their heads as they entered—just as we did. We had seated ourselves on the pews to the left. They too the right. At the altar I stood face to face with a collection of four men. Each of them were aged, grizzled, and discontented.

"Good morning, gentlemen. Fine weather we're having today," I said, looking out the window at the pale-grey skye. It was a dry day—a good omen.

"Did they send a boy to do a man's work?" asked the eldest of the four gentlemen. The patches on their clothes indicated what little regard they had for decency. "Does your Ghijsbrecht think so damn little of us?" Such foul language I would not normally tolerate - certainly not in a house of God. But, I had a mission. I would not let my emotions guide me. I could tell them their place once the Count and the Prince-Bishop had been dealt with.

"I am the son of his closest friend," I replied. "My Father fell in Frisia. I am here in his place."

"Well deserved—how many of our sons and brothers

won't return home?" said the eldest.

"I'm sorry for your loss," quickly added another. The eldest gave him a cold look. Division—I would have to work with this. Clearly, the elderly gentleman who stood before me would be the most stubborn of the lot.

"Much appreciated," I replied. "He was a man of the Cross, a Knight Templar. He had recently returned from the Holy Land."

"His service to Christ is met with grace," said the second man.

"What are we here for?" said the eldest. To tranquilize myself, I took in a deep breath, and released one.

"Gentlemen, I have summoned you here…"

"Hold on, what makes us so gentle?" asked a third man. Had he never been called a gentleman before? I suppose he wasn't, but to not even know its meaning…

"I apologize, it is a term of respect."

"Don't cloak your meaning, boy, speak straight with us. You've hacked our sons and brothers and fathers to bits over the past week or so, not to mention the horrors your war parties brought with you marching through these lands," said the eldest. The fourth man now decided to open his mouth for the first time. The binding over his eye seemed fresh.

"Have you the slightest clue why we fight?" he asked. I had to think for a moment, to collect my thoughts.

"It is my understanding your lords have failed you," I replied. "They have not fulfilled their oaths to steward the land…"

"Our lords let ten thousand men march through our homes, have their way with our wives, and our children, and bring with them death and disease. They took our livestock, our harvest, all of it. We are fighting to survive, Floris."

"I understand," I replied. "I had not known how grave the situation truly was. I believe this was unknown to my comrades as well."

"No wonder," said the second. "Since the first rock was thrown, not a single man has come to parlay. Not a single man has chosen to speak with us. You are the first. For that, we are grateful."

"I deeply apologize for this," I replied. I suppose that our only chance at cooperation would include a degree of concession. I respected that he chose to extend the olive branch, and I would gladly take it. "This has been a grievous error trespassed upon you. We mistakenly placed our faith in the whim of the Count. We received orders to come and fight, and so we did so, with complete faith that we were justified in restoring order. It would appear we were wrong," I said.

"Is that what you came here to say, boy?" asked the eldest. "That you were wrong? Hundreds of ours lay dead. Not just men. Women and children too. They fell by the blades of your men. Likely your own sword too…"

"Stonesplitter has not spilled the blood of any Dutchman." I replied. It was true—she had only been tested against the flesh of Frisians and wolves. This seems to have taken the men by surprise.

"What you say now, you say before God," said the third

man. "Your lies will be your own peril here."

"This is the truth," I replied. "With God as my witness. I have come here to make peace with you." the men now appeared to be very much taken aback. "A threat looms on the horizon. We have no use in slaying one another when the true enemy rides out in force."

"What tales are you spinning, lad?" asked the eldest.

"As of two mornings ago, we have received word that the Count himself, alongside the Prince-Bishop of Utrecht, are on the march to come and squash this rebellion. They also come to make battle with our forces."

"You are not men of the Count?"

"We were," I replied. "Until two mornings ago. We have been betrayed. Just as you have. We have been failed by the Count and his close families. With your aid, we will fight together and hang the traitors." The men simply looked at one another. The fourth now took leadership.

"You speak of endless rivers of blood. We simply wish to return to our lives, seek aid for our wounded, food, work. We want to farm our lands again, and eat what we grow."

"That you shall have. That is something I can promise. Together we have the power of seven baronies. By the time we are done, we will have the entire Wassenaer, and, of course, Kennemerland. As well, I should expect a good number of dissatisfied nobles in the courts of Hollant and Utrecht to join us, not to mention our hungry neighbours and Brabant, Friesland, Flanders, and Gelrelant who, I'm sure, would love to carve out pieces of their own."

"And what if the Emperor comes?" he asked.

"There is no Emperor—let the Germans find one first before they come to deal with some petty land dispute in the corner of their empire."

"How can we believe you?"

"What choice do you have? Regardless, the same problems remain—but we wish to provide you with trained men, arms, armour, educated command, food, surgeons, livestock, you name it. We can join forces—the choice is yours. Either we stand together, or we both fall to the scarlet lion," I replied.

"You speak well, boy," said the man. "Some of those words I've never heard a country boy utter. We'll need time to discuss," he said.

"That you shall have," I replied. "Think well, gentlemen. And best of luck in the times to come—whether or not you accept our offer. Regardless, there will be a struggle, and many men, men sworn to either of our causes, will fall." The fourth man replied with a nod. I descended from the altar as they began to speak quietly among themselves. I had supposed it would take them several days to relay this information to their superiors and to come to a consensus. Thus, I summoned my men, and made my way to the church doors. The floorboards creeked. I remember this moment well—it is burned in my mind. Before I could even place my hand on the door, the elderly man called out. I looked back at them through the rood screen.

"Wait!" he shouted in the loudest tone he could muster through his aged esophagus.

"We have an offer of our own." I made my way back to the altar. I don't know what my men did.

"Do we have terms?" I asked. The fourth man stared into my soul with his good eye. "You want our lands?"

"Nay, I want to live," I replied. He smiled.

"We have peace," he said, extending his hand. I had never shaken hands with a peasant before. His handshake was firm, like I was gripping hands with an ox. I suppose years of pushing a plough would do that to a man. "Our children need food. If you betray us, we will kill you," he said. I smiled.

"Likewise."

+ Piet +

"Traitors and brigands!" shouted the town criers. You could hear this message throughout the streets as they read from their scrolls—several times a day, as well. "Traitors and brigands all! The dishonourable Ghijsbrecht van Amstel and his cronies have taken advantage of the Kennemer Opstand and now stand at the helm of the rebel army! The rabble dogs have named him their Hooftman! Our good Count voes to restore order to the County! The gracious Jan van Nassau, Prince-Bishop of Utrecht, is raising an army to bring with him to help our noble Count bring the sword of Imperial justice!" The shouting could be heard through the windows, even when we closed the wooden shutters.

"Are you ready for the trial?" I asked Master Waleran.

"Today will be an important day, Piet," he replied. "I suppose we are as ready as we will ever be." He knelt down

373

to match me at my height, placing one hand on my shoulder.

"Remember to treat the burghers with the utmost respect. The Aldermen are the supreme law in this court, alright?"

"Alright," I said with a big nod. Miss Filomena came and gave me a massive hug from behind, nearly crushing my bones.

"You intelligent little lad," she said joyfully. "My little knight in shining maille.

Master Waleran told me everything you've done for your Lord Hillebrant, and might I say that you are quite the little man," she said through a broad smile. "I've made a fresh batch of cookies, just for you," she said, poking me on the nose. She handed me a sack. "They're all in here—don't eat them all at once."

"Thank you!" I said with a smile. I felt my stomach rumble at the thought of the delicious cookies inside. "Are my brothers up yet?"

"Not yet—those poor boys have been through quite a lot." Miss Filomena replied. "I'll make sure that when they do decide to leave those beds of theirs, they'll be treated to a nice, hot meal and an ice-cold ale. Don't you fret. Now, off you go—time to go free your Lord little lawyer," she said, ushering the two of us out the door.

"Until this afternoon, madam," said Master Waleran.

"Until this afternoon," she replied, waving us off before shutting the door.

The trial was to take place in the Stadhuis, or town hall,

a venue reserved only for the most important litigations. Others were held in various smaller courts across the town. The Stadhuis itself was a tall building on Bread Street—the sweet smell of fresh bread did little to ease the butterflies that fluttered about in my stomach. The building was solid, made of brick, with a main hall and a tall tower. Master Waleran told me that the walls were built to be twice as thick as any others in the town, except for the surrounding walls, of course, to keep in all the noise and make sure that no sneaky people can listen in.

Two watchmen of the schutterij stood guard at the tall, oaken doors, brandishing great, spiked goedendags.

"Name and occupation?" they seemed to ask everybody as they walked through the doors. A scribe, sitting at a desk just beyond the doors, marked down their answers with precision before allowing each guest to pass.

"Waleran vanden Ijssel, a scholar in the employ of the accused," said Master Waleran. "The boy is with me." After a few moments of careful script, the scribe allowed us passage into the main champer. It lay behind enclosed doors. It was a dimly lit room—what little light there was had either entered through the tall, gothic windows, or the candelabras which stood on also tall metal stands. The room was also silent. As men and women shuffled in, we occupied the seats which stood at the edges of the room, with a central table set up at the room's head, in front of the hearth. In front of the table was a clearly demarcated place where I supposed the speakers would be doing the speaking. Behind the table sat thirteen men, each garbed in long, flowing cloaks, and brightly-coloured conical felt hats which demarcated their status. The man in the centre wore a chaperone of fine cloth. After many people had shuffled in and found their seats, the churchbells rang 10:00 am. Promptly, the man in the chaperon stood up.

"Good afternoon, gentlemen and ladies," he announced. "It is ten hours passed midnight—let us begin promptly. You are all gathered here for the trial of Lord Hillebrant ver Heyen, a lawyer registered in the City of Leyden. We here before you today are the burghers of the Council of Law of Leyden—appointed aldermen charged with the task of administering justice and order in this town. You are to refer to myself and my colleagues by the title *Master Alderman*. Any action against doing so will be seen as non-compliance, and will be disciplined accordingly. Right, with that speech out of the way, let's get to it. Wardens of the court, please present the accused." From the back of the hall emerged three men. Two crude-looking guardsmen escorted Lord Hillebrat, hands bound behind his back. He looked sickly. He remained in the same clothes in which he was abducted. Reluctantly, his feet shuffled across the hall. "Hillebrant, you stand accused of treachery, treason, and embezzlement of the highest order."

"Yes, Master Alderman," Lord Hillebrant replied sheepishly.

"We have requested that you come before the court twelve-handed. Have Lord Hillebrant's twelve advocates been assembled?" the Alderman asked. Master Waleran rose to his feet.

"Yes, Master Alderman," replied Waleran.

"Excellent. If God is good, we will be finished by

lunch," replied the Alderman. The trial proceeded witness by witness, each testifying to the morality of Lord Hillebrant. Many of them were his clients, mostly burghers, some moneylenders or tradesmen, a few neighbours, members of the church community, and several of the brothers in his confraternity, all of whom said that Lord Hillebrant was an honest, hard-working man. It was very boring.

Luckily for me, one of the wardens of the court saw that I was nearly falling asleep at points, and kicking my legs at others, so he'd make funny faces at me every now and then to keep me occupied. Sometimes, he'd pretend to scratch his helmeted head with his goedendag. Other times, he'd mockingly mimic the long, drawn-out nature of the testimonies.

Then, the twelfth testimony came from Master Waleran himself. He approached the table with a folded document— our list of each and every transaction outside of Leyden, and where they may be found in Lord Hillebrant's records. As he spoke, the burghers passed the paper to one another for observation. Some of them were so old that they resorted to reading stones which they kept in their pouches just to read the regularly sized text.

"Master Alderman, every testimony that you have heard here is true," said Master Waleran. "Lord Hillebrant is a just and honourable man. He is intelligent, and diligent, and supremely hardworking."

"We have no doubt as to his industriousness," replied the Alderman. "It has been a long day, Master Waleran. This court has heard the testimonies of men and women from many walks of society here in this town. We do not doubt that you have kind words for him, and we have been shown that he is an asset to the community. But, our reports do still indicate that he has been funding the opstand. Do you have any evidence to offer in Hillebrant's defense?"

"I do," replied Master Waleran with a confidence. "I'm sure the parchment I have provided will reach you in a moment. I, myself, and Lord Hillebrant's page, young Pieter van Duivenvoorde over there, have pored over his documents, day and night, for nearly the past week. We ask that you, as respected men of the law, exude the same effort to discover for yourself the validity of this baseless claim. I can assure you that each and every stuiver is accounted for."

"That is quite the claim," said the Alderman. "I wouldn't suppose my books would be so accurate."

"Lord Hillebrant is an extremely diligent man," replied Master Waleran. "He leaves no stone unturned, and left not detail unwritten."

"I am impressed," replied the Alderman. "This is, frankly, the first testimony of substance. It's a shame that it's the last testimony. We must take a moment to discuss." he told Master Waleran. I saw Waleran's hands tremor as he waited patiently. The thirteen men all retired to the room behind the hall to discuss. After several moments of waiting, they appeared to have reached a consensus. Shuffling out and settling back in with their old, slow bodies, the spokesman announced his verdict.

"Do you, Waleran vanden Ijssel, swear to the Holy Father, Saint Jacob, and Saint Martin that you speak the truth? Can you truly guarantee that Lord Hillebrant's records will disprove any claims made against him?" the Alderman asked.

"I swear, by all the saints and the Father himself, that Lord Hillebrant's records will refute any accusation of knowingly funding the rebel cause," replied Master Waleran. The Alderman nodded his head.

"Good. Very good. You, sir, should commend yourself. Of course, I am not to speculate any sentencing, and certainly not on behalf of my colleagues, but I would personally, be inclined to believe that you have victoriously won your master, at the very least, one fortnight. And you spoke of a page? Where is he?" asked the Alderman. Master Waleran ushered me to stand. When I did stand, I was no taller than I was sitting down—the chair on which I was seated left my legs dangling, you see. So I decided to climb the chair and stand on top of it. I noted a few of the alderman smiled when I arose. "A young scholar," the Alderman said with a grin. "Perhaps I have now proven myself to be a fool to wholeheartedly trust the work of such a young gentleman, but alas, a decision has been made." he arose from his seat. "This court decrees that Lord Hillebrant's accounts shall be made available to officers of the Council of Justice, and that these accounts are to be read through in full. A court hearing of this gravity requires a complete investigation. With that said, let's get some food, gentlemen. I am famished. Men and women of the court, you are all dismissed."

+ Maarten +

The sea turned some of the men green. It wasn't uncommon to hear some of the boys in the night yacking their guts out through the oar holes. It wasn't easy to get a good night's sleep—certainly not in the cold with little but a few old cloths to keep us warm. The deck was always wet, too. No matter where you went, water found its way in some how, either through small leaks in the lower deck or crashing waves over the upper deck. I thought of the warmth of the kilns—the blazing fire which provided for us. I thought of the colour of the charcoal when we pulled it out, and the homely warmth that erupted from the kiln as we pulled off the bricks and shoveled out its contents into barrels. That was a life worth living. I thought of Kees and Felix, and wondered what those two dummies were up to. Probably still adventuring in Frieslant, if I had to guess. Although perhaps the war was over. Perhaps peace had been restored, and the boys could finally go back to their homes and their wives. What a feeling that must be, to come home, sword at your side, but to kneel down and embrace your children. To be met with a hot meal and a warm bed. I wished it on all the men, even those that ran in the face of the enemy, and even those that did the unimaginable when they lost their wits. They were good men. At least I think they were. Nay, they are—or they will be, I suppose. They will be good men again when the killing is done.

"Wake up, Dutchies, ye snore like a bunch of animals," barked the overseer. Some of the kapmonnen came and threw buckets of seawater on those that didn't wake up quickly enough. "You lot had better keep your quiet, yeah?" he said. "You're all Frisian traders like the rest of us. If you tell these Bretons you're anything but I'll string you up by your ankles and let your juices flow before I throw you overboard." What Bretons, I wondered? As far as I knew, Brittany was a cross between France and a magical forest— teeming with the fairies and spriggans of pagan times.

Sure enough, through some holes in the side of the ship, I saw a warship headed our way. The beast had both fore and stern castles, and it towered over the waives like a great palisade of wood and light. The light of its lanterns shone brightly on the waves, setting fire to the darkness. They were my hope—I had to get myself on this boat. Once I saw that the boat had linked up with ours, I made my move. I assumed that the Frisians wouldn't make a fuss if I joined them on the upper deck—I was pretending to be one of them, after all.

Besides, what would they do, beat me? I couldn't even feel the wounds from the last one, and to do any more than that would be to damage their own merchandise. So, I ascended the stairs, catching the cool, sea breeze as I ascended to join my Frisian 'comrades.' The overseer saw me immediately.

"Oh, look who decided to join the party late," he said with a broad grin. Of course, his eyes told a much different story—one that would sound as menacing as any other time he spoke to me. I looked out into the dark waters—a storm was on the horizon. The moonlight lit up the night—the sky was a greyish lavender. The Frisians had begun to practice their French as we passed through the channel. I had been listening to their practice—hoping to learn a bit more for myself. Of course, French was spoken differently wherever you went, just like Hollanter, or Luxembourgish, or Brabantian, Deuts, Flemish, or any other language, really.

"I am Seigneur Harvey, Viscount of Léon," said the first man to approach the ship. He pulled back his cloak, revealing a livery collar bearing a black lion on gold—presumably his heraldry. "In the name of the Duke of

Britanny, the crew of this ship asks to search your cargo." He was dressed in sailor's clothes—durable, hardy things, with a hat and cloak to keep him warm. Many of his comrades appeared the same in the darkness, their cloaks flying amid the ocean spray.

"Of course," replied the captain, taking off his own hat, and bowing before them. The party of men passed through onto our deck. I noticed, as they passed, that the viscount made not of my bare feet. Among other things, he appeared to be quite suspicious of the Frisians. After a while of searching, he turned to the captain.

"May we see your lower deck?" he asked. I saw the captain freeze.

"Might we ask what you are looking for in particular, my lord?" asked the overseer. "If you are good, God-fearing men, you will have nothing to worry about." The viscount replied. I felt myself smile. Only a little, though, before I quickly corrected my expression.

"Of course," replied the captain, now getting a grip on himself. "Right this way." The viscount and the men with him were ushered down through the door that led to the lower deck. There, as he descended down the stairs, he found the other Hollanters shivering among the cargo, huddling against one another for warmth. He turned to the captain.

"That's a lot more men than I expected," he said.

"It's always good to have a few extra hands," replied the captain. The viscount appeared unconvinced. I felt a shimmer of hope grow in my stomach.

"Let's get back up to the upper deck and have a chat,"

the viscount said. The captain had no choice. When we had all made our way back upstairs, the viscount asked several armed men in maille shirts and with swords to come onto our deck. The captain's expression changed. "What's your name, captain?" asked the viscount.

"Roan the Raven." the captain replied. "I've traversed these waters many times before."

"But you've never run into me," replied the viscount. "I can't say I have."

"I know you haven't—I'd remember a face like yours," he said. "Come, now, you don't expect me to believe that those poor souls are shipmen, do you?"

"What are you getting at?" asked the captain.

"You know precisely what I mean—I know how you lot do your business. I'm surprised there's no girls down there too."

"Please, we're not monsters…"

"I can't say the same for your kinsmen," the viscount replied. "I've seen many of you folk come in these waters on your way down to Araby. Horrible things I've seen."

"What can I do to prove to you these are my men?" asked the captain.

"What's on the table?" asked the viscount. My hope now turned to disgust.

"Please, you have to help us!" I blurted, stepping forward now, to which I was held back by a couple of the kapmonnen. The viscount now looked at the captain.

"That one doesn't seem to be a shipmate, now does he?" he said.

"Please, they'll beat us now," I replied. "Now that I've given up the act they'll come for all of us."

"They won't beat you too hard, boy, they need to sell you still," he told me with a grin. "But you've cost them a whole lot more money now."

"Fine, thirty francs," said the captain. I was angry now. If I was going down, I wasn't going down without a fight.

"They have ten times that in the captain's room." I blurted. The overseer came and punched me square across the jaw. I threw one back. He was surprised—he must never have received one from a slave before. But, when I wound up for a second, I found my arm caught by a kapmon. The man stepped down on the back of my knee, driving me to the floor. The overseer, on the other hand, loomed over me with his cane now. Just as he raised it high in the air, the viscount spoke.

"Thirty francs and that one," replied the viscount. He pointed to me. "Unharmed," he added. "Well, no more than has been done." The overseer paused, waiting for the captain's reply. The captain considered for a moment.

"A man like that could fetch a fortune down south," he said.

"A man like that won't be goin' anywhere passed Nantes if you don't hand him over," the viscount replied. The captain turned to me and eyed me up and down. I saw the storm brewing in the night sky, inching ever closer.

"You're a lucky man, Salamander," the captain told me in the most rancid Dutch imaginable. "Get the coffer!" he ordered.

Chapter 19. The Rebirth: Floris

I peered over the brick ramparts of Heemskerk Castle. I felt the morning air sweep across my face. My stubble was freshly shaven—the wind clasped my cheeks with a firm and smooth embrace. The view reminded me of Duivenvoorde Castle—the moss-adorned moat, the surrounding farmland, all of it. I breathed in the damp air, and let a deep breath out. Today was the day.

"Floris?" asked Guillaume. I turned around to see the templar in his crisp white robes, beard combed, standing patiently for me. It felt strange to have such a moment of peace and tranquility, knowing the storm that was coming. "The ceremony has begun," he said with a smile. I couldn't keep my own from sprouting.

I looked down upon the fresh, white tunic of my own and my sanguine cloak. I felt sleepy—sleepy and excited. I'd spent the entire night in the chapel kneeling before the altar. I pictured Stonesplitter, laid before me below the effigy of Christ. The first few hours were excruciating. Now, I had come to peace. I was ready. The hours in silence transformed me, I felt. They settled my mind, calmed my waters.

Before my night in the chapel, I had bathed myself thoroughly. My face was smooth. I had purged myself of my wrongdoing. I took the ceremony seriously—it was a right of passage. It was my entrance into the world of my peers. I had earned this.

"Follow me, brother," Guillaume said kindly.

"When you were knighted, was it like this?" I asked him as we walked.

"Which time?" he asked. "When I was first knighted I was just a boy—and my ceremony was being ripped from my father's hands by those of my new master. The second time, I knelt before the Father just as you will now, in the Holy Temple of Solomon, and I was embraced by him, and his arms embraced me in the mantle of the Knight Templar. You, brother, will feel this warmth today," he told me. I could sure hope so.

The doors of the chapel cracked open. The hall was filled with lords and ladies, many friends, many brethren. I paused before descending the steps. This was it—this was what I'd been waiting for. Of course, I had expected it to be my father standing where Ghijsbrecht stood now—beside the priest, baring a pennant with my blazon. My squire-to-be, a young man selected from among the ranks of my men-at-arms, carried my sable greathelm. Today, as fate would have it, marks the day of my birth—befitting sight for this transcendent occasion. I suppose that today I would be reborn, in a sense. I would have to detach from all that I was to become the man I was born to be. I would be a knight.

The priest began to sing in Latin as I approached the altar, reading from a heavily decorated book of psalms. My Latin was not up to standard, but I recognized its discussion of God and duty. Upon reaching the altar, I knelt before him. The priest gave me a solemn nod of approval as I looked up at him. I began to pledge my vows.

"I, Heer Floris van Duivenvoorde, son of Heer Arend van Duivenvoorde, Baron of Duivenvoorde Castle, pledge here, on this day, anno domini 1272, to do battle with wrongdoers, protect widows, protect orphans, protect the poor, and lead the plight of the good people of Hollant. I vow never to still my blade against the forces of evil and to show mercy to those deserving." The Priest lifted Stonesplitter, with the flat of its blade tapping lightly my left shoulder.

"In the name of the Father," he said, now moving to my right, "the Son," and now back to my left, "and the Holy Ghost, I dub thee, Sir Floris, a knight of the Holy Roman Empire, defender of the faith, disciple of Saint Michael and Saint George. Be valiant and mighty," he said to me. He then proceeded to bless Stonesplitter, imbuing her with great power and bidding her only to cut the enemies of God. He then gave way to Ghijsbrecht who now stood before me. Crisply and firmly, he slapped me across the cheek.

"Suffer now the last blow you will take without recompense," he told me sternly. "And arise, my brother, a knight." I took his hand and rose to my feet. Promptly, my new squire girded my sheathed sword onto my waist while Ghijsbrecht's squire fastened my spurs to my turnshoes. Like a swarm of locusts, my fellow knights were upon me, each shaking my hand and congratulating me.

"You've earned this," said Guillaume. "Gherrijt lives through you." I couldn't help but smile.

"Always remember this day," said Ghijsbrecht. It was a joyous occasion. Amidst the chaos, I struggled to turn to the audience.

"Let the feast begin!" I hollered as best I could.

+ Maarten +

"Have you ever tasted freedom, boy?" asked the viscount. He spoke slowly so I could understand him.

"I have only been a slave for a few days, maybe half a fortnight at most," I replied. The man seemed kind—a welcome change, but I knew that beneath the lacquer of kindness hid something darker. I saw it in his eyes—he was an aged man. And he was tough, tough as iron. You heard it in his voice; it was the sort of voice that could pass for a serf, a sailor, or a knight, or, not that I've ever heard one, a king, I reckon. He seemed like a free man. He didn't seem to have the shackles of duty or liege lords or anything of the sort looming over him. I couldn't be sure if this was what he'd meant—this feeling of true freedom which he exuded, and yet, I could only answer with regards to my slavery.

"I mean real freedom, boy," he said to me, discarding his livery collar into a box with other things. It was clear to me now that this was precisely what he'd meant, and that he was no viscount at all.

"Never," I replied confidently. "But I don't crave it," I told him. "I made an oath to my beloved Yda that I would return to her, even if that means bartering myself into serfdom."

"But you are here," he told me. "Freedom is something all men crave," he said, "the serf and the duke." He placed his hand on my shoulder. "But few find it."

"Is there freedom to be found here?" I asked. "Have you escaped it?"

"Nobody truly escapes it," he replied. "But we can all try—and I think we've gotten dangerously close," he told me. "What's your name, boy?"

"Salamander," I replied. I suppose it had become my new identity. If I ever returned to Duivenvoorde or anywhere in the Low Countries, I might not want my past to come with me. And that could go in either direction. "Who are you?" I asked. He smiled at me.

"I am just a man," he told me. "And a man who doesn't keep other men bonded to him."

"Are you saying I'm not your slave anymore?" I asked.

"You never were," he replied. "You are free to go, just as any other man on this ship.

But, if you choose to, know that you are selling yourself back into the life you once lived."

He offered me a pair of clean linens out of a chest. "The life which landed you here," he added.

"You're a pirate?" I asked.

"I'm a free man," he replied. "Call me what you will."

"You don't seem so free, locking yourself away on this ship, unable to flee, barely able to dock in port without rousing the real viscount, I reckon. If there is one."

"But to be here is my choice," he said. "I love the sea. It released me, just as it has you, and when I die it will embrace me." He then dispatched his pouch from his belt and jingled it about, proving its weight. "And the sea pays handsomely," he said with a smile. "Enough to live the freest life one could ever ask for." The man had sincerity in his voice. I suppose I may only have trusted him because he granted me my freedom—something I would be eternally grateful for from any man. But, in truth, I believed every word that came from his mouth. At the very least, I believed that he believed them. This was, indeed, a man who had managed to wriggle free from the crushing social order. And, clearly, he had not been smote by God. He had yet to be a pillar made to salt the waves. I accepted the man's offer. He told me he could use a man like me—I had no doubt. I was a soldier, and I was strong from shoveling the coals. I suppose I was what one might look for in a pirate—without, of course, the seamanship.

The days were long, but they were good. I had a lot to learn. One of the men, Eustace, an Occitan, showed me the ropes, quite literally. I had learned a little from my time on the Frisian cog, but managing a warship such as this one was a whole other matter.

"You keep your body strong and your hands hard; you'll be a true seaman in no time," said Eustace. He was a tough man—he'd seen things. He told me of his family and his life back home. He told me about how they were outsiders in their village—they'd fled Albi long ago during the heresy. That was something that all of Christendom spoke of when the words 'Occitania' or 'Langedoc' met their ears. It wasn't a pleasant thought—the physical proof of the wrath the church might bring upon any outspoken man. Our grandfathers called it a defense of the faith, no different from the conquests in the Holy Land and Prussia. How times change—we civilize like our Roman ancestors. Eustace told me of how he left the village—ostracized, with little faith, only now to find himself with more food in his belly and coin in his purse than any peasant could claim. He'd grown big on the ship. He was a fighter.

But not all the men were good to me—I rubbed shoulders with the occasional sneer monger. One man in particular, Bertrand, was more than eager to run his muck-ridden boots over my freshly mopped floors or tug at my ropes, claiming they weren't good enough. I knew how to tie a damn knot as well as any other man. I never indulged him, though. There were a few moments when he'd offered me a strike—he'd slap his cheek, plunging the stubble of it in my face like it was a hay bale at an archery contest. I never struck him, no matter how hard my fist clenched in rage or how badly I wished I could send his teeth across the deck. Of course, that would risk my life. I was new, and the little faith the captain put in me would not be risked for such a loss of control. I simply stood my ground most times.

One time, however, was different. There was an arm wrestle tourney happening below deck. The men had been drinking—so had I. I think I was about three ales deep when I'd gotten word on the top deck that Bertrand and Eustace were facing off below. Of course, I had to see it for myself. Eustace, with his bright red chinstrap beard, stood hulking over the table, as Bertrand, cracking his knuckles and walking steadily so as to maintain his balance on the waves and the pints, slammed his bottom down in front of him. Their sleeves rolled—the men locked in. The captain, marshalling the competition, counted them off. Three. Two. One. And then erupted a contest of titans—the two beastly men grabbed firmly onto one another's hands and the table—I was certain if they'd gone on for long enough, the thing would've snapped in half. Of course, cheering filled the stifling air of the deck. There was no clear crowd favourite—after all, we were one crew. We all knew one another, and whether we liked it or not, we could all kill one another in our sleep. Suffice it to say, we had an easy habit of making mates of each other.

Finally, the tide began to turn in Eustace's favour. With the burst of a great wave that hit the hull, Eustace came out on top, slamming Bertrand's hand into the table. He then stood up and roared something in Occitan so vulgar I couldn't follow. Bertrand didn't look happy—he was used to being the strong man. He was used to being trusted with the rigging and the offloading of the greatest number of barrels. He wasn't one to lose.

"He cheated," he said with a slur. Nobody heard him at first, although I'd taken note of it. He repeated himself a little louder the second time. Now he'd gotten their attention.

"What did you say?" asked Eustace. As far as I'd seen, the man had done nothing wrong. Truthfully, it wasn't in his character. I'd hesitate to call him a godly man, but a cheat he certainly wasn't.

"You 'erd me," said Bertrand. Eustace's smile faded.

"I smashed that hand of yours harder than an ox pulling the plough, and you're calling me a damn cheater?"

"I said what I said," said Bertrand, standing now. "You stepped on my foot."

"I did not."

"You most certainly did, you bloody ginger."

"What did you just call me?" asked Eustace, now squaring up with the man. The captain stepped between them. He had such a commanding presence that the tankards in their bellies were not enough to cloud their minds. They stood back.

"Bertrand says Eustace step on his foot. Did anybody see their feet?" asked the captain. Immediately, I stepped forward out of the crowd, only realizing how smashed I was when I couldn't find my balance. Leaning on a beam, I spoke.

"I did, sir," I said. "Eustace's feet were right where they'd ought to have been."

"And where was that?" asked the captain.

"Are you playing, little Salamander?" asked Bertrand.

"Up Bertrand's arse," I replied the captain. That's when I realized I'd made a mistake.

I felt a set of four, bony knuckles plant themselves firmly into my forehead. My skull then thudded against the wooden beam I'd been holding onto. I plummeted to the floor. I just heard Bertrand and a few of his lackeys erupt in their drunken laughter. *Get up.* I told myself.

Bloody get the hell up. After a few deep breaths, I found my feet. I patted my eye—it was already swelling. Feeling the black ring forming sobered me a little. He saw me standing.

"Come at me, you little bootlicker," he said. I walked up to him as if I were squaring up with him.

"I'd ought to throw you in the water," I said to him. The captain tried keeping us apart. Bertrand placed his hands on my chest. From the inside, I swatted them aside, placing mine on his. He thought I was just squaring up. From there, as the taunts continued, I launched an upper cut with my right fist. I heard his teeth bite through the very tip of his tongue. While he was still dazed, I grabbed the back of his head with both hands, and rammed my knee into his groin. I then tore him, over my left foot, to his knees, where my elbow came a few times to his forehead. After a few blows, he managed to get up and tackle me over at the same time. A brawny fist slammed harshly into my nose. When it came back a second time, I felt my eyes widen. I moved my head as far to the side as I could, letting his paw make contact with the wooden deck. He cried out in frustration. I managed to roll him over, at which point we just began grappling. At one point, I think I dug my nails into his arm. At another, he bit my shoulder. The fighting continued until a great bucket of seawater drenched us both.

"Enough!" cried the captain. We both found our wits almost immediately. The salt burned the wounds. "Save it for the enemy," he grunted. "You two," he said, pointing to two other shipmates, "keep these men apart." I felt myself breathing heavily—he was too. We'd exerted ourselves.

"You fight like a bloody demon. I'll give you that much, Dutchman," he said. I couldn't help but smile a little—I knew my teeth were bright red.

"You fight like a rabid dog," I said with a chuckle, showing him the bite mark. "You smell like a fishmonger's catch," he said with a laugh.

"You two idiots nearly turned the boat over," said Eustace, giving us both a hand. He turned to Bertrand. "Suffice it to say, I won, eh?"

"If I knew you'd have this ship rat to fight a duel for

you, I wouldn't have started nothing," he said with a smile. "Who the damn hell are you, Dutchman?" he asked me.

"I was a charcoal burner," I said. "And then a soldier."

"Did you scratch your enemies, soldier?" he asked, showing me his arm.

"Nay, I was fighting in Friesland. If it came close enough for that, scratching would do me no use against those wolves of men." I told him.

"I heard that a Frisian fights no different from an ape," said Eustace.

"They are far more terrible," I replied. "An ape uses his fists out of instinct. He fights because God put the idea in his head. A Frisian fights for his home. His wife and his child."

"And for a good coin or two," said Bertrand with a laugh. "The Frisian merchants that come out here would sell their wives or their children for a chest of silk, I tell ye." I gave him a look of disdain.

"I've felt their blood on my skin," I said. "I know these men. They are warriors, all." I told him. That's all I could say—every kapmon would pick up a blade if the time was right. I knew that to be a fact—no matter how much gold he craved. Seagulls interrupted our conversation.

"You hear that?" asked Eustace. "Seagulls, out here?"

"We're too far from shore for these bastards," said Bertrand. Many of the sailors drunkenly stumbled our way to the upper deck. Sure enough, swarms of the little white demons circled above us, riding the winds like kites.

"A storm is coming," said the captain. "All hands!" he

barked. The *all hands on deck* meant only one thing—the captain expected the storm to be large. Sure enough, through the dark of night, revealed only by the purple tint of moonlight, I saw it—a wall of black and grey thundering toward us. The rain picked up. Eustace took me by the shoulder.

"Man, the damn oars," he said, the pouring rain now sticking his hair to his face. "The winds are bad. We have to row ourselves out." Without a word, I followed his instructions. I echoed his orders.

"Man, the bloody oars!" I shouted. Firmly gripping one of the long, wooden beams and plunging it through the side of the ship into the waves below, I prepared myself for a long night.

+ Piet +

There was not a single quiet moment in the house anymore. Scores of record-keepers and other men working for the burgher council came and went as they pleased, muddying the carpets in Lord Hillebrant's office. This was a victory, for now at least. Lord Hillebrant was still alive as long as these men pored over the endless scrolls and books and loose leaflets of parchment.

"How long will they be here for?" I asked Master Waleran over dinner one night.

"For as long as they need to be," he said, looking at the reactions of the other pages and servants. "Miss Filomena, a little more pea soup?"

"Do you think Lord Hillebrant is okay?"

397

"They will not let him fall ill," said Master Waleran. "If they do, and he dies because of it, they will have failed at law."

"Is there anything else we can do?" I asked. He gave me a warm look. "You've already done more than enough," he replied.

"You're a little hero," said Miss Filomena. "And heroes get extra pork in their soup," she said, dropping a few more hunks of pink meat into my bowl. "To grow strong and fit like a knight," she smiled.

"Will I be a knight?" I asked.

"If you'd like to be," she said. "Or, I suppose, you could be like Lord Hillebrant."

"A knight of the pen," said Master Waleran. "Far mightier than any sword I've seen."

"A sword would do Lord Hillebrant good," I said. "That way, he could make his mistake, and nobody would have to read all these pages of parchment." Master Waleran and Miss Filomena laughed.

"Little lad, you're quite a troublemaker, aren't you?" asked Miss Filomena. "I know what you can do to help. Lord Hillebrant has had all the legal help he can muster, but the Lord is always watching, and I believe an eloquent young man such as yourself might just sway him." Master Waleran scoffed.

"What would you have him do, say his daily prayers?" he asked with sarcasm. Miss Filomena scowled at him.

"The boy needs God in his life—he can't just read those

math books of yours and think he knows the world." She turned to me. "Why don't we go to the beguinage tomorrow. We will ask the sisters there to pray for our Lord Hillebrant."

"Why do we need them to do it?" I asked.

"It never hurts to have a few sisters of the church on your side in matters of fate," said Miss Filomena.

"Yes, yes, you two go off on your adventure. I'll be here, watching the books," said Master Waleran.

The next morning came early—the sun peaked through the windows and pulled me out of my slumber. I hopped out of bed and donned my clothes while the other servant boys stayed fast asleep. Of course, Miss Filomena was already up and about, stirring in the kitchen. A servant girl was working there with her.

"Go now to the market and fetch us another few sacks of grain, will you? She asked the girl, handing her a few coins."

"Yes, miss," said the girl with a curtsey. Quickly, she was on her way.

"Don't think I don't notice you stirring about, young man," said Miss Filomena with a smile. I peeked out from around the corner. "Come here and give me a hand with the bread," she said. I walked over to her to see what I could do.

"Why don't you just buy bread from the baker instead of flour?" I asked. She let out a short but hearty laugh.

"Lord Hillebrant is wealthy, but not *that* wealthy," she said. "If we were to buy bread every morning for all of you boys down here, you'd eat the town empty," she said with a smile. She paused. "Did your mother ever teach you how to make bread?" she asked.

"No," I replied, shaking my head. "She always said it was women's work. She taught my sisters." Miss Filomena clicked her tongue and shook her head.

"You won't get too far if you don't know how your trencher's made," she said. "A boy like you'd ought to learn. Here," she said, "Here, fill up one of those wooden bowls to a half with flour." She told me. I did as I was told. "Now, add a hunk of old dough. Here," she said, handing a small handful of it to me. "And now, let's just add some water," she said, taking water out of a bucket with a ladle to wet her own bowl, and then doing the same for mine.

"Now what?" I asked.

"Now we mix it all up, and when it all feels the same, we knead it to pick up all the leftover flour and oats," she said. "Just like this." Her hands were strong—you could see the veins in her knuckles pop every time she pressed down into the mixture. They moved quickly like they'd done this a thousand times before. I reckon they had. I tried my best to mix my own dough together—it was hard work. After a while, I let Miss Filomena take over for mine, too. Again and again, she pressed down into the dough, letting the air slowly but surely seep out of it. It was a tough process—it took a long time. I watched and watched as she continued. We spoke as she worked. We talked about bread, what made good bread good, and why the bread rises. She said it was a little miracle every time the dough naturally grew when we left it. But, she said that we always had to add a bit of old dough for good luck. She knew a lot about bread. She spoke about how the colour of the bread determined how good it was —the darker it was, the more stalk and oats it had, so it wasn't as high quality. For the House of ver Heyen, only the best quality there was. They only every bought flour as white as snow.

"What sort of bread do they eat at the beguinage?" I asked. I'd never been to one before. I couldn't have imagined they'd have anything quite as nice, but, of course, those were burgher daughters there in the cloisters, not simple women.

"I suppose you'll have to ask them yourself when we go there." Miss Filomena replied.

The building itself was quite plain. Brick, of course, as all the important buildings were, the crimson cloister could have passed for any old church attached to a few halls if I hadn't known beguines lived in there. They were religious women, like nuns, but they lived in the towns. Mother always said a nun's place was in the countryside, away from the world—but she wasn't one, so who's to say if she was right?

When we were let inside, the place filled me with a calmness—it had a serenity to it that couldn't be found anywhere else in the city. Nowhere else but tucked way in my bed back at the manor, I suppose. Short walls surrounded the building, creating an inner bailey of sorts matted with lanes of green grass for the beguines to enjoy the outdoors without too much interaction with the outside. There were small cells attached to the wall where a few recluses lived, acting as a hermit medium between the beguinage and the outside world.

"Good morning, Mother," said Filomena, bowing her

head to one of the beguines who came to meet us. She looked less like a nun, and more just like a wealthy old lady. The only thing that kept her apart from other women, I suppose, was the white scarf that wrapped itself in all sorts of strange ways upon her head. For the rest, her dress and all was nothing I hadn't seen before on the streets of Leyden.

"Good morning, madam," said the lady in a calm, gentle voice. "May I be of assistance?"

"Yes, Mother, we are here to pray for a dear friend of ours. Our liege lord, Heer Hillebrant ver Heyen," replied Miss Filomena. A troubled look marked the face of the woman.

"Ver Heyen, you say?" she asked. "Word of his arrest has found its way even inside this wall, madam. You must, indeed, be concerned."

"Yes, Mother." Miss Filomena replied. "Tell me what we must do."

"Leity are not usually allowed inside these walls…" said the beguine. I lost her when I saw, out of the corner of my eye, two young girls, seemingly stacked on top of one another, trying to reach the top of a cabinet down the hall. I squinted my eyes. It couldn't be! Before even thinking, I felt my feet race down the brick-lain hallway.

"Merin! Florie!" I exclaimed. Like a stack of linens, I saw Merin wobble from side to side before tumbling down.

"Pieter!" they both said in unison. I ran over to them, where I was soon squeezed by a massive hug.

"We looked all over for you!" they said.

"What are you doing here? In the beguinage?" I asked, confused.

"The nuns at the abbey said we were causing too much trouble," said Merin.

"So they granted us to the beguinage," added Florie with a smile.

"Maurits and Thiel are in the city too!" she said.

"I know!" I told them. "I found them in the stocks!"

"Did they end up getting out?" asked Merin.

"A man named Lauerens helped them," I said. "He's a friend of Lord Hillebrant's…"

"What are you three little panotti doing making all this noise?" asked the beguine, who I now realized had caught up to us. Miss Filomena did not look impressed. The beguine towered over us.

"I'm sorry, Mother Margareta," said Merin.

"The three of you, if you wish to speak, speak outside," said the beguine. As we were told, we shuffled our way out of the building and into the courtyard. Here, the noise of all the hustle and bustle of the city was muted by the thick brick walls. The grass was green, and small gardens were tended to by the beguines.

"Did you know that this whole place was built by the beguines?" Florie asked.

"I didn't know that," I said. "That's a lot of work."

"It must have been," Florie said. "Did you help?"

"It was built before we came here."

"Oh," I said. We walked around a little bit, talking about the adventures we'd gone on. I learned about their lives at the abbey and how they finally came here. I told them everything about Lord Hillebrant and my time there as a page, and also about the trial. "You've read a lot!" said Merin.

"I have," I said. "When you're both beguines, I suppose you will too…"

"I don't know if we will be," said Florie.

"Why not?" I asked.

"Well, we aren't from one of the burgher families. We're serfs, remember?"

"So?"

"*So*, we can't just be *allowed* to be beguines," said Merin. "It's not like you, who was just taken in by a noble."

"Hey, that's not fair. I'm working hard at the manor," I said, feeling my face flex into a frown. "He's training me to be a lawyer, like him," I said. "I read all day, and when I don't, I'm always being tested and working hard."

"Piet, you have a good future ahead of you," said Florie. "You'll be a lord someday. We aren't nobles. We'll be working for the beguinage until we're old."

"Then, when I'm a noble, you can come live with me," I said with a broad smile. "You won't have to work another day," I said. Merin gave me a smile. Florie did not.

"But what if you forget about us," she said. I could see

water welling in her eyes.

"Mother's gone," she said. I could feel her fighting back tears. "Since Mother gave us away, we've all been apart." I saw water now rushing from her eyes and nose. I offered my sleeve to wipe it off, but she used her apron instead.

"When we're older, we'll all get back together. It'll be just like back in Duivenvoorde," I said. "I promise."

"Now that we're here," said Merin, "You can come visit us," she said.

"Of course!" I said. "I'll visit as much as I can." I felt at the coin purse that hung at my belt. "I have a few coins," I said. "What do you say we get ourselves some sweet waffles?" I asked. Florie nodded. I felt horrible—she was right. I was living in the warm manor, eating my pork and eggs and buying my sweets, while Merin and Florie were here sweeping the floors and helping in the kitchen and doing what they had to do. It wasn't fair; they were right. I promised myself that I would visit as much as I could. And when the time came, and I had a house or a space to myself, they could live there too, for as long as they wanted. Florie could make her art, and Merin could read her books, sing her songs, or do whatever she wanted to do.

The day was good, and when it became dark and it was time to go, it was hard to leave. When I nestled into bed that night, I couldn't stop thinking of the beguinage and the life that Merin and Florie found themselves in. It was peaceful, sure, but it was quiet, boring, and stale. They seemed tired. No matter how much I knew they loved talking in the garden and listening to the nuns sing, I also knew that they needed to explore and eat sweets and play. I smelled smoke.

"Lads, do you smell that?" asked one of the servant boys in one of the cots beside me. There was silence and the ruffling of attentive ears rising in woolen blankets. Then I heard a faint crack.

"Godverdomme, there's a fire!" shouted another. Immediately, most of them sprung into action. Miss Filomena came rushing into the room.

"Everybody up! Everybody up, let's go!" she shouted.

"Water, fetch some water!" shouted Master Waleran. There was chaos, complete and utter chaos. I felt myself picked up by Master Waleran, who took me to the upper floor on our way to the front door. I looked upstairs through the bannister. Lord Hillebrant's office was set ablaze. A vivid and ferocious orange raged in the room—bright as the sun.

"The accounts." Master Waleran muttered as he placed me on my feet outside. He went charging back into the building. "Save the accounts! Water! Water! To his office!" he shouted. It was cold outside—the night was dark, and there was no sun to be seen. I had wanted to help, but there was nothing I could do. Nay, that's what they'd say, but that's what they said about Lord Hillebrant, too. I rushed back into the house to fetch a pale. Then, I ran out to fetch more water from the canal one street over. Once I'd filled it up, I lifted the wooden bucket with all my might and quickly marched it back to the house. Energetic hands took the burden off of me and rushed up the stairs to throw it into the fire.

Armoured feet clanked down the street. I saw the lanterns and goedendags of the town watch hustling towards the house.

"There's a fire!" I shouted. "Fire!" By now, most of the neigbours had also been awoken and poured out into the streets. All of them came to help, fetching water from the nearby well and the canals, all rushing to dump it on the fire. Servant boys carried out all of Lord Hillebrant's most valuable possessions—his jewelry, chests of fabric and clothes, and, of course, all the alcohol. God knows what would happen if his cellar ignited. The fire was eventually kept at bay. Slowly but surely, they were all able to contain it and fight it back. But Master Waleran was right—the accounts, all the records of transactions and credits and debts and all of it, were all crisp and blackened. They were gone. They were all gone. And with it, I feared, Lord Hillebrant would be too.

When all the fire was blackened again, and only charred wood with orange tips remained, a man stepped out from the crowd. It was the Alderman, apparently he'd come to help fight the fire. But, his news was bleak. He stepped forward to speak to Master Waleran, with the assemblage of town watchmen behind him.

"I am so sorry this happened to you, Master Waleran," he said, placing his hand on Master Waleran's shoulder.

"It couldn't be helped, I suppose. Perhaps a candle was left lit and spilled over," he replied. "I give you my thanks for rushing here with your water so quickly."

"It is the mark of any good citizen," the Alderman replied, his hat conspicuously absent, adding curious informality to his demeanor. "Unfortunately, however, it was not a candle but a man who set the office ablaze,

Waleran," he said.

"Nay, nay, nay, that would make no sense, who would…"

"We do not know," said the Alderman. "The watchmen saw him, and he is being hunted down as we speak—that dastardly rogue. In the meantime, the trial of Lord Hillebrant is to be paused."

"Please, let him live here—if he is to pay later, he will pay his fine. He is growing weak, Alderman. He is an older gentleman…"

"Enough," said the Alderman. "You have had your moment to plea in court, and a decision was made then."

"Clearly, circumstances have changed. How are we to prove his innocence if the records are all burned?" asked Master Waleran.

"You cannot," said the Alderman with the most foul expression imaginable. "Your plea is lost, Waleran. I suggest you get used to Lord Hillebrant no longer around."

"Godverdomme…"

"Schutterij," the Alderman ordered, "Help clean up this mess," he said. He made intense eye contact with Master Waleran. "And make sure the citizens remain calm," he added. The big guardsmen nodded, hanging back as the Alderman sauntered off into the black.

Chapter 20. The Snake: Wollefram

"A nest of damned serpents, the lot of them, those Amstellanders. Bloody traitors. They spit on my father's good name. They spit on his Godverdomde legacy," shouted the count. His mailed fist pounded through the war table, nearly splintering its finely carved edge to bits.

"Settle down, Florens," replied Jan van Nassau, Prince-Bishop of Utrecht. He bore the character of a godly man well—his calm demeanour contrasted that of the count's in all ways of contending. "You are still just a boy."

"And?"

"And, Alexander only conquered the Orient with twenty-two years of age. You only have eighteen. You have already made a name for yourself—tales of the chivalrous knights questing out to vanquish the heathen have made their way across the Low Countries and far beyond. They cheer your name."

"They do?" asked the count.

"They do, indeed," the Prince-Bishop replied.

"But I have only subdued a heathen backwater—a set of barbarians and inbreds," said Florens. He was right—his rare moment of self-reflection had cast a dangerous shadow of doubt among the men that filled the war tent. Jan paced about the table as if to plan the army's next moves carefully. "Why, again, do you wish to war with the count of Amstel?"

"He disobeyed my orders, has now aligned himself with the horde of unwashed filth, and has no doubt made a covenant with the Devil himself," Florens replied. I couldn't help but smirk. Us ver Heyens were ruthless, we knew that. This wasn't a game; this was war. It was coming; it was inevitable. All we had to ensure was that our enemies were all neatly packaged together.

"It would be unwise to act with haste," said Jan.

"Oh, would it now? A blight of unholy revolution burns across *my* lands, *my* people, and you would tell me to slow my hand?"

"Your father had the mind of an emperor. He *was* an emperor," said Jan. "Are you calling me weak of mind?" asked Florens.

"Nay, only that you have yet to achieve his mastery of the battlefield. You only lack… experience," said Jan. "We have more resources than they do. We are upper nobility for Christ's sake," he hastily made the sign of the cross to correct his lapse in performance. "I am both a man of the cloth and of the sword. What these peasants do is foul, and any man who would help them, even my own vassal, Ghijsbrecht, is a traitor unto God and unto the realm. Rest assured; I would smite them just as Archangel Michael smote Lucifer to the abyss."

"We should crush them while we have the chance. We bring it to a great battle, draw out their masses of dung-covered low-borns, and ride them down."

"Then who would till your fields, Count?" asked Jan.

"They deserve to water my fields with their blood—they have foregone their right to reap my crops," said Florens with a rage that singed the air. I glanced at the nobles, who all stood around the two men, listening to the conversation at hand.

"They *deserve* a chance at redemption once they have seen what we can truly unleash upon them," said Jan. "We show them the very might of God. We bring them hell. We burn everything, slowly but surely. We force them to run south. We take every castle, burn and loot every village until they have no choice but to submit and return to their homes to rebuild. What say you men of the war council?" he asked.

"Aye" came from most of the men, accompanied by hesitant nods from others. My head remained firm. The ver Heyen lands were safe and secure. I only wanted to hunt down the men of the Wassenaer. The Duivenvoorders would be crushed once and for all.

"Prima, I suppose it is settled," Jan said to Florens. "Have you any further suggestions?" he asked, perhaps out of sarcasm, to humiliate the young count. After all, he was the adult here now to swoop in like a gryphon to clean up his mess. Florens gave him a sneer.

"I will prove that Hollanter knights fight like lions," he said. He grabbed his dagger and plunged it into a parchment with a list of manorial fiefs on it. "We will restore order to this land. I swear it, by Saint Paulus and the Virgin Mary."

"That was quite the spectacle, eh Wollefram?" said a Johannes vander Wassenaer, making his way out of the tent with the rest of us. I don't know what compelled him to begin conversation with me. I suppose he wanted something— that's the only incentive a man of the House of Wassenaer could have to bring himself to speak with us. I felt bad for him, of course, he had lost a son. But, in this world of war and politicking, there is no time for mercy nor remorse. For all intents and purposes, he was a coward. I saw him as one, as did my father, and my uncle. His nephew ran about playing knight with Ghijsbrecht and his crew of outcasts, while his uncle, Johannes, chose to stand by the crown. An impressive display of loyalty and oathkeeping, to be sure, but a severe lack in judgement. He was outnumbered here. He was a rotting fish with no water to swim back to among these men—he had the traitor's blood in his veins. A growing suspicion about him ran deep among the nobles in the loyalist camp. Trust was important in war. One had to know that his brother-in-arms would not flee the field. One had to know that such a man would slay his own nephew, would the time arise. I do not believe he would.

"I suppose," I replied. I believe he only chose to speak to me as I am the youngest ver Heyen here. Unce Renier was a gruff man—he prized his martial prowess as a marker of his knighthood. It was immensely important to him, as were loyalty and integrity—escutcheons impassable to Johannes' naked blade.

"Have you heard the news of your uncle, Hillebrant?" Johannes asked. He caught my attention now. "Your father, Lodewijk, is a busy man, I am well aware, but I believe this may be of import to him."

"You should speak with him, then," I replied.

"Would you pass on the message?" asked the Hollanter.

"What of him?" I asked.

"He has been found guilty of embezzlement and treachery to the Count by the Burghermeister of Leyden," said Johannes.

"Hold your tongue, you viper," I replied. "What have you done?" I saw a crooked smile reveal the teeth he had left below his unkempt moustache.

"This decision was made by the aldermen of Leyden and the judicial council alone," he replied. His expression said otherwise.

"We are allies, Johannes. You treacherous bastard."

"You listen here, boy," said Johannes. "I know you poisoned the count's ear against my family. I remain loyal to him—it is my duty as his vassal, but if you grubby ver Heyens believe you will ever set foot in the Wassenaer, you are sorely mistaken. Once the young Duivenvoorde and his boys are wrung by their necks for treachery, my brother's estate is mine. Why don't you go pass that on to your father."

"You dishonourable pig of a man," I replied. "If one hair on my uncle's hair is removed, I will personally have you pried out of your maille and hacked to bits." I felt the rage of a thousand suns burning in me.

"You have my word," replied Johannes. He extended his hand for a handshake to mark the deal.

"Save yourself the effort—neither of us wish to catch a fever," I replied. "Go run off now to your plotting and scheming. You knights of the Wassenaer only ever think of yourselves."

"I do this for my family."

"You have betrayed your family," I replied. "And you have betrayed allies of your sworn liege, Florens. You lack honour, sir."

"Since when did a ver Heyen ever care about honour?"

+ Floris +

"Lions of Hollant, stand at the ready!" I shouted to the motley crew of farmers and town dwellers who stood before me. Pitch forks, threshing flails, clubs, wood axes, and what have you. A few of them held lootes voulges or spears or polearms of the sort. The mob of men didn't move. Nearly two hundred of them stood before me. "Alright, what formations have you been using?"

"Formations?" asked one of them. "Like what?"

"Like, how do you stand when you are ready to do battle as an army?" I asked. Most of them shrugged or looked confused. "For the love of God, please tell me you weren't just planning on rushing at the enemy as an undisciplined mob," I said.

"With all due respect, not a man here's fought in a battle before these past few weeks.

Nobody here's been trained for war like you knights," he said. "But what we've been up to seems to do the trick— the trained waffenknechten and schutterij usually crumble to bits after a good charge at them."

"But how many do you lose in the process?" I asked. "How many of your brothers fall because you lack discipline?" I nodded to my men who waited on the sidelines of the field.

A few wagons full of fresh gambesons and goedendags were ready to be distributed there. "Here, we have purchased a new bulk load of quilted armour and goedendags, real weapons, for you all to carry into battle. We will teach you how they are to be used. I suggest, if you have an axe or a dagger, or a kitchen knife, or something of the sort, you keep it girded to your belt, just in case. The distribution process was sluggish. As the peasants walked up in several lines to receive their arms and armour, I noted that many of them were not truly fit to fight. Some of them were injured, others were elderly, and others were boys of no more than fourteen or fifteen years of age. I suppose I had my work cut out for me—I would transform this horde into a well-trained, well-disciplined unit.

By the time the armouring was done, they had looked a little more uniform now.

"Look at yourselves, men," I said with a grin. "You're soldiers now—fighting men. The armour hides all imperfections. Those jackets can take several arrows before giving in and can stop the strike of a mace or even the cut of a sword. Feel confident, men," I said. I began to pace up and down the line. I began to transform my voice into my command voice. "Now, form a line!" I shouted. "Shoulder to shoulder! I don't want Kees, that massive bastard there, to be able to break through you, even if he charged at full speed." They slowly shuffled together to form their line. It was thin in some parts and thick in others; I had some of the Duivenvoorders even it out a little and straighten it. "You move as one," I said. "You march as one. You are one beast—one dragon. Every one of you is a scale in its mantle. You do not survive as a warrior—you are a soldier, you protect your brothers, and they protect you." I looked to Kees. "Alright, boys, now drop your goedendags, all of you," I said. They did as they were told. I nodded to Kees, who took a heater shield and charged straight into the lines. As expected, it wasn't long before he managed to plough through five men and tear a hole in the line—it crumpled like paper soon after. "Again, hold firm this time." They repeated the drill again; this time, the ox-man charged a different section of the line. I had a few more Duivenvoorders join in now, and I repeated the drill again and again until the rebels managed to hold their own, turning the field into a pushing match between two large scores of men.

They were fast learners, and each baron in Ghijsbrecht's army received just as many of these Kennemers. We called them Kennemers—they were really a mix of Kennemers, Amstellanders, Frisians, Waterlanders, and the like.

It was time to change things up. I mounted my destrier.

"You can stop a few men now," I said. "But the enemy will not break your line with men alone. You will need to have enough mass to stop a horse," I said. Of course, when I rode at them, the line crumbled once more as it had at the beginning—no man in his right mind would stand to face the impact of a horse and his rider.

"You're out of your Godverdomde mind!" shouted one of them.

"Nay, nay, whatever hits you take now will only strengthen you. But, you are right," I said. "Never stand a horse without a weapon in your hand. Pick up your goedendags." I looked to my men. "You three, Felix, Kees, and whatever your name is, stand to face my horse," I ordered. I stood in front of the line of men so that they all could see. "Three men should take one horse," I said. "One man, the man directly in front of the animal, should pierce it with his goedendag to stop the animal. Next, the man behind him, to his right, should use his spike to peirce through the maille of the rider on his approach. At the same time, the man behind him to his left should use the club head to hit the rider off his horse, where the two supporting men can now pin him to the ground while the first man finishes him with his dagger. Understand?" I asked. The group of men looked a little confused. I had my men-at-arms come to help them practice. "Divide yourselves up into groups of three, and pick a rider. Together, you will go through the motions. My Duivenvoorders will come by to instruct you," I said.

Their training was progressing well. In a matter of days, the Kennemers had gone from mere rabble to drilled, trained soldiers. They had the heart for it—they trained every moment they had when they weren't required to labour, or hunt, or keep watch. They were fighting for their homes, their families. I could see it in every swing of the goedendag, and every practice charge. They practiced like the devil stood before them. They saw the enemy in their eyes. They knew him well—the hatred they held for their lords burned hot. Of course, they were natural beasts. Their labour in the fields rendered them hard, and what they'd seen, harder. They were big men, most of them, those whose meat hadn't shriveled from a diet of leftover grain.

Ghijsbrecht was a king to them. I remember the moment the first emissaries came from loyalist lords who wished to turn sides. The whole army had come out to see Ghijsbrecht marched toward them. I remember the rustling of his maile hauberk drowned out by the ferocious cheers, "Hooftman! Hooftman! Hooftman!" They lacked composure, as one might expect.

These were not the diligent, disciplined serfs or waffenknechten we were used to—we couldn't call them rats or pig-dogs or maggots; they were men. They expected to be treated as men.

Several other lords flocked to us. They turned sides the moment they saw Florens break composure. Of course, the Prince Bishop was also not entirely popular—several barons trickled in from Utrecht and Cologne to support our cause as well. They were welcomed with open arms— each retinue was given at least fifty Kennemers to bolster their ranks. The Kennemers knew the land, and the barons knew the order of battle.

"They're progressing well," said Guillaume to me one night after dinner. We were looking out together over the merlons of Slot Heemskerk. He had weight in my mind—he was an experienced warrior. He knew what would become of untrained men.

"Well enough?" I asked him. We made cheers with our tankards.

"Only time can reveal what God has in store for them. You are doing all you can," he said, placing a hand on my shoulder.

"Their lives are in my hands," I told him. "No knight has ever been afraid of a sod-painted low-born."

"Do you remember the books your father used to read you when you were a boy?" asked Guillaume. "The books on knighthood, and chivalry, and the proper demeanour of a nobleman."

"I do," I replied. "Although I can't recount much from them now. It feels like the tenets they preached have all fallen by the wayside now."

"Never mind that," said Guillaume. "Do you remember the drawings, Brother Robbrecht left in the margins? The snails and the blemmyes and the two-legged gryphons?" I felt myself laugh. I thought he was being serious.

"What about them?" I asked with a smile.

"Think about how terrifying a man-sized snail would truly be. No matter how slowly the beast moved."

"I suppose. What do you mean?" I said. I was lost with this one—I wasn't sure what his lesson was meant to be this time.

"You treat each Kennemer as a snail. Small, insignificant, harmless. Easily crushed beneath a mailed boot," said Guillaume. "But they are not alone. They are the man-sized snail. They are headed by scores of men like you—experienced, trained since birth, and eager for war. They are in large numbers—enough to swallow the enemy whole. They know the land. These are *their* fields. *Their* villages. They are dangerous, Floris. Feel the power you wield. Florens does. Jan, too—he wouldn't have entered the war if he hadn't. Those lords are trembling in their decorated tents, sipping their Italian wines. But, rest assured, they are trembling. And planning. And they will do all they can to reap victory because they know you are a threat. Do not underestimate them, and do not underestimate yourself." I suppose he was right. These men at my command were each experts in their own right. I could use this. I stood up. I turned to my squire.

"Fetch me a few volunteers," I told him. "Under cover of night, I wish to ride out and learn this land. I want to know everything there is to know about it. Every dyke, every windmill, every wood. Oh, and fetch men who can ride."

+ Wollefram +

"The preparations have been made, gentlemen," said the Prince Bishop. Jan appeared quite contented with himself. By now, Florens sat behind him, shunned from the discourse.

"In the name of God and the Empire of Holy Romans, we shall begin our assault today. No quarter for the heathen. No quarter for the pretenders. Bring me their heads, gentlemen," he ordered. That wrapped up our meeting or today. We all had our orders. But, there was one matter left for us ver Heyens.

"One moment, gentlemen," said my father.

"What is it, Lodewijk?" asked Jan.

"It has come to my attention that there is a rat in our midst," he replied. Father was an honourable man. He would always appeal to authority when needed, and in this case, it was the proper course of action. "Heer Johannes vander Wassenaer threatened my brother's life through my son yesterday. I will not stand by idly without reporting such an offense to my liege." Florens arose from his seat.

"This is troubling news, Lodewijk. Why would my vassal Hannes decide to do such a thing?" asked Florens.

"A simple spat between houses, sir. Our houses have been feuding since our grandparents' generation. More recently, I believe you ruled in favour of my brother, Lord Hillebrant ver Heyen, in his petition to liberate the child Pieter van Duivenvoorde."

"Ah yes, I remember now," said Florens. His eyes turned to Johannes. "Heer Lodewijk would challenge your honour, Johannes. What say you to this?"

"I have lost my one and only son, and you plague me with these ridiculous accusations?" asked Johannes. "Your brother, Hillebrant, was arrested and tried for embezzlement and funding the Kennemer rebels. When the investigation was underway, he had his records burned so that no representative of the courts could sift through them. He is a guilty man and a traitor, Lodewijk."

"I give you this one chance to reconsider your words, Johannes," said my father. I had never seen him grow so red. Even Uncle Renier reached for his blade.

"I have no evidence nor time for this," said the Prince Bishop. "I cannot speak to your Johannes' integrity either. I know him not. I leave this in your hands, Florens."

"Well," said Florens, "I know both of these families well. I find myself torn between my duties to the Empire and my loyalty to my vassals. What's more, as you said, Jan, we have not been presented with any evidence."

"This must be dealt with," said Jan.

"Please, Count Florens, seek justice. My brother is an innocent man," said my father. I felt his urge to ask for the corroborating words of the other Gelrelanter barons, but it occurred to me that my father was practicing restraint as Lord Hillebrant was, after all, a lawyer, not a knight. He supported the merchants in the towns and the burghers—he supported the very forces which saugth to uproot noble society. We would find no support among the nobility here. Us ver Heyens would have to stick together.

"I suggest you resolve this *spat* among yourselves," said Florens. "You are grown men and respectable lords. Figure it out," he said. My father grew even more red.

"Fine then," said Uncle Renier, stepping in now. "I would not have resorted to such extreme measures, but an innocent man lies deep behind the territory of the enemy, and his jailor stands before us." I did not know what he was about to do. He stepped forth to Johannes, who stood with the composition of a damned stone. I could see the fear in his eyes, though. Renier pulled one of his riding gloves from his belt. I couldn't help but smirk.

Johannes stood no chance. He then slapped the man's moustached cheek, and dropped the glove before him on the ground. And then he spat on the ground, and said the words. "Baron Johannes vander Wassenaer, I, Sir Renier ver Heyen, hereby challenge you to a duel to the death, a trial by combat, to settle the dispute of the trial of Lord Hillebrant ver Heyen. May God decide the righteous victor." Johannes grew pale. God have mercy on his soul. He looked to Florens. Florens provided no recourse.

"Your response, Johannes?" the count asked. Johannes scanned the room—how could he dare to refuse? He was in a war tent, surrounded by knights and men of the sword. If he could not stand up for his actions with the might of a sword, how could he dare to lead a damn army? "I accept your challenge," replied the baron. "When would you have us do battle?"

"Here. Now," replied Renier. "My brother rots in a cell, and every moment we waste, his jailors inch closer to his execution."

"You heard the man, Florens; let us draw up the documents," said Jan.

"Hannes, you have sorely miscalculated," said Florens. "I wish both competitors the best of luck and the Grace of God."

They met on a polder near the camp. All the great barons came to watch the duel unfold. Florens and Jan stood on either side of the competitors. Renier and my father spoke for a long time. Finally, they touched foreheads.

"Good luck, brother," said Father. "Send the bastard to hell."

"I do this for Hillebrant," replied Renier. "When the day is done, by God, let that fat bastard come live with us in Gelrelant."

"God willing," Father replied. "Give him naught but steel." Renier nodded, slamming his knuckles together as he approached the green. Across from him, Johannes stood, sword and buckler in hand.

"Alright, gentlemen, you know what happens now," said Jan. "Two men enter the field, and one leaves. Have you made your peace with God?"

"I have," both replied in unison.

"You may touch blades, gentlemen. May God have mercy on you both."

"May the better man win," said Renier.

"God knows His own," replied Johannes with a sneer. The two men touched their blades together, and then the battle began. It was slow and methodical. They switched between stances and guards—they wore not armour, only the cloth they dressed in daily.

Renier's coif kept his long hair to his head. Johannes' bowl cut sluttered in the heavy wind. It was a cold day— brisk. The wind made it worse. The earth of the polder was soft, caving in beneath their feet. At places, it was slippery, even. I prayed for Renier's safety. The clashes of sword and buckler were brief and violent. And they were awkward.

Their sword arms moved as fluidly as water. Well, Renier's were somewhat more efficient than Johannes's, who were elegant but ineffective. He frequently misjudged his spacing and quickly became tired, failing to move his buckler along with his sword hand, exposing it. It was only a matter of time before Renier's blade would hack his wrist. The art was to do it safely without being cut himself. Both of them, like myself, would have been taught to fight with sword and buckler since childhood. It was not an art in war, but it was essential to knighthood.

It was how gentlemen were to fight. It showed a degree of bravery to fight another man without armour, risking one's own life. But no life was lost that day—only a few fingers.

Renier managed to catch Johannes' blade in a bind with his sword and buckler. He then cast the blade aside with his buckler. Johannes had no more energy to lift his own buckler, leaving the perfect opening. Renier found his angle, slashing at Johannes' hand.

Immediately, the baron dropped his blade. Three of his fingers flew into the water. Like a coward, he dropped his buckler as well, falling to his knees. The dirt squelched below him—he was wet and muddy. He begged for mercy. Renier looked to Florens and Jan, who both signaled that the fight was over.

"God has chosen His victor," said Jan. "Now he must claim his prize." The document stood on a wooden table which had been brought out to the field. Renier didn't even pay any more attention to Johannes. He simply left him in the mud to reel in pain. "Johannes van der Wassenaer is hereby found guilty of perjury and fabrication." He turned to the bloodied baron, struggling to rise to his feet. "We have no room for criminals in our camp. Get out of the Low Countries. If you return to this diocese, Johannes, you will be hunted and slaughtered like a wild pig. You are hereby banished as an outlaw." The sentence was harsh. I suppose, to Jan, God did truly decide this day. Johannes' expression was that of utter despair. We had crushed the man—robbed him of everything. Justice had been done.

He couldn't read—Lodewijk corroborated that the clauses were correct. Renier stamped the document with his seal. After his hand was wrapped, Johannes did the same with his left hand. The day was done. Once the wax had dried, Lodewijk took the document in haste.

"Come, we have no time to lose," he said, trodding through the wet soil and making a gap in the crowd. "We make haste to Leyden."

Chapter 21. The Retribution: Maarten

I'd gotten used to the stormy waters. I felt less green now than I had when I'd left Frisia. Every few days, we'd come across a boat worthy of plundering. Usually, the crew capitulated without much of a fight. Sometimes, we had to bloody a couple of them before they knew we were serious. It made me sick to watch, although I'd never admit it. Not to the other shipmates, at least. I loved the freedom of it. The open water, the fresh sea breeze, every part of it. It was the life of camaraderie I'd found with the Water Board and the Duivenvoorde retinue, only there was no noble or overseer barking orders at us. Only the captain, and even he saw himself as one of us. He ate with us, slept on the same deck as us, and gave us gifts for good work. We were all in this together—what we plundered meant what we could buy. It meant what we could eat and for how long we could dock. Life in port was the greatest. The captain wasn't wrong when he said this was the greatest form of freedom. We had coins from the farthest reaches of the world. We roaved as a band—laughing in taverns, drinking, eating, and coming back to the ship to sleep. And the girls, by God, the girls loved seamen. They found their way into the taverns—I managed to strike some luck with a few. And after all of it, we'd repent at mass in church on land. That is, as long as we were not at sea on a Sunday.

We'd sailed out of the channel, up and down the coast of France, before returning north and sailing through the channel to the North Sea. All the while, we hunted for merchant cogs, most often towering over them in our beast of a vessel. We were titans; even a sea beast wouldn't dare to do battle with us. We saw many of them out on the high seas—the odd tail flick of a sea serpent or washed-up bodies of krakens. I suppose it would only be a matter of time before we'd run into the leviathan itself. We broke storms and waves like a bloody bodkin tip. The ship, she was a damn mountain.

One night, Eustace, up in the crow's nest, caught sight of a ripe little ship, ready for the plunder.

"She's not flyin' no coat of arms; she's merchant vessel," he shouted out. Sure enough, on the horizon, I caught sight of the small, flickering torch lights reflecting in the water.

"Danish make?" asked the captain.

"French," Eustace replied.

"Alright, lads, you heard the man. We set course for the little cog—to glory, boys!" the captain barked.

"Man, the ropes!" shouted Bertrand.

"Full sail!" added the captain. "The winds are with us."

"By Saint Nicholas, I spot chests upon chests of booty!" shouted Eustace with an excitement seldom seen. "Let's spook 'em, lads before they toss 'em in the drink!" Before long, we were hot on their course, with not another boat nor land in sight. The little cog had teeth. By the time we'd found ourselves gearing to board, three crossbowmen were launching bolts at us. They lodged themselves firmly in the side of the ship and the shields of the men. Those who had shields, of course. One shipmate took a bolt to the leg. A few others had to abandon their duties to aid him. Nevertheless, a band of twenty pirates hopped the bannister and climbed down on ropes and ladders to take the vessel. There were not nearly enough of them to stand a chance. Axes, maces, and falchions flashed, with a constant hail of bolts descending from the crow's nest.

"Surrender, you bloody sea dogs!" shouted the captain. But they chose not to. What could they be hoping for? The door to the lower deck flung open. Out from the doorway poured men clad in red and white livery.

"Bloody hell, there's an entire army here!" shouted Bertrand. Last out of the door came a knight, clad in maille from head to toe, swinging about a broad, war axe. The light of the ship lanterns gleamed off of his armour. He appeared left-handed, with his right hand heavily bandaged, slipped out of the sleeve of his hauberk, and only his little finger and thumb wrapped around the haft of the weapon. I recognized his moustache. He must have been travelling in secrecy—nothing about the boat indicated there was a noble on board. The merchants were French, not Dutch.

"There's a knight!" shouted a pirate. "There's a fucking knight!" another echoed.

"Holy shit. Saint Nicholas, have mercy. Mother Mary!" Before I knew it, the steel-clad man began hacking his way through the pirates. Their axes and maces did little to him as they glanced off his cervelliere and his coat of plates. The man was as fearsome as a scaled dragon in that armour.

"Have none of you louts faced a bloody knight before?" I asked. I was met with only terror. I'd have to do this myself. I took my handaxe in one hand and a buckler in the other. I will be honest; it took a few deep breaths. But I didn't have enough time to think it over—I rushed toward him. His strike would've taken me out if I hadn't instinctually stepped to the side. I rammed my buckler into his nose and then began wailing down on him with the axe head. With the haft of his two-handed axe, he shoved me back, preparing to strike again.

Godverdomme. I did my best to tackle him—he didn't move. He weighed twice that of any man in that hauberk of his. He tossed me aside, now pointing his axe at Eustace. Bravely, Eustace stood with his fauchard in both hands. One more try. I drew my dagger. From behind him, while he was busy, I grabbed his forehead and held my dagger at his lip— his throat was covered by his maille coif. Another pirate rammed a spear through the steel links behind his knee. The knight fell to the deck.

"Call off your men!" I barked in Hollanter. "You're Dutchman?" he asked.

"Call them off, now!" I shouted. He complied.

The next morning, the remaining crew had all been tied up and seated around the mast. Once most of their cargo had been loaded onto our ship, it was time to discuss the fate of the knight.

"You, Salamander, you're a Dutchman. Do you know this knight?" the captain asked.

"I recognize his heraldry," I replied. "Let me speak to him."

"Be careful, boy, we can ransom him for a good coffer of silver. Don't bloody him up too badly," he said. I nodded.

I crouched down to speak with him. He wouldn't have it, only looking at the wooden planks of the deck.

"Something caught your interest between the floorboards?" I asked.

"I won't speak to you, filthy pirate," he said. He spat on my shoe. I smirked.

"Not used to the filth?" I asked. "You'd better be used to it if you're escaping Hollant."

"What tells you that?" he asked, looking up at me now. I had his attention.

"Hiding on a ship like a common merchant. Give me a break," I said. "What are you doing out here?"

"Secret mission," he said. "Bollocks."

"Secret mission for the count," he said. "Official business."

"And he sent you out with only a handful of men?" I asked. "Lie to me again, and you'll lose those bloody teeth of yours."

"Give me some water, and I'll talk," he said. I thought about it; it wouldn't be too hard. But what would it tell the captain? I decided to do it anyway. In truth, I felt bad for the man—he'd done nothing wrong. Well, to my knowledge.

I brought him a gourd of clean water.

"Drink up," I told him as I poured the liquid down his throat. When it began coming back out, I put the vessel down. "Now speak."

"My name is Baron Johannes vander Wassenaer," the

man said.

"Wassenaer?" I asked. "I lived in Duivenvoorde for quite some time." He smiled as much as he could.

"So you knew my brother, Arend?" he asked.

"I saw him fall in Frisia," I replied. His eyes widened.

"A soldier?" he asked.

"For the House of Duivenvoorde," I told him. "What word of the war in Frisia?" Johannes' expression soured.

"It's no longer just in Frisia," he said. "The Kennemers rebelled. Then the Waterlanders and the Amstellanders. And then the Friske joined them. Bastards, all. The entire damn country's ablaze," he said. "You have family in Duivenvoorde?" he asked. "Because they're not safe anymore," he said. This was horrific news. I felt myself grow pale and cold. I made an oath to Yda, and now, when she could be butchered, I wasn't there.

Godverdomme, who had I become? A damn pirate? Nay, nay, nay, I couldn't stand living like this while Kees and Felix would still be marching about, now fighting other Dutchmen. Nay, I had to join them. The thought of myself staying as a pirate haunted me. How could I be so stupid? Running away? I chose to stay out here and not go back.

"Are you willing to pay a ransom?" I asked.

"Yes," he replied. "But I'm not going back to Hollant."

"Are you a coward?" I asked. "Or a traitor?"

"Nay, an outlaw," he replied. "You know how the count can be, the bloody saffroned peacock of a boy," I smirked.

"Secret mission for the count." I teased. "I'll deliver your letter of ransom myself."

+ Floris +

A feast was prepared for the war camp. At the high table, beside Ghijsbrecht and his command, we were served chicken with rice and almond milk. In the center was presented a swan presented in in full plumage. The gellies and such were all delicious, but it was difficult to relax at this moment. There was a war afoot. This was our last celebration before making heavy contact with the enemy. Skirmishes had been consistently breaking out near Vredelant and the northern border. The raids grew heavier. The time had come.

Messengers frequently rushed into the hall, requiring immediate action. New raids, minor victories, minor defeats, all across the country. Ghijsbrecht and his circle had their hands full. One messenger thought his information so valuable he thought to announce it to the entire hall. The doors burst open with his entry. Panting, he shouted, "The ver Heyens ride South! The ver Heyens make haste to Leyden! With a host of men! They seek safe passage, my lords!"

"Safe passage?" asked Ghijsbrecht.

"Yes, my lord," the messenger said breathlessly. "Is this a joke?"

"Nay, my lord," the messenger replied.

"Will you grant it to them?" asked Harmant.

"This is no time for mercy. They have clearly made a

mistake. We must exploit it," said Ghijsbrecht.

"So you will refuse their demands, yes?" asked Zweder.

"Nay, we accept. And then we ambush the bastards," said Ghijsbrecht. The news brought me joy, in honesty. These were the men who were to blame for this chaos. They were treacherous dogs. I would have my vengeance. I immediately rose to my feet, girding my arming sword.

"I will ride out to meet them, uncle," I said. Ghijsbrecht studied my disposition for a moment. Then, he gave me a nod.

"Show no mercy," he told me. "Bring us victory—failure is not an option. You have every advantage. Do not let your men be seen, and finish it quickly." I bowed before him. I would return victorious or not at all.

The land was wet and misty—perfect conditions. We had one day to prepare for their arrival. I chose to cut them off near the small village of Rijsenhout. I stood upon the dyke that separated the village from the Westeinderplatsen River to survey the landscape. It was flat, completely, aside from a woodland which divided the local demesnes, perfect for hiding our men. The road to Rijsenhout itself sunk low into a small gorge, which would be a perfect place for the ambush. The winds were almost blinding.

"I hope this mist holds unto the morrow," said Guillaume.

"God willing," I replied. I brought a good three hundred men with me, most of whom were rebels and a handful of men-at-arms. "If we attack from this grove here and station our archers on the hill, they will be able to safely rain down arrows while we advance without hitting our men," I noted.

"Excellent plan, Floris," he replied. "Perhaps you should have some men fire practice shots to know their range?"

"Good idea," I said. "When the wind dies."

"It is paramount that the ver Heyens do not break through our assault. I hear most of their host is mounted. My scouts will return with their numbers," said William, the Englishman.

"You are right," I said. "What do you men suggest, a fallen tree to block their path? Or a reserve in the village itself?"

"There is no guaranteeing they will run on the road when the ambush strikes," said Guillaume.

"We need someone who knows this land better," I said. "Have the bannerets ask their retinues if any man is well acquainted with this part of the country. And if they have any suggestions. We will need all the insight available."

"Aye, my lord," replied Gaspard as he rode off to relay the order. A rider came rushing along the road. We could hear him long before we could see him in this mist.

"Who goes there?" asked Guillaume.

"I come in peace!" he shouted. "A scout of the Lord William fitz Roy."

"What news bring ye?" asked William.

"We sorely underestimated their force, my lords," the man said as he dismounted and took a knee before us.

"By how much?" I asked.

"They number over one thousand men," he said, looking me in the eyes now. I saw the fear in his. I certainly felt it swell in myself as well. I looked at Guillaume.

"You have to retreat, Floris. We will remuster and meet them with a real army."

"But I swore to return victorious…"

"That would be madness, Floris. Don't throw yourself away, and these men. Ghijsbrecht wants to win this war, he can't do that if…"

"They will ride in a single column, correct?" I asked. "Yes, but…"

"Then we do not have to engage them all at once. We cut off the vanguard, overwhelm them with superior force, and let the rest run North," I said.

"That is a gamble," said Guillaume. "You are playing dice here, Floris."

"It is a gamble I am willing to make," I said. "We achieve glory here, tomorrow, or we die trying." Guillaume sighed.

"I suppose we achieve glory, then."

The sun quickly hid behind the clouds. A storm was coming—it would beat down on us all night. But it would rain down on them too—and it would further muddy the road. These were favourable conditions. After dinner, a couple of Duivenvoorders were brought to my tent.

"My lord?" asked one of them. I recognized him.

"Ah, Felix, Kees, come in," I said. "What brings you here?"

"We believe we could be of some assistance, my lord," said Felix. "My mate here, Kees, had an idea earlier."

"Go on."

"Well," said Kees, "Today we were standing at the dyke. And the water was low then, but with the rain, it will be high tomorrow. When we were working as charcoal burners for the Water Board of the Rhineland, we saw how they managed the water. We saw how much water they could bottle up by a dyke. If we dig a hole in the dyke, the water will flood through. But, if we do it now, we can patch it up with a wooden board, like a few tables nailed together, and then, when we need to, we can release it, flooding the land." I felt myself smile. This, for lack of a better term, oaf, had, frankly, been struck with a stroke of genius.

"Kees, you beautiful man," I said, "show me."

In the dark, under the rain, we walked along the dyke. We found it, the perfect spot.

When needed, it would be released. I said a quick prayer, and then I had a unit of hand-picked Duivenvoorders come to quickly dig it out and fill it in again with a wooden sluice. Stealthily, they dug, braving the cold, keeping any lights and fires to a minimum.

Come morning, it was done, and it looked glorious. The river was high indeed, nearly at the height of the dyke itself. The plan was solid.

"Get your men into position," I ordered the bannerets.

"And double the rations for the men who worked on the dyke—it'll give them a reason to live today."

In haste, like ants on the road, the units scattered about the landscape, finding nooks and grottos covered in foliage in which to hide. We had precisely the section of land we wished to cut off and control. We had several great trees tied and dislodged, such that when the time came, we could simply cut the ropes, and their army would be segmented.

"We cut the head off the snake today, gentlemen," I said with excitement.

"One thousand of them, Floris. Remember, do not bite off more than you can swallow," said Guillaume.

"This is our day, Guillaume," I said.

"Then have courage, Floris," he replied. "And know that your father watches over you." I nodded.

Scouts consistently rode to us to inform exactly how far out their force was. The church bells of Rijsenhout kept time for us. By midday, the time had come to sit in wait.

Silence blanketed the land. Not a man was to make noise. The mist had remained, mostly, allowing us to better conceal ourselves. All conditions were favourable. We would be victorious. Slowly, but surely, we heard the rumbling of their marching approach. Their scouts came by with haste, spotting nothing, or being hastily dispatched with. Our priests made silent prayers, granting our men peace with the Almighty. Finally, they were right before us. The green ver Heyen banners flew high, aggressively fluttering in the lowland winds. They sung a marching song as they marched, something about a girl named Maria and her lover Hendrik. It was all normal—familiar even. I felt the excitement building—many of the rebels appeared genuinely eager to charge forth. So I let them.

I gave the signal when the time came, and a bellowing blast of horns followed my order. Just as planned, the trees came crashing down. The vanguard was exposed and cut off, and a horde of goedendagers were now upon them. Shouting filled the air. Chaos and confusion reigned. I saw the ver Heyens now riding about, frantically reaching for their swords and shields and spurring their horses into action. And, amid all the cacophony, I heard the roaring of a river. Down into the gorge, the water began to pour. It first soaked the earth, rendering it even more slippery than before. Then, the water kept coming, bathing men up to their knees. Those who fell in battle were drowned beneath the rushing water. Horses neighed frantically amid all the confusion, launching their riders off their backs and running off in every direction. I felt myself smile. Guillaume put his mailed hand on my shoulder.

"The day is not won yet," he told me. He was right, it was now our turn to ensure that reinforcements would not arrive. Around the chaos and slaughter that now took place in the valley, we mounted up, and led the men-at-arms to run down any forces hoping to join the fray. Surely enough, disorganized units of ver Heyen and other loyalist soldiers rushed through the wooded area into the plains just north of the ambush. The second they reached grass, we ran them down. What thin lines they could hastily muster were nothing compared to tens of mailed knights and their caparisoned destriers thundering across the field. My lance found its way into three men before splintering. We watched as further reinforcements looked helplessly at their brothers in arms, retreating back northwards into the treeline. Victory. As the final hammer strike, we rode our men-at-arms back to the site of the ambush, where the struggle continued. Now, we entered the melee. There was no semblance of battle lines nor formations, only men wrestling one another in what was now waist-high water, smacking around with the goedendags. Some of the men-at-arms dismounted to engage; others simply rode their horses into the water, trampling any poor souls caught below.

The day was won. It was quick, and vicious, just as Ghijsbrecht had requested. The men cheered.

"Sir Floris! Sir Floris! Sir Floris!" echoed its way through the trees. I had specifically ordered that the ver Heyen brothers be kept alive. Along with the other knights for ransom, they sat, stripped of their weapons, surrounded by rebels who would happily poke them with the ends of their goedendags, if given the chance.

I rode up to them, my horse's barding drenched in pink water.

"There comes the Duivenvoorder boy," said Renier. "Damn backstabbing, dishonourable, son of a—"

"Watch your tongue, brother," interrupted Lodewijk. "You have been bested. Take it as a man." I carefully dismounted, taking great care not to catch my stirrup in the soaking caparison.

"He's right," I said. "There's no need to act honourable, we've shown none."

"You gave us your word, you bastard," said Renier.

"After all you've done to us?" I asked. "Nay, you were fools to trust your enemies."

"We were only headed to liberate our brother," said Lodewijk. "He stands falsely accused. Please, have mercy on him."

"Your brother?" I asked. "One thousand men to free your brother?"

"Yes," Renier replied. "In case we ran into you whoresons."

"Well, you did," I replied. "And I suppose it didn't go as planned." I looked to Wollefram, who sat sulking in the dirt, his facial birthmark more red than ever. "And you? Wolf? What do you have to say for yourself? How many peasants felt your sword today?" He simply spat and said nothing.

"Don't toy with us. Show us the tip of your blade or show us mercy. What will you do?" asked Renier.

"There is little time for this," I laughed.

"Little time for this? You act as though your lives are not forfeit. You act as if I did not just deal you a crushing blow…"

"Because you didn't," said Wollefram.

"Excuse me?" I asked.

"You didn't. We freed that Pieter boy and his family. Your father lies dead in a Frisian ditch. Gherrijt too. Your cousin, the Wassenaer boy, was also slain. Your uncle, Johannes, is now in exile, leaving the Wassenaer completely unguarded. It will not be long before we take it. Either that, or your count does, and in that case, guess to whom he will gift it?" I felt a rage burn inside me. I hit him. It was dishonourable. But I did it. I couldn't contain myself. The fool grinned.

"Your father screamed like a girl," he said. "And that one we can't take credit for. That was all your doing."

"You take that back, you ass!" I shouted.

"You're so content that you defeated us when we were vulnerable. Remember our duel in Duivenvoorde? Remember our duel then? Remember how quickly you hit the dirt?"

"Times are different now…"

"We should have taken all your Godverdomde serfs!"

"What are you doing, you fool? I could have you executed. I'd ought to…"

"Maybe I'm just sick of your garbage, Floris," he shouted. "Maybe I've heard enough from your stupid mouth."

"Wolf!" said Lodewijk.

"Nay, Father, I will tell him how small of a man he truly is. I heard you were knighted, Floris. Do you think that makes you a man? A warrior? You are nothing. Nobody. You *and* your father will be erased with the passage of time."

"Get up," I told him. He hesitated. "I said rise, wretch." I ushered two wapenknechten to come and lift him if he did not comply. He did comply, though, and he squared up with me as if to pick a fight. He was slightly taller than I was—I could see he was exploiting that. "This war between us is stupid," I told him. "We have no more reason to fight, to slight each other like this. Both of our houses have been horrible to one another, killing and tricking and playing politics, and for what? Honour?"

"Today, you slew nearly every waffenknecht in the service of the House ver Heyen. This cannot go unpunished," said Wollefram.

"Wolf, sit down," said Lodewijk.

"Listen to your father, Wolf," said Renier.

"Nay, this offense cannot go unpunished. You two have lived your lives of honour and chivalry—I must still earn mine," he said. "Give me a damn sword, and we settle this here and now. A rematch, if you like," he said. Without hesitation, I asked that a sword be returned to him—more than that—lance, horse, and helm. We were to do this properly.

I'd proven nothing by winning in battle this day—as Ghijsbrecht said, every advantage was in my favour. If I was to prove myself as a knight, as *Sir* Floris, I would have to do so on equal footing with my enemy. That opportunity was now here.

We clasped our maille mittens with one another, and then spurred our horses to take positions at either side of the road. Our squires stood awaiting us, each with multiple lances in reserve. Both of us took a lance, and Sir Guillaume took charge of the marshalling.

"Marks…" he called, raising his hand in the air. "Charge!" he cried out, dropping his hand like a blade befalling an enemy. I dug my spurs into my destrier's flanks, hoping to accelerate as quickly as possible. I could feel the earth shake as I rode. On the first pass, both lances splintered against our shields. Neither of us had been dehorsed. We wheeled about and reached for another lance from our squires. Again, we strode forth, and again, we both hit our targets. My left shoulder ached now from the blow. I couldn't imagine he felt any better. On the third pass, instead of for me, his lance drove itself through the chest of my horse. The beast tumbled below me. The monster, still atop his own horse, gave a cry of victory. This was not over yet. But, it was eerily reminiscent of our battle of the Duivenvoorde green. Once again, I stood defenseless as he came now with another lance. Once again, I'd hide behind my shield. This time, I was ready. As he charged toward me on his horse, I drew Stonesplitter. I felt the balance of the blade. I felt its grip in my hand. And when he approached, this time, instead of soaking his strike, I stepped to the right, to the side of his offhand, at the last moment, so that he couldn't shift his lance over to my side. From there, I was able to slice his reins, remaining unscathed. The leather he held in his hand was now useless. I heard him curse through the breaths of his greathelm.

"Dismount and fight me like a man!" I shouted, unbuckling my greathelm. He did the same before lunging at me, now, with his own sword. Back and forth we struck one-another, exchanging blows, parrying, redirecting strikes, hoping to find a way around one-another's heater shields and land a blow to one of the soft spots. And then, it happened. Just over the tip of my shield, I managed to launch a thrust which glanced at his forehead. Struck, and in pain, the young knight stumbled backwards, landing on his back in the wet, river-soaked muck.

Immediately I pounced on him, pinning down his sword arm and driving my dagger up his ventail.

"Surrender," I told him. "Plead for mercy." The call never came. I looked at Guillaume. "You're a knight now, Floris. Act like one," he told me. I looked back at the foolish boy, now struggling for any hope of escape. In vain. Why wouldn't he just surrender? Why wouldn't he just surrender? *Surrender, damn it!* He spoke.

"When we had duelled in Duivenvoorde," he began, "If you had gained the upper hand, would you have ended me then?" he asked. I took a moment to think about it.

"No," I replied, as I slid the dagger into his throat. "This is for all the men who will fall in this mess you started. Make sure Saint Peter knows I sent you."

Lodewijk and Renier didn't cry out in anger nor anguish. They just sat there, watching. I suppose they knew this was to come of it. Wolf had signed away his life for his honour. The problem was that, in truth, he had none.

"He will receive a proper Christian burial," I assured them.

"May we take him with us to Utrecht?" Lodewijk asked.

"Of course," I said. "Now go and free your brother," I told him. "And run from Hollant. If I see you in this land again…"

"If you see me again, you will look upon a man with a vengeance in his eyes and rage in his heart," replied Lodewijk, fighting the battle that was very clearly raging inside of himself.

"I look forward to it," I replied. I cleaned the blood off of my dagger and mounted a fresh horse that was brought for me. I turned to Guillaume, mounted beside me.

"Did I make a mistake in killing him?" I asked.

"If you made a mistake today, it was only in letting the other go," Guillaume replied.

"They are just men," I said. "Their armies are crushed."

"I suppose so. No matter, for now, we must report your brilliant victory. Your father would be proud."

"Have a pigeon fly a report of today's happenings to Lady Mehaud," I replied. "I expect a feast upon my return home."

Chapter 22. The Return: Maarten

Planting my feet in Duivenvoorde again felt surreal—as though I was walking through a memory. So much had happened since we marched out, and yet everything was here just as it was before. I was relieved by that—that the war had not yet come to this village.

But it was also obvious the men had not yet returned. Much of the fields were left uncultivated. The first place I went was the alehouse. I'd supposed it would be nice to see a friendly face there. The dirtied rushes were a nice reminder of old times—when we were the ones dirtying them.

"I haven't seen ye in quite some time," said the barkeep. She was right. "You're the first of those boys to return. What of the others?" she asked. It took genuine courage to tell her the truth.

"Nay, it's been some time since I've seen them too," I replied. "I've seen too much of the world," I said. "I'm back where I need to be."

"No such thing as seein' too much," the barkeep said, cleaning out a tankard for me. "Travellers come by here, always tellin' tales of all the lands they'd seen. I'd pay a real good bit of silver to travel like that. I suppose I could take a pilgrimage, but you know the Lady Mehaud." She smirked. I'd forgotten what a witch she was. "I'm off to see her later," I said. "Any suggestions?"

"She's only soured since her son left," she said. "The castle seems empty."

"Doesn't seem like the worst place to be," I said, taking a sip of the nice, cool ale she handed me. "How much do I owe you?" I asked.

"On the house," the barkeep said. "For a war hero," she added with a wink. I gave her a smile.

"Much appreciated," I replied.

The enclosed area that surrounded the castle—the thin line of trees that veiled the wooden palisade and connected to the gatehouse, had overgrown. It was clearly in need of tending to. I suppose that, with many of the household retainers off to war, even the groundskeepers were gone or understaffed. I supposed it may be less likely than I though that Johannes' ransom would be paid. After all, from what I'd heard about his sister-in-law, she was quite the vile woman.

"Who goes there?" bellowed a guard from atop the gatehouse.

"My name is Maarten. I used to be one of the charcoal burners out on the Vliet. I fought in Frisia in the retinue of the House of Duivenvoorde," I said.

"What news of the chaos in the countryside?" the guard asked.

"I've been gone for quite some time," I replied. "I was taken a slave, and then I was freed, and now I have business with the lady of the castle," I said. The man came down from his tower to speak with me in front of the gates. "Usually, aren't the gates open during the day?"

"Times have changed," the guard said. "You never

know what could happen now with all these rebellious peasants afoot."

"I have a message regarding Baron Johannes," I said. The guard seemed intrigued. "It is only for the Lady Mehaud," I added.

"Alright," the man said. "But no funny business, yeah?" he asked. I nodded.

I was received in a small room. It was ornately decorated, with tapestries on all the walls and small heraldic decorations on the ceiling beams. There were crescent moons everywhere—I suppose it made sense as it was their house sigil, but perhaps it was presented a little *too* much. I was seated on a wooden chair in front of a table, on the other side of which was another wooden chair—that one lined with a sheepskin on its seat.

An evidently hurried and stressed Mehaud briskly paced into the room. She paused when she saw me. Did she recognize me? I felt an anxious inkling seep within me.

"Usually, it is commonplace for a peasant to stand for their lord," she said. "Even a free one." Embarrassed, I fumbled to find my feet.

"Apologies, my Lord… uh, my Lady," I said.

"Sit down," she told me. I did as she commanded. "I hear you have news of all that mess with my brother-in-law?" she asked. I felt even more embarrassed now, given the circumstances of my visit.

"Here," I said, handing her the letter I held. It had his stamp of approval. "Johannes…"

"*Heer* Johannes," she corrected. "Go on."

"*Heer* Johannes has been captured by a band of pirates off the coast of Flanders," I told her. "They have taken him to an undisclosed location on land and will keep him there as a guest, as is customarily afforded to nobles, until his ransom is paid," I replied. I watched as the lady's face grew red.

"And you? What role did you play in all of this?" she asked.

"I am just a messenger," I replied. "I am a levyman of the House of Duivenvoorde—I fought under the command of your husband and later your son. I offer my condolences." I replied.

"My son?" she asked. "Did you fight at Rijsenhout?" she asked.

"Nay," I replied. "Rijsenhout? What happened there?"

"I received a pigeon this morning." Lady Mehaud said. I watched as her expression changed. "My son won a brilliant victory over the loyalists," she said. I smiled—if Kees and Felix were to be anywhere above ground, they would have been there.

"My most heartfelt congratulations," I replied.

"He has done a great honour to his name," Mehaud said. "May God watch over him."

"I plan to return to the war," I said. "If you wish to send a note to him, you can send it through me."

"That's quite a bold offer," said the lady. "You have proven yourself to be a capable messenger thus far. I suppose you might do well. Just remember to bow when you give it," she added. "And to call him your lord."

"I apologize again for my lack of grace, my Lady. I spent too long abroad."

"No matter. Just make sure the message reaches him," she said.

While Mehaud wrote her message, I decided to see if I could find Yda anywhere.

With every step I felt more nervous, in honesty. It would be cowardice not to see here—but why did this feel more frightening than any battle I'd marched to? I didn't even know what I would say. I didn't even know what I was going to say… I simply walked, ready to face my own word. I made my way down the slopes, looking out over the fields and the village. The sun was bright today—everything was peaceful. The clanging of the smithy was just as obnoxious as it was. The foul stench of the tanner's was also just the same. I saw Yda's brother, Sam, working the bellows at the smithy. I was happy that he had earned his apprenticeship— the boy always wanted to be a smith.

And then I saw her, beautiful as ever, working the fields with her scythe, collecting bushels of barley. She was exactly as she was. And then I remembered all the foulness I'd done. All the loose girls in France. The way I'd given up in Frisia. How could I approach her? How could I even speak to her? For a moment, I thought she caught sight of me, but it mustn't have been the case, as she kept swinging her scythe, hacking the barley. The sun shone straight on her— her ruby hair gleaming. I missed those good days. The days before I left. I couldn't muster the courage to speak to her. I just watched, leaning in the shade of an oak tree. I began to play with the cross necklace that still hung around my neck. The rope was frayed, the wood worn, but it was still there— even after everything. It had seen it all.

Eventually, she put down her scythe. Then, to my shock, a man came. He was a young man of a muscular frame— good-looking. He had good, strong hair and a clean face. And they spoke. And she twirled a lock of her ginger hair. And they laughed. And they stood close to one another. They touched one another's forearms when they talked. They didn't have to, but they did. She'd ought to be doing her work—so should he. But they stood there and spoke and inched closer. I was happy for her. Perhaps she thought I was dead. Perhaps word reached Duivenvoorde of my capture. I felt no need to meddle in her life again. I was gone; he was not. I made my way up the hill toward the castle. Kees and Felix, God keep them alive, awaited me.

+ Piet +

Lord Hillebrant was a much thinner man now than he had been a month ago. His release was sweet like honey— there was he, knelt down to give me a hug, and ruffled my hair, and said I would be a fine lawyer one day. We threw a feast in his honour, and in the name of his brothers, who finally came to rescue him. All it took was a letter from the Count.

Joy filled the air. Minstrels played their tunes and recounted their tales of heroic knights battling giants and monsters and rescuing damsels. The great swans presented to us came in full plumage as if they were sitting there on the pewter dishes. I merrily ate my saffron chicken cut and wildberry jellies. Archimedes happily weaved his way about the dance floor, picking up food scraps. It was a good evening. It was a very good evening.

The tables had been arranged in a square around a dance floor where the guests enjoyed themselves hopping about and dancing joyously. I listened to the tales of the bards while I watched Master Waleran and Miss Filomena dancing on the center floor. They looked at each other with a contentment that had been absent since Lord Hillebrant's capture. Life had been restored.

Lord Lodewijk and Lord Renier did not appear very happy, though. They spoke as if they were discussing serious matters, even at the dinner table. Wrinkles creased their brows. I didn't know where Wolf was—they always travelled together.

"Tell me, Piet, how in the world did you manage to investigate my finances at your early little age?" asked Lord Hillebrant, indulging in his honeyed and peppered pork.

"You taught me," I said, "and, I suppose, all that reading helped," I said.

"Have you kept up with it?" Lord Hillebrant asked. I nodded. "Good lad," he said, pinching my cheek with a saucy hand. I wiped it off with my sleeve. "Ah, ah, ah, manners, Piet, you must use trenchers for that," he said, handing me a piece of bread. "You know, with such fine reading and writing skills, I could send you wherever you like across the world for your squirc's training," he said. "I reckon even the Duivenvoorders would take you if you wished to return home." I thought about it for a moment. I thought about how sweet it would be to return to old times with Mother, and Yda, and Sam. I would be only a few minute's walk away, living in a castle, training to be a knight in shining armour. And then I remembered the knights at the tourney. And then I remembered that Maurits and Thiel and Merin and Florie were all here in Leyden. And my books, how could I leave my books? And, most of all, Lord Hillebrant? I just got him back—now I'd plan to leave him?"

"Can I stay here?" I asked.

"Here?" he asked. "But you could not be a knight if you stay here; there are few knights in Leyden," he said.

"I could be a lawyer," I said.

"Or a burgher." Lord Hillebrant laughed.

"You may be the first boy I've ever heard of who'd wish to be a lawyer," he said. I smiled. "But it can certainly be done. You are the best squire I could ask for."

"I have one condition, though," I said. Lord Hillebrant lifted an eyebrow.

"Go on, little negotiator. Have you been spending too much time with the merchant children?" he asked. I laughed.

"Maurits and Thiel are hungry every night, and Merin and Florie hate the Beguinage. Can they stay with us and help around the house as I do?" I asked.

"Piet, this is not a large house," Lord Hillebrant replied, growing less joyous. "And the cost of the repairs…"

"You could build it higher," I said. "You could add a floor, and then, since it won't be level with the other houses, you can get rid of those clay roof tiles you hate," I said. He gave a reluctant smile.

"You know what?" he began. "You make a good argument. You will, indeed, prove to be a good lawyer. It will be done. You have my word," he said with a warm smile. I couldn't help myself, so I wrapped my arms around his great, big belly. Miss Filomena interrupted.

"Might I have this dance?" she asked me, sticking out her strong, caring, working hands. I looked to Lord Hillebrant.

"It's impolite to turn down a woman," he said with a smile. Happily, I jumped up and joined her and Master Waleran in the center. The music filled the air, the candles kept the room bright, and the tapestries kept us warm.

It was a good night.

www.ingramcontent.com/pod-product-compliance
Lightning Source LLC
Chambersburg PA
CBHW070303310726
48976CB00005B/1554